What the Magnate Wants

JOANNE ROCK

MILLS & BOON

THE MAGNATE'S
MAIL-ORDER BRIDE

JOANNE ROCK

To Maureen Wallace, the empathetic and efficient property manager on-site at the vacation rental where I finished this book. When construction work outside my rental made writing impossible, Maureen listened to my tale of woe and found another spot for me, making sure I could get work done the next day and have a gorgeous water view to boot!
Thank you for going above and beyond to help.

One

"It's no wonder her performances lack passion. Have you ever seen Sofia date anyone in all the time we've known her?"

Normally, Sofia Koslov didn't eavesdrop. Yet hearing the whispered gossip stopped her in her tracks as she headed from the Gulfstream's kitchen back to her seat for landing.

A principal dancer in the New York City Ballet, Sofia had performed a brief engagement with a small dance ensemble in Kiev last week. Her colleagues had been all too glad to join her when her wealthy father had offered his private plane for their return to the United States. But apparently the favor hadn't won her any new allies. As one of the most rapidly promoted female dancers currently in the company, Sofia's successes had ruffled feathers along the way.

She clutched her worn copy of *A Midsummer Night's*

Dream to her chest and peered toward her father's seat at the front of the jet, grateful he was still engrossed in a business teleconference call. Vitaly Koslov had accompanied the troupe on the trip to the Ukraine, his birthplace. He'd used their rare time together as an opportunity to pressure Sofia about settling down and providing him with grandchildren who might be more interested in taking over his global empire than she'd been.

"That's not fair, Antonia," one of the other dancers in the circle of four recliners snapped, not bothering to lower her voice. "None of us has time to meet people during the season. I haven't had a lover all year. Does that make me passionless when I go on stage?"

Sofia told herself she should walk back to her seat before the pilot told them to buckle up. But her feet stayed glued to the floor. She peered down at her notes on Shakespeare's play, pretending to reread them for an upcoming role as Titania if anyone happened to notice her.

"But Sofia's been with the company since ballet school and have we ever heard her name connected romantically with anyone?" Antonia Blakely had entered ballet school at the same time as Sofia, and had advanced to each level with the company faster than her. "Actually, her dad must agree that she's turning into a dried-up old prune, because—*get this*." She paused theatrically, having relied on showmanship over technical skill her entire career. Now, she lowered her voice even more. "I overheard her father talking to the *matchmaker* he hired for her."

Sofia's stomach dropped even though the plane hadn't started its descent. She gripped the wooden door frame that separated the kitchen from the seating area. For over a year she'd resisted her father's efforts to hire a matchmaking service on her behalf. But it was true—he'd stepped up the pressure during their visit to Ukraine, insisting she think about her family and her roots.

Marriage wasn't even on her radar while her career was on the upswing. Would Dad have signed her up with his matchmaker friend without her approval? Her gaze flicked back to the proud billionaire who made a fortune by trusting his gut and never doubting himself for a second.

Of course he would proceed without her agreement. Betrayal slammed through her harder than an off-kilter landing.

"Seriously?" one of the other dancers asked. "Like a private matchmaker?"

"Of course. Rich people don't use the same dating web sites as the rest of us. They try to find their own kind." Antonia spoke with that irritating assurance shared by know-it-alls everywhere. "If Papa Koslov gets his way, there'll be a rich boy ready and waiting for his precious daughter at the airport when we land."

Sofia lifted a hand to her lips to hold back a gasp and a handful of curses. She wasn't wealthy, for one thing. Her father might be one of the richest people in the world, but that didn't mean she was, too. She had never even spent a night under his roof until after her mother's death when Sofia was just thirteen. She'd followed her mother's example in dealing with him, drawing that financial line and refusing his support a long time ago. Her father equated money with power, and she wouldn't let him dictate her life. Ballet was her defiance—her choice of art over the almighty dollar.

Her father knew he couldn't control her choices. Not even Vitaly Koslov in all his arrogance would arrange for her to meet a prospective date in front of twenty colleagues. Not after an exhausting overseas dance schedule and nine hours in the air across seven time zones. Would he?

A ringing noise distracted her from the question and she peered around, only to realize the chime came from her pocket. Her cell phone. She must not have shut it off for the plane ride. Withdrawing the device, she muted the volume, but not before half the dancers on the plane turned to stare. Including the group nearby who'd been gossiping about her.

None of them looked particularly shamefaced.

Sofia hurried toward an open seat and buckled into the wide leather chair for descent. She checked the incoming text on her phone while the pilot made the usual announcements about the landing.

Her closest friend, Jasmine Jackson, worked in public relations and had agreed to help Sofia with a PR initiative this year to take her dance career to the next level. Jasmine's text was about the interview Sofia had agreed to for *Dance* magazine.

Reporter and one camera operator for Dance will meet you in terminal to film arrival. We want you to look like you're coming off a successful world tour! Touch up your makeup and no yoga pants, please.

Panic crawled up her throat at the idea of meeting with the media now when she was exhausted and agitated about the other dancers' comments. Still, she pulled out her travel duffel and fished around the bottom for her makeup bag to comply with Jasmine's wise advice. Chances were good that Antonia had misinterpreted her father's conversation anyhow. He might be high-handed and overbearing, but he'd known about the *Dance* magazine interview. She'd told him there was a chance the reporter would want to meet her at the airport. He wouldn't purposely embarrass her.

Unless he fully intended to put her on the spot? Prevent her from arguing with him by springing a new man on her while the cameras rolled?

Impossible. She shook off the idea as too over the top, even for him. She already had the lip gloss wand out when her phone chimed with another message from Jasmine.

WARNING—the camera person freelances for the tabloids. I'm not worried about you, of course, but maybe warn the other dancers? Good luck!

The plane wheels hit the tarmac with a jarring thud, nearly knocking the phone from her hand. Capping the lip gloss, she knew no amount of makeup was going to cover up the impending disaster. If Antonia was correct about her father's plans and some tabloid reporter captured the resulting argument between Sofia and her dad—the timing would be terrible. It would undermine everything she'd worked for in hiring a publicist in the first place.

Celebrated choreographer Idris Fortier was in town this week and he planned to create a ballet to premiere in New York. Sofia would audition for a feature role— as would every other woman on the plane. Competition could turn vicious at the slightest opportunity.

Maybe it already had.

Steeling herself for whatever happened in the terminal, Sofia took deep breaths to slow her racing heart. Forewarned was forearmed, right? She should consider herself fortunate that her gossipy colleague had given her a heads-up on her father's plan. With cameras rolling for her interview, she couldn't afford the slightest misstep. She could argue with him later, privately. But she wouldn't sacrifice a good PR opportunity when she had the chance of a lifetime to be the featured dancer in a new Idris Fortier ballet.

She would think of this as a performance and she would nail it, no matter what surprises the public stage had to offer. That's what she did, damn it.

And this time, no one would say her performance lacked passion.

"Don't do something stupid because you're angry." Quinn McNeill tried to reason with his youngest brother as he strode beside him toward the terminal of the largest private airport servicing Manhattan. They'd shared a limo to Teterboro from the McNeill Resorts' offices in midtown this afternoon even though Quinn's flight to Eastern Europe to meet with potential investors didn't leave for several hours. He'd canceled his afternoon meetings just to talk sense into Cameron.

"I'm not angry." Cameron spread his arms wide, his herringbone pea coat swinging open as if to say he had nothing to hide. "Look at me. Do I look upset?"

With his forced grin, actually, yes. The men shared a family resemblance, their Scots roots showing in blue eyes and dark hair. But when Quinn said nothing, Cameron continued, "I'm going to allow Gramps to dictate my life and move me around like a chess piece so that I can one day inherit a share of the family business. Which I don't really want in the first place except that he's drilled loyalty into our heads and he doesn't want anyone but a McNeill running McNeill Resorts."

Last week, Quinn, Cameron and their other brother, Ian, had all been called into their grandfather's lawyer's office for a meeting that spelled out terms of a revised will that would split the shares of the older man's global corporation into equal thirds among them. The news itself was no surprise since the McNeill patriarch had promised as much for years, grooming them for roles in his company even though each of them had gone on to develop their own business interests. Malcolm McNeill's apathetic only son had taken a brief turn at the company helm and proven himself unequal to the task, so the older man had targeted the next generation to inherit.

None of them *needed* the promised inheritance. But Cam was the closest to their grandfather and felt the most pressure to buy into Malcolm McNeill's vision for the future. And the catch was, each of them could only obtain his share of McNeill Resorts upon marriage, with the share reverting to the estate if the marriage ended sooner than twelve months.

Out of overinflated loyalty, Cameron seemed ready to tie the knot with a woman, sight-unseen, after choosing her from a matchmaker's lineup of foreign women eager to wed. Either that, or he was hoping a ludicrous trip to the altar would make their grandfather realize what a bad idea this was and prompt him to call the whole thing off.

It had always been tough to tell with Cam. For Quinn's part, he was content to take a wait-and-see approach and hope their grandfather changed his mind. The old man was still in good health. And he'd conveniently booked a trip to China after the meeting in his lawyer's office, making it next to impossible to argue with him for at least a few more weeks.

"Cam, look at it this way. If it's so important to Gramps that the company remain in family hands, he wouldn't have attached this new stipulation." Quinn ignored the phone vibrating in his pocket as he tried to convince his brother of the point.

"Gramps won't live forever." Cameron raised his voice as a jet took off overhead. "That will might be ludicrous, but it's still a legal document. I don't want the company to end up on the auction block for some investor to swoop in and divvy up the assets."

"Neither do I." Quinn's coattails flapped in the gust of air from the nearby takeoff. "But I'd rather try to convince the stubborn old man that forcing marriage down our throats might backfire and create more instability in the company than anything."

"Who says my marriage won't be stable? I might be on to something, letting a matchmaker choose my bride. It's not like I've had any luck finding Ms. Right on my own."

Cameron had a reputation as a playboy, a cheerful charmer who wined and dined some of the world's most beautiful women.

Quinn shook his head. "Since when have you tried looking for meaningful relationships?"

"I don't want someone who is playing an angle." Cameron scowled. "I meet too many women more interested in seeing what I can do for them."

"This girl could be doing the same thing. Maybe you're her ticket to permanent residence in the United States." Shouldering his way through a small group of businessmen who emerged from the terminal building stumbling and laughing, Quinn opened the door and held it for his brother. "How much do you know about your bride? You've never even spoken to this woman. Does she even speak English?"

Where the hell was their master negotiator brother, Ian, for conversations like this? Quinn needed backup and the reasonable voice of the middle son who had always mediated the vastly different perspectives Cameron and Quinn held. But Ian was in meetings all day, leaving Quinn to talk his brother out of his modern-day, mail-order bride scheme.

All around him, the airport seethed with activity as flights landed and drivers rushed in to handle baggage for people who never paused in their cell phone conversations.

Cameron led them toward the customs area where international flights checked in at one of two counters.

"I know her name is Sofia and that she's Ukrainian. Her file said she was marriage-minded, just like me." Cam pulled out his phone and flashed the screen under Quinn's nose. "That's her."

A picture of a beautiful woman filled the screen, her features reflecting the Eastern European ideal with high cheekbones and arched eyebrows that gave her a vaguely haughty look. With her bare shoulders and a wealth of beaded necklaces, however, the photo of the gray-eyed blonde bombshell had a distinctly professional quality.

Quinn felt as if he'd seen her somewhere before. A professional model, maybe?

"This is probably just a photo taken from a foreign magazine and passed off as her. Photography like that isn't cheap. And did you pay for a private flight for this woman to come over here?" Not that it was his business how his brother spent his money. But damn.

Even for Cameron, that seemed excessive.

"Hell, no. She arranged her own flight. Or maybe the matchmaker did." He shrugged as though it didn't matter, but he'd obviously given this whole idea zero thought. Or thought about it only when he was angry with their grandfather. "Plus she's *Ukrainian*." He stressed the word for emphasis. "I figured she might be a help once you secure the Eastern European properties. Always nice to have someone close who speaks the language, and maybe Gramps will put me in charge of revamping the hotels once I've passed the marriage test." He said this with a perfectly straight face.

He had to be joking. Any second now Cameron would say "to hell with this" and walk out. Or laugh and walk out. But he wasn't going to greet some foreigner fresh off an international flight and propose.

Not even Cameron would go that far. Quinn put a hand on his brother's chest, halting him for a second.

"Do not try to pass off this harebrained idea as practical in any way." They shared a level gaze for a moment until Cameron pushed past, his focus on something outside on the tarmac.

Quinn's gaze went toward a handful of travelers disembarking near the customs counter. One of the women seemed to have caught her scarf around the handrail of the air stairs.

"That might be her now." Cameron's eyes were on the woman, as well. "I wish I'd brought some flowers." Pivoting, he jogged over to a counter decorated with a vase full of exotic blooms near the pilots' club.

Vaguely, Quinn noticed Cameron charming the attendant into selling him a few of the purple orchids. But Quinn's attention lingered on the woman who had just freed her pink printed scarf from the handrail. Although huge sunglasses covered half her face, with her blond hair and full, pouty lips, she resembled the woman in the photo. About twenty other people got off that same plane, a disproportionately high number of them young women.

Concern for his brother made him wary. The woman's closest travel companion appeared to be a slick-looking guy old enough to be her father. The man held out a hand to help her descend the steps. She was waif-thin and something about the way she carried herself seemed very deliberate. Like she was a woman used to being the center of attention. Quinn was missing something here.

"She's tiny." Cameron had returned to Quinn's side. "I didn't think to ask how tall she was."

Quinn's brain worked fast as he tried to refit the pieces that didn't add up. And to do it before the future Mrs. McNeill made it past the customs agent.

The other women in front of her sped through the declarations process.

"So who is supposed to introduce the two of you?" Quinn's bad feeling increased by the second. "Your matchmaker set up a formal introduction, I hope?" He should be going over his notes for his own meeting overseas tonight, not worrying about who would introduce his foolish brother to a con artist waiting to play him.

But how many times had Cameron stirred up trouble with one impulsive decision or another then simply walked away when things got out of hand, leaving someone else to take care of damage control?

"No one." Cameron shrugged. "She just texted me what time to meet the plane." He wiped nonexistent lint off his collar and rearranged the flowers, a glint of grim determination in his eyes.

"Cam, don't do this." Quinn didn't understand rash people. How could he logically argue against this proposal when no logic had gone into his brother's decision in the first place? "At least figure out who she really is before you drag her to the nearest justice of the peace." They both watched as the woman tugged off her sunglasses to speak with the customs agent, her older travel companion still hovering protectively behind her.

"Sofia's photo was real enough, though. She's a knock-out." Cameron's assessment sounded as dispassionate and detached as if he'd been admiring a painting for one of the new hotels.

Quinn, on the other hand, found it difficult to remain impassive about the woman. There was something striking about her. She had a quiet, delicate beauty and a self-assured air in her perfect posture and graceful walk. And to compound his frustrations with his brother, Quinn realized what he was feeling for Cameron's future bride was blatant and undeniable physical attraction.

Cameron clapped a hand on his shoulder and moved toward the gate. "Admit it, Sofia is exactly as advertised."

Before Quinn could argue, a pair of women approached the doors leading outside. They were clearly waiting for someone. Both wore badges that dangled from ribbons around their necks, and one hoisted a professional-looking camera.

Reporters?

Cameron held the door for them and followed them out.

And like a train wreck that Quinn couldn't look away from, he watched as Cameron greeted the slender Ukrainian woman with a bouquet of flowers and—curse his eyes—a velvet box. He'd brought a *ring*? With his customary charm, Cameron bowed and passed Sofia the bouquet. Just in time for the woman with the camera to fix her lens on the tableaux.

Quinn rushed toward the scene—wanting to stop it and knowing it was too late. Had Cameron called a friend from the media? Had he wanted this thing filmed to be sure their grandfather heard about it? Whatever mess Cam was creating for himself, Quinn had the sinking feeling he'd be the one to dig him out of it.

Cold, dry, winter wind swept in through the door and blasted him in the face at the same time Cameron's words hit his ears.

"Sofia, I've been waiting all day to meet my bride."

Two

Sofia had mentally prepared to be approached by a suitor. She had not expected a marriage proposal.

In all the years she'd danced Balanchine on toes that bled right through the calluses, all the times she'd churned out bravura fouetté turns fearing she'd fall in front of a live audience, she'd never been so disoriented as she was staring up at the tall, dark-haired man bearing flowers and…a ring?

The way she chose to handle this encounter would surely be recorded for posterity and nitpicked by those who would love nothing more than to see her make a misstep offstage. Or lose a chance at the lead in Fortier's first new ballet in two years.

In the strained silence, the wind blew Sofia's scarf off her shoulders to smother half her face. She could hear Antonia whispering behind her back. And giggling.

"For pity's sake, man, let's take this inside." Sofia's father was the first to speak.

Vitaly Koslov maintained his outward composure, but Sofia knew him well enough to hear the surprise in his tone. Was it possible he hadn't foreseen such a rash action from a suitor when he arranged for a matchmaker for her without her consent? The more she thought about it, the more she fumed. How dare this man corner her with his marriage offer in a public place?

She stepped out of the wind into the bright lobby, wishing she could just keep on walking out the front exit. But the camerawoman still trailed her. Sofia needed to wake up and get on top of this before a silly airport proposal took the focus of the *Dance* magazine story away from her dancing.

"Ladies." Sofia turned a performer's smile on the reporters, willing away her exhaustion with the steely determination that got her through seven-hour rehearsals. "I'm so sorry. I forgot I have a brief personal appointment. If you would be so kind as to give me a few moments?"

"Oh, but we've got such a good story going." The slim, delicately built reporter was surely a former dancer herself. She smiled with the same cobra-like grace of so many of Sofia's colleagues—a frightening show of sweetness that could precede a venomous strike. "Sofia, you never mentioned someone special in your life in our preliminary interview."

The camera turned toward the man who'd just proposed to her and the even more staggeringly handsome man beside him—another dark-haired, blue-eyed stranger, who wasn't as absurdly tall as her suitor. They had to be related. The second man's blue eyes were darker, frank and assessing. And he had a different kind of appeal from the well-muscled male dancers she worked with daily who honed their bodies for their art. Thicker in the shoulders and arms, he appeared strong enough to lift multiple ballerinas at once. With ease.

Tearing her eyes from him, she pushed aside the wayward thoughts. Then she promised the reporter the best incentive she could think of to obtain the respite she needed.

"If I can have a few moments to speak privately with my friend, you can film my audition for Idris Fortier." Sofia recalled the magazine had been angling for a connection to the famous choreographer. As much as she didn't want that moment on public record—especially if she failed to capture the lead role—she needed to get those cameras switched off now.

Her father wasn't going to run this show.

After a quick exchange of glances, the reporter with the camera lowered the lens and the pair retreated to a leather sofa in the almost empty waiting area. In the meantime, the rest of the troupe who had traveled with Sofia lingered.

"May we have a moment, ladies?" her father asked the bunch. And though some pouting followed, they went and joined the reporters, leaving Sofia and her father with the tall man, still holding a ring box, and his even more handsome relation.

Belatedly she realized she had mindlessly taken the orchids the stranger had offered her. She could only imagine how she looked in the pictures and video already captured by the magazine's photographer.

The same woman her publicist warned her moonlighted for the paparazzi. How fast would her story make the rounds?

"Sofia." The tall man leaned forward into her line of vision. "I'm Cameron McNeill. I hope our matchmaker let you know I'd be here to take you home?"

Even now, he didn't lower his voice, but he had a puzzled expression.

She resisted the urge to glare at her father, afraid the reporter could use a long range-lens to film this conversation. Instead, Sofia gestured to some couches far removed from the others, but her suitor didn't budge as he studied her.

His companion, still watching her with those assessing blue eyes, said something quietly in the tall man's ear. A warning? A note of caution? He surreptitiously checked his phone.

"How do I know that name? McNeill?" Her father's chin jutted forward in challenge.

"Dad, please." After a life on stage studying the nuances of expressions to better emote in dance, Sofia knew how easily body language could tell a story. Especially to her fellow dancers. "May I?" Without waiting for an answer she turned back to Cameron. "Could we sit down for a moment?"

Her father snapped his fingers before anyone moved. "McNeill Resorts?"

As soon as he uttered the words, the quiet man at Cameron's shoulder stepped forward with an air of command. He seemed a more approachable six foot two, something she could guess easily given the emphasis on paring the right dance partners in the ballet. Sofia's tired mind couldn't help a moment's romantic thought that this man would be a better fit for her. Purely from a dance perspective, of course.

He wore the overcoat and suit of a well-heeled Wall Street man, she thought. Yet there was a glint in his midnight-blue eyes, a fierceness she recognized as a subtler brand of passion.

Like hers.

"Vitaly Koslov?" Just by stepping forward into the small, awkward group, he somehow took charge. "I'm Quinn McNeill. We spoke briefly at the Met Gala two years ago."

A brother, she thought.

A very enticing brother. One who hadn't approached her with a marriage proposal in front of a journalist's camera. She approved of him more already, even as she wondered what these McNeill men were about.

She needed to think quickly and carefully.

"Sofia's got family in New York," Cameron informed Quinn, as if picking up a conversation they'd been in the middle of. "I knew she wasn't some kind of mail-order bride." He smiled down at Sofia with a grin too practiced for her taste. "The reporters must be doing some kind of story on you? I saw their media badges were from *Dance* magazine."

"Mail-order bride?" Her father's raised voice made even a few seen-it-all New Yorkers turn to stare, if only for a second. "I'll sue your family from here to Sunday, McNeill, if you're insinuating—"

"I knew she wasn't looking for a green card," Cameron argued, pulling out his phone while Sofia wished she could start this day all over again. "It was Quinn who thought that our meeting was a scam. But I got her picture from my matchmaker—"

"There's been a mix-up." Quinn stood between the two men, making her grateful she hadn't pulled the referee duty herself. "I told my brother as much before we realized who Sofia was."

Sofia couldn't decide if she was more incensed that she'd been mistaken for a bride for hire or that one of them wanted to marry her based on a photo. But frustration was building and the walls damn well had ears. She peered around nervously.

"Who is she?" Cameron asked Quinn, setting the conspicuous velvet box on a nearby table. Sofia felt all the eyes of her fellow dancers drawn to it like a magnet even from halfway across the waiting area.

"Sofia Koslov, principal dancer with the New York City Ballet." He passed Cameron his phone. He'd pulled up her photo and bio—she recognized it from the company web site. "Her father is the founder of Self-Sale, the online auction house, and one of the most powerful voices in Ukraine, where I'm trying to purchase that historic hotel."

The two brothers exchanged a meaningful look, clearly wary of her father's international influence.

While Cameron whistled softly and swiped a finger along the device's screen, Sofia's father looked ready to launch across the sofa and strangle him. Maybe her dad was regretting his choice of matchmaker already. Sofia certainly regretted his arrogant assumption that he could arrange her private life to suit him.

"You call that a *mix-up*?" Her father's accent thickened, a sure sign he was angry. "Why the hell would you think she needed a green card when she is an American citizen?" Her father articulated his words with an edge as he got in Quinn McNeill's face. "Do you have any idea how quickly I can bury your hotel purchase if I choose to, McNeill? If you think I'm going to let this kind of insult slide—"

"Of course not." Quinn didn't flinch. "We'll figure out something—"

Sofia missed the rest of the exchange as Cameron leaned closer to speak to her.

"You're really a ballerina?" He asked the question

kindly enough, but there was a wariness in his eyes that Sofia had seen many times from people who equated "ballerina" with "prima donna." Or "diva."

"Yes." She lifted her chin, feeling defensive and wondering if Quinn could overhear them as he continued to speak in low tones with her father. The older brother drew her eye in a way men seldom did. And was it her tired imagination or did his gaze return to her often, as well? "I competed for years to move into a top position with one of the most rigorous and respected companies in the world."

Men never apologized for focusing on their careers. Why should she?

Cameron nodded but made no comment. She sensed him rethinking his marriage proposal in earnest. Not that it mattered—obviously a wedding wasn't happening. But how to dig herself out of this mess for the sake of the cameras and her peers? If she wasn't so drained from the long flight and the demanding practice schedule of this tour, maybe her brain would come up with a plausible, graceful way to extricate herself.

She noticed the members of her dance troupe moving steadily closer, no doubt trying to overhear what was going on in this strange powwow. Every last one of them had their phones in hand. She could almost imagine the tweets.

Will Sofia Koslov be too busy with her new fiancé to give her full attention to Fortier?

The dance world would go nuts. A flurry of speculation would ensue. Would Fortier decide he didn't want to work with a woman who didn't devote all of her free time to dance?

Her stomach cramped as she went cold inside. That would be so incredibly unfair. But it didn't take much to lose a lead role. It was all about what Fortier wanted.

"And you were not actively seeking a husband?" Cameron asked the question with a straight face.

Did he not realize she'd forgotten him completely? Her eyes ventured over to Quinn, hoping the man truly had an idea about how to fix this, the way he'd assured her father.

"No," she told him honestly. "I didn't even know my father had hired a matchmaker until shortly before we landed. He signed me up without permission."

"Then I apologize, Ms. Koslov, if I've caused you any embarrassment in my haste to find a bride." Cameron lifted her hand and put it to his lips, planting a kiss on the back of her knuckles. The gesture had the flair of a debonair flirt rather than any real sentiment. "My brother warned me not to rush into this. And, once again, it seems the ever-practical Quinn had a good point."

He straightened as if to leave, making her realize she would be on her own to explain this to the reporters. And the dance community. But she didn't blame Cameron. She blamed her father.

"You were really willing to marry someone without even talking to them?" She couldn't imagine what would drive him to propose to a stranger out of the blue.

"I was leaving it in the hands of professionals." He shrugged. "But next time, I will at least call the bride ahead of time. Good luck with your dancing, Sofia." He stuffed his hands into his coat pockets. "Quinn's flight doesn't take off for a few hours. If you need help with the reporters, my brother has a gift for keeping a cool head. He'll know what to do."

"You're…leaving?"

"I only came to the airport to see you. It's Quinn who has a flight out." He nodded toward his brother, who had captured the full attention of her father. "But he'll come up with a plan to help you with the reporters first. He's the expert at making the McNeills look good. I'm the brother who seems to stir up all the trouble."

It didn't occur to her to stop Cameron McNeill as he pivoted and stalked away from her, the necks of her traveling companions all craning to follow his progress through the airport terminal. She noticed other women doing the same thing.

But then, these McNeill men were uncommonly handsome.

The whole thing felt too surreal. And now the two reporters turned from the large windows on the other side of the terminal and headed her way again. The sick feeling returned in the pit of her stomach. She should have been using this time to come up with a plan. Maybe she could tell the reporters that the proposal had all been a joke?

Except she'd trip over any story she tried to concoct. Unlike her PR consultant, Sofia was not a master of putting the right spin on things. Besides, her colleagues' words about her not dating still circled around in her head.

About her lack of passion.

What would they say now that her suitor had ditched her publicly?

Her father and Quinn McNeill converged on her.

"You should listen, Sofia. McNeill has a fair plan." Vitaly nodded his satisfaction at whatever they'd decided.

Fear spiked in her chest as the reporters drew closer. These men didn't understand her world or the backlash this little drama would cause. How could she win the part in the Fortier ballet while her whole dance company gossiped gleefully about her five-minute marriage offer?

"No. I will handle this." She looked to Quinn Mc-Neill. "I need to save face. To come up with something that doesn't make it look like I've been jilted—" Hell, she didn't know what she needed. She couldn't even explain herself to Quinn. How would she ever make sense in front of the reporters?

Quinn's blue eyes gave away exactly nothing. Whereas his younger brother was all charm and flirtation, this man's level stare was impossible to read. He seemed at ease, however. He leaned closer to her to speak softly while her father discreetly checked his watch, positioning himself between her and the oncoming dancers.

"Your father is livid at my brother's antics." Quinn's voice was like a warm stroke against her ear. It gave her a pleasant shiver in spite of her nervousness. "I'd like to appease him, but it's more important to me that you're not embarrassed by this. How can I help?"

She blurted the first thing that came to mind. "Ideally, I'd like a fiancé for the next three weeks until I have a ballet part on lockdown." As soon as the words tumbled out, of course, she realized that was impossible. Cameron McNeill was already gone.

But Quinn did not look deterred. He nodded.

"Whatever I say, please know that it's just for show." His hand landed on her spine, a heated touch that seeped right through her mohair cape. "We'll give a decoy statement to the media and then you and I can iron out some kind of formal press release afterward. But I can have you happily engaged and out of here in less than five minutes. Just follow my lead."

She didn't even have time to meet his eyes and see for herself his level of sincerity, because the cameras were rolling again, the bright light in her eyes. Excited whispering from the other dancers provided an uncomfortable background music for whatever performance Quinn McNeill was about to give.

Strange that, when her reputation hung in the balance, the main thing she noticed was how his hand palmed the small of her back with a surety and command even a dancing master would appreciate.

Her father hung back as the flashing red light on the Nikon handheld swung her way. Blinking while her eyes adjusted, she thought she saw her father reclaim the velvet ring box Cameron had left behind and hand it to Quinn. Which made sense, she supposed. The brother of empty gestures left a diamond behind while the practical brother reclaimed it. Hadn't Cameron assured her Quinn would take care of everything?

"Ladies." Quinn's voice took on a very different quality as he turned to the camera and the small audience of her colleagues who clutched their cell phones, surely eager to send out updates on this little drama. "Forgive me for spiriting away Sofia earlier. In my eagerness to see her again, I failed to remember her interview with the magazine. I didn't mean for a private moment to be caught on film."

Sofia could almost hear the collective intake of breath. Or was that her own? Her stomach twisted, fearing what he might say next while at the same time she couldn't make herself interrupt. Like any strong partner, he led with authority.

Besides, he said it was only for show.

"Where is your brother?" one of the reporters asked. "He said he couldn't wait to meet his bride."

No doubt they'd all been surfing the internet to figure out who Cameron and Quinn were.

"My brother was teasing. Cameron hadn't met Sofia yet and, in the way brothers sometimes do…" He de-

ployed a charming grin of his own, one even more disarming than his brother's had been, only now she realized
how practiced the gesture could be. "Cam only said that
to rattle me on the day he knew I was going to ask her
something very important myself."

Quinn turned to her now, his blue eyes locking on her
with an intensity that speared right down to her belly to
stir an unexpected heat. Even when she knew with one
hundred percent certainty it was all an act.

"He just so happened to have a ring in his pocket?"
the reporter asked, gaze narrowed to search out the truth.

"I had no idea he brought an old ring of our mother's
from home," Quinn continued easily. "Then he grabbed
some flowers from the customer service desk." He
pointed out a half-empty vase nearby. "Trust me when I
tell you, my brother doesn't lack for a sense of humor—
a somewhat twisted one."

Even Sofia found herself wondering about his story.
Quinn looked convincing enough, especially when he
gazed down at her as if she was the only woman in the
world.

She licked her lips, her mouth gone suddenly dry.
She should say something. Prevent this farce that no one
would ever believe. But then again…hadn't she promised herself she would make this a performance worth
watching?

A show of passion?

"Now—" his gaze never left hers even as he continued to address the media "—I am going to ask you to
check Ms. Koslov's schedule for a new interview time
tomorrow. Because tonight, we have something private
and wonderful to celebrate."

Somewhere behind that bright light the camerawoman
gave a quiet squeal of excitement while someone else—

a colleague from the ballet company, no doubt—made a huff of disappointment. That the story hadn't panned out how she'd wanted? Or that she'd have to wait until tomorrow for answers? A few people clapped halfheartedly. The dancers who had hoped for a scandal were clearly disappointed while Sofia wondered how she'd ever dared to ask Quinn McNeill for a temporary fiancé. She couldn't believe he'd granted her wish.

And not with his brother but with Quinn himself as her fake groom.

The cameras captured every moment of this absurd dance as she clutched the bouquet in one hand while Quinn tucked the mysterious black-velvet box into the other. Then, leaving no doubt as to his meaning, he slanted his lips overs hers and kissed her.

Three

Normally, Quinn McNeill knew how to stick to the talking points. He'd delivered enough unwelcome news to investors during his father's failed tenure as the McNeill Resorts' CEO that Quinn had a knack for staying on script.

But all bets were off, it seemed, when an exotic beauty fit into his arms as if she'd been made for him. One moment he'd been delivering the cover story to explain Cam's behavior and still give Sofia Koslov a fiancé. The next, he was drowning in her wide gray eyes, her full lips luring him into a minty-flavored kiss that made the mayhem of the airport fade away.

This was so not the plan he'd come up with to smooth over business relations with Sofia's ticked-off and powerful Ukrainian father. He'd told Vitaly Koslov he would publicly apologize and explain away the proposal as a joke between friends. But when Quinn had seen the panic on Sofia's face, he'd known his only option was to help her in whatever way she needed.

Although, it occurred to him as he kissed her…

What if she'd meant she wanted that fake engagement with his brother?

Forcing himself to edge back slowly, Quinn peered down at her kissed-plump lips and flushed cheeks. She couldn't have possibly meant she wanted anything to do with Cameron. Not after that kiss.

Still, he'd just complicated things a whole lot by claiming her as his own.

"So you're engaged to Ms. Koslov?" one of the reporters asked him while the other one flipped off the power button on her camera.

"A full statement will be issued tomorrow morning," Vitaly Koslov snapped before Quinn could respond, the older man's patience clearly worn thin as he shot a dark glare at Quinn.

The hotel deals he was working on in Kiev and Prague were now seriously compromised. The man had threatened to block the sales by any means necessary if Quinn didn't smooth things over with the media, and Quinn was guessing that taking Cameron's place as Sofia's suitor wasn't what Vitaly Koslov had in mind.

Right now, however, Quinn had promised the man to get his daughter out of the terminal and home as quickly and privately as possible.

"Come with me," Quinn whispered in Sofia's ear, a few strands of silky hair brushing his cheek as he bent to shoulder her bag for her. "Your father will divert them. We are too happy and in love to pay attention to anyone else."

He started walking toward the exit, hoping she would continue to play her part in this charade. She did just that, moving with quick, efficient steps and glancing up at him in a way that was more than just affectionate.

Hell. Those gazes sizzled.

"How fortunate we are," she muttered dryly. Her tone was at odds with the way she was looking at him, making him realize what a skilled actress she was.

Had the kiss been for show, too? He liked to think he could tell the difference.

"I regret that we have to do this. I hope my brother at least had the decency to apologize before he made his escape." Quinn had already texted his pilot to reschedule his own flight, a delay that would add to the considerable expense of closing this deal that might never happen anyhow.

He held the door for Sofia and flagged the first limo he spotted, handing off her luggage to the driver to stow. The wind plastered her cape to Quinn's legs, bringing with it the faint scent of a subtle perfume.

"He did apologize." She tucked the mohair wrap tighter around herself, waiting on the curb while the driver opened the door and she relayed the address of her apartment. "He told me he was sorry right before he assured me you'd take care of everything." She slid to the far side of the vehicle, distancing herself from him. "Tell me, Quinn, how often do you step in to claim his discarded fiancées?"

He understood that she was frustrated, so he told himself not to be defensive.

"This would be a first," he replied lightly, taking the seat on the opposite side of the limo. "I tried to talk him out of hunting for a wife in this drastic manner, but he was determined."

The driver was already behind the wheel and steering

the vehicle toward the exit. Darkness had fallen while they were inside the terminal.

"It would not have been so awkward if there hadn't been any media present." She seemed to relax a bit as she leaned deeper into the leather seat, pulling the pink scarf off her neck to wrap it around one hand. "Then again, maybe it would have been since I had the rest of the dance ensemble with me and there are those who would love nothing more than a chance to undermine my position in the company."

"Your father told me that you were recently promoted to principal." He only had a vague knowledge of the ballet, having attended a handful of events for social purposes. "Does that always put a target on a dancer's back?"

"Only if your name is mentioned for a highly sought-after part in a new ballet to premiere next year. Or if you rise through the ranks too quickly. Or if your father sponsors a gala fund-raiser and angles for you to be featured prominently in the program." She wound the scarf around her other hand, weaving it through her fingers. "Then, no matter how talented you are, the rumor persists that you only achieved your position because of money."

In the glow from the streetlights, he watched her delicate wrists as she anxiously fumbled with the scarf. She hadn't been this skittish back in the airport. Did he make her nervous? Or was she only allowing herself the show of nerves now that she was out of the spotlight?

He found himself curious about her even though he should be focusing on the details of their brief, pretend engagement and not ruminating on her life. Her kiss.

"You move in a competitive world." It was something he understood from the business he managed outside of

McNeill Resorts since his bigger income stream came from his work as a hedge fund manager. His every financial move was watched and dissected by his rivals and second-guessed by nervous investors.

"The competition led me to hire a PR firm at my own expense, which is costly, considering a dancer's salary. But they secured the feature for me in *Dance* magazine."

He had no idea what a professional ballerina earned, but the idea that she'd hired a publicity firm suggested a strong investment in her career. Quinn found it intriguing that she would pay for that herself considering her father's wealth.

That wasn't all he found intriguing. The spike of attraction he felt for her—a heat that had intensified with that kiss—surprised him. He'd been adamantly opposed to his grandfather's marriage ultimatum and yet he'd found himself jumping into the fray today to claim Sofia for his own.

Not just for McNeill Resorts. Also so Cameron couldn't have her.

As soon as he'd seen her today, he'd felt an undeniable sexual interest. No, hunger.

"I realize that my brother created an awkward situation and you have every right to be frustrated."

"And yet you helped me out of a tricky situation when I was tongue-tied and nervous, so thank you for that." She settled her hands in her lap and stared out the window at the businesses lining either side of Interstate 17 heading south toward Manhattan. "I have a difficult audition ahead of me and I know I wouldn't have been able to focus on it if the debacle in the airport was the topic on everyone's lips." She gave him a half smile. "If I didn't have a fiancé, everyone would badger me about what happened. But since I actually *do*? I don't think anyone will quiz me about it. Sadly, my competitors are more interested in my failures than my successes."

He understood. He just hoped her father would support her wishes regarding their charade.

"Yet tonight's events leave you a loophole, Sofia, if you want to give a statement that you refused me." He hadn't thought about it until now, but just because he'd implied he was asking for her hand didn't mean she would necessarily accept. "If you change your mind about this, I can have someone work on a statement for the press that expresses my admiration for you, my disappointment in your refusal—"

"Expedient for you, but not for me." She tipped her head to the window, her expression weary. He noticed the pale purple shadows beneath her eyes. "Just because I issue a statement that says it's over doesn't mean there won't be questions about my love life given the backstabbing in my company this season. An abrupt breakup when everyone wants a story could make the press start digging into how we met. And until I know the truth about where Cameron got my contact information, I'm not comfortable letting the media look too closely at how we connected. I never wanted anything to do with a matchmaker, and I'm concerned that whoever my father hired posted my information in a misleading way. I don't understand why your brother thought I was Ukrainian. Or why he didn't know I was a dancer."

"We could work on a cover story—"

"I am exhausted and my body thinks it's midnight after the time I spent in Kiev. I have rehearsal tomorrow at ten and what I need is sleep, not a late-night study session to keep a cover story straight." She folded her arms and squared her shoulders, as if readying herself for an argument.

Did she realize how many complications would arise if they continued this fictional engagement? He'd really thought she would jump at the chance to say she'd turned down his proposal. But then again, he couldn't deny a surge of desire at the prospect of seeing her again.

"I'm willing to continue with the appearance of an engagement if that's simpler for you." He wanted to right the mess Cameron had made. And this time, it wasn't for Cameron's sake.

It was for Sofia's.

"It would be easier for me." She twisted some of her windblown blond hair behind her ear and he noticed a string of five tiny pearls outlining the curve. "Just for three more weeks. A month, at most, until the rumor mill in my company settles down. I need to get through that important audition."

She glanced his way for the first time in miles and caught him staring.

"Of course," he agreed, mentally recalibrating his schedule to accommodate a woman in his life. He would damn well hand off the trip to Kiev to Cameron or Ian since Quinn would need to remain in New York. "In that case, maybe we should draw up a contract outlining the terms of the arrangement."

With Vitaly Koslov threatening to block his business in Eastern Europe, Quinn needed to handle this as carefully as he would any complicated foreign acquisition.

"Is that wise?" Frowning, she withdrew a tin of mints from her leather satchel and fished a couple out, offering him one. "A paper trail makes it easier for someone to discover our secret."

He took a mint, his eye drawn to her mouth as her lips parted. He found himself thinking about that kiss again. The way she'd tasted like mint then, too. And how an engagement would lead to more opportunities to touch her. The idea of a fake fiancée didn't feel like an imposition when he looked at it that way. Far from it.

"Quinn?" Her head tipped sideways as she studied him, making him realize he'd never responded. "If you really think we need the protection of a legally binding contract—"

"Not necessarily." He should keep this light. Friendly. Functional. "But we'll want to be sure both of our interests are protected and that we know what we're getting into."

"A prenup for a false engagement." She shook her head. "Only in New York."

"Your father will want to ensure your reputation emerges unscathed," he reminded her.

The limo driver hit the brakes suddenly, making them both lurch forward. On instinct, Quinn's arm went out, restraining her. It was purely protective, until that moment when he became aware of his forearm pinned against her breasts, his hand anchored to her shoulder under the fall of silky hair.

A soft flush stole over her cheeks as he released her and they each settled back against their respective seat cushions. The awkward moment and the unwelcome heat seemed to mock his need to put the terms of this relationship in writing.

"That's fine," she agreed quickly, as if she couldn't end the conversation fast enough. "If you want to draw up something, I will sign it and you can be sure I will not cause a fuss when we end the engagement."

She wrapped her mohair cape more tightly around her slight figure, the action only reminding him of her graceful curves and the way she'd felt against him.

Damn. His body acted as though it'd been months since he'd been with a woman when...

Now that he thought about it, maybe it had been that long since he'd ended a relationship with Portia, the real-estate developer who'd tried to sell him a Park Avenue penthouse. In the end, Quinn hadn't been ready to leave the comfort of the Pierre, a hotel he'd called home for almost a decade. He hadn't been ready for Portia, either, who'd been more interested in being a New York power couple than she had been in him.

Somehow he'd avoided dating since then and that had been...last year. Hell. No wonder the slightest brush of bodies was making him twitchy. Gritting his teeth against the surge of hunger, he told himself to stay on track. Focused. To clean up his brother's mess and move on.

The sooner they got through the next month, the better.

Sofia breathed through the attraction the same way she'd exhale after a difficult turn. She ignored the swirl of distracting sensations, calling on a lifetime's worth of discipline.

She controlled her body, not the other way around. And she most definitely would not allow handsome Quinn McNeill to rattle her with his touch. Or with his well-timed kisses that were just for show, even if the one she'd experienced had felt real enough.

With an effort, she steered him back toward their conversation, needing his captivating eyes to be on something besides her.

"I'm curious about the plan you developed with my father. I'm certain it didn't involve us being engaged." She would rather know before her father contacted her. Her powerful parent would never stop interfering with her life, insisting he knew best on everything from which public relations firm should promote her career to hiring a matchmaker she didn't want.

They'd butted heads on everything since her mother had died of breast cancer during Sofia's teens, ending her independence and putting her under the roof of a cold, controlling man. Until then, she and her mother had lived a bohemian lifestyle all over the US and Europe, her mom painting while she danced. When her mother died, she'd been too young to strike out alone and her father had been determined to win her over with his wealth and the opportunities it could afford.

She'd wanted no part of it. Until he'd found that magic carrot—ballet school in St. Petersburg, Russia, an opportunity she truly couldn't ignore. But she'd been paying for the privilege in so many ways since then, her debt never truly repaid.

"He wanted me to write off Cam's behavior as a private joke between old friends." Quinn shifted conversational gears easily. "But I'm sure he'll be glad that your preferences were considered."

"Vitaly has never concerned himself with my preferences." She already dreaded the phone call from him she knew was coming. He would be angry with her, for certain. But she needed to remind him that *he* wasn't the injured party here. "But he is not the only one affected by his decision to hire a matchmaker without my permission. I need to call him and demand he have that contract terminated immediately. I don't want my photo and profile posted anywhere else."

"Would you like me to tell him?" Quinn asked. She must have appeared surprised because he quickly added, "I don't mean to overstep. But he and I have unfinished business and I plan to find out exactly where Cameron found your profile. I'm not sure who is at fault for the miscommunication between your matchmaker and his, but I plan to look into it as a matter of legal protection for McNeill Resorts since your father threatened to sue at one point."

Sofia sighed. "I'm ninety percent sure that was just blustering, but I honestly don't blame you. And since I'd rather not speak to my father when I'm so upset with him, I'd actually be grateful if you would handle it."

It was a sad commentary on her relationship with her father that, while she hardly knew Quinn, she was already certain he would deal with her dad more effectively.

"Consider it done. And for what it's worth, he seemed to care a great deal about you when I spoke with him." Quinn said the words carefully. Diplomatically. No wonder Cameron relied on him to take care of sticky situations. "But I'm most concerned about your expectations going forward." He narrowed his gaze as he turned back toward her. "For instance, how often we need to be seen together in public. If we're going to do this, we'll need to coordinate dates and times."

"Really?" She was too tired and overwhelmed by the events of the evening to maintain the pragmatic approach now that it was just the two of them. "Although it's been a while since I dated, I'm sure that we managed to schedule outings without a lot of preplanning. Why don't I just text you tomorrow?"

His short bark of laughter surprised her as the limo descended into the Lincoln Tunnel toward Manhattan. Shadows crossed his face in quick succession in spite of the tinted windows.

"Fair enough. But maybe we could find a time to speak tomorrow. I'd like to be sure we agree on a story about how we met since you'll be talking to the media."

A stress headache threatened just from thinking about how carefully she would have to walk through that minefield, but damn it, she'd worked too hard to land that feature in *Dance* magazine to allow her pretend love life to steal all the spotlight.

"I have a rehearsal tomorrow at ten and I'll be jet-lagged and foggy-headed before that." She could barely think straight now to hammer out the details. "What if I just avoid reporters until we speak later in the day?"

Tomorrow's challenges would be difficult enough. She couldn't believe she'd also offered for *Dance* magazine to film her private audition with Idris Fortier the following week. She would be stressed enough that day without having her mistakes captured on video.

"This news might travel fast." He frowned, clearly disliking the idea of waiting. "But I understand about jet lag making conversation counterproductive in the morning. Can I pick you up after rehearsal then?"

His voice slid past her defenses for a moment; the question was the kind of thing a lover might ask her. Was it certifiable to spend so much time with him this month? He was the antithesis of the kind of men she normally dated—artists and bohemians who moved in vastly different worlds from the Koslov family dynasty. Quinn, on the other hand, was the kind of polished, powerful captain of industry who liked to rule the world according to his whim. The tendency was apparent from the moment he'd strode into her personal drama today and quietly taken over.

His assistance had been valuable, without question. But would she regret letting herself get close to a man like that? Especially one with such unexpected appeal?

"After rehearsal will work." She steadied herself as the limo driver jammed on the gas, trying to make some headway down Fifth Avenue despite the rush-hour traffic. "I'll be done by four. Do you know where the theater is?"

"Of course." He shifted his long legs in front of him, his open overcoat brushing her thigh when he moved. "Is there a side door? Somewhere to make a more discreet exit?"

She crossed her legs, shifting away from him.

"Good idea. There's a coffee shop on Columbus Avenue." She checked the address on her phone and shared it with him as the car finally turned down Ninth Street in the East Village where she lived. Her phone continued to vibrate every few minutes, reminding her that the whole world would have questions for her in the morning.

"Do you live alone?" he asked as the car rolled to a stop outside her building.

The question shouldn't surprise her since the neighborhood wasn't the kind of place where hedge fund managers made their home. Her father hated this place, routinely trying to entice her into rooms at the Plaza or a swank Park Avenue place.

"Yes." Her spine straightened as if she was standing in front of the ballet barre. "I love it here."

He got out of the car to walk her to the door while the driver retrieved her bag. In the time it took her to find her keys in her purse, two older men stumbled out of a local bar, boisterous and loud. She noticed that Quinn kept an eye on them until they passed the entrance to her building.

"Thanks for the ride." She opened the front door and stood in the entryway, very ready to dive into bed.

Alone, obviously. Although the thought of diving into bed with Quinn sent a warm wave of sexual interest through her.

"I'm walking you to your apartment door," he insisted,

eyes still scanning the street out front that was filled with
more bars than residences.

Too weary to argue, she gave a clipped nod and led the
way through the darkened corridor toward the elevator.
She was vaguely aware that he had taken her bags from
the limo driver and was carrying them for her. A few
moments later, arriving at apartment 5C, Quinn stepped
inside long enough to settle her luggage in the narrow
foyer. Strange how much smaller her apartment seemed
with him in it. She watched as his blue gaze ran over the
row of pendant lamps illuminating the dark hardwood
floor and white grass-cloth walls covered with dozens of
snapshots of ballet performances and backstage photos.

Maybe it was a sudden moment of self-consciousness
that made her grab her cell phone when it vibrated again
for what seemed like the tenth time in as many minutes.
Checking the screen, she realized the incoming texts
weren't from curious colleagues or her father.

Half were from the publicity firm she'd hired. The
other half were from the ballet mistress. A quick scan
of the content told her they were all concerned about the
same thing—social media speculation had suggested
she wasn't serious about the Fortier ballet and was focusing on her personal life. She felt her muscles tighten
and tense as if she were reading a review of a subpar
performance, the stress twisting along her shoulders and
squeezing her temples.

"Is everything all right?" Quinn's voice seemed distant compared to the imagined shout of the all-caps text
messages.

"You were right. News of our engagement traveled
quickly." Swallowing hard, she set the phone on an antique cabinet near the door. "My publicist urged me to
wear an engagement band tomorrow to forestall questions

until she writes the press release." Anger blazed through her in a fresh wave, shaking her out of her exhaustion. "It is a sad statement on my achievements that a lifetime of hard work is overshadowed by a rich man's proposal."

She wrenched off her scarf and fumbled with the buttons on her cape, anger making her movements stiff.

"It's because of your achievements that anyone is interested in your private life," Quinn reminded her quietly, reaching for the oversize buttons and freeing them.

She might have protested his sudden nearness, but in an instant he was already behind her, lifting the mohair garment from her shoulders to hang it on the wrought-iron coatrack.

"It still isn't fair," she fumed, although she could feel some of her anger leaking away as Quinn's words sank into her agitated mind. He had a point. A surprisingly thoughtful one. "No man would ever be badgered to wear a wedding ring to quiet his colleagues about his romantic status."

"No." He dug into his coat pocket and took out the small, dark box that had caused such havoc at Teterboro. "But since you've been put in a tremendously awkward position, maybe we should see what Cameron had in mind for his proposal."

He held out the box. The absurdity of the night struck her again as she stared at it. Who would have suspected when she boarded her plane in Kiev so many hours ago that she would be negotiating terms of an engagement with a total stranger in her apartment before bedtime?

"Why not? It's not like I'm going to be able to sleep now with all this to worry me." Shrugging, she backed deeper into her apartment, flipping on a metal floor lamp arching over the black leather sofa. "Come in, if you like. I haven't been home in three weeks so it feels nice to see my own things. I'm glad to be home even if it has been a crazy day."

She gestured toward the couch, taking a seat on the vintage steamer trunk that served as a coffee table.

"Only for a minute." He didn't remove his coat, but he did drop down onto the black leather seat. "I know you must be ready for bed." Their eyes connected for the briefest of moments before he glanced back at the ring box. "But let's take a look."

He levered open the black-velvet top to reveal a ring that took her breath away.

Quinn whistled softly. "You're sure you never met my brother before today?"

"Positive." Her hand reached for the ring without her permission, the emerald-cut diamond glowing like a crystal ball lit from within. A halo of small diamonds surrounded the central one, and the double band glittered with still more of them. "It can't possibly be real with so many diamonds. Although it looks like platinum."

"It is platinum." He sounded certain. "My brother goes all-in when he makes a statement." Gently he pried the ring from the box. "And given how much trouble his statement caused you today, I think it's only fair you wear it tomorrow."

Dropping the box onto the couch cushion, he held the ring in one hand and took her palm in the other. The shock of his warm fingers on her skin caught her off guard.

"I can't wear that." She sat across from him, their knees bumping while his thumb rested in the center of her palm.

Awareness sparked deep inside her, a light, leaping feeling like a perfectly executed cabriolé jump. Her heart beat faster.

A slow smile stretched across Quinn's face, transforming his features from ruggedly handsome to swoon-worthy.

"We agreed on an engagement. Don't you think it makes more sense to use the ring we have than to go shopping for a new one?"

The insinuation that she was being impractical helped her to see past that dazzling smile.

"I never would have guessed your brother would spend a small fortune on a ring for a woman he never met." She edged out of his grip. "I thought he was a romantic, not completely certifiable."

Quinn's smile faded. "I assure you, Cameron is neither." He set the ring on the steamer trunk beside her. "I'll let you decide whether or not to wear it in the morning. And in the meantime, I'd better let you get some rest."

He rose to his feet, leaving a priceless piece of jewelry balanced on last month's *Vogue*.

"Quinn." She stood to follow him to the door then reached back to grab the ring so she could return it. "Please. I don't feel right keeping this here."

He turned to face her as he reached the door, but made no move to take the glittering ring.

"If you were my bride-to-be, I would spare no expense to show the world you were mine." His blue eyes glowed with a warmth that had her remembering his kiss. Her breath caught in her chest and she wondered what it might be like for him to call her that for real.

Mine.

"I'm—" *At a total loss for words.* "That is—" She folded the diamond into her hand, squeezing it tightly so the stones pressed into her soft skin, distracting her from her hypnotic awareness of this man. "If you insist."

"It's a matter of believability, Sofia."

"It's only for one month." She wasn't sure if she said it to remind him or herself.

"We'll work out the details tomorrow." He reached to smooth a strand of hair from her forehead, barely touching her and still sending shimmers of pleasure along her temple and all the way down the back of her neck. "Sleep well."

She didn't even manage to get her voice working before he was out the door again, leaving her alone in a suddenly too empty apartment.

Squeezing the ring tighter in her fist, she waited for the pinch of pain from the sharp edges of the stones. She needed to remember that this wasn't real. Quinn McNeill had only agreed to this mad scheme to clean up his brother's mess. Any hint of attraction she felt needed to be squashed immediately, especially since Quinn was cut from the same mold as her father—focused on business and the accumulation of wealth. Her world was about art, emotions and human connections.

Her mother had taught her that people did not fall into both camps. In Sofia's experience it was true. And since she wanted her own relationships to be meaningful bonds rooted in shared creativity and ideals, she was willing to wait until she had more time in her life to find the right partner. Romance could not be rushed.

"It's only for a month," she said aloud again, forcing herself to set the engagement ring on the hallway table.

Surely she could keep up her end of a fake engagement for the sake of appearances? She'd made countless sacrifices for her career, from dancing on broken toes to living away from her family on the other side of the globe to train with Russian ballet masters.

Ignoring the sensual draw of Quinn McNeill couldn't possibly be more difficult than those challenges.

Yet, even as she marched herself off to bed, she feared she was lying to herself that she could keep her hands off the man anywhere near as easily as she'd set down the ring.

Four

Four

Quinn pulled an all-nighter, working straight through until noon the next day. He rearranged his schedule to accommodate more time in the city over the upcoming month. He'd avoided the office and shut off his phone for all but critical notifications, not ready to address the questions about his relationship with Sofia until they'd worked out a game plan.

Sofia.

Shoving away from the overly bright screen on his laptop, Quinn leaned back into the deep leather cushioning of his office chair. His grandfather's old chair, even after decades of use, seemed to retain class and grace, a steady touchstone in a career that constantly demanded invention and innovation to stay competitive. Eyes wandering to the corner of his walnut desk, he absently skimmed over the open newspaper. Even with news apps on his phone, Quinn still read the paper every morning, feeling a sense of connection to the ink and paper. And he couldn't ignore what was printed in today's society section—a photograph of the lithe ballerina.

She hadn't been far from his thoughts all morning and now was no different as he shut down his computer and headed out of the office building to his chauffeur-driven Escalade. And damn if Sofia didn't continue to dance through his mind as he rode toward the site of McNeill Resorts' latest renovation project in Brooklyn. Quinn powered down his laptop and stored it in the compartment beside the oversize captain's chair. He tried to prep himself for the inevitable confrontation with Cameron, who was slated to be on site in their grandfather's absence.

Even though his brother had walked away from his would-be ballerina bride yesterday, Quinn guessed that Cameron would still have something to say about the turn of events after he'd left. And though Quinn hoped he'd quelled some of Sofia's father's anger, he knew the engagement would make waves with his brother. If anything, Quinn hoped that this would make Cameron come to his senses about tying the knot with a woman he'd never met.

Running his hand through thick hair, Quinn let out a low sigh. He needed Cameron to be rational today.

He pressed the switch for the intercom as the Escalade rolled to a stop.

"I shouldn't be long, Jeff," Quinn told his driver before he stepped out of the vehicle in front of the converted bank on Montague Street in Brooklyn Heights. Coffee in hand, he headed onto the site, his well-worn leather shoes crunching against the gravel and construction dust.

Glancing at the scaffolding on the building, he nodded at the progress as the smell of fresh-cut wood and the sounds of hammering filled the air.

"Morning, Giacomo." Quinn nodded to the site foreman before picking up a hard hat to enter the building.

Giacomo—a sought-after project manager who specialized in historic conversions—gave a silent wave, his ear pressed to his cell phone while he juggled a coffee and a tablet full of project notes. The guy pointed to the roof of the building, answering Quinn's unasked question about his brother's whereabouts. Out of respect, the only time the McNeills showed up at each other's job sites was to talk family business.

Or, in this case, family brides.

Mood darkening as he anticipated an argument, Quinn climbed the temporary stairs installed during the renovation stage to connect the floors that had been stripped down to the studs. A swirl of cement dust kicked up from some kind of demo work on the second floor, and he quickened his steps. He passed some workers perched on scaffolding outside the fourth floor, debating the merits of salvaging some of the crumbling granite façade. Quinn had practically grown up on job sites like this, frequently travelling around the country with his grandfather to learn the business.

At least, that had been the family's party line. The larger reason was that, during the six months of the year his father had custody of his sons, Liam McNeill was usually too busy thrill-seeking around the globe to bother with parental duties.

Cliff-jumping in Santorini, Greece, or white-water rafting down a perilous South Korean river always seemed like more fun to Quinn's father than child-rearing. So Malcolm McNeill had stepped in more times than not, teaching his grandsons about property development and the resort industry from the ground up.

Reaching the rooftop, Quinn spied his brother looking out at the skyline from the structure's best feature—a sunny oasis on the roof that would one day be a space for outdoor dining, drinks and special events. Even at noon the view was breathtaking. But at dusk, when the sun slipped behind the Manhattan skyline, there was no finer perspective on the city than right here.

Cameron sat in a beat-up plastic patio chair that looked like a Dumpster salvage, the legs speckled with various-colored paints. He had dragged the seat close to the edge of the roof, his laptop balanced on his knees and his hard hat sitting on a section of exposed trusses at his feet. His dark jeans sported sawdust, his leg bouncing to some unheard rhythm.

Quinn must have made a noise or cast a shadow because Cameron looked toward him.

"I'm not sure I want to see you right now." Cameron didn't smile, his attention returning to his computer screen. "The headlines I've seen so far don't exactly fill me with confidence about what went on last night after I left."

"The key point there being—you left." Quinn had never connected as well with Cam as he did with Ian, and that made it tougher to see Cameron's side now when his younger brother seemed so clearly in the wrong.

"So you felt compelled to stick around and play white knight?" Cameron flipped the screen of his laptop to face Quinn, showing a headline that read Two McNeill Magnates Propose to Former Sugarplum Fairy.

The accompanying photo showed Sofia pirouetting across a stage in a tutu. Damn. So he hadn't really imagined how hot she was. The levelheaded, practical side of

Quinn reeled at the absurd headline and the media circus that would continue to send in the clowns until the official "engagement" story aired.

But his rational side didn't seem to be in full control. Sofia's petite body, her lean and limber pose, made him recall their kiss and the heat of that impromptu moment.

Cameron set his jaw, daggers dancing from his eyes. Accusatory and angry, sure. It was all Quinn needed to be drawn back to the problem at hand.

Quinn crossed his arms, undaunted. Cam had to realize what was at stake.

"You piss off her father, one of the wealthiest men in the world, who also happens to have enough Eastern European connections to run our deal for the new resorts into the ground, and call it none of my business?" Quinn shook his head and dragged a crate over to where Cameron was sitting. He planted a foot on it.

Cameron's mouth thinned, his voice a near growl. "You crossed a line into my personal affairs and you know it. You don't just propose to your brother's girl five minutes after they're through." Cameron tipped back in the plastic chair like it was a rocker. It teetered on two legs.

The move put Quinn's teeth on edge but not nearly as much as his words. Cam would think no more of walking across exposed truss beams at two stories than he would at twelve.

"Sofia was never yours," Quinn reminded him, more irritated than he ought to be at the idea, as a protective fire suddenly blazed in the pit of his chest. "And you lost any chance you had of salvaging something with her when you walked out of the airport yesterday."

For once, however, Quinn couldn't be disappointed

with in Cam's impulsive ways. The thought of her sharing that kiss with anyone but Quinn was intolerable.

"Think what you want of my motives, but I saw how you were looking at her." Cameron drummed his fingers along the back of the laptop case.

That stopped him. He couldn't deny that he'd felt something as soon as he'd seen her in person.

Cam shook his head. "And I still wouldn't have walked out, except I saw her looking at you that same exact way. It's one thing for me to turn my back on a bar fight or a heated investors meeting, but, contrary to popular belief, I wouldn't leave the woman to fend off nosy journalists if I hadn't seen the looks darting back and forth between you two."

"In that case…thank you." Stunned by a depth of insight he'd never given his brother credit for, Quinn wasn't sure how to handle the new information. Had Sofia been as drawn to him as he was to her? "After speaking to her father, I'm beginning to think her privacy was compromised by the matchmaker he hired. Bad enough Vitaly Koslov contracted the consultant without her knowledge. But I don't think he would have ever sanctioned his daughter's photo and contact information on the kind of pick-a-bride profile site you described to me."

"I thought the same thing after I left the airport yesterday." Cameron turned his laptop screen so Quinn could see the web banner for a Manhattan matchmaker, Mallory West. "I called my own matchmaker and she reminded me that I knowingly chose a match off a third-party web site Mallory West's clients can access, so I was informed ahead of time that Ms. West didn't know those women personally. She simply facilitated the meet. She gave me a full refund and assured me she would speak to the person who vetted the women on the web site I viewed."

Quinn sank down onto the crate and looked out across the bay on the sprawl of Lower Manhattan anchored by the Freedom Tower. Now that he'd seen firsthand how much havoc Cameron's bride hunt had caused for Sofia, he was thoroughly invested in the whole debacle.

"How can a matchmaker match people she doesn't actually know?" That sounded unethical. "I didn't think that's how they worked."

Cameron nodded as he signed into a private web page.

"They don't. But I was in a hurry and didn't want to jump through a lot of hoops since I wasn't really looking for true love everlasting." Cameron shrugged. "And Mallory's right—she was just a facilitator. I was paying special attention to the women listed on that third-party web site."

"Defeating the whole purpose of a matchmaker." Quinn ground his teeth together. "You might as well have gone shopping for a bride online. Why the hell would you pay the rates for a private matchmaker only to meet a woman whose name you pulled out of a damn hat?"

Cam seemed to take the question seriously. "I wanted to speed up the process and I hoped that the matchmaker's résumé lent credibility to the women I met."

Quinn wished he'd paid better attention when Cameron had first told him about his visit to the matchmaker's office, but at the time, he'd been focused on talking Cam out of jumping into a marriage.

"So she's taking no responsibility and she gave you your money back, which makes me wonder if she's worried about that web site, too. Can you still access that page?"

"No. Now that I've given up my membership with

Mallory West, I can't, but Ms. West said Sofia's profile is no longer included on the page."

"And once you told her you were interested in meeting Sofia, she texted you the flight details?"

"Correct." Cameron closed the laptop.

"I'll pass that information along to Sofia's father. I'm hoping to defuse some of his anger. After all, he was the one who released her photo in the first place. It's not your fault he hired an incompetent matchmaker." Quinn raised his voice as a jackhammer went to work somewhere in the building. The roof vibrated with the noise.

"I find it ironic that I ran out to marry a woman because of Gramps' will, and Sofia was my match based on her father's equally manipulative tactics to see her wed." Cameron picked up his hard hat and juggled it from one hand to another, his eyes never leaving some distant point to the northwest.

"Right. But I don't understand why Vitaly was surprised to see you in the airport if he shared the flight information with Sofia's matchmaker, who shared it with yours." Quinn's teeth rattled as the vibrations under his feet picked up strength. "I don't think his surprise was an act. Which means something doesn't add up."

He'd already hired a guy in his company's IT department to research any information about Sofia Koslov that had been posted online in the last month. Even if the third-party web site had deleted her profile, this guy could usually find reliable traces. For Quinn, it would help to show Vitaly where Cameron had found Sofia's profile. How could Sofia's father block the sale of the hotels the McNeills wanted if they were blameless in this matchmaking snafu?

But hiring an investigator served a second purpose, too—protecting Sofia's privacy.

Rising to his feet in one fluid motion, Cameron picked up his hard hat and shoved it onto his head.

"It makes sense to figure out what happened with Sofia's personal information before you move forward with your engagement." Cam checked his phone and put it in his pocket. "Or your wedding."

"Whoa." Quinn clapped a hand on his brother's back. Hard. "We're not getting married, as you damn well know."

The thought of spending a night with her revved him up fast, though. He didn't need that image in his head when he was on his way to meet her and talk through a plan for their fake engagement.

Then again, it wasn't as if he'd promised to keep his hands off her or anything. And she wanted the engagement to be believable. Already he was giving himself permission to get closer to her.

Much, much closer.

"You keep on telling yourself there's nothing going on." Cam shook off his hand and stalked toward the stairwell. "But no matter how much you play it off like Gramps' will doesn't matter to you, I know it's got to be in the back of your mind that you need to get married." Cameron rested a hand on the brick half wall that housed the stairs and faced Quinn. "Soon."

A dark expression clouded Cameron's features as he turned away, his steps echoing in the sudden silence as the jackhammer stopped. Quinn watched his brother walk away before he could argue. He was not getting married for the sake of McNeill Resorts, damn it. He was just running some damage control for the family business after his brother had made such a damn mess of things.

But maybe Cameron had a point. Quinn was attracted

to her. He had to pretend to be her fiancé. There was no reason in the world he couldn't use this time to get closer to Sofia.

To enjoy Sofia.

To find out if that kiss had been a fluke or if the heat between them was every bit as scorching as he imagined.

Five

Sofia braided her wet hair in the large, shared dressing room after her shower, unwilling to attend her meeting with Quinn while drenched in sweat from her second class of the day. The writer Anton Chekov had once famously said that he knew nothing about the ballet but that the ballerinas "stink like horses" during the intervals, and the man had a point.

Digging in her bag for a hair tie, she scuttled past some of the junior dancers before she dropped into a chair near one of the makeup mirrors. The afternoon classes tended to have more of the sixteen-to eighteen-year-olds who could give her a run for her money physically, which had been just what she'd needed. After a day in the air yesterday, her body had felt off during her first class of the morning. So after her show rehearsals, she'd joined an afternoon session as well to will her body back into show shape. A day missed, and a dancer noticed. Besides, cramming every second of her day with hard work meant there were less opportunities for her older colleagues to quiz her about yesterday.

Or the huge rock on her finger.

She hadn't left the breathtaking ring on for long, but she'd worn it from the cab to the dressing room before removing it for dancing, causing a room full of whispers and raised eyebrows before the dancing master put everyone to work. She retrieved Quinn's gift now that she was in street clothes and slid the beautiful piece onto her finger. The few junior ballerinas remaining at the end of the day were in a heated discussion about the romantic availability of one of the male dancers.

"Holy crap, honey, look at that thing." Jasmine Jackson's voice surprised her, even though she should have been expecting her friend and publicist to meet her backstage for a quick meeting.

Jasmine rushed toward her, the heavy exit door banging shut behind her as she wove around stored stage lights and rolling racks of costumes covered in plastic. Petite with glossy hair so black it looked blue in certain light, Jasmine had attended ballet school with her in North Carolina for a year before Sofia's mother had caught the travel bug to tour Europe. Jasmine had quit dancing at thirteen with the arrival of hormones and serious curves. Many women would envy her figure, but Sofia had taken the phone calls from her distraught friend when her breasts had moved well into C-cup range—one of many physical changes that made dancing more difficult and casting directors overlook her. She'd been devastated.

Jasmine had ended up attending Syracuse University for communications and went on to work in advertising and promotions for the fitness industry. Her job paid well and brought her to New York, much to Sofia's delight. They'd shared an apartment for two years before Jasmine's budget had seriously outstripped hers and her friend had upgraded to a bigger place.

Sofia squeezed her hand in a fist to keep the ring in place. "I know. I'm terrified of losing it. And it seems really weird that it fits me, doesn't it?" Had her father shared such personal details with the matchmaker he'd hired? She had considered speaking to him today to assess how much her privacy had been breached. But she was still so angry with him over his presumptuous matchmaking tactics.

Jasmine bent to lift and examine Sofia's hand. A strand of silky black hair trailed over Sofia's wrist as her friend peered at the ring in the lights of the makeup mirror. As always, Jasmine looked so put together—her knee-length, gray-and-taupe sweater dress was formfitting underneath a tailored swing coat she left open. Bracelets clinked as she moved, everything about her girly and feminine. By contrast Sofia sported leggings and a man's dress shirt left untucked, with a black blazer—kind of her go-to work outfit in the colder months. With her wet hair braided, she felt more than a little dull next to glamorous Jasmine.

"Wow. Those diamonds are the real deal." Her Southern accent had softened over the years, but the lilt was still there. "Come on. Let's walk and talk so I can bring you up to speed before we meet with your very sexy fiancé."

Leave it to Jasmine to maintain the façade of this fake engagement in public. She was great at her job and a great friend, too. Jasmine had tried refusing payment for the work she did to promote Sofia's career, but she wouldn't hear of it. As it was, she knew the rate Jasmine gave her was far less than what her friend billed her corporate accounts.

"You're going into the coffee shop with me?" Sofia led the way out of the building, taking the less conspicuous path over West Sixty-Fifth Street instead of cutting through Lincoln Center. "I've been second-guessing myself and nervous about seeing him all day." She squeezed Jasmine's arm like a lifeline, grateful for a true friend after the past weeks of being on her guard at all times.

"Well, I hadn't planned on it." Jasmine frowned, oblivious to the male heads she turned as they navigated streets getting busier as rush hour neared. "The two of you have a lot to figure out."

"I know. But you're a major part of that." If Jasmine was there, it was like a business meeting—a way to coordinate schedules.

"Since when do you need a babysitter for a date? I'll say hello, but then I've got to go. I have an appointment downtown for happy hour drinks." Her work in PR happened over dinner and cocktails as often as it happened in a boardroom. "So fill me in on what happened today."

"Not much, thankfully." She'd been pleased with her plan to avoid talking about the engagement by outworking everyone in the room. "The only one who really cornered me about it was the ballet mistress, and she just warned me to remember that Idris Fortier would surely prefer any woman he worked with to devote one thousand percent to his ballet."

"Did you tell her that one thousand percent was a bit much?"

"Would I still have a job right now if I did?" The lighthearted moment ended quickly as Joe Coffee came into view and Sofia thought about seeing Quinn again.

Had she overestimated his appeal last night in her trancelike jet lag? She hoped so.

"How are your knees?" Jasmine asked. It was the only question that could rattle her more than Quinn.

Prone to knee problems, Sofia had injuries the same way all dancers had injuries. That is, always. Ballet was hard on the body and a dancer never knew when her time might be up. She feared for the length of her career, especially when she remembered the devil's bargain she'd made with her father as a teen. Two months after her mother died, he'd refused to let Sofia pursue a dance opportunity in St. Petersburg, insisting she finish her education in the US. But after weeks of begging and crying—it was what her mother had wanted for her—he'd offered her a trade. She could go to Russia for dance school, but only if she promised that when her dance career was finished, she would come to work for him.

Which was not happening. He couldn't hold her to a deal she'd made as a teen. But she worried for her future with no backup plan after dance. Saying no to him when she had no prospects would be difficult. Staying in this expensive city would be virtually impossible. She willed away the ache in her knee and vowed to ice it longer tonight. It'd have to do.

"I had some twinges in my right knee in Kiev, but nothing that kept me off the stage." She tucked her shoulder bag closer as a family with two strollers pulled up beside them on the crosswalk. Horns and squeaky brakes mingled with the occasional sound of a doorman whistling for a cab in a cacophony her ears welcomed after six hours of Tchaikovsky and Stravinsky.

"Don't overdo it," Jasmine warned. "Staying healthy is more important than Idris and his ballet, no matter what you think."

"On the contrary, Idris and his ballet are my ticket to a post-dance career." She knew that a starring role and working closely with the superstar choreographer would completely change her profile in the dance world. It would open doors for a creative project she had in mind, but she needed someone like him to be on board. So she just had to nurse her knee through this opportunity.

Jasmine laughed. "You're the same as ever, Sofia. I think I could replay the conversations we had at nine and they'd be exactly the same ones we have today. You've always had a plan, I'll give you that."

Sofia slowed her step outside the door of Joe Coffee, grabbing Jasmine's arm.

"Not with Quinn McNeill, I don't." She wasn't intimidated by him or his money. Yet there was something about the way he made her feel that kept her anxious. Was it just physical attraction? Or did that anxiety mean something more worrisome?

Was it her gut telling her he was untrustworthy?

A messenger on a bicycle slammed his bike into the rack near them before entering the coffeehouse. The scent of fragrant Arabica beans and baked goods drifted through the door in his wake. Hunger reverberated in Sofia's stomach. Her diet was controlled and disciplined. Most days, she didn't mind. The sacrifice of cheesy fries and pizza had yet to outweigh the worth of her dream. But the smell of food tempted her so.

"He's just a man. The same as any other." Jasmine pursed her lips. "Your everyday average billionaire." She linked her arm through Sofia's and tugged her ahead. "Come on. I've got a few details to go over before I head out."

Squaring her shoulders, Sofia headed inside, determined not to let Quinn see that he made her uneasy. Distracted.

And far too interested in the attraction she'd felt for him the first moment their gazes had connected.

* * *

Head high, Sofia Koslov strolled into the coffee shop like a dancer and Quinn took notice from his seat at a table in the back corner. She carried herself differently than other women, a fact he'd picked up on yesterday before Cameron had proposed to her.

At that time he hadn't known what it was about her perfect posture and her graceful movements. Now he recognized it as her dance training that made her move like that. He couldn't picture her ever playing the Sugar Plum Fairy, however, despite the news clippings.

The Black Swan in *Swan Lake* maybe. She had a regal elegance, a sophistication. Her hair was pulled back into a damp braid that highlighted the long neck traditional in ballerinas. Her clothing was simple and understated so that the only thing that shone was the woman herself. And the ring on her left hand, he amended with satisfaction. Even staring at her across a crowded coffee shop, Quinn wanted her.

Damn.

He rose to greet the two women as they made their way through milling patrons juggling cups and cell phones. Her friend continued to shadow her step for step, a fact that disappointed him since he'd been eager to speak to Sofia privately. Or as privately as he could in a Manhattan java shop. He would have lobbied to meet at his apartment or in a quiet restaurant, but Sofia had been tired and rattled last night when they'd made these plans and he had the impression she'd purposely chosen someplace more public.

"Sofia." He greeted her the way he would greet a woman he loved, sliding an arm around her waist and kissing her cheek, mindful of the public atmosphere but still appropriately warm. He thought it better to be cautious since he didn't know her friend and wanted to be sure he played the part of Sofia's husband-to-be at all times.

Besides, it felt good to touch her.

The cool skin of her cheek warmed as his lips lingered for a moment. When he backed away, he spied the hint of color in her face before he extended a hand to her friend.

"Quinn McNeill," he introduced himself.

"Jasmine Jackson. I'm the best friend as well as the publicist. And total keeper of all her secrets." Her grip was firm and professional, and her eyes made it clear she knew full well about their ruse. "Shall we have a seat so I can go over my suggestions for the two of you?"

"Of course. Right this way." He gestured toward the table he'd secured in the back. Jasmine went first, and he palmed the small of Sofia's back to guide her along. Having his hands on her again made him realize how much he'd looked forward to acting out the part of fiancé.

He claimed the seat beside Sofia while Jasmine took the spot across from them and set down the leather binder on the maple surface between them.

"I've made copies of my ideal social calendar for both of you." She slid matching papers their way. "I've already sent Sofia the digital file so she can forward it to you, Quinn."

Taking in the extensive notes on dates and events, he was impressed. She had details about the status of their invitations, directions, suggested attire, a who's who list of people they should try to speak to at each event and potential spots for photo ops. Clearly, the woman had done her homework and she'd done it in a hurry.

"I see you know the New York social calendar," he remarked, wondering if his company's PR firm would do half as good of a job. "This is ambitious."

As Sofia's finger followed the lines of type, the diamond engagement ring caught the last of the pale winter sunlight. As impressive as the piece was, and he was glad she'd worn it, he felt a ridiculous urge to replace it with something of his own choosing.

He hoped that normal brotherly competitiveness accounted for that instinct and not some latent sentimental notions. No way would he let his grandfather's dictate to marry get to him. He had decided to use this time with Sofia as a way to enjoy their obvious attraction. Not romanticize it.

"As I said." Jasmine closed her binder and folded her manicured fingers on top of the leather. "This is simply a wish list that would serve several purposes at once for Sofia."

"You got in touch with *Dance* magazine to reschedule our interview?" Sofia asked, her finger now stalled on a line item toward the bottom of the page.

"Yes. I told them today was full for you but that you could meet with them Friday night during the welcome reception for Idris Fortier." Jasmine reached across the table to point out the event listed at the top of the paper. "In the meantime, I promised to release your statement about yesterday's events to them first." Jasmine pulled another set of papers from the binder and passed them across the table. "Here's a tentative release. If you could make your changes and send the digital file back to me before seven tonight, I can get it to the reporters for a blog post spot they're holding for you."

Quinn scanned the release, approving of the minimal personal details it included.

"'When we met'?" Sofia read a highlighted yellow section aloud. "'When we fell in love'? Is that really necessary?" Her gray eyes darted his way then back to her friend.

"Those are two questions everyone will ask. Better to save yourself answering it twenty times over and put out the information up front that you want people to see." Jasmine gave Sofia's forearm an affectionate squeeze. "But I will let you two discuss that since I need to run to another appointment."

Secretly pleased to have Sofia all to himself, Quinn rose as Jasmine took her leave. Sofia neatly folded the papers and tucked them into the black leather satchel she carried.

"Maybe we could talk through the rest of this while we walk? The park is close by. I know I suggested this place, but I wasn't thinking about how noisy it would be."

"Good idea." He left the waitress a tip even though they hadn't ordered, then escorted Sofia out onto the street. With a hand on her hip, he could feel the tension vibrating through her. Stress? Nervousness? He had a tough time reading her. "I live on the other side of the park. We could at least head in that direction."

The traffic would be gridlocked soon anyhow and he knew the paths well enough on the southern end of Central Park.

"Sounds good." She seemed slightly more relaxed outdoors. "And I'm sorry if this situation is cutting into your time. I probably wasn't in the best frame of mind to make decisions yesterday."

"Attending these events will only benefit my business." He turned down West Sixty-Ninth Street toward the park, plucking her bag off her shoulder to carry it for her. Fake fiancé or not, she would be his top priority for the upcoming weeks. She didn't seem like the type of woman who allowed other people to take care of her.

But from where Quinn stood, she was in need of some spoiling—something this media ruse might let him do for her. "I haven't done much networking in the last year and it always lifts the company profile."

He wanted her at ease. Enjoying herself. Hell, he wanted to get to know her better and this would be the perfect time. So the less she worried about inconveniencing him, the better.

"That's a generous way to look at the situation. Thank you."

"I wouldn't call it generous." He tipped his head up to the skies as a few snowflakes began to fall. "Are you going to be warm enough for this?"

Her blazer was heavy but now that the sun was almost down, the temperature was hovering just below freezing.

"My cape is in my bag," she said, pointing to the satchel on his shoulder. He lifted his arm so she could rifle through it and pull out the same mohair garment she'd worn the day before.

"Let me." Drawing her to the quieter side of the street near the buildings, he took the cape and draped it over her shoulders, then turned her so he could fasten the two big buttons close to her neck. His eyes met hers and, for half a heartbeat, that same awareness from their kiss danced in the air between them.

"I can get them," she protested, trying to sidle away politely.

He held fast, hands lingering on the placket as the snowfall picked up speed, coating her shoulders.

"But the more comfortable we get with each other now, the easier it's going to be to fool everyone on Friday." He looked forward to it.

Very much.

Part of it had something to do with the way her heartbeat quickened at his touch. He could feel the quick thrum beneath his knuckles right through her layers of clothing. He wanted to kiss her again, to taste her rosy lips where a snowflake quickly melted. But instead, he reached for the wide hood of her cape and drew it over her head to keep the snow off.

"Then I will try to think of this day as a dress rehearsal." She sounded so damn serious.

That, combined with some of the things she'd shared with him the night before, reinforced his notion of her as highly driven. He admired her work ethic and her dedication to her career. He'd always been the type to pour himself into a work project, too. Duty and perseverance were the cornerstones of his approach to the world.

"In that case, we can't go wrong." Readjusting her bag on his shoulder, he pressed a light hand to the small of her back to guide her through a left on Central Park West and the quick right to get on the path that would take them toward his apartment. "From what I gleaned about you last night as I read up on your career, it sounds like you've succeeded at everything you've set out to accomplish."

Even with the hood pulled up, he could see the way she smiled.

"Either that or I have an excellent publicist."

That surprised a laugh out of him as they strode deeper into the park, which seemed a bit busier than usual, the fresh snow bringing out kids and kids-at-heart. They passed people walking dogs and packs of middle-school-aged children in uniforms, still wearing backpacks.

"Jasmine does seem determined to package your career—and you—in the best possible way."

"She's a good friend and an equally awesome public relations manager."

"And this reception she wants us to attend. That's

for the choreographer you mentioned who's putting to-gether the new ballet." He'd read about the guy a good bit last night. "The media can't use enough superlatives about him gracing New York with his presence." It had been a bit much in Quinn's mind, but then, he was far from an expert.

"You have been doing your research." She rewarded him with an approving smile that renewed the urge to kiss her.

But he also liked finding out more about her that would help him get closer to her. He would wait.

"This is a dress rehearsal for me, too, Sofia." He watched a few kids try to shake a radio-controlled heli-copter down from some tree limbs; they were attracting an audience. "I'm trying to get my part down."

"You're doing well. If you were one of my students, you'd be promoted to the next level."

"You teach?" He paused on the outskirts of the crowd.

"A lot of the dancers do." Sofia's gaze went up to the helicopter and the kids shaking any branches of the old oak they could reach. "It's a way to pick up some extra income and give back to the company. The School of American Ballet is like our farm system…it feeds the City Ballet."

"Give me one second." He hated to interrupt her, but he also couldn't let the kids kill a tree that—for all he knew—could predate the damn park itself. He set down Sofia's bag and grabbed a football at one of the boys' feet as he strode into the group. "Guys, back up a minute."

The group did as he asked, a few calling out taunts that he'd never be able to reach the branch where the he-licopter teetered. Which he welcomed, of course, since the ribbing only ensured that he'd throw twice as hard.

He'd grown up with brothers, after all. He spoke the language.

"I get three shots," he insisted. "Only because I haven't warmed up my arm."

"I'll give you six, old man," shouted a wiry redhead who seemed to be the ringleader. "That thing is straight-up stuck."

Old?

Quinn told himself that he was only interested in saving the tree, but with a beautiful woman he wanted to impress watching from the sidelines, there was a chance he was fueled by another motivation altogether. Far from old…he was acting like a damn kid.

Backing up a step to adjust his aim, he cocked his arm and let the football fly.

Like in an ESPN highlight reel, the thing connected with the toy helicopter on the first try, earning cheers of admiration. And, because it had been so high up, the kids had time to run underneath the tree where the mouthy redhead caught it, scoring some of the victory for himself.

"Sorry about that." Quinn jogged back to Sofia, who stood on the path under a halo of light from a cast-iron street lamp. He grabbed her bag and hitched it higher on his shoulder.

With her hooded cape and the snow falling all around her, she looked like some exotic character from one of her ballets. A Russian princess, maybe.

"You appeared to have performed that trick a few times before," she observed.

"With two brothers? Of course. We got plenty of things caught in trees as kids. Kites were the worst to get down. By comparison, the helicopter was a piece of cake." His warm breath lingered in the cool air, making it seem as though his words hung in the space between them. A gust of wind sent a slight chill through him. Glancing at Sofia, he noticed her hair was still wet.

"I can't imagine what it would be like to have siblings." The loneliness in her words was evident.

"Your bio doesn't say much about your family." He knew because he'd scoured it for details about her.

"In the past, I tried to keep my personal life and work life separate. Not that I have a lot of personal life to speak about." She stared up at Tavern on the Green as they passed. The restaurant looked sort of otherworldly in the snowfall with the trees and white lights all around. "But my mother died when I was thirteen and I am not close with my father."

"I'm sorry about your mother." He took her hand for the dash across West Drive before they reached quieter roads through the middle of the park. "That must have been a really difficult age to lose a parent."

He didn't let go of her hand since her fingers were chilled. And because he wanted to touch her. Besides, they would be in the public eye again soon enough, where they would have to sell themselves as a loving couple.

As if she understood his motivations, she leaned into him and the spicy smell of her currant perfume wafted up to him. Hooking her arm through his, she drew closer.

"I was devastated. All the more so because my mother hated my father, which meant I hated him, too. Then, suddenly, after her death I was left with him." Sofia pushed off her hood as they reached denser growth that limited how much snow fell on them. Maybe she'd just been looking for a reason to untwine their fingers. "To this day, I don't know what drew the two of them together since he represented everything she despised. She called the privileged wealthy a 'soulless culture.'"

"What about you?" Quinn wondered where that left him in her world view. "Do you agree with your mother?"

"Wait." She turned around to look at the path they'd just traveled, tugging on his arm so they stood off the walkway to one side. "Let's stop for a second and take it in."

She didn't have to explain what she meant. This part of the park was beautiful on any given day. But in a fresh snowfall, with the Tavern on the Green glowing from within and the tree trunks and branches draped in white lights, the view was like no other in the city. The snow dulled the sounds from the streets nearby, quieting rush hour to white noise.

Standing with Sofia at his side made it all the more appealing. The glow of the white lights reflected on her face.

"Beautiful." His assessment, while simple, was heartfelt.

"But you know what my mother taught me about beauty?" Sofia asked, a mischievous light in her liquid silver eyes. "It is not a matter of just looking beautiful. It should surround us." She held her hand out, palm up to catch snowflakes. "Feel special." Inhaling deeply, she smiled with her eyes closed. "Have a unique scent when you breathe it in. And if you can catch it on your tongue, the taste will be beautiful, too."

He watched, transfixed, as this aloof and disciplined dancer stuck her tongue out and tipped her head to the sky.

Another time, he might have laughed at her antics. But she seemed lost in a happy childhood memory, and he didn't want to spoil it. Reaching for her hand full of snowflakes, he warmed her palm with his and peered upward through the white branches at the hint of stars beyond.

"You're right." He felt the beauty around him, that much was certain. But it had more to do with the slide of her damp fingers between his. With the tattoo of the pulse at her wrist that he felt on his palm.

"Did you catch one?" She lowered her chin to meet his gaze, her eyes still alight with a glow of happiness.

But she must have seen another expression reflected in his face because her smile faded.

"No." He reached for her jaw to thumb a snowflake from her creamy cheek, her skin impossibly soft to the touch. Capturing her chin in his hand, he angled her lips for a taste. "But I'm about to."

Six

Transported by the snow, the city and the man, Sofia hadn't been expecting the kiss, and maybe it was her total lack of defenses that let her feel the pleasure of it. She delighted in the warm pressure of his mouth in contrast to such a cold day. The soft abrasion of his chin where the new of growth of whiskers rubbed over her tender skin oversensitive from the wind. The gentle way he touched her face to steer her where he wanted, to better delve between her lips.

Answering his demand by stepping closer, craving the warmth of the man, Sofia lost herself.

Quinn's kiss was the second act of *Swan Lake*. Or maybe *Giselle*. Or maybe it was every romantic moment she'd ever danced and never felt deeply until this moment. She squeezed his hand where he'd entwined their fingers, enjoying the way her body fit against him. They weren't like two dancers with bodies that complemented one another. But like a man possessing a woman, lending her his strength so she didn't have to draw from her own.

It was a moment of heaven.

When he slowly pulled away from her and she felt the snowflakes fall on her skin again now that he did not completely shelter her, the cool ping of the tiny drops urged her out of her romantic swoon. And no doubt about it, she stood in Central Park swooning on her feet for a man she'd met the day before.

"Quinn, we have a lot of work we should be doing." She blurted the words with no segue and zero grace. "If we want to get that press release out on time, that is."

Untangling her fingers from his, she brushed by him to continue walking…east? Her brain scrambled to regain thought. Yes, east. What on earth had gotten into her? Had that kiss been part of the role he seemed determined to play for her? Or had he truly felt inspired to kiss her?

"You're right." Quinn didn't need to walk fast to keep up with her as she practically jogged through the park. His longer strides ate up the ground easily. As he glanced at her, the light reflected devilishly in his eyes. "But I want you to know I liked kissing you, Sofia. Very much. There's no reason we shouldn't enjoy ourselves over the next few weeks."

Sharp, cold air entered her lungs. "Just because we are within easy reach doesn't mean we should automatically start touching." She didn't want to be a convenient outlet for him. "But what's our story for how we met or when we met?"

"I was introduced to your father at the Met Gala. Were you there with him?"

"Of course not. Do you have any idea what a ticket costs to that event?" At moments like this she could understand how her mother might have come to believe the wealthy were living in a different universe from regular people. The Met Gala was so far beyond her price range it was laughable.

"Actually, no." He stuffed his hands into the pockets of his overcoat, his profile in shadow as they walked. "I was on the guest list because I made a donation to the museum."

Right. Which meant he'd paid more than the ticket price that was almost half her annual salary. Like her father, Quinn belonged to a world of wealth and unreality. A world she had purposely avoided.

"Suffice it to say, we didn't meet there." She wished she'd worn warmer clothes for their walk. Her knees were feeling the effects of the cold.

"What if we say we met here? In the park? We bonded over rescuing a kid's toy stuck in a tree last spring." As a bicyclist churned through the growing snow cover, Quinn slid a protective arm around her, his hand an enticing warmth through her cape before his touch fell away again. "At least we don't have to make up something fictional. We base it on today, but say it happened when I was walking home one evening and you were taking a break in the park."

"That could work." She nodded, locking down the time frame in her mind and trying to envision today's scene in a different season. "Although I would never give a stranger I met in the park my contact information."

"Maybe I started taking that route home every day, hoping to see you. Two weeks later, bingo. There you were again. We fell in love over the next few months, and that should be all we need to fill out Jasmine's press release." He slowed as they passed Central Park Zoo and headed toward Fifth Avenue. "Are you all right?"

"Of course," she answered automatically. "Why?"

"You're limping."

"No I'm not." She couldn't be. Refused to be. She excelled at hiding injuries on stage. Perhaps she just didn't give much thought to her gait in her private time. "Just hurrying to get home."

She couldn't read his expression in the dark.

"I should have insisted on a car. We're almost there."

"I'm fine. And if you can point me to the closest subway station? I thought there was one on Fifth?"

"Come inside and warm up first. I'll drive you home."

"That's not necessary. As you pointed out, we have enough for the press release. I'll send it over to Jasmine when I get home."

"We haven't firmed up plans for the Fortier reception." As they emerged from the park, he crossed Fifth Avenue at East Sixty-First. "Besides, my building is right here. I can send out that release for you, and I'll call you a car afterward." He stopped outside the Pierre.

He lived in the hotel?

Of course he did. It was a gracious, old New York address with five-star service. The small part of her that was still her father's daughter could already envision the kind of food room service provided here.

"Sofia." Quinn lowered his voice as they stood under the awning in front of the building. "We're committed to this course now. Let's be sure we deliver a believable performance."

"Believable because we show up for all of those public appearances as a couple?" She lowered her voice even more in deference to the doorman who was pulling open a cab door for a newcomer. "Or believable because we're kissing in our spare time?"

Quinn seemed to weigh the idea carefully. "If you truly think that the kiss was a bad idea, we'll make sure all future displays of affection are strictly for show and limit them to the public sphere."

She wasn't sure if she was disappointed or relieved. Maybe a little of both.

"That might help." At least then she'd be prepared before he kissed her again. She'd have her guard up. Her body would receive a warning before he stoked it to life with a mere flick of his tongue. "Thank you."

"Will you come inside, then? We can have dinner sent up while we fill in the blanks for Jasmine and send out the statement." Quinn had been both patient and reasonable.

Of course, he was only doing any of this for the sake of his business concerns, protecting the McNeill interests from the threats her father had made at the airport last night. She needed to remember that, even if his kisses told a different story. Quinn was simply more experienced. Worldly. Maybe even jaded. Some people could kiss solely for passion's sake, not love, but she'd never been that kind of woman.

Or so she thought. Maybe she'd just never met a man she could truly feel passionate about? Unlike her friends, she'd never been a boy-crazy teenager. Her attention and love had always belonged to the stage.

"Okay," she agreed, the chill in her bones making the decision for her, damn it. Or maybe it was the promise of something more delicious than the banana and crackers that awaited her at home.

It wasn't Quinn's fault she was far more attracted to him than she'd ever been to any man. Deep in thought as they entered the hotel, they rode a private, key-operated elevator to his floor. Even the elevator was opulent, inlaid with gold, and the deep rich scarlet carpet showed no signs of wear. The doors swished opened into a large foyer and a view through the living room to Central Park.

The apartment took up an entire floor.

She should have guessed from the engagement ring she still wore that he would live this way. His family owned a resort chain, while he himself managed a hedge fund. Exactly the kind of man she would have never envisioned herself with. But in spite of the multimillion-dollar views, his apartment was decorated with tasteful restraint. Coffee-toned walls were a warm backdrop for sleek, gray furnishings punctuated with some rust-colored accents—a vase, matched roman shades that covered the top third of the huge windows. Comfortable and attractive, the room pulled her forward as Quinn switched on the fireplace and put in a call to the hotel's kitchen.

An hour later, picking over the remains of her chicken fricassee while seated on a giant leather couch that wrapped around a corner of Quinn's apartment, Sofia had to admit she felt glad to be there. The snow had stopped outside the living room windows, but peering down into the park with all the street lamps lit was sort of like looking into a dollhouse with hundreds of different tiny rooms. He was putting the finishing touches on the press release on his laptop. A fire crackled in the fireplace, warming her feet and knees, and she'd even accepted a throw blanket made of the softest cashmere ever.

With silent apologies to her mother, Sofia decided that no one truly soulless would help a scrappy thirteen-year-old retrieve a toy. Or help Sofia carry off a mad scheme to pretend to have a fiancé. Quinn was an exception to her mother's rule about rich people.

"Just confirming…when did we know we were in love?" Quinn had taken the easy chair diagonally across from her, maintaining a professional amount of space between them.

"How about when you ordered the chicken fricassee for me?" she offered, trying to stick to the truth the way he'd showed her earlier.

"No one could blame you for being wooed by the food here." He quit typing and peered over at her in the firelight.

They hadn't put any other lights on in this room, although there was a glow from the kitchen. Sofia had been enjoying looking outside and the view was easier to appreciate with less light behind her.

"Dancers are perpetually starving," she admitted. "So I'm more susceptible than most to good food."

"Why are you always starving?" Quinn set aside the laptop long enough to clear their plates and set the dishes on a serving cart that had been delivered half an hour ago.

"It's a figure of speech. I expend a great deal of energy, for one thing. And, for another, the body preferred by most directors is very slender."

The topic had come under more debate over the last few years with a move to recognize healthy bodies of all sizes in dance. But ballet was rooted in traditions on every level, and she didn't know any company that truly embraced this philosophy yet.

"I'm surprised. I would think the moves require a great deal of strength."

"They do. But we need to build that strength in different ways. Repetition of lighter weights, for example."

"But why?" He took the seat closer to her now, sharing the couch even though he was a couple feet away. He'd brought his laptop with him but hadn't opened it yet.

"Choreographers like a company of dancers that are all roughly the same size and build. There's more symmetry to it when we all move."

"And you'd still get that if you all agree to be ten

pounds heavier. And wouldn't more muscle minimize injury?"

"Yes and no. Some say a lighter frame puts less strain on the joints."

"You can't eat enough. You work constantly. You're subject to intra-squad jostling for position—so much so you're willing to fake an engagement to keep your detractors quiet." He counted off the negatives on his fingers. "So if you're willing to go through all that, I have to think there's one hell of an upside for you."

"There is." She shifted positions, straightening as she warmed to her subject. "I watched *Sleeping Beauty* with my mother as a child. It was a performance in the middle of nowhere—a tiny troupe traveling through Prague. And I was captivated by Aurora like any other little girl who attends the ballet." Sliding off the couch, she moved to an open spot on the floor to show him. "I thought the dancer was the most beautiful and elegant woman in the world." She took a position for the Rose Adagio dance in her stocking feet, imagining a princely suitor before her as she mimicked Aurora's questioning pose with one leg raised and curved behind her. "When she took the roses from each of her four suitors…" She mimed the action, having danced the role many times herself. "I knew I wanted to *be* her. Not just Aurora, but the dancer who brought her to life."

Quinn's blue gaze tracked the movement of her arched foot as she lifted it in the exaggerated extension that her Russian teachers had stressed. The warmth in his eyes—his attention to her body—did not inspire the same feelings as when she captured an audience's imagination on stage. This felt personal in a way that heated her skin and made her all too aware of her appearance.

Not just her body, which was perpetually displayed in

dance. But the stroke of her braid against one arm. The rush of air past her lips as her breath caught.

"So you dance for the love of it. Because it was your dream." He kept the conversation focused, which she appreciated since she'd forgotten what they were talking about for a moment, distracted by the sparks that crackled between them.

"I have never wanted to do anything else." Which was why she feared the end of her career, a moment that could sneak up on her on any given night, with her body constantly battling injuries.

She needed to reach the top of her field now—as quickly as possible—to achieve the fame necessary to parlay the experience into success afterward. And she needed to dance the starring role for Fortier to make that happen.

"Ballet is your passion." Quinn let the word simmer between them for a long moment before returning his attention to the laptop. "And I think I know when we fell in love."

He began typing.

"You do?" Her heartbeat stuttered in her chest. She forced herself to sit back down and resume normal conversation in spite of the nerve endings flickering to life all over her body.

Too late she realized she had sat closer to him than she'd been before. She told herself that was only so she could peer over his shoulder at whatever it was he was typing. She caught a hint of his male scent, something clean like soap or aftershave that made her want to breathe deeply.

"It was the first time I saw you dance." His fingers paused on the keyboard, the sudden quiet seeming to underscore the moment and stirring to life a whole host of complicated feelings.

His words should not affect her this way. Especially since they were spinning tall tales for the media and not discussing anything remotely real.

"Name the performance. I'll tell the whole world how your movements on the stage captured me. When I watched you dance, I saw how passion guides you and knew we were a match."

"You toy with me," she accused, scuttling back to her previous position on the couch. "Your words are like your kisses—all for show. But I find them confusing."

"I'm not toying with you." He passed her the laptop. "You should read this over."

How could she concentrate on the words when her blood ran too hot and she kept imagining the way his eyes had followed her body while she danced?

"I'm sure it's fine." She set the laptop on the couch between them. "Jasmine will review it before she sends it out."

"Sofia?" He moved the laptop to the coffee table, edging closer. "I don't know how else to approach this to make you more comfortable. But *you* wanted to put on this show. I'm trying to help you."

His voice, deep and masculine, sent a shiver through her.

"Thank you. But I would prefer if this remained a performance for the benefit of others. I don't want to play at the game when we are alone." She felt his nearness in the same way that she knew without looking where her dance partner would be at all times. Except that was practiced, a trick she'd learned through study and repetition. With Quinn, her cells seemed to seek out his presence, attuning themselves to him without her even thinking about it.

"The only reason I kissed you in the park is because I'm attracted to you. I won't pretend otherwise." With a shuddering breath, his eyes, which a moment ago blazed with heat, seemed to ember as his voice lilted with resignation. "But I can put a rein on that, and I have."

"How? How do you put a rein on it, as you say?" She wondered if he had tricks of his own. Something she might learn for herself.

"It's not easy. And it gets tougher the longer I'm with you." He lifted his hand toward her face the way he'd done in the snowfall right before he'd kissed her. But then he lowered his fingers again, hand falling to his side. "We have an agreement, however, and I'll do what it takes to see it through. If that means we play this your way, I'm going to do everything in my power to keep my hands to myself unless we're in public."

"The way we will be on Friday." At the reception for Idris Fortier. Her first real public appearance with Quinn as a couple, and it would be a major moment in her career.

Butterflies fluttered through her belly at the thought of being on this man's arm all evening. Feeling his hand at her waist or grazing her hip through a thin evening gown.

Pretending to be in love.

Her lips tingled as she wondered if he would kiss her.

"Yes." His gaze dipped to her mouth as if he could read her mind. "I'm already looking forward to it."

Seven

Tossing generous handfuls of Epsom salt into the tub, Sofia ran the hot water, anticipating the effects of the bath. Her muscles ached and it was only Wednesday.

As she let the water fill the tub, she pumped toning soap onto her hands and then her face, before splashing water from the faucet to wash away a day of sweat and stress. A candle flickered on the sink's countertop, sending a soothing scent of lavender into the air. When she was a small girl, her mother would always burn lavender candles after a long day. Although only a small connection to life before her mom passed away, the fragrance still relaxed her.

And she needed that now more than ever.

Deep breath in. Deep breath out.

Washing the rest of the soap from her face, Sofia tried to focus on preparing for the private audition for Idris Fortier in less than a week. That should be her sole thought.

But instead thoughts of Quinn pushed into her head. It had been two nights since they'd walked through the park and a day since her interview with *Dance* magazine where she'd relayed the love story she and Quinn had manufactured. The details seemed all too real. And she kept replaying their brief time together. His lips, his touch. How she was attracted to him, though she knew better.

Even after her bath, she was frustrated as hell. She stepped out of the tub, water dripping from her body onto a bath mat, and tested her knee carefully. And, thank heaven, it held. It felt better if not perfect. She shrugged on a short, fluffy bathrobe and yanked the tie into a knot.

Patting her face dry with a semi-plush hand towel, she examined her reflection in the mirror. She could do this. She could nail the audition and be the star that Idris Fortier wanted for his next ballet. That connection would do so much for her. Give her career legs after her physical ones quit giving her the lift and height she needed on her jumps.

Stashed on the corner of the countertop was a collection of reviews from the most reputable critics about Fortier's last ballet. Jasmine had sent this particular stack over to her apartment. When Sofia had an audition on her radar, she always poured over press releases and reviews, trying to glean a better sense of her audience.

Sifting through the documents once more, a headline caught her eye.

Affair.

She eased herself down onto the edge of the tub and put her feet back in the water as she devoured the article. Apparently the choreographer had had an affair with the star of his last production. The weight of that information unsettled her.

Her phone chirped, startling her. Pulling it out of the pocket of her robe, she glanced at the screen.

Quinn.

"Hello." Heart fluttering, she felt a mixture of excitement and nerves crash in her chest.

"Hello, Sofia." His voice incited a flush of warmth over her skin beneath the robe.

"Quinn." His name felt like an endearment on her tongue. "Hello," she said again. To cover her surprise.

She closed her eyes and saw him there—with her—in the tub. Her mouth went dry.

"I thought you might like an update about the matchmaker situation," he continued.

Something that felt an awful lot like disappointment pounded in tandem with her heartbeat. Had she really just wanted him to call for no reason? If this faux engagement was going to work, she'd have to keep her emotions in check.

"Of course. Tell me." The news clipping about Idris's affair was still in her hand; she stared at it while Quinn's baritone voice filled the speaker, willing her pulse back to normal.

She hadn't called her father since announcing her engagement at the airport, despite how angry she'd been with him at the time. That night, she'd been too exhausted to do battle with him, and Quinn had told her he would take care of making sure her dating profile was removed from wherever it had been posted.

"I'm not sure if I mentioned that Cameron's matchmaker is Mallory West. He contacted her for an explanation the day after he proposed to you."

The name meant nothing to Sofia, but as her dancing peers had noted, she wasn't part of the Manhattan singles scene.

"Did she say where she got my flight information?" She had thought about that more than once. How could Cameron's matchmaker have known her arrival time in New York, while her father claimed to be ignorant of Cam's appointment to meet her?

She dipped her hand into the bubbles in the tub, skimming her fingers across the soapy tops.

"She told Cameron she would look into it." Quinn's voice was as potent as his touch. If she closed her eyes, she could imagine him beside her. "But since then, her phone has been disconnected and her email generates an autoreply that she's out of the country on an extended trip."

Sofia forced her eyes open, thinking about that bit of peculiar news. Her cheeks puffed with a hefty exhale. "What do you think it means?"

"For now, it simply means that she is a dead end in our hunt for information. I'm sorry, Sofia. But I will continue having my IT technician hunt for any sign of her online. And, for what it's worth, he's seen no traces of a dating profile for you online, so I think the matchmaker your father hired made good on her promise to pull it down."

"At least that part is good news." She really needed to call her father and ask him more about the situation herself, if only to find out whom he'd hired to help her with her dating prospects. She would feel better once she told that person in no uncertain terms that she wasn't interested.

"It is. And we'll figure out the rest of it, Sofia," Quinn assured her before his tone shifted and his voice got lower. "But that isn't the only thing we have to figure out."

"No?" Sensations tripped down her spine at that sexy rasp in his voice. "What else should we be discussing?"

A half laugh sounded from the other end of the call and nothing else, no background noise, just him. He must be somewhere private. Alone. "Something more fun. So, Sofia, what kind of dress should I buy you to wow and woo the crowds at Idris Fortier's reception on Friday? Do you have a favorite boutique?"

Buy her a dress? The gesture was sweet. But it was too much. Far too much.

"That is kind of you, but definitely not necessary." Still, she imagined what he would choose for her. What it would be like to slide on a garment handpicked by Quinn?

"I'll take you shopping anywhere you'd like."

She tried not to think about the beautiful things a man like Quinn McNeill could afford.

"You are thoughtful, Quinn, but I can't accept more gifts." She felt guilty enough about wearing that massive diamond on her left hand, but he'd convinced her the ring was a necessity. "And I already have something in mind." She didn't mean for her voice to sound so clipped.

"Are you nervous?" he pressed, the deep tones of his whiskey-rich voice warming her moist body.

Her instincts kicked in; she could tell he was interested. He actually wanted to know.

"A bit. I…I just…" Her voice trailed off. Social gatherings and big parties were not her thing. She disliked superficial small talk, preferring meatier conversations.

Music.

Dancing.

"Yes?" he prompted.

"I'm terrible at galas. And around large masses of humanity in general."

"Seriously?" Surprise colored his voice. "But you dance in front of large audiences."

"Yes, seriously. I have stage fright in social scenarios

where I'm forced to talk. But when I'm on stage, ballet feels like poetry, like breath. It's different. Completely different." Chewing her lip, she felt a ball of anxiety begin to form.

Deep breath.

"Luckily for you, I'm quite the pro at these galas. I'll be there to guide and help you, if you want to follow my lead, that is."

"If you can speak in coherent sentences, you'll be one step ahead of me. I'm notoriously awkward in interviews. Jasmine has tried to coach me, but I get very tense."

"I hope that having me there helps. But either way, we'll get through it. And if you want to leave early, I'll give everyone the impression that it's my fault because I can't wait to have you all to myself."

The images that came to mind heated her skin all over again. So much so, she needed to pull her feet out of the hot water.

"How generous of you," she observed, feeling tongue-tied already but for a very different reason.

"I do what I can." The smile in his voice came right through the call. "So can I ask what you plan on wearing?"

A playful tone from him? Now, wasn't that a surprise. Smiling, she glanced out of the bathroom and into her bedroom, eyeing her closet where she had exactly nothing appropriate.

While her father would have loved to write her monthly checks or set up a trust fund for his sole heir, she'd resisted all of his efforts to share his wealth with her in any way. Her mother had always blamed him for his refusal to focus on the things that really mattered in life. Like love. Family. Art. All the things that mattered most to Sofia.

She would do without a dress.

"Something stunning," she told Quinn finally, wondering if she could get something on loan from the costume department.

"Something sexy?" He pressed and she heard his smile through the phone.

"Extremely," she said, forgetting that she was supposed to keep herself in check around him.

Chuckling, his voice was low like a whispered promise. "I look forward to seeing every sexy inch of you on Friday."

And before she could close her gaping jaw, he'd hung up.

Quinn stepped from the limo outside Sofia's apartment building shortly before seven on the night of the reception for her big-deal choreographer.

He hit the call button near the door and waited to be buzzed in before heading inside and taking the elevator to her floor. They'd spoken by phone the last two nights and their conversations had allowed him to get closer to Sofia without the in-person surge of attraction getting in the way. She seemed more at ease on the phone, as if she needed that cerebral connection before she'd allow herself to admit the physical chemistry that had been apparent to him since the first moment he'd seen her.

He'd even talked her into letting him send her a gown for tonight, a feat it had taken him a lot of effort to pull off. He'd only gotten his way by arguing that it would make their engagement more believable. He would absolutely want his fiancée to appear at such an important event for her career in an unforgettable, one-of-a-kind dress. Especially since this would be their first formal public outing as an engaged couple.

Now, as he rang the bell outside 5C, he mentally reviewed the game plan. *Let the attraction build. Don't rush her.* But once they were in the spotlight and she needed to sell their relationship as a stable, happy union that wouldn't detract from her dancing, he planned to deliver. She would be in his arms as often as possible to prove it.

And he looked forward to that more than he'd anticipated any date in a long time. So much for the idea that all this was for show or to smooth over relations with her father. Quinn wasn't going through with it just to ease those European deals and to save his brother from embarrassment.

When the door opened, the sight of her hit him in his chest like a physical blow. Not because she was beautifully dressed, although she damn well looked incredible in her navy-silk gown with subtle, breezy feathers covering much of the skirt to the floor-length hem, her blond hair artfully arranged so it was half up and half down, the tendrils snaking along her neck. He would have been affected if she'd been in a T-shirt and shorts.

He'd missed her. And that realization rocked him.

"You look incredible, Sofia." She looked like the woman he wanted more than any other. Her wide, smoke-colored eyes picked up hints of silver when she wore navy. Diamond roses glittered in her ears.

"You clean up rather nicely yourself." She reached to touch him, surprising the hell out of him in the best possible way, but in the end she merely rubbed the fabric of his tuxedo sleeve appreciatively. "That's a gorgeous tux."

"Thanks," he answered absently, his mind on stun at a simple brush of her fingers. He wanted her touching all the rest of him that way. But he breathed deep and stuck to the game plan.

"Are you ready to go?" He stepped inside her apartment, following her while she retrieved a beaded purse.

"Almost. I couldn't get the hook at the top." She presented him with her back. A soft scent like vanilla mingled with musk drifted up from her hair as he swept aside some of the blond tendrils to find the clasp.

What was it about the nape of a woman's neck that drove a man insane? The vulnerability of it? The trust in exposing it? Quinn wanted to lean closer and lick her there, kiss his way to the back of her ear and then down the column of her throat again.

He settled for taking his time with the clasp, his knuckles lightly brushing beneath the fabric of her dress. He felt the answering quiver in her body. They were that close. Sealing his eyes shut for a moment—needing to control his runaway thoughts—he finished the job and reached around her to take the evening wrap, settling it on her shoulders.

"Time to leave," he urged, wanting nothing so much as to get her in public so he could touch her. How backward was that? Most men couldn't wait to get a woman home to be alone. But he'd promised her their physical contact would be just for show. "Do you have a coat?"

Quinn needed a public audience as an excuse to put his hands on her.

But maybe tonight would change that. Make Sofia realize the effort of staying away from each other wasn't worth it when they could explore the heat between them to their thoroughly mutual satisfaction.

"A cape." She reached for a long black cape with fur around the oversize hood. Lovely. Elegant. Like her.

Before she could move further, he took it from her and draped it reverently over her shoulders. She looked like a timeless screen star in that movie *Doctor Zhivago*.

Damn, he was getting downright sentimental. He needed air. Bracing, cold air.

Leaving her apartment behind—thank God the elevator was crowded to keep him in check—he offered his arm and was glad she took it as they walked toward the vestibule. As a dancer used to working on her toes, she must be comfortable in the sky-high silver heels he glimpsed beneath the dress hem as she walked. But with damp spots on the hall floor from the snow tracked indoors, it helped that she could hold on to him for support.

Once they were inside the limo and headed uptown to the gala venue, Sofia placed a hand on her chest.

"Can I just tell you I'm a nervous wreck?"

"Just remember, you're a professional at the top of her career about to impress a choreographer who is probably already very eager to work with you." Quinn had read up on Idris Fortier over the course of the week, as well as the dance world's frenzied reaction to his New York arrival.

"You don't know that. Some of my reviews are solid." She spoke quickly, settling her purse beside her as they stopped at a red light. "But I have received plenty of harsh criticism, too, and I know my own shortcomings, so Fortier might decide—"

"I read your reviews, Sofia. They're more than solid." He wanted to halt her before she strayed too far down that road of what-ifs and worry. "Some say you favor technique over artistry, the sport of it over the dancing, and you don't trust your partners enough." He'd scoured the praise and the criticism in an effort to understand her more, to be closer to her. "But I compared your reviews to the rest of the stars in the company, and I don't see anyone who comes away more favorably. In fact, critics agree you are the most exciting talent to work here in

years. If I can glean that as a novice, an insider like Fortier will be well aware of you."

"I'm not so sure about that." She wound one of the
long, loose feathers of her skirt around her finger where
the cape had fallen away. He noticed how her nails were
polished a clear pink, and her engagement ring was practically glowing in the limo's dome lighting.

But her movements suggested she was more than a
little nervous.

"May I make a suggestion?" He covered her hand
where she'd gently destroyed the single feather, breaking
his own rule about not touching her in private.

"I don't suppose it could hurt." The tension in her
body was so obvious she practically vibrated with it.
"What is it?"

"Considering that you're visibly anxious about tonight…" he began. But before he could propose the
idea, she made a small sound of distress. Uncrossing
and re-crossing her legs in the opposite direction, her
foot nudged his calf and then began to jitter.

"Oh, God." She swallowed hard. "I *will* get it together.
Even though there is so much riding on making a good
impression—"

"Listen. We make a good team. Remember how easily we ran off the journalists from *Dance* magazine at
the airport? I know your goals tonight and I'm good at
things like this. Follow my lead and you'll be fine." He
twined his fingers through hers, hoping to impart some
calm, not just because he wanted to touch her.

"You think I can after reading how I don't trust a partner?" she asked dryly. "I've gotten dropped on several
occasions. It doesn't inspire confidence."

Sofia's forced smile and raised brow struck him. He

needed to assure her that he wasn't one of those types of partners. He'd be there.

Pulling her gaze away from his, she stared out the window, eyes actively scanning the buildings and pedestrians on the sidewalk.

"I can imagine." He smoothed his thumb over the back of her hand, liking the feel of her skin and the way his touch relaxed her. He could sense some of the tension leaking away as her musky vanilla perfume seemed to invite him closer. "But I would never let you fall."

"Well. Thank you." Her gaze fell to their locked fingers, as if she were surprised to see the way they were connected. "I will admit that I could use a steadying presence tonight."

A car horn blared outside and a faint crescendo of sirens filled the air. Oh, New York.

"Good. Now, about my suggestion." He traced the outline of her engagement ring with his finger, extraordinarily aware of her calf still grazing his knee. "It might help if you allowed me to distract you."

"Distract me?" She arched an eyebrow at him, skeptical but no longer nervous. Her jittering foot came to a rest.

If anything, the sudden stillness of her body suggested she just might be intrigued.

"It's completely up to you." He wanted nothing so much as to gather her up and settle her on top of him. But he had a plan and he would take his time. Let her get used to the idea of enjoying every moment of their time together. "But we could rechannel all that nervous energy. Give it a different physical outlet."

Her jaw dropped.

"I am not the kind of woman who has sex in a limousine," she informed him, not looking quite as scandalized as she might have.

He, on the other hand, was plenty surprised her mind had gone there.

"Well, damn. That's an incredible thought, but I wasn't suggesting we take things that far. You look too beautiful to mess up before your big night, Sofia."

"Then be more clear," she snapped, her cheeks pink and her eyes alight with new fire. "Because I have no idea what you mean."

In a blink, he shifted positions, releasing her hand so he could bracket her shoulders between his arms, pinning her without touching her. He held her gaze, lowering himself closer until his chest came within inches of her breasts. Even with her dress and cape between them, he could see their gentle swell.

He spoke softly in her ear.

"Distraction." He articulated it clearly so there would be no mistake. "I could kiss you somewhere that wouldn't mess you up. A spot along the curve of your lovely neck, maybe." His eyes wandered over her, assessing the possibilities. "Or beneath your hair."

A shiver ran through her while his breath warmed the space between her skin and his mouth. Careful not to touch her, he let the idea take hold. If nothing else, he felt damn certain just this conversation would rewire her thoughts for a while, taking them off the choreographer she was so anxious to impress.

The notion satisfied him. A lot.

"That is a crazy idea," she whispered back. "Letting you kiss me might give me more heart palpitations than I was having before."

He wanted a taste of her. So. Badly.

"But the heart palpitations I could give you would be the pleasurable kind." Dragging his attention off the rapid pulse at her throat, he heard her quick intake of breath, saw her eyelids flutter once. Twice.

"You are way too sure of yourself, Quinn McNeill." Her hands lifted, hovering near his shoulders as if she debated touching him there.

He willed her palms closer.

"No. I'm sure of what's between us even though you don't want to acknowledge it."

"We're only pretending," she insisted, her eyebrows furrowing as the limo slowed to another stop, jostling her closer to him. She braced her palms on his chest. Torture. Pure torture.

He hoped their destination was another hour away because he was locking that limo door if anyone tried to open it now.

"I only agreed to pretend because I was attracted to you to start with." The words were out of his mouth. He couldn't take them back, and what surprised him was he didn't want to.

"What are you saying?" She shook her head, squinting as she tried to process. "Next month, this will be all over—"

"I know." Gently he edged her wrap back and smoothed aside a few locks of silky hair that curled around her neck and rested against the fur-lined hood. "But until then, I want this."

Pressing his lips to the curve of her shoulder, he soaked in the warmth and fragrance unique to this woman. Sweet and musky at the same time, her scent made him instantly hard. Not moving, he wanted to take his cue from her, only advancing this game as far as she'd let him.

When her hands finally landed on his shoulders, for a moment he thought she might push him away. Instead her fingers tunneled under his open coat, then farther inside his jacket, splaying out over his tuxedo shirt until he could feel the soft scrape of her short nails through the cotton.

The sensation raked over his senses, arousing a fierceness in him that had no place in a limo five minutes before a party. He opened his mouth to taste her, lick her, nip her. His chest grazed her breasts, her delicate curves arching hard against him as she pressed deeper into him.

Her response was everything he wanted, everything he could have hoped for, and the damn reception of hers was just a minute farther up the road. But his heart slammed in his chest in a victory dance, his body too caught up in the feel of hers to get the message that this was not the time to take all he wanted.

Damn. Damn.

"Sofia." He kissed her neck below her ear, bit the tender earlobe just above her earring and forced himself to lean back. "We're here."

Eight

Games and lies, Sofia reminded herself later that night while Quinn fielded another question about their relationship from the reporter who wanted to do a follow-up interview with her and her fiancé. They were seated in a private room off the skylight lounge where City Ballet was holding the party for Idris Fortier, the music from a chamber orchestra filtering in through the open door along with the sounds of laughter, clinking glasses and the rumble of conversation.

The space was crowded and warm, especially for those who danced.

Or those who were overwrought with the sensual steam of longing.

Quinn and Sofia had been dealing in games and lies all week, so she could hardly be upset with her handsome, charming date for spinning a moving tale about how he fell in love watching her dance. She'd signed off on the story, after all. She'd agreed that it was easier to root the lies in some element of truth so they had shared memories to trot out at moments like this.

How could she fault Quinn now for being a much better liar than her, especially since she was the one who'd pressed for the pretend engagement?

"But I won't take the focus away from Sofia's dancing," Quinn was saying as they sat side by side on a black leather sofa in the sparse, modern room full of bistro tables and areas for private conversations. "If you'll excuse me, I'll let her finish up the interview." He turned toward her, his tuxedo not showing a single crease as he stood and kissed her hand. "Save me the first dance when you finish?"

His blue eyes had a teasing light. It bothered her that he was good at this, rousing suspicions of his motives no matter that he claimed to be attracted to her.

"Of course. Thank you." She smiled up at him, playing her part but knowing she wasn't as skilled as he was. And her body still hadn't completely recovered from the kisses in the limousine.

If he hadn't pulled away when he had back in the vehicle, she would have sacrificed the most beautiful gown she'd ever worn to press herself against all that raw masculine strength and follow where the attraction led.

"Your future husband was one of the city's most eligible bachelors, Sofia," the reporter—Delaney—observed. The woman's eyes followed Quinn as he strode out the open door into the party in the lounge. "The McNeill heirs are rich, charming and exceedingly good-looking." She tore her eyes from Quinn as she picked up her digital tablet where she'd been taking notes. "His brother must have made quite an impression on you when he proposed at the airport. But I'm surprised you dated Quinn for so long without meeting Cameron? Cameron tends to be the most visible of the three."

Sofia fought back nerves, not wanting to drop the ball after Quinn had set her up so skillfully to talk about something else.

"That may be, but I don't have much time outside of ballet for socializing. What time I do have, I spend with Quinn. But I'd prefer to talk about work, if you have any questions for me."

Delaney pursed her lips in a frown.

"Very well." She changed screens on the tablet. "Perhaps you'd like to address your critics. Your work has been called mechanical and without artistry. What makes you think you will capture the leading role in the Fortier project when the choreographer is such a decided fan of mood and emotion in his work?"

The biting tone of the query told Sofia just how much she'd accidentally offended the reporter by asking to change the subject. Maybe she should have asked Jasmine to be here for this follow-up interview to help smooth over awkward moments and ensure Sofia didn't embarrass herself. But it cost enough just to have Jasmine set up these kinds of appointments, and she had attended a video interview earlier in the week.

The upside of all the press coverage was that she ought to have a great feature piece by the time they were finished, right?

"I strive every day to balance the physical demands of the dance with all the artistry I can bring to each piece. I hope that I'm always improving on both fronts. An artist should always aspire to improve." She should explain how. Give the reporter more to work with. Except that her nerves had returned in full force.

"And what is your impression of Mr. Fortier so far?" the woman asked, tapping her stylus on the tablet.

Was she waiting for the quotable bit that would torch Sofia's career for daring to stick to the topic?

"I have the same impression everyone else has. He's a brilliant talent and our company is extremely fortunate to work with him." She couldn't believe she'd invited this woman to her private audition with Fortier.

The last thing she needed was to be nervous on that day, too. She was usually so solid when she danced. She didn't need Delaney getting in her head.

"Are you aware that his last two featured leads have moved in with him during the creative process?" The woman watched Sofia's reaction closely. "That he was romantically linked to both of them?"

She hadn't known about that. Although she had read about the affair with the previous one, she'd assumed that was just a one-time thing. People working together fell in love all the time.

But the same scenario twice?

"No." With an effort she coaxed her lips into a smile. "I'm sure it's not a requirement for the job."

Outside the private room, the chamber group paused in their play and someone took the microphone. Sofia peered over her shoulder, wondering if Idris was about to be introduced.

"I'm sure it's not." Delaney gestured toward the open door. "But don't let me keep you. I plan to speak with several more of your colleagues tonight."

"Have you got all the material you need?" Sofia had hoped for a feature in the magazine, not a snippet about her engagement to a hedge fund manager.

"Plenty." Delaney flipped off her tablet and stood. "And I'll be there to film your audition for Mr. Fortier, which will be something our readers will want to hear all about."

Sofia knew she'd made a misstep with the woman, but had no idea how to correct it now. She settled for being polite as she rose to her feet.

"Thank you, I look forward to it," she lied, although not nearly as well as Quinn could have in this situation. Funny how he'd become her biggest ally this week, their unlikely partnership providing her with an outlet at a stressful time in her career.

Maybe she shouldn't be so quick to write off his ability to put on a façade in public. She would do better to learn the trick from him.

"Enjoy that handsome fiancé of yours," the reporter called after her. "You're so lucky to have found someone special. I was thinking of resorting to a matchmaker myself."

Sofia nearly tripped over her feet, the shock of the words like an icy splash to her nerves. Turning, she saw Delaney tapping her chin thoughtfully with her stylus.

"You don't happen to know any good ones, do you?" the woman asked.

A gauntlet had been dropped.

Sofia understood the implication. The woman knew something about what had happened at the airport. Had she learned that Sofia's father had hired a matchmaker? That in itself was certainly not a big deal. But what if she knew more than that? That her engagement was a lie. That Sofia had only done it to quiet the gossip among her peers so she could focus on her dancing.

Maybe she should have straightened it out that night. Stuck with the truth. But since she was in no position to untangle any of it right now, Sofia simply smiled.

"I don't, but I've heard that's a very popular option

these days." She rushed to melt into the crowd and find Quinn.

In the pressure cooker of her work world, her fake fiancé had become her best source of commiseration.

And he wanted to be even more than that. He wanted to give her pleasure, a heady offer that had teased the edges of her consciousness all evening long. With her heart ready to pound out of her chest, she realized he was the only person she wanted to see right now.

If only she could truly trust him. But even as she raced to find him, she reminded herself to be careful. He might genuinely be attracted to her. But he wouldn't be helping her right now if it didn't serve McNeill interests.

"I need to speak to you."

Sofia's whisper in Quinn's ear was the sexiest thing he'd heard since that small gasp she'd made in the limo when he'd kissed her neck. He'd been ready to get her alone ever since then.

Maybe this was his moment.

He stood on the fringes of the crowd listening to the guest of honor speak at a podium about his eagerness to work in New York and to let the city inspire him. The guy said all the right things, but something about him irritated Quinn from the moment he'd opened his mouth. Perhaps it was just because he held power over Sofia's career and Quinn didn't like thinking that the subjective opinions of one man could mean so much to her.

More likely, it was because Idris Fortier laughed at his own jokes and occasionally referred to himself in the third person. The well-heeled crowd in attendance hung on his every word, however.

"Should we listen to this first?" Quinn asked Sofia quietly, surprised her interview had finished so soon.

"The reporter asked me if I could recommend a good matchmaker." The soft warmth of her breath teased over his ear, but the seductive sensation couldn't cancel out the anxiety in her words.

And no wonder she was nervous.

"He's almost done speaking." Quinn wrapped an arm around her waist, to bring her as close as possible, wanting to give every appearance of being deeply in love and lost in one another. "It will be easier to talk once the dancing begins." His lips moved against the silk of her hair. "And I don't want your reporter friend to see us darting off in a corner to whisper."

Nodding, she relaxed against him ever so slightly. That small show of trust was something he'd been working hard for all week long. He'd put her needs first, letting Cameron fly to Kiev to handle the hotel acquisitions. He'd asked his brother Ian for help running down more information about Mallory West, giving himself more time to gain Sofia Koslov's trust.

To help her, of course. They'd agreed to as much. But things had gotten more complicated as he admitted the depth of his attraction. He wanted her. And after the heat they'd sparked in the car on the way over here, he thought he knew where things were headed between them.

Would she act on that attraction if she knew this engagement was helping him as much as it helped her? That he'd purposely delayed drawing up that contract he'd discussed with her that first night they'd met because he now wondered if the relationship could help him around his grandfather's marriage dictate.

Quinn still hoped he could help Malcolm McNeill see that he didn't need to call the shots in his grandsons' love lives. That he could trust them to find spouses on their own terms and in their own time. Quinn would at least try to talk him into scrapping the marriage stipulation from the will. But failing that? He was confident he could work out some kind of agreement with Sofia that would help him to fulfill the terms.

As the crowd around him erupted into applause for the choreographer, a violinist struck a dramatic, quavering note. It cracked through the air, stirring the room. The unmistakable trill of a Spanish bandoneon followed in the opening note of a tango, a rare dance Quinn knew well. It transported him back to the small Buenos Aires pub where he'd learned the steps afterhours with his work crew while overseeing renovations on one of the family's resorts. He recalled the packed dance floor crowded with passionate couples and knew, with fierce certainty, that he wanted to share this with Sofia.

"Dance with me," he murmured in her ear, his nostrils flaring at the vanilla scent of her skin. It rose around him and heated his blood.

Her large gray eyes were hesitant, questioning as they swerved to his. He trailed his fingertips up her spine, feeling the sweet curve of her back through silk. "I am classically trained," she murmured in a breathy rush. "The tango is a ballroom dance."

"Then it will be a welcome chance for me to partner you on the floor." He drew her toward the square parquet tiles near the musicians.

"Since when do hedge fund managers learn sexy Argentinian dances?" She was light on her feet as she backed into position, joining the handful of couples taking the floor.

"I must have known I'd need to impress a woman one day." He tightened his grip on her, urging her closer as they entered the counterclockwise flow. Her lithe body moved gracefully against his, but this wasn't a pretty dance. It was primal and raw.

She watched the other dancers long enough to gather her bearings, then turned her gaze back to him.

"You are full of surprises, Quinn McNeill." For an aching moment her body cradled the growing hardness concealed by his tuxedo. Then she twisted her hips sideways and kicked her foot through the long slit up one side of her dress, shooting him a coquettish look from beneath the sweep of her long lashes.

At last he'd distracted her completely. She was no longer worried about the reporter, the choreographer or her career. All her focus was on him.

The throbbing notes of the violin wove with the cry of the bandoneon and echoed the seething heat she stirred inside him.

Before she could slip too far away, he hauled her close again then bent her backward. Her spine arched and her head dipped to the floor, exposing the creamy, satin skin of her elegant neck, the slender column of her body. Their hips brushed as they swayed and then he snapped her upright so that their mouths touched. They breathed each other in and their gazes tangled.

Tension whipped between them. His body grew taut; need and craving pounded through him. He felt the pressure of it all licking through his blood. When he stepped with his left foot, she followed, her limbs seeming to loosen and grow molten, her movements more languid. The arm curled around his neck singed his flesh and her fingers burrowed into his hair, her nails raking his skin.

He steered her expertly, felt her respond to the lightest of touches, the smallest pressure. She seemed to surrender to the dance, to him, as her eyes closed and she let him lead her the way he wanted to.

Yet just when she looked defenseless, a staccato rhythm seemed to break her trance and she whirled around him, improvising mouthwatering steps as he stood rigid, watching. Wanting. He couldn't tear his eyes off her. She held his hand then shimmied lower, her body sinuous. She rose slowly. Out of nowhere, her lips curved into a tempting smile, her expression full of promise.

His mouth dried and his tongue swelled. They cross-stepped for several more beats and the world fell away. His senses narrowed, homing in on the beautiful woman who didn't back down when he pushed forward, who stood her ground and stalked him as well until at last, they stood, foreheads pressed together, breaths coming in fits and starts as the tango ended.

"Come home with me," he commanded. Her eyes burned into his and dimly he heard another song, slower, strike up.

Her grip tightened on his. "Yes."

Victory surged through him. He wanted to pick her up and carry her out of the crowd and downstairs to the waiting limo this minute. But he didn't want to end her time at a work function without accomplishing one more key goal that her friend Jasmine had clearly laid out as an objective for the evening.

"Excellent." He released her slowly, peering through the crowd to find the man who held Sofia's professional future in his hands. "We'll pay our regards to the man of the hour and then we're free to spend the rest of the night however we choose."

He felt her go still beside him. But she didn't tremble or fidget the way she had earlier in the evening.

"Good idea." She nodded. "I'll say hello and then I'll text Jasmine from the car to let her know about Delaney's comment to me. I want to give Jasmine some advance notice if the reporter plans a story about the matchmaking mix-up."

"I'll ask my own public relations department to circulate some stories about our engagement, as well."

That would lend their union all the more credibility. And for the first time Quinn found himself wondering what Sofia would say if he asked her to extend a fake engagement into a year-long marriage like his grandfather's will stipulated...

But of course he wouldn't do that. His grandfather's terms were out of line and unfair. He needed to talk him into rewriting the will. Right now, he would keep his focus on Sofia.

They stood waiting while an older woman dressed in an exotically colored caftan finished her conversation with the famed choreographer. When Sofia turned worried eyes toward him, Quinn took great pleasure in skimming a touch along her hip. And discreetly lower. Her eyes went wide so that she was thoroughly distracted by the time the older woman bid Fortier good-night.

"Sofia Koslov." The boyishly built Frenchman opened his arms wide. "My dear, I've been dying to meet you."

Quinn released her so she could be swept into a hug he personally found too damn enthusiastic, but then, he might have thought as much about anyone who put their hands on a woman he wanted this badly.

"Welcome to New York, Mr. Fortier," she greeted him. Her wooden delivery was an endearing sign of her nerves, Quinn realized.

He liked knowing things about this very private woman that other people didn't.

"Call me Idris. I insist." The man didn't spare a glance for Quinn as his eyes raked over Sofia with what Quinn hoped was professional interest.

Her body was the medium for her dance, he reminded himself even as he ground his teeth together.

"Idris," she corrected herself with quiet seriousness. "We are thrilled to host you at City Ballet. We are all excited to hear your plans for your new work."

Quinn found himself hanging on her words, wanting her to succeed since it clearly meant so much to her.

"And I sincerely hope you will be the first to hear those plans, Sofia. I look forward to your audition."

Before Sofia could reply, the celebrated choreographer turned to greet a young man who'd come to stand behind Sofia, effectively dismissing her.

Sofia tucked against Quinn's side with gratifying ease, whispering, "Did I offend him?"

If she wasn't so intent on securing the man's good opinion, Quinn might have told her that—on the contrary—Fortier's behavior had been rude. But he didn't want her to worry.

"You were perfect," he assured her honestly as he guided her through the crowd toward the coat check. "Jasmine would have been thrilled."

"Speaking of Jasmine." Sofia opened her purse and withdrew her phone. "I need to let her know what happened with that reporter." She lowered her voice for his ears only. "We should be prepared if the woman releases a story about me using a matchmaker."

Quinn nodded his agreement as he excused himself to retrieve their coats. But he already knew his plan B if the matchmaker story leaked. If anyone questioned the legitimacy of their engagement, it would pave the way to convince Sofia to marry him for a year and secure that damned inheritance anyhow.

Just in case.

Nine

Twenty minutes later Sofia watched the numbers light up above the elevator in Quinn's building as they waited for the private conveyance.

Ten, nine, eight…

Quinn's hand brushed the small of her back and circled, his touch burning her as it had on the dance floor. The white-gloved bellhop near the concierge desk spoke with a deliveryman wheeling in a silver cart full of insulated dishes—presumably a five-star meal from an area restaurant. Behind them, an elegantly attired elder gentleman strode through the building's thick glass doors, the smell of diesel and roasting nuts carrying on the rush of crisp, evening air that trailed after him.

Was she out of her mind for being there?

Probably.

Their arrangement was for public events only, yet here she stood, ready—no, *wanting* this intimate privacy with Quinn.

Seven, six, five...

Every nerve ending had come alive since the moment he'd guided her through the most passionate dance she'd ever performed. Only, it hadn't been a performance. Every unchoreographed move had been born out of the sensuous desire he'd incited. Never before had she completely let go that way and she felt so empowered. Impassioned.

Nearby, other elevators with more white-gloved attendants took patrons to their floors, but she and Quinn were waiting for the private one direct to his floor.

Four, three, two...

Yet she hadn't come home with Quinn just because she was crazy with lust. She wanted to take this risk with him and open up as she had on the dance floor. He'd helped her navigate a stressful time in her life just as he'd led her through the tango—with certainty, command, giving as well as taking.

While she'd appreciated his strength and cool head this week, his passionate moves had given her another glimpse at the enigmatic man, made her want to know him more. Following his lead, as she had earlier, gave her confidence to let go and trust that he wouldn't let her down.

In fact, she suspected he would bring her to greater heights than she'd ever known. Her past relationships had all been as careful as her professional life, each step rehearsed until she felt safe about moving forward. And where had that gotten her?

It had been bloodless companionship that amounted to little more than friendships, causing her peers to think she led some kind of sad, passionless existence.

There was nothing passionless about what she felt for Quinn. Nothing scripted. Just heat and wild fire.

The elevator bell chimed, the doors opened and he

ushered her inside the wonderfully empty space. She held her breath as the door swooshed closed and, in an instant, he backed her up against the paneled wall. Hand burrowing in her hair, he loosened the few pins that held its shape so that the fragrant locks tumbled around her face, releasing the scent of her shampoo. Her cape slid from her shoulders to pool on the floor and she shoved his wool overcoat off in a quick, deft sweep.

She melted at his appreciative, predatory growl. When his lips brushed hers, she rose on tiptoe and fit her body against the hard length of him. A feminine thrill shot through her when he deepened the kiss. His tongue slid over the seam of her mouth, demanding entrance, and she moaned in the back of her throat. She felt winded, light-headed and incredibly turned on as he crushed her to him, his mouth slanting over hers, their tongues tangling in their own passionate dance.

His heart drummed against her chest, hard enough that she could feel it through his tuxedo jacket. Her head tipped back at the crescendo of sensations as he dropped his mouth to the crook of her neck, his tongue sweeping in intense, hot circles, his breath sounding harsh in the small space.

She gasped when he traced the outline of her rib cage through her dress. Her breasts swelled and ached as his fingers skimmed over her neckline before dipping inside to tease each tight peak. A sizzling tremble ran rampant through her body. His blue eyes burned into hers when the elevator lurched to a halt and he stepped away.

She pressed her hand to her chest as though she could slow the runaway beat of her heart. This was all going so fast, but she needed that speed now that she'd made up her mind not to wait anymore. She'd wanted Quinn, probably had from the moment he'd captivated her full attention at the airport even through her jet-lagged exhaustion. No more holding back. Their tango had been a prelude of what was to come and she wouldn't waste another minute out of his arms now that she'd made the decision to take this risk.

To trust her partner.

When the elevator arrived at his floor, he backed her inside the apartment, guiding her through the vaulted great room and open kitchen that she remembered from the first time she'd been there. Tearing at each other's clothes, they moved as one down a hallway she hadn't seen before, and into a dimly lit bedroom where a lamp shone on a large painting of the Manhattan skyline. In the sitting area, she spied a large desk against one wall and a bank of shade-covered windows on another. When he made as if to tumble them both to the bed, she sidestepped at the last minute.

Just long enough to catch her breath.

Her lips burned from his kisses, her skin tingling everywhere underneath the sensuous silk gown he'd had delivered to her apartment today, complete with a tailor to ensure the hem fell just right. Then the gown had felt like a lover's caress against her skin, the hand-sewn, designer original a decadent luxury. But now, she only wanted the real thing—Quinn's hands all over her. No extravagant dress would do.

"Are we moving too fast?" he asked, brushing his knuckles down her bare arm. "We can slow things down. Take our time. Would you like a drink?"

"No." She didn't need anything to cloud her head. "I just want a moment to take it all in. Savor the sensations."

She rested her hands on his broad chest, admiring the contrast of her pink nails against the crisp white tuxedo shirt, her glittering ring a reminder of all they pretended to be to each other. But she needed this much to be real.

He lifted her hand to kiss the back of her knuckles. The back of her hand. The inside of her wrist. Even that brush of his lips in such an innocuous spot made her simmer inside.

Somewhere in the suite of rooms, a clock chimed twelve. A fairy-tale time…only she wasn't turning into a pumpkin or the girl she'd been before tonight.

Now that she'd stepped onto this path, she was desperate to see where it led. What she would discover. Most of all, she wanted to dance with him. The kind of dance they'd begun at the party and would continue here to its fiery conclusion.

She turned her back and peered over her shoulder. "I might need a hand." She pulled her hair to one side, revealing the zipper. "I want to be careful with the gown."

"Damn the gown." His teeth flashed in the darkened room. "I want what's inside." He eased the zipper down past her hips and she felt the room's temperate air caress her bare skin.

"Are you sure?" She slid the fabric from one shoulder and smiled at him, loving that he let her go at her own pace, giving her time to enjoy this kind of teasing pleasure.

"Lady, I've never been more sure of anything in my life," he growled, unadulterated male appreciation roughening the edges of his voice. Still, he held himself back and she loved the command he exerted over every aspect of his life—even hers. It steadied the out-of-control tilt of her world and made her feel as though she might stop spinning for tonight at least.

The silk whispered as the gown fell around her silver heels. She stepped out of it then turned slowly. He gaped at her, his amusement gone, replaced by an intent, hungry expression that made her stomach clench and warmth pool at the apex of her thighs. As a dancer, she'd always been aware of her body. She'd felt every muscle, sinew and bone, commanded them to move and pose at her will. Yet now she felt less in control and more aware of her body than ever. Standing there half-nude in her black lace bra and panties, she felt her skin heat everywhere his gaze fell. With Quinn, she wasn't just a dancer but a woman brimming with desire and needs that transcended her ambitions, her career, her future. She wanted to gulp down every second of this encounter with him.

When she slid each bra strap down over her arms, his eyes grew hooded. Exhilaration fired through her at his reaction. She commanded attention in a way that had nothing to do with her training, her skills, and everything to do with who she was…or maybe who she was discovering herself to be.

She turned again, unhooked her bra then dangled the scrap of lace from an extended hand, letting the lingerie drift to the polished wood floor. At his guttural groan she smiled, pressed an arm across her aching breasts and turned, crossing one leg over the other as his eyes drifted down then rose slowly, lingering.

"Enjoying yourself?" She stepped between his legs and her knees brushed the edge of the bed.

"Not as much as I'm about to," he vowed then tumbled her down on top of him.

Sofia absorbed the feel of him, from the hard planes of his chest through the starched cotton shirt to the silken glide of his pants along her bare thighs. The metallic pinch of his belt buckle pressed against her abdomen, just above the jutting length of his erection.

He cupped her bottom, fitting her to him in a way that aligned the neediest part of her with that straining length.

"I've thought about doing this," she admitted, skimming a finger along the edge of his jaw. "All week, I thought about it when I was on the phone at night with you."

"When we were talking about the missing matchmaker? Our career hopes and the demands of ballet?" He captured her finger in one hand and brought it to his lips for a gentle bite. "All that time, you were thinking about being naked on top of me?"

"Maybe not every second. But the idea definitely crossed my mind a few times. Especially right after I disconnected the calls." Those had been oddly lonesome moments. She'd felt a growing attachment to him but she hadn't been sure if it was friendship, a sense of being allies at a time when they needed one another, or if it was simply attraction. But each night when confronted with the silence of her apartment, she'd thought about how much she wanted to see him again.

Touch him. Undress him.

His expression grew serious. "I thought about you then, too. It was like the quiet echoed louder once we stopped talking."

His words so nearly matched the way she felt she fought a desire to squeeze him tighter and kiss him senseless. She was already taking a risk tonight in being with him. She wasn't ready for a more emotional leap that might bare too much of her soul.

So, instead, she kissed him.

And for the first time she took the lead in the kiss, exploring the fullness of his lips and taking teasing swipes at his tongue. She tasted and tested, liking the feel of his body under her as she moved around him. Her nipples tightened at the friction of the pleats on his shirt. Her hair slid down to pool on top of him, curtaining them in silky privacy. She could have kissed him for hours, but then he ended the game by rolling on top of her.

A new game began, becoming hotter and more fervent until she became lost in him and the way he made her feel. He palmed her breasts, cradling each in turn as though they were precious weights, his thumb gliding over each tip until the peaks ached with sensitivity. Only then did he lower his tongue to first one, then the other, making her back arch to increase the delicious friction.

She lifted her hands to his shirt, flicking open the buttons and tugging the fabric from his pants. He must have loosened his tie and the top button earlier, because the knot slipped free easily, his shirt suddenly open to her questing hands.

He felt even better than she'd imagined, his bare skin simmering with heat. From the sprinkling of hair on his chest, she followed the lightly furred line down the center of his abs to his pants, but he reared up on his knees and stopped her, unfastening the buckle himself and lowering the zipper to her avid gaze.

Built like an athlete, he had the thighs and butt of a soccer player, his whole composition heavier than a dancer's. Sturdier. Immovable. And yet he'd been light on his feet when he'd taken her around the floor in that surprising tango tonight. Proving he knew how to use all that muscle to enticing effect.

"I want you inside me." She didn't know she'd said the words aloud until her throat rasped on a harsh breath. Reaching to touch his hip, she followed the path of his boxers as they slid from his thighs.

"And I can't wait to be there." He stretched over her, his thigh parting hers as he gave her more of his weight.

Sofia sighed into him, wrapping her arms around his neck, molding her breasts to his chest and fitting her hips to his. He rolled them, as one, to the side of the bed where he tugged a box of condoms from a nightstand drawer. He left them there, a tangible assurance she would get what she wanted.

She cried out when he shifted against her, his thigh pressed at the juncture of hers where she ached for him. Where she wanted more of him. But in an instant, he replaced his thigh with his palm, his fingers playing lightly along the damp silk of her panties, now the only scrap of clothing between them.

Their gazes collided in the half light and the intensity of his expression quieted her hunger for a moment since she could see the same need in his eyes. He wanted her, too. Badly. But he must be holding back for the right moment, spinning out the beauty of the dance until act three instead of jumping straight to the climax.

Who would have thought she'd be the one desperate for more, faster, while Quinn took his time with every delicious sensation, burning this night into her memory—she knew—forever. So, closing her eyes, she gave herself over to him and his sure hands, allowing her mind to savor each shock of pleasure he ignited with his fingers. He pressed gently, testing what made her sigh and gasp, only sliding beneath the silk when she twisted her hips in a silent plea.

And, *oh*.

The slick glide of one blunt finger down the center of her set off one heady contraction after another, her body racked with spasms in a release that shook her to her toes. The waves of pleasure broke over her again and again.

Quinn whispered sweet words in her ear, beautiful encouragement she only became dimly aware of as she floated back from her brief trip to carnal oblivion.

"I can't wait to taste you," he breathed against her ear, the sensual promise alone almost sending her body into another orgasmic frenzy.

"I'm too new to this," she reminded him. "That is, I'm not *totally* new to this, but it's never been like this for me before." She kissed his shoulder, her tongue tasting a hint of salt on his skin. "I might lose consciousness if I have much more pleasure in one night."

He grinned, his male pride evident as he tightened his hold on her waist. "I don't think that's possible, but it could be an interesting experiment."

"I think I'd rather be fully in control of my senses for all of this." She roused herself to draw the arch of her foot up the back of his leg, gratified to see his smile slip, his pupils dilate. "You could take it easy on me this first time."

"As long as there are more times." Hooking a finger in her panties, he dragged them down and off, the action stirring a feather that must have fallen in the sheets from her discarded dress.

Quinn plucked it from the air, drawing it over her hip and up her rib cage, circling her breast. Sweet chills skipped along her nerve endings.

"There will be more times," she promised, knowing this night had to mean something more than simple pleasure. Didn't it?

Refusing to overthink it, telling herself that simple pleasure might be a very good thing, she helped herself to the box of condoms and withdrew a single packet.

Handing it to him, he set aside the feather and went to work ripping open the foil. She took the opportunity to kiss along his biceps, feeling the muscles flex against her lips as he moved. The raw power in his body fueled the fire in her.

When he positioned himself between her thighs, she bit her lip at the sensation of him right there, where she needed him most. Their eyes met. Held. He gripped her hips with one hand and tilted her chin toward him with the other.

Brushing her lips with his, he took his time entering her, letting her get used to the feel of him. Even if it hadn't been a long time for her, it still would have felt brand new for being so different. Quinn wasn't like any man she'd ever met and he treated her body in ways no one ever had before.

So by the time they were joined fully, the sweat on his brow told her how much his gentleness cost him. She kissed his cheek and his jaw, grateful for the tender care. But now, with her body easing around him and the delicious pleasure building again, she could give herself over to the sensations. Let him guide her.

Rolling them over again, he settled her on top of him, giving her a sense of control. His hands remained on her hips, though, setting the pace for each toe-curling thrust. For long moments she lost herself in it—the heat of the friction, the musky scent of his skin, the silken sheets that brushed against her calves. But then, remembering the way Quinn's eyes had heated on the dance floor earlier, she swiveled her hips with the grace and strength that a ballerina had at her disposal, taking him with her on a sensual slow ride.

His eyes closed as he hissed a low, ragged breath, giving her a tantalizing peek at the man behind the sleek, controlled exterior. When his eyes opened, she saw blue fire even in the dimly lit room.

Spinning her to her back, he kept one arm anchored beneath her, his forearm aligned with her spine, one hand at her neck. Nose to nose, he thrust deeply—again and again—until the pleasure was too much to bear. She came in a blinding rush, a cry rising from her throat while the spasms trembled through every part of her.

Quinn held her tight, his release following hers a moment later so that his breathing was as sharp and ragged as hers in the quiet afterward. They lay together in the middle of the king-size bed, limbs still twined and sheets wound around their feet in a soft love knot.

Sofia wanted to remain there, boneless and sated, for as long as possible. She felt so good, for one thing. And for another, she had no idea how to follow up something like that with casual conversation. All her life, she'd been better using her body to express herself than her words and she'd done that tonight, as well.

But as Quinn tucked her against his chest and stroked her hair, she knew there was one significant difference. She'd built some kind of friendship with him, too. That long walk in the park and their talks on the phone at night had all helped her to feel closer to him and to give her the sensation that maybe he cared about more than just protecting his resorts business from the wrath of her father.

She might have been able to drift into sleep on that hopeful note, but one disturbing truth had emerged from the party tonight. As their breathing returned to normal, Sofia couldn't help but share her worry.

"I hope that journalist was just taking shots in the dark tonight when she brought up the matchmaker." She didn't want that story to come out now. Or ever. Antonia Blakely could whisper her gossip all day long, but if there was no proof her father hired a matchmaker, she wouldn't share the story with the media.

Antonia might be venomous, but she wouldn't risk casting a shadow on her own career.

"It seems an awfully specific detail to pick out of a

hat," Quinn observed in a dry voice. He pulled the blankets over her, tucking her in next to him.

Even so, her skin cooled thinking that Delaney from *Dance* magazine might really have her big scoop.

"Jasmine texted me that she'd look into it." Nervous tension crept into Sofia's shoulders, spoiling the languid pleasure she'd been feeling.

"And you know she will. If she has any advance notice, she'll let us know." His hand roved rhythmically along her arm, then rested on her hip. "But if the reporter actually writes that your father hired a matchmaker, we simply toast to the fact that you got lucky on your first try. And then stay engaged for as long as you need to prove you were committed to finding true love." The five-o'clock shadow on his jaw caught against her hair, a tender intimacy that would have soothed her if not for the direction of a conversation that made her worried.

"I can't tie you up forever." She scooted up to a sitting position, her shoulders tensing. "Maybe we should just come clean. It was all a mix-up anyhow."

Quinn shook his head.

"We're in too deep now. And the backlash could hurt my family's business as much as you."

Those tentative, hopeful feelings of trust she'd put in him earlier now seemed misplaced. Quinn really was staying with her to protect his business interests. To ensure her father's goodwill by doing what she'd asked of him.

"So what would you suggest?" she asked, clutching the sheet to her chest.

"If it comes down to it, we can always get married for real." His teeth flashed white in the darkened room, but his expression was more grimace than grin. "No one would dare to question our love then."

"Only our sanity." Frustrated, she debated calling Jasmine anyhow—if only to reassure herself she was worrying needlessly. She wanted real answers, not a glib treatment of the problem. "I'm serious, Quinn."

"Unfortunately, so am I." He leveled a look at her from across the pillow before dropping a kiss on her temple. "Instead of a fake engagement, we make it a fake marriage. We give it a year and call it quits. Our critics are quieted. Scandal averted."

"You would be willing to go that far?" To *actually* marry. "To share a name, a house and a life when it's all for show?"

And she thought she was the performer in the relationship. Perhaps Quinn was a better actor than she knew. Even with her.

"There's too much at stake now. It's not only your career or your father's threats to McNeill Resorts' European acquisitions." His arms went around her, but the temperature in the room had cooled considerably. For her, at least. He didn't seem to realize the effect his words had as he continued. "My name is on a hedge fund. My clients could pull billions of dollars out if they don't trust my word."

She let the realizations roll over her, remembering all the times her mother had warned her to follow her passions and not chase material successes. As much as she'd tried to do that, she still found herself naked in the arms of a man who would always put his fortune first. It was a timely reminder not to wade any deeper into her feelings for Quinn.

But that didn't stop the truth from cutting deep.

Ten

Two days later, Quinn paced around his personal library at the McNeill Fund headquarters in the Financial District, one floor above the McNeill Resorts' offices.

His brother Ian had returned from Singapore earlier in the week. After giving him a day to recover from the trip, Quinn had asked for his help tracking down Mallory West to ask her some follow-up questions after Cameron's too brief interview with her. Ian had texted both Cameron—returned that morning from Kiev—and Quinn to meet this afternoon to share new information that concerned them both.

Now, with Ian leaning a hip on the front of Quinn's massive desk and Cameron commanding the leather executive chair behind it, Quinn stood at the window looking out over the view of the city, the Woolworth Building in the foreground with other towers stretching as far he could see in the wintry, gray haze.

"So is it true that Mallory West closed up shop?" Cameron asked, pushing back from the desk to test the range of positions available on Quinn's leather chair. "When I spoke to her the last time—"

"That wasn't her you talked to." Ian slanted a glance at their younger brother over his shoulder. Closer in height to Quinn than Cameron, Ian had more of their Brazilian mother's coloring—dark eyes and deeper skin tone—but the shape of his face and features echoed the rest of the McNeills.

His clothes were the most casual today—dark jeans with a gray blazer and a button-down. But that was normal since Ian spent most of his time on job sites around the globe.

"Dude. I think I know who I talked to." Cameron smoothed a hand over his bright blue-and-yellow tie that was as unconventional as the wearer. He might sport a Brooks Brothers suit, but his socks were usually straight out of a Crayola box or else covered with weird graphics from video games. "It was the same woman who spoke to me the first time. Who was helping me find a wife."

"Right," Ian told him dryly. "First of all, you don't order a wife the same way you get a snack from the room service menu. Second, the woman you spoke to on both occasions was Mallory's assistant, Kinley."

"She lied to me?" Cameron stopped messing with the settings on the chair and sat straighter.

Quinn pivoted back toward the room, giving Ian his full attention.

"Kinley has been lying to all of Mallory's clients for nearly a year—almost since the inception of Mallory's debut as a matchmaker—impersonating her employer to protect the woman's real identity." Ian hitched his leg higher on the desk so he could face his brothers better.

"I'm trying to trace her real identity now. But I wonder if part of the reason the matchmaking service closed down was because something went wrong with Cameron's date."

"But the more relevant question is where did Sofia's contact information originate, and who would have added her to the web site that Cameron viewed?" Quinn asked. "The obvious answer is that it was the matchmaker her father hired, but Vitaly swears the woman he hired speaks little English and was tasked to find a Ukrainian husband for Sofia through personal connections, not online." Quinn wanted to bring reassurance to Sofia after the way things had ended on a strained note two nights ago.

He'd run through the events dozens of times in his mind, trying to pinpoint exactly when her attitude toward him had shifted from red-hot interest back to overly cautious regard. Was it simple morning-after awkwardness? Or had he upset her and not realized it? Whatever it was, he had the sense they'd taken one step forward and two steps back after the Fortier reception.

She certainly hadn't liked the idea of marriage. And he wasn't any more eager to go down that path than her, even if it would fulfill his end of his grandfather's will. But if he had to marry to help Sofia with damage control in the press? Then he'd be an idiot *not* to at least stick with the marriage for a calendar year to take that family pressure off him.

"Are you kidding? If the woman doesn't speak English, it's all the more likely she was confused about what she posted online." Cameron folded his arms on the desk and pulled himself forward on the wheeled chair. "Talk to Koslov's matchmaker and your problem is solved."

"Possibly." Quinn regretted exploring this end of the matchmaking equation more when he'd already guessed it was a dead end. But how much did he dare look into the Ukrainian woman who was Vitaly Koslov's personal friend?

After assuring Sofia he would ask her father to make sure her dating profile was removed from circulation, Quinn had phoned Koslov, but the guy hadn't exactly been forthcoming with much information. All Vitaly had told him was that he'd hired a close personal friend named Olena to search for a husband for Sofia. But when Quinn suggested the woman must have given out Sofia's travel plans to a US matchmaker to relay to Cameron, Vitaly had gotten angry all over again about Cam's public proposal.

"I'm still going to look for Mallory West, just for the principle of the thing." Heading over to the bookshelves, Ian tipped a silver weight that was part of a perpetual motion machine, sending the oddly shaped pendulum piece swinging and glinting in the fluorescent lights.

"Thank you for all you've done." Quinn appreciated the way his brothers came together as a family even if they didn't always see eye to eye. "If Sofia's father doesn't want to come clean about the role he played in all this, I'm not sure I want to ruffle his feathers anyhow. I had one of my IT techs search for any traces of Sofia's dating profile, and he found nothing. So I feel sure her digital privacy is intact."

"It's unlike you to use company resources for something personal," Ian noted while Cameron just grinned. And grinned.

And grinned.

Damn it.

"Obviously the guy needs overtime and I'm paying him out of pocket." Hadn't that been clear? "And what happened in Kiev, Cam? What's the holdup now on those hotels?"

His brother had taken Quinn's place at the most recent round of meetings on the Eastern European acquisitions, but no paperwork had come through for the purchase.

"Officially, we're waiting on some government bureau to sign off. But if you ask me, it's an excuse they trotted out to hide the fact that Koslov is blocking the sale. His name came up more than once during the meeting."

Thwarted on every front, the day was going to hell in a hurry. "Why would he interfere with the deal after I made it clear I acted in his daughter's best interests?"

"Maybe he's waiting to see how it all plays out," Ian offered. "She's not off the hook yet, especially if that reporter is hinting that she knows something about a matchmaker."

"Which would be his fault, not ours." Quinn hated having to dance to the guy's tune, but as far as the hotel deal went, clearly Sofia's father had plenty of foreign influence.

Quinn debated speaking to that reporter himself to get a better feel for what was going on. He could run interference for Sofia while she was auditioning since the same reporter would be covering it for her magazine.

Besides, he wanted to see Sofia again. Soon.

His cell phone vibrated on the desk, but before his brothers could use the call as an excuse to leave the meeting, the Caller ID flashed their father's name.

"It's Dad," Quinn announced. "Maybe you'd better stick around."

Both of his brothers went stone silent. Their father communicated with them less than ever since he left the family business. He hadn't been in New York for over a year.

"Hi, Dad," Quinn answered, finger hovering over the

button to broadcast the call to the room. "I'm with Ian and Cam. Mind if I put you on speakerphone?"

"No," Liam answered, his voice sounding unusually hoarse. "That will save me having to call them, too."

Concerned, Quinn turned on the feature. "Is everything okay? Where are you?"

A perpetual thrill-seeker, Liam McNeill had gotten himself into some tight spots over the years.

"I'm in China. I figured I'd check out that Mount Hua Shan ascent since your gramps is over here anyhow."

Quinn hadn't heard of it, but he knew the kinds of climbs that attracted his father's attention. "You're with Gramps?"

"Not yet, but I'm heading to Shanghai now. He called me to see if I could come get him out of a local hospital."

All three brothers froze. Quinn could feel the tension in the room as a chill shot over his skin.

"Why?" Ian barked into the phone. "What's wrong?"

"He was on a tour of the city, I guess, and the guide brought him in. There are language barrier issues, of course, but apparently they think he had a minor heart attack and they want to keep an eye on him."

Cameron swore quietly, speaking for every last one of them. No matter his age, Malcolm McNeill had always seemed invincible.

"How far are you from the hospital?" Cameron asked, already loading a map on his phone.

It occurred to Quinn, while his brothers took down the necessary information, that they had taken over his usual role as the leader. He'd froze the first moment he'd heard the word *hospital*.

"Call us when you see him," Quinn barked, finally adding to the conversation. Their father agreed to do so and ended the call.

The three of them didn't say much as they parted. Their father was already in China, so it wasn't as if they needed to jump on the first plane. He'd let them know if they should come to Shanghai.

After his brothers left, Quinn could think of only one person he wanted to see. Needed to see.

And it wasn't about marriage, damn it, even though honoring his grandfather's will now seemed like something he needed to take more seriously.

Right now, he didn't care about that. He just wanted Sofia's arms around him and he was too numb to think about what that might mean.

The night before the most important audition of Sofia's life, the downstairs intercom buzzed.

"Hello?" she asked, not expecting anyone and figuring it was probably a fast-food delivery guy having a hard time getting in the building. How many times had her neighbor ordered a pizza and then decided to walk her dog or get in the shower?

"Sofia, it's Quinn. I need to see you." His tone set off an answering response in her body before her brain had the chance to think it through.

But something in his voice alerted her that it was serious. This was not the sound of her tango-dancing lover or even her friend who could talk her through her nervousness. Something was wrong.

"Of course." She buzzed him inside and shut down the video of one of Fortier's first ballets she'd been watching. She was dancing a piece from it for her audition, hoping to capture the mood of it better than his star had at the time.

But now her focus shifted to Quinn, as it had so often since they'd met, and even more often since they'd shared a night together. Yes, she needed to guard her emotions more around him. Yet she couldn't simply turn her back on their pact when it had been her idea to stay together for appearance's sake.

Or maybe she just really wanted to see him tonight. The idea seemed like a worrisome possibility as she checked her reflection in a mirror over the couch. Her eyes were bright and her color high. She tugged her black cashmere cardigan closer around her, covering the pink tank top she was wearing with silky, gray lounge pants.

"Get a grip," she reminded herself as she moved toward her front door. She was almost there when a sharp rap sounded.

As she swung the door wide, Quinn's gaze snapped up to meet hers. Everything about him looked tense. His flexing jaw. The flat line of his mouth. The set of his shoulders beneath a black wool coat tailored to his broad form.

And yet some of the tension seemed to ease as he looked at her.

"Sofia." He didn't step inside even though she'd made a pathway clear. "May I come in?"

She waved him in and shut the door behind him. He brought a hint of the cold air with him and a slight hint of the aftershave that she remembered on her skin following the night they'd spent together. Like an aphrodisiac, it pulled her closer and she breathed deep for a moment while she stood behind him.

"Can I take your coat?" Idly, she wondered what he thought of her tiny apartment as she hung the beautifully made wool garment on a simple iron coatrack she'd bought at a salvage shop in Long Island.

She might have connections to Quinn McNeill's extravagant world through her father, but she'd never let herself be a part of it. Last week's ill-fated private flight aside, she paid her own way in life in spite of her father's wealth.

"I apologize for stopping by unannounced. My grandfather had a heart attack twelve hours ago." Quinn's stark statement changed the track of Sofia's thoughts instantly.

"I'm so sorry." She'd never forget the pain of her mother's battle with cancer. The hurts were etched on her forever, pain that went so much deeper than anything her profession could ever wreak on her knees or her feet. "Is he okay?"

She reached for him, needing to offer some kind of comfort in spite of all her warnings to maintain her guard around him. She could never deny someone comfort in the face of that kind of hurt.

"I'm waiting for my father to call from Shanghai with an update, but with the time difference…" He shrugged, still wearing the jacket of his black, custom-tailored suit that looked like something off Savile Row. His burgundy tie and crisp, white shirt were an elegantly simple combination. "I don't know how long it might be." He glanced around the apartment beyond the small foyer. "Am I interrupting anything? I told the driver to wait in case you were busy."

Of course he did. Because hedge fund managers didn't just drive themselves around the city. But even that reminder of their very different lives didn't stop her from wanting him to stay.

"I was just going over some notes for my audition tomorrow—"

"I forgot." Shaking his head, he halted his steps before the living area. "Hell, Sofia. I know how important that is—"

"It's fine. I was only getting more nervous anyhow."

She drew him forward, gesturing toward her well-worn couch. "I don't want you to wait for that phone call alone."

No matter that she'd hoped to put up more barriers with him.

He'd been kind to her when she'd been nervous at the reception for Idris. Helped her maintain a façade of an engagement when she'd asked him to. She wouldn't betray their unlikely friendship even if he was better at guarding his heart than she was.

"If you're sure." He still didn't take a seat, however. "I'll stay a little longer." He stopped at a framed photo above an antique wooden rocker. "Is this your mother?"

"Yes." She remembered that moment so well, standing on a rocking boat deck, her mother's arm slung around her shoulders and a new sunburn already making her skin itch. "That's the summer before she died. We went to Greece and sailed with a group of art students around the islands."

"What a year that must have been." He reached to trace Sofia's face in the photo, a gesture she swore she felt on her own skin. "From so much happiness to mourning her."

"She gave very explicit instructions about that." Her throat tightened as she remembered. "We were supposed to celebrate her life. Not mourn. She wanted her ashes taken out to the Aegean so she could sparkle in the sunlight one more time." Sofia smiled at the memory of her saying the words. "She said if I did it, maybe she'd come back as a mermaid. Which, in all my thirteen-year-old wisdom, I called bullshit. But she said I would understand the truth about beauty and magic when I was older."

"And you have." Quinn turned away from the photo, his eyes full of warmth.

"Not really." She rubbed her arms briskly to ward off

a sudden chill despite the cashmere cardigan. "I work hard to create beauty on stage, but I still haven't found anything magical about the sweat, blood and stress fractures that go into ballet."

She hated to sound like a cynic. But perhaps she resented—just a little—that she hadn't inherited more of her mother's free-spirited joy.

"But you saw it that first time you watched *Sleeping Beauty* when you were a girl," he reminded her. "It showed when you told me about that performance. And you admitted yourself that the skill wasn't necessarily impressive. Maybe you only see the magic from the audience."

"Maybe." She conceded the point mostly because she didn't want to bring him down on a night that was already stressful for him. "What about you?" She tugged him to sit beside her on the couch. "Do you see your mom often? I think I read that she's a Brazilian native."

A surprise smile appeared on his handsome face. "Studying up on your fiancé?"

"I had to be prepared to field questions about you since we've been dating for months." She had a lot of her own questions about him. She felt like the man she knew wasn't necessarily the one she read about online.

Lowering himself to the couch cushion beside her, Quinn gave a tight nod. "My mother moved back to Brazil after the divorce. She has a place just outside Rio de Janeiro. I make an effort to call her often, but…"

"But it's complicated?" she offered, touching his hand softly, then linking their fingers.

His mouth cocked into a jaded smile and he rubbed his thumb along the inside of her wrist. "Families are usually more complicated than they seem, aren't they? My parents were married for seven years. My father, for lack of a better description, marches to his own drummer. He's a thrill-seeker, an adrenaline junkie who swept my mother off her feet. He showed up at a bar where she was singing one night after he'd had a close call with a hang glider on a mountain near Rio."

Giving his hand an encouraging squeeze, she nodded at him. "Your mother sings?"

"Not often anymore, but yes. She has a beautiful voice. The night they met, she thought my dad finally saw the error of his ways and was going to stop taking stupid risks." Quinn barked out a low laugh. "But that didn't last long. By the time the rib fractures healed, he was right back to his old tricks. After seven years together, she said she wouldn't follow him anymore and be complicit in watching him kill himself."

From her quick internet searches, Sofia had read that Liam McNeill was a reckless adventurer. And from what she could tell about Quinn, he was almost the exact opposite. Quinn's practical, steady and calculating nature was probably part of what made him such a successful hedge fund manager. His fund set records two years straight for its profit margins. In some ways he reminded her of her own father.

"Your dad didn't try to change?"

"No. He got a lawyer to divide things up evenly—much to my grandfather's frustration—and my mother returned to Brazil permanently. My brothers and I split our time between Rio and New York. Six months with Dad, six months with Mom."

Sofia's brow rose in surprise. "Do you speak Portuguese?"

"Not as well as I did as a child, but yes. Some Spanish, too. The languages definitely help both my businesses, but I'm not sure I'd recommend raising children on two continents to make it happen." The genuine regret in his voice gave her a small peek into his upbringing and the things he must have overcome. How hard would it have been to be away from his mother for half the year at such a young age?

She wanted to know more about him. But with him sitting so close and her feelings about him all over the map, she didn't know how wise it would be to keep up this intimate conversation when their thighs were almost touching.

Plus, he might ask more about her and her own complicated relationship with her wealthy father.

"A man of many talents," she said, pushing off the couch. "Tea?"

She needed to put some distance between them, even just for a moment, to resurrect some fragile emotional boundaries.

"Please. Thank you, Sofia."

Her apartment was small and she moved quickly from the couch to the kitchen area. Sofia kept her teakettle on her stove for easy access. Filling the yellow kettle with water, she placed it on the burner, twisting the knob to high.

"So that tango at the gala…your globe-trotting background explains why you moved so beautifully. It's part of your identity." Leaning up against the stove, she stared at him, remembering the way his body had kept rhythm with hers.

Apparently going to the kitchen wasn't going to prevent her from wanting him. He looked far too good in her home.

"Yes. But I always gravitated more toward life with my grandfather, who ended up caring for my brothers and me more than my dad. Gramps was the one that pushed

me—and my brothers—toward responsibility and pro-
ductivity. In some ways, I'm much closer to him than I
am to either of my parents." His expression darkened. No
doubt he was worried about the older man.

"I'm sure we'll hear some news about him soon." She
remembered the fear of wondering if a loved one was
going to be okay. There were nearly two months of her
life she'd spent waiting and terrified when her mother
was sick. For the first time she really thought about the
fact that her father hadn't been much comfort. But then,
he was one to lose himself in work—the same way he
pushed her to do now and then. Work more. Dance more.
Move forward with life and quit worrying about what
might be, until sometimes she felt like she was pirouetting so quickly her world was a blur—

The kettle whistled, startling her from her thoughts,
and she poured the boiling water into two teacups. They,
like the kettle, were flea market finds. Mismatched. But
sturdy, full of character. Artistry of a different kind. She
plopped the tea diffuser into the cups, the jasmine green
tea mixture instantly turning the water a pale, spring
green.

As she placed the cups on the fancy serving tray—another mismatched item—she felt his eyes on her. Glancing around her apartment, her cheeks flushed.

What did he think of her and her piecemeal apartment
when his life operated at a whole different frequency?
She shouldn't care. And it didn't matter. But she felt a
rush of stiff-necked pride anyhow.

She carried the tea to the sofa, nearly spilling the
whole thing when his cell phone rang. The chime seemed
to blare through the small space, unnaturally loud. Rushing to settle the tray, she sat beside him as he answered
the call.

"Dad." Quinn sat forward on the couch, his elbows on his knees, all his attention focused on the call.

Sofia wondered if she should give him privacy. But what if he needed her? She moved closer to him in spite of everything. Damn it, she would have wanted someone sitting by her any of those times she'd gotten bad reports about her mom from doctors who didn't know who else to tell. Her father hadn't been there, unaware of her sickness since Sofia's mother hadn't wanted to tell anyone.

"So that's encouraging news, right?" Quinn glanced over his shoulder and their gazes collided.

She hoped, for his sake, that his grandfather would make a strong recovery. Quinn listened to his father while Sofia stared at Quinn's broad back. Even now, she wanted the right to touch him, to be the woman who sat by his side and could loop her arm through his whenever she chose. What madness was this that gave her such strong feelings for him so fast?

Her heart thumped hard as she took a careful sip of the scalding tea and tried not to eavesdrop. But she was so very worried for him.

"You sure you don't want me to call them?" Quinn was asking. "Thanks, Dad."

He disconnected the call and set aside the phone, pivoting to look at her.

"It was minor and they are keeping him for two days for observation. Gramps' doctor in New York is being consulted, because even though it was minor, they want to put a pacemaker in."

"Can it wait until he comes home?" Arranging for medical care in foreign countries was a challenge. She and her fellow dancers had experienced that more than once in their travels.

"We'll let his doctor make the call after he reviews

the tests from the hospital in Shanghai. But Dad says Gramps looks good." Quinn looked better, too. Some of the tension seemed to have rolled off his shoulders since he'd walked through her door.

"I'm so glad to hear it." She set her cup aside and reached for him. She planned to rub his shoulder, maybe. Or squeeze his forearm.

But as she moved toward him, he opened his arms wide and hugged her. Hard.

"Thank you, Sofia." He stroked her back with his big hands, tucking her against his chest. "I was so damn worried."

She would have replied, but her cheek rested against his chest, preventing her from speaking. His arms still squeezed her tight. She settled for planting a kiss on his shirt to one side of his tie. His body was warm beneath the fabric. She could feel his heartbeat beneath her ear. Hear how it picked up rhythm. For a moment time stood still as she thought about what that rapid heartbeat meant. And how the rest of this night might unfold.

He would leave if she asked him to.

She knew without question that how things proceeded from here was her call. But as she edged back to look up at him, she knew she didn't stand a chance of sending him away. Not when her own heart beat faster and her whole focus had narrowed to him.

He was the only man she'd ever met who could make the rest of her world disappear. And the night before the most important audition of her life, maybe she needed the chance to lose herself in the raw passion only Quinn could give her.

Eleven

He wanted to lose himself in her.

Quinn had tried giving her an out, offering to leave so she could focus on her audition. But she had insisted he stay. And after the hellish worry of the last few hours, he was only too glad to shift gears. All that pent-up, tense energy found an enticing outlet in the irresistible woman beside him.

"Sofia." He threaded his fingers through her hair and pulled her to him.

Everything about her was soft and welcoming, from the cashmere sweater to the creamy-smooth skin beneath. He brushed the backs of his knuckles under the cardigan to trace the edge of her tank top. The slow hiss of her breath between her teeth stirred him, calling him to touch her just the way she wanted. Just the way she needed.

"I've missed you." He'd thought about her so often since their last night together. Had it only been two nights ago?

It seemed like two months. He'd wanted her in his bed every moment since.

"I thought I dreamed how good this felt." She kissed the words into his cheek as she undid the buttons beneath his tie.

Quinn tugged at the knot, wanting all the barriers between them gone. He'd taken off his jacket earlier. Now he cursed French cuffs to the skies and back as he undid one and Sofia unfastened the other.

"It was no dream." He tore the shirt off, tossing it on a slipper chair nearby. "I was there, remember? It was better than anything I could have imagined."

"For me, too." She studied his exposed chest. Her gaze hot and admiring, but he wanted her hands all over.

Closing the distance between them, he lifted her against him, startling a squeak of surprise from her while she wrapped her arms around his neck and—much to his pleasure—her legs around his waist.

"Bedroom." He gripped her splayed thighs, cradling them at hip level as he started walking toward a hallway in the back. Her vanilla and floral scent teased his nostrils, bringing back heady memories of things they'd done that night after the welcome reception.

He hadn't wanted to shower the next day, but wanted to savor her fragrance on his skin.

"On the right," she murmured between kisses, her teeth raking gently down his neck. "Hurry."

Her hands smoothed over his back and shoulders, feeling everywhere she could reach. As she moved, her hair stroked his chest, a tantalizing brush of silk each time. She reached to flick a light switch dimmer as they entered the hallway, casting a warm glow where he'd bared one shoulder.

Black cashmere falling away, he nudged aside the tank top strap with his teeth.

"You taste so good." Selfishly, he wanted to keep her up all night, tasting her and tempting her, driving her to that precipice again and again.

But he knew she needed her rest for the audition. This time together had to be enough for tonight.

"You can tell from just one bite?" she teased in a whisper, the hint of her passionate nature setting him on fire.

"I'm hoping like hell I can confirm the facts." He turned them sideways to edge through a partially open door and into her bedroom.

A very white bedroom. A single bedside reading lamp illuminated a high, four-poster painted white with hints of gray details around the carved woodwork and an eggshell-colored duvet atop floor-length pale linens. An antique chandelier hung over the bed. Even in the dim light from the bedside, the glass prisms cast small rainbows around the room. Behind the bed, there was a triangular bookcase instead of a headboard, hundreds of leather-bound volumes adding the room's only color.

Quinn set her in the center of the bed, hating to let go of her, but giving himself a moment to unfasten his belt and step out of his shoes. Sofia watched him, rolling one shoulder and then the other out of her sweater until she was down to her pink tank top and pajama pants. When her eyes lowered to where he unzipped his pants, his blood rushed south, turning him to steel.

It made the unzipping an effort, but seemed to inspire Sofia to sidle out of the cotton spandex, revealing that she was wearing absolutely nothing underneath her shirt. At the sight of her pink-tipped breasts, he forgot about his pants and dived onto the bed with her, drawing her down into the thick duvet with him.

Her moment of laughter turned to a gasp of pleasure as he fastened his mouth around one taut peak, drawing her in for a thorough exploration. She twisted beneath him, her hips seeking his. No woman had ever lit him up as fast as she did, heat blistering across his back, and they weren't even naked yet.

Hands raking off the rest of her clothes—the lounge pants and bikini panties—he traced the muscles of her bare calves and thighs, hugging her legs to his chest as he worked his way back up her body. He kissed a path along her hips, relishing the growing warmth in her skin and liking that he'd put it there.

Heart hammering, he ignored his own needs to focus on hers. Parting her thighs to make room for himself there, he kissed her deeply. Thoroughly. Listened to every sigh and hitch in her breath to learn what she liked best as he stroked her over and over with his tongue.

He brought her close to release twice, feeling her body go taut and still. Both times he backed off, not ready to finish. If this was his only time to be with her tonight, he wanted her fully sated. Boneless with the pleasure he gave her. But the third time she tensed, her fingers gripping his shoulders, he took her the rest of the way, helping her savor every last sweet thrill until she collapsed beneath him.

Elbowing his way higher on the bed, he undressed the rest of the way while she caught her breath. He retrieved a condom from his wallet before he tossed aside his pants, placing it on the bed nearby. When he was done, he moved to cradle her against him so he could stroke her hair while she recovered. He wasn't expecting her to rise up from the bed like some kind of pagan goddess and straddle him, but she did just that, arching her eyebrows at him as though she was daring him to object.

As if he ever would.

"You're beautiful," he told her simply, watching her as she positioned herself above him.

She bent low to kiss him and retrieved the condom. She unwrapped it and rolled it into place, her touch tempting him far too much. He took deep breaths. Steadied himself.

Damn, but he wanted her. Now.

When she lowered herself on him, he ground his teeth together to hang on to the moment. And when she started to move, her beautiful body a tantalizing gift, he knew that moment would be seared on the backs of his eyelids forever. She gave him this and so much more tonight.

His body roaring with a new fire, he had no choice but to roll her to her back and hold her there for a long moment. Pulling himself together, he steeled his body for the incredible sensual onslaught of this woman.

After a long pause he kissed her, thrusting deep inside her. She surrounded him with her softness and her scent, her arms winding around his neck, her feminine muscles clamping him tight. Sweet sighs turned to needy cries as he increased the pace, but she met every thrust, driving him higher.

By the time the heat in his blood reached a fever pitch, he'd brought Sofia to that heady precipice again, her body tensing under his. Sweat beading on his brow, he drove inside her once more, propelling them both over the edge.

Breath, limbs and shouts tangling, they held on tight to one another while the pleasure swelled and spent itself. They lay there, heartbeats syncing as they slowed.

Quinn pulled a corner of the duvet over her, covering her pale limbs with the white, downy spread. Her blond hair danced along her jaw as the air shifted around her from the movement of the blanket.

She lay her cheek on his chest and he had a sudden pang at the realization that it all felt too damn right. After the way she'd welcomed him, her care for him extending to his family when she'd urged him to stay until his father called, Quinn couldn't pretend this arrangement of theirs was strictly for show. Something had shifted between them and it was a whole lot more than sex.

He didn't know what it was. But he'd dated women for months without feeling the kind of connection he had to Sofia after a week together. And with his grandfather's health on the line now—because, damn it, the heart attack had scared the hell out of him—Quinn couldn't ignore the idea that had been rolling around his head to cement their relationship.

Too bad she'd already told him that marrying for show was a bad idea. He still didn't understand how that was so much worse than a fake engagement, but he knew where she stood in regard to a fake marriage.

But what if it was for his grandfather's sake?

"I can almost hear you thinking," she said, peering up at him from her spot on his chest, her hair a tousled, sexy mess. "Everything okay?"

Quinn could fulfill the terms of the will and keep her by his side in one move. And maybe help her focus on her career instead of all the drama surrounding her demanding job. It would be good for both of them.

"I have an idea." Shifting her in his arms, he raised them to a sitting position, lifting a pillow behind her back. "And I want you to hear me out."

"I'm ready." She practically glowed from their lovemaking, so it was probably as good a time as any to pitch his idea.

"That night Cameron proposed to you, we were so focused on damage control that we never really talked about why he was in such a hurry to find a wife."

"I thought he was an impulsive guy." Frowning, she raised one bare shoulder in a delicate shrug.

"That's part of it. But he was also unhappy with our grandfather for writing up new terms in his will that dictate each of his three grandsons marry in order to secure a third share of McNeill Resorts. He thought it would ensure the company's future." Quinn felt bad he hadn't told her about it before. But there'd been a lot to learn about each other in a short space of time. He'd been busy trying to acquaint himself with her world while she'd been preparing for her audition and managing the fallout of Cameron's public proposal with the media.

"That sounds…heavy-handed." Sofia straightened beside him, her slight withdrawal feeling like an absence. "Why would he think that forcing his heirs into marriages would give his business more stability? Surely he must know those unions won't necessarily be durable."

"He refused to elaborate on his motives before he left for a month-long trip overseas. Privately, I've wondered about his state of mind, and whether my father's very expensive divorce from my mother was a factor in Gramps' decision." The legal termination of their marriage had made her a rich woman able to live anywhere in the world she wanted. Unfortunately it wasn't anywhere near her sons. "But Gramps had his lawyer unveil the new will three weeks ago and so far he's refused to change it. As it stands, each of our portions of the company will be sold at auction if we don't follow the rules and stay married for at least a year."

The air between them stilled. He felt her body tense further, like a wound spring.

"So Cameron wanted to marry me to save his shares

in the company?" Her voice hardened, her eyes wide as she swung on him. "He really was looking for a modern-day mail-order bride. And you knew this all the time? Oh. My. God."

Quinn hadn't expected such a strong reaction, especially since she'd met Cameron in person. His brother—while headstrong—wasn't a bad guy.

"Cameron was the most incensed about the terms because he is close to my grandfather and is most invested in the family business. I think he hoped a rash engagement might make Gramps see he'd pushed us too far." At least, that was the reasoning as Quinn understood it. With Cameron, who knew?

Cameron had yet to give him an explanation that made any sense in his mind.

"So, basically, to hell with me and my feelings. I was just supposed to be the wife of convenience for him." Sofia shook her head, then took a deep breath as if trying to hang on to her patience. "I hope he's not going to try that again with someone else."

The silences between her words seemed to grow longer, more deliberate and awkward. Was he being shut out?

She paused, her voice getting quieter. "What about you, Quinn? Are you going to marry and follow your grandfather's rules?"

He couldn't read her right now. Didn't know if she was already thinking he was ten kinds of ass for considering it. Or if she could possibly have the same idea in mind as him: that a marriage between them could be beneficial all the way around since she'd been pressured by her father to settle down, as well.

"I wasn't planning on it." He chose his words carefully, well aware he was walking on thin ice here, not wanting to lose what they'd just shared. He still wanted to explore where it might lead. Might? Where it damn well was heading at the speed of light. "But I'll admit that having my grandfather's health in question now makes me rethink how much I want to dig my heels in about protesting the will."

"Meaning?" She lifted an eyebrow in silent question.

"Meaning…" He was in too deep to turn around, but he realized midstream he probably should have prepared more. Had a real ring that was from him and not Cameron. Thought about what to say. But, too late now. He'd come this far already and he was a man used to making executive decisions quickly, firmly, decisively. "Why don't you and I get married?"

How could a man she'd only just met break her heart in such a short space of time?

She'd known Quinn for a week, but it had been an intense time with a lot of personal upheaval for her. Maybe that's how she'd come to care about him far too much, far too quickly. The turmoil had forged a bond between them, yoked them together. The heat of their passion and the high stakes of preserving her public relations campaign had driven her into the arms of a man that could not emotionally provide for her.

He'd slipped around tattered defenses when she was battling injuries, professional jealousy and worries her career could end before she had a plan B in place. Before she knew it, she was opening her heart to a man wholly inappropriate for her.

It wasn't his fault that her heart ached so fiercely she wanted to hold on to her chest to try to ease the pain. No. The fault was all hers for not protecting herself better, especially when she'd known that he was getting under her skin and making her care.

"Sofia?" Quinn's fingers brushed along her jaw, tipping her face up so he could see her better. She wanted to fold into his touch, melt into him again. But things between them had changed. Everything had. "It could solve a lot of problems for both of us. Quiet the speculation about our engagement with the reporters and with your peers so you can focus on the art that's most important to you. And, of course, it would secure my grandfather's legacy and fulfil his lifelong dream for his grandsons to run the company. At least where I'm concerned."

"If he'd really wanted that," Sofia interjected, leaning away from Quinn's touch, the chill of the apartment flooding the space where his fingers had lingered, "he could have just given you each a third of the business."

"I think he wanted to—"

"No," she said, forcing strength into her voice. She couldn't pretend to listen seriously to this idea when Quinn had crushed a piece of her by even suggesting it. "I know I agreed to hear you out, but I understand what you are proposing."

The thought ripped through her, wounding her more deeply than any injury dance could ever give her. Ballet could never betray her like this.

"It would only be for one year," he clarified. "Like dating with incredible benefits for both of us. I could help you solidify your career plans during that time so when you're ready to quit dancing you have a future you're excited about."

He understood her practical needs so well. Unfortunately he didn't have any idea about the emotional end of the equation.

"Most people don't put a time limit on a marriage, but

thank you for making that perfectly clear." She shot out of bed, dragging a sheet with her, unable to sit quietly by while he spouted more ideas that were like small knives to the naïve vision she'd had of continuing a relationship. "I really thought we had a connection, Quinn."

Stepping behind a screen, she flipped the sheet over the top because damned if she was baring any more of herself to him. She found her tank top on the floor and yanked it back on. Then she slid her pants into place, desperate to put boundaries between them, any sort of boundary at this point.

"We do. I never would have suggested this otherwise." She heard the creak of the mattress and the whisper of his clothes as he slowly got dressed. "I don't understand why you're so upset."

"I'm upset you never mentioned this will and the need for all the McNeill men to marry, when it feels highly relevant to our arrangement." Stomping out in her tank and pants, she found her sweater and punched one arm through each sleeve. "You even suggested marrying if worse came to worst and the *Dance* magazine writer published something unsavory about me. That would have been the perfect time to clue me in about the will and how—by the way—it would check off some boxes for your goals, too."

"How is me using a marriage to satisfy the terms of my grandfather's will any different than you using an engagement to smooth over your public relations agenda before a big audition?" Quinn stood, his clothes on but his shirt unbuttoned, the tie loose around his neck.

"I was trying to maintain focus on my career during a drama that had *nothing* to do with me. You're trying to protect your bottom line." She lobbed the accusation at him and hoped it found its mark.

"No." A new stillness went over him, alerting her that she'd at last gotten through to him. "Actually, it's about protecting family, which is the most important thing to me."

Watching the pain flash across his face sent a tiny prick of regret stabbing through her. She couldn't forget how devastated he'd looked when he'd walked into her apartment tonight. But, damn it, he had hidden the truth from her.

"You told me that billions of dollars of investments would be at risk if people don't trust you, but how are you worthy of trust if you treat a person as deceptively as you've treated me?" she reminded him. Reminded herself. She kept having to do that. "So, to a certain extent, it is about the money."

"If it was just about the money, I would find another way. I know it doesn't mean much to you, but I'm fairly good at making it." His mouth twisted. His jaw flexed. "I only care about making sure my grandfather's life's work is not lost to strangers because of his desire to see the family settled."

He waited for her to say something. But she was at a loss, empty after a night where passions had run high. Her emotions were spent and she didn't know what—or whom—to trust.

She stared at the rainbow colors leaping from her engagement ring in the muted light of her bedroom. It was the physical manifestation of every lie and deception.

With more bravado then she felt, she twisted the ring from her finger, hoping that with its absence, she'd be able to focus on why she was here in New York. On why she didn't get involved.

"I'm sorry, Quinn. But I don't know how to move forward from this. I know I asked you to pretend we were engaged to help me, but I release you from our agreement." Handing back the ring, she was done with false promises and a relationship that was just for show.

She'd finally learned to put some trust in her partner, and it had been a mistake that had cost her dearly.

Quinn stared at the ring in his open palm for a long moment.

The moment echoed between them. Her heart hammered; she was wretched. If he would just walk away now, she'd be able to curse him, move on. But he just stood there, a lingering shadow of what could have been.

"I know that people are important, Sofia, not the bottom line." His hand closed into a fist around the ring, the whites of his knuckles showing. "Has it occurred to you that you're so busy seeing the bottom line—in my case, a wealthy one—and that you're not seeing the person behind it?"

His eyes held hers. Challenging her.

"I don't know what I see anymore," she said tightly, barely hanging on to the swell of raw emotions seething just below the surface. She wrapped her cashmere sweater around her like shrink wrap to hold herself together. "I don't know what to believe."

"I'm not going to be the one to break our engagement." He set the ring on a whitewashed narrow console table by the bedroom door. "Keep this in case you need it to stem unwanted questions from reporters about its absence. And good luck tomorrow."

He walked out of her bedroom. Out of her apartment. The door shut quietly behind him. Only then did she allow her knees to give out beneath her. Curling on her bed, she wouldn't let herself her cry. Not when she had the most important audition of her life tomorrow.

There would be time enough for heartbreak afterward.

But as she closed her eyes, a tear leaked free anyhow. Despite her famous iron-clad professional discipline, her body had its limits for what it would do based on sheer will. She could dance on stress fractures and bunions, pick herself up after her dancing partners dropped her on a hard, unforgiving floor that would leave her body bruised for weeks.

Yet she'd discovered tonight that her eyes would go on crying even if she told them not to. And her heart would keep on breaking the longer she thought about Quinn. In spite of all reason and practicality, she'd fallen head over heels in love with this man.

Twelve

Turning around the stage in petit jeté jumps, Sofia prepared to dance for Idris Fortier. The choreographer sat in the middle of the small practice theater, which would be a closed set for the next hour. He'd allowed Delaney to sit off to one side with her camera, but had requested she not film during the session.

Even Delaney had been too cowed by Fortier to gainsay him. Sofia smiled to think how quietly the journalist had slunk to the sidelines to watch Sofia perform.

"Are you ready, darling?" the choreographer called up to her now, his accent lingering over the endearment even though his eyes were still on his tablet screen.

"I'm ready." She'd barely slept the night before and wondered if her parting with Quinn was going to cost her this audition, too.

The role of a lifetime. The cementing of her place in the ballet world. Some dancers were principals twelve, fifteen or even more years. Sofia knew her knees were on borrowed time. She might come back after the surgeries she would one day need, but a dancer never knew if she would be as skilled afterward.

She needed her career on fast forward in order to have the kind of post-dance life she envisioned for herself. To still work in the field and be able to hold her head high.

"What will you be dancing for me today?" He put his tablet aside and adjusted the small, round spectacles on his nose, giving her his full attention.

Sofia had planned for weeks to dance one of Fortier's dances. A flattering compliment. Plus, dancing a younger choreographer's work meant that there were fewer ballerinas she could be compared to. New pieces allowed a dancer a little more room for interpretation. But after the tears she'd shed last night, she'd arisen from bed this morning with the Black Swan in her heart and ready to burst through her toes.

"Black Swan. The final act in the Grigorovich version." She could dance that one without a partner since there was less emphasis on the pas de deux so important in the Balanchine version.

"An interesting choice, Ms. Koslov. Wholly unexpected."

She had no way of knowing what he'd expected. But most experienced dancers left the world's most well-danced pieces alone for situations like this since they left too much room for comparison. Today, Sofia did not care. She strode to the side of the stage to start her music, which gave her a twenty-count of silence to walk to position. She wanted to dance the hell out of a virtuoso piece and demonstrate the technical skill her critics all agreed she possessed.

And if she couldn't add the extra layer of emotion that

some say was occasionally missing from her work? She didn't deserve the part. Because today, she was nothing but raw emotion with Quinn's parting words still echoing in her head.

You're so busy seeing the bottom line...you're not seeing the person behind it.

As if *she'd* been the one to focus on his wealth.

Banishing the thoughts from her head, she took solace in the music and let Odile's seduction blast away everything else. She didn't want to be hapless Odette who lost Siegfried even though she hadn't done a damn thing wrong. Right now, she needed the fiery passion of Odile to lure Siegfried to his lonely end.

With multiple pirouettes spinning her across the stage, Sofia articulated every phrase, letting the music fill her as she poured out the role. Space-devouring leaps ate up the stage. Fast fouettés flowed naturally, one after the other. She didn't dance so much as she burned—all the heedless energy and longing of the night before torched through this one outlet she understood.

When she reached the end of the coda, the final fouetté perfectly timed, Sofia held her position into the silence, her breathing so heavy the pull of air was the only sound in the theater.

Until one person clapped. The fast, excited clap of genuine praise. And since Sofia could see her evaluator seated, unmoving, before her, she knew it hadn't been him doling out enthusiasm. Had Delaney truly been impressed? It didn't matter, but after tossing and turning about this dance all night, Sofia felt gratified to think someone had liked it. The journalist might be motivated by gossip scoops that would sell more magazines, but the woman would certainly know her ballet.

"Thank you, Ms. Koslov." Idris Fortier rose to his feet

and glanced sharply to his right. "I'd like a moment alone with my dancer, please?"

Sofia went to shut off her music while she heard Delaney making moves to leave the theater. As she wiped down her face with a clean towel, Sofia caught her breath and turned to find Idris standing very close.

"Oh." She stepped back to give herself room. "I didn't hear you." Her shoulders tensed; she hated to feel crowded and had anxiety in social situations where the professional pressure was high. For a split second she wished Quinn would show up—

And how ridiculous was that?

Her brief engagement was over, her ring still at home on the console where he'd left it.

"You have my full attention for this position, Sofia." Fortier's accent—French by way of Tunisia—had a peculiar but pleasant inflection.

"I realize you still have several dancers to audition." She should be pleased, she knew. She'd hoped to impress him and she seemed to have accomplished that.

But why was he standing so close? She folded her arms.

"The part is yours now if you are willing to work hard for it." He took her arms and unfolded them, extending them. He studied her body. "Black Swan really shows off your Russian training. You have beautiful extension."

Her body was part of her art, she reminded herself. Ballet was incredibly physical and she'd been touched often in her career by other dancers, directors and choreographers. So while Idris's touch felt a bit too informal for their first true professional meeting, it certainly wasn't out of bounds.

And…he'd said she had the part? Excitement trembled through her as she became aware of rehearsal music in the next studio over. A group was working on an interpretation of Vivaldi's "Four Seasons."

"I am prepared to devote everything to the project," she told him sincerely. She'd pinned all her professional hopes on it.

His hands lingered on her wrists as his dark eyes met hers.

"What will your new fiancé think of you spending all your time with me?" He didn't move. Didn't release her.

She stepped back, pulling her wrists from his hold but easing any offense with a smile.

"He will be proud of my success." She refrained from mentioning that her engagement had ended. With the strange dynamic at work in the room, she felt that it would be good protection from any misguided notions Idris might have about her becoming his lover, the way his last two featured performers had.

"Will he?" The choreographer narrowed his gaze and backed up a step. "Many new relationships are full of jealousy. That can destroy a dancer's focus."

It would destroy anyone's focus. But she could see his point. Besides, using her relationship with Quinn for show was exactly what she'd said she wouldn't do anymore. She'd wanted honesty about their relationship, not more subterfuge.

"Actually, our engagement is off," she confided. "We aren't announcing it to the press, but it was all so sudden—"

"This is very good news, Sofia." He smiled in a way that unsettled her.

It was almost as if he'd been expecting her to say that. She'd known the man for less than an hour and already she didn't like him. Artists could be strong personalities though. Maybe that accounted for it. And sometimes, the more successful, the more eccentric. Backing up another step, she bent to retrieve her phone, disconnecting it from the external speaker that had played her audition music.

"For me, as well. I couldn't be more pleased to work with you on a new ballet." When she straightened, he was still there, closer than ever.

His eyes were fastened to her left hand. He picked it up and kissed her ring finger before she could yank her hand back.

"Just happy to see this place is bare and that you are free," he explained, finally stepping away from her. "Let's go to lunch and celebrate the launch of our new partnership."

"I can't today." She hadn't even showered. She'd barely slept. And she had a very strange vibe from him that she needed to seriously consider. "I have another appointment."

"And I thought you were prepared to devote everything to this project?" The man's tone withered.

Damn it. She wasn't going to play this game. She'd worked too hard for her spot at the top of the company to be treated this way—even by a major star of the industry.

"Everything within the bounds of professionalism. And since I knew you had two other dancers to audition, I haven't cleared my schedule yet to begin working on new development."

"Perhaps you shouldn't bother. I can see you're not excited to begin." He gave her body a meaningful look, one she'd seen too often leveled at a dancer desperate for a break.

"If you're looking for a creative partnership, Mr. Fortier, I can't wait to begin." She didn't want to lose the role on a misunderstanding or because she was admittedly testy today.

Then again, she wasn't going to let him touch her, kiss her finger and stare at her body without calling him out.

"What if I'm looking for more, Ms. Koslov? What if I've read your reviews about passionless performances and I think I could be the man to inspire a creative fire that would make you unforgettable in every viewer's eyes?"

Anger simmered. She knew her Black Swan had just contained so much damn passion she'd burned down the room with it.

"How exactly would you accomplish that?" she asked, hearing a scuttling noise in the backstage area.

Had someone else entered the small theater or was that just wishful thinking?

He leaned closer, not touching her, but lowering his voice considerably. "Put yourself in my hands, Sofia, and you will see."

She didn't know if that was intended to be seductive, but she'd had enough of walking the edge of creepiness with him. And maybe her time with Quinn had given her enough confidence in herself to know she had all the passion she needed inside. This man couldn't undermine her with his smarmy insinuations.

A voice niggled at her, making her wonder if she could have walked away so confidently a week ago.

"I wonder if you actively seek out the most insecure women for your games, Mr. Fortier?" She backed away from him. "But I am not one of them, I assure you. I know my own worth. And I can admire your artistic excellence without being madly in love with you. I hope you will respect me enough to do the same for me."

Padding across the floor in her ballet shoes, Sofia left him to splutter condemning warnings about the future of her career. He threatened to tell the world she'd flubbed the audition and that's why she didn't get the part. And while that hurt, she refused to engage with him any further. She gathered her dance bag to change in a more private dressing room when she ran into Delaney.

The reporter held up a quieting finger as if she didn't want to be discovered, then waved her out into the corridor while Fortier ranted about naïve girls who didn't understand the way the world worked. What a disappointment the man had turned out to be. Usually news about people like him—a lecherous creep in the ranks—traveled along the dance grapevine quickly. She wondered if she'd alienated her fellow dancers too much in the past and that's why she hadn't already heard it for herself.

"Sofia, I taped a little of your audition," Delaney confided privately. "And I stayed behind even when he told me to leave—"

"My God." Sofia slammed through another door into a private dressing room empty except for open bags and discarded street clothes; everyone else was rehearsing right now. "Are there any lengths you wouldn't go to in order to get a story?" she fumed.

"No." The reporter set a small disk on the makeup table in front of Sofia. "But in this case, you should be thrilled since this can prove you danced your freaking toes off. You were amazing back there."

"You think so?" So maybe the self-worth she bragged about to Idris Fortier wasn't quite as steadfast as she'd pretended. Who didn't love to hear good reviews?

"I know so. And the footage I got shows it." She tapped the disk. "I heard that bastard threaten to tell people you flubbed it. I couldn't hear everything that happened before that, but it sounded like he was coming on to you?"

"Yes." Sofia dug through her bag for her facecloth. "I tried to tell myself he was just eccentric, but in the end, there was no mistaking he was angling for me to kiss his ass. And more."

"Bastard." Delaney frowned. "I took the footage hoping to use it to persuade you to give me a story about Cameron McNeill using a matchmaker."

"Excuse me?" She set down the cleansing cloth, shaking her head in disbelief.

"I moonlight for a gossip magazine on the side. It pays better." She shrugged, unapologetic. "It's expensive to live anywhere near this city. I was a dancer once, you know. A halfway decent one. But after I got hurt, my options were limited. I'd like to write about ballet and only ballet. But there's no money in it."

"What did you hear about Cameron using a matchmaker?" Sofia asked, needing to know what she was up against. Now that she'd ended her relationship with Quinn, she wouldn't have his help figuring out what to do next.

"Just that he hired Mallory West to find him a bride. I'm going to publish that much, but if you can give me anything else to add…"

"You're trying to trade the audition footage for information?" Sofia was going home and going to bed for a week. She couldn't deal with this toxic environment. Especially not with her heart breaking over Quinn and her career very likely in the dumps now that she'd told off the most respected choreographer of her time.

"I thought about it. But I can't do it." The journalist shoved the disk closer. "I can't stand it when guys try to use their position to manipulate women. Consider this me cheering on your rejection of his slimy suggestions."

"In that case—" Sofia put the disk in her bag along with her pointe shoes "—thank you. I can't help you with any information about the McNeills, though."

"Is your engagement really over with Quinn?" the other woman asked. "Or were you just saying that to convince Fortier you could do the role?" Delaney pointed to Sofia's bare ring finger.

"No comment." Sofia smiled brightly to hide the fact that just hearing Quinn's name hurt today.

He'd been such a generous lover the night before. Could a man so giving in bed really want to deceive her as thoroughly as she'd accused him of doing? She wished she had some perspective on the situation. Later, she would call Jasmine and ask for her best friend's advice. For now, she needed to go home and wrap her sore knees.

"Fine. But if you want my two cents, I would not let that man go." She shoved the strap for her black leather satchel onto her shoulder and checked her phone. "Besides being one of the city's most eligible bachelors, he seems to only date people he really cares about, you know? You won't see his name in the gossip rags, that's for sure." The woman headed for the door, shoving her phone into the back pocket of black jeans under a quilted blue parka. "And there was an older woman looking for you backstage earlier. With an accent. Oleska? Olinka?"

"Olena?" Sofia stilled. Olena Melnyk was one of her father's oldest friends from Ukraine. They'd visited with her briefly in Kiev after one of Sofia's performances. What was she doing in New York?

Delaney snapped her fingers. "That's it. I told her you'd probably be in the main theater after this."

Grabbing her bag, Sofia left the dressing area to peer inside the main theater. She didn't feel guilty about going home for the day. She didn't have any rehearsals scheduled and she'd substituted her audition for a class to keep her limber. The audition had been as physically demanding as two classes—a fierce workout for certain.

"There you are." A voice sounded behind her, the thick Ukrainian accent familiar since it still colored her father's speech.

"Olena." Sofia turned to find the petite, round-cheeked woman pacing the halls outside the theater. "My father didn't mention you were coming to New York. How nice to see you."

Olena wore a red scarf around her head and tied under her chin, the bright silk covering hair that had faded from blond to gray, but still gleamed with good health in the bright overhead lights.

"I go to Des Moines to visit my son. But I stop in New York when I find out your father, he is angry with me." She gestured with her hands, agitated.

Sofia spoke very little Ukrainian, so she was grateful for Olena's English. Although, at the moment, she wondered if her father's childhood friend had chosen the right words. Why would her father be mad at her?

"I can't imagine why he would be." Sofia hadn't spoken to her father since the flight home from Kiev, letting Quinn intervene on her behalf because she'd been so upset with him. She'd been ignoring his calls for days. "He was so glad to see you the night after my performance—"

"He is furious I did not choose Ukrainian husband for you. That I allow New York rich man to meet your plane." Her round cheeks deflated with her frown. "I am so sorry, my girl."

"*You're* the matchmaker he hired?" Sofia leaned into the back of a nearby theater seat, revising her perspective on her father's underhanded scheme.

Something about "hiring" his good friend from the old country—a woman who had helped him with his history homework in grade school—seemed far more forgivable than if he'd contracted an expensive global dating agency.

While still underhanded of him, at least there was something personal about the approach.

"Yes." She gave an emphatic nod. "He told me, 'Olena, find our girl a good man.' But afterward, Vitaly very angry I did not choose man from old neighborhood."

"He never told me that he wanted to hire a matchmaker." And the more she thought about that, the more she remembered how his pressure to get married had undermined her. As did his insistence she take his money. Had her father been holding her back from becoming self-confident all this time? Yet a voice inside her persisted; something had changed to give her a newfound strength and belief in herself. "And then, my photo and contact information ended up on a web site for men seeking wives—"

"I did this." Olena patted her chest to make it clear. "Come, we walk and talk. I explain where walls do not have ears." She glared at a young ballerina who had come out into the hallway, probably just trying to find a place to smoke.

The girl skittered back into the theater while Sofia tried to process what the woman was saying.

"You posted my photo on a site for men seeking a quick marriage?" Sofia asked as they walked out into the chill of a New York winter, a crust of snow covering most of Lincoln Center.

"My nephew helped. But I am very clear." Olena pounded one fist against the palm of her hand, her heavy silver rings glinting in the sun. "I say, my girl only date men ready to marry."

Sofia closed her eyes briefly, letting that news wash over her. Her father had asked an old friend to find her a Ukrainian husband. Instead, Olena had gone online to advertise her. No wonder Cameron had only gotten half of Sofia's details. The older woman was hardly a professional matchmaker. Just a well-liked woman from her father's hometown.

"So you told someone about my plane landing in New York?" Sofia wasn't ready to fight her way through the crowds on the subway yet. Maybe she'd walk for a while to let the fresh air clear her head and sooth the ache in her heart.

"First, I check the name of the man who asks about my Sofia. Very rich. Very handsome. I give details of flight." She shrugged her shoulders. "But you are not happy?"

Halting on the sprawling mezzanine outside Lincoln Center, Sofia let the snow fall on her as she watched the lunchtime traffic fill the streets. She wasn't about to delve into a long explanation of why she hadn't want her father in charge of her dating life. But she didn't mind sharing why she wasn't happy.

"I am only unhappy that my father thinks he can control my life. That he could manipulate me into marrying a wealthy man who moves in the same kind of circles as him." Her hands fisted inside the bright yellow mittens that a fan had knitted her long ago—a young ballet student who hadn't been invited into the company after graduation. The girl had moved back to Nebraska, but had given the mittens to Sofia as a thank you for inspiring her.

Oddly, looking down at them now made her realize that was a little bit of magic in her career. She'd told Quinn there wasn't any—only hard work. But that wasn't entirely true. Touching someone else's life, making a difference—that was beauty and magic combined. An insight she wondered if she would have realized without Quinn.

"It is not the point to be rich." Olena gripped her shoulders with her weathered hands. "It is the point to be a good man. And this McNeill, he is smart and successful. His smile is kind."

"So the fact that he is wealthy was incidental?" She shouldn't be hung up on it. The fact that she protested it only proved Quinn's point that she was too focused on the bottom line and didn't see him for himself.

Had she made a horrible mistake in sending Quinn away?

"Rich man focus on you instead of struggle to make life for himself. But there are good men everywhere." Olena spread her arms wide to point to the whole city. "You look beyond this small corner where dance is all you do. Find different men who give you new look at world, yes?"

"Yes." Sofia agreed, although in her heart she knew that search wouldn't be happening for a long time.

"Good. Then I have done my job." Olena patted her cheek. "I will not help anymore, as you ask. Tell Vitaly that we spoke, yes? He will forgive me then, I think." The older woman pulled her in for a hug and a kiss on each cheek. Exchanging goodbyes, she turned on her furry boots and stalked toward the subway station through the crusty snow.

Totally spent on every level, Sofia turned toward downtown to start the walk home. She might give in and get the bus in a dozen blocks or so, but right now she needed the fresh air. Striding across the mezzanine, she neared the crosswalk when a black Escalade rolled to a stop at the curb. She wasn't sure why her eye went to it.

But when Quinn McNeill stepped out of the back door of the chauffeured vehicle, she felt his presence like an electric shock.

"Sofia." He beckoned her through a veil of snow-flakes. "Can I give you a ride home?"

Her pulse sped, her mouth going dry at the sight of him. How had he gotten more handsome since the night before?

"No. Thank you." She could hardly resist him from ten yards away. She would have no chance of denying him anything if she sat beside him in the warm comfort of that luxury SUV. Especially after Olena's pep talk about finding someone who made her see beyond the confines of her narrow world.

She questioned her feelings for Quinn, what she'd learned from him, but, damn it, this was still so new.

But her refusal didn't make Quinn jump back in his ride and leave. He exchanged a word with the driver before dismissing the vehicle. Then he strode toward her, his long, denim-clad legs covering the space quickly.

Even before he reached her, she knew she was toast. She'd stood up for herself to Idris Fortier. Held her ground with Delaney the nosy reporter. Danced the best piece of her life.

She didn't have the reserves for the temptation that Quinn McNeill presented.

He paused a few inches away from her.

"We need to talk."

Thirteen

Quinn had had his driver circle Lincoln Center for the last hour so he wouldn't miss Sofia after her audition. Jeff had promised to keep an eye on the exits so Quinn could work, but he couldn't have concentrated on anything else anyway.

Thoughts of the woman now standing in front of him had consumed him ever since he'd walked out of her apartment the night before. He'd felt that she'd needed him to leave, so he had. And he'd been offended that she'd reduced their relationship to economic differences that didn't matter. But, apparently, they mattered to her. Today, he realized that if he was serious about her, he needed to take her concerns seriously, too. That meant he was going to do a better job listening and paying attention, not just lining up his questions while already thinking ahead to his next move.

He had a few ideas for how to show her he was committed to her and not some temporary marriage to fulfill the terms of a will. But that's all they were—vague ideas. And he hated not having a solid game plan to win her back. In a short space of time she had become his most important priority and he was shooting from the hip with her.

She defied business logic.

She was art.

She was magic.

And, by God, he wanted her to be his.

"I was going to take a walk," she told him, looking so damn beautiful in her dark bomber jacket with a shearling collar pulled up to her heart-shaped face. Her hair looked like it had been in a ballet bun at one point, the ends all wavy and still a little damp. Tall boots covered most of her leggings, so she looked warmer than the last time they'd taken a walk together. Her bright yellow mittens reminded him of the sunny teacups she'd used the night before when she'd made him tea. But she was full of those contrasts—the worldly sophistication next to her more bohemian tendencies made her who she was.

A very special woman able to stand on her own feet.

Or tiptoes.

"I'll go wherever you like," he assured her. "But if we walk through the park again, we might have more privacy."

Also, he hoped traveling that route held happy memories for her, too. He needed every advantage at his disposal to ensure she didn't turn her back on him forever.

"That's fine." She nodded, heading toward Central Park the way they had after the meeting at Joe Coffee the week before.

"How was the audition?" he asked, knowing how much it meant to her. He reached for her bag, but she didn't give it to him to carry and he didn't press her.

"I nailed it," she said flatly, snowflakes swirling around them. "He offered me the role."

"That's incredible, Sofia. Congratulations. But I would have thought you'd be more excited." Maybe she was as tired as him.

Had she spent half the night thinking about the way they'd parted, too? He wished she would have agreed to join him in the Escalade where he could have spent his time watching her expression and gauging what she was feeling instead of looking out for traffic.

"It was clear to me that he expects to have an intimate relationship with his feature lead." She shoved her yellow-mittened hands into her coat pockets. "I made it clear to him I would be thrilled to work with him if our relationship is strictly professional. But honestly? I didn't like him, and I'm not sure I'd work with him even under the best of circumstances."

Anger surged through Quinn and he vowed right then and there he would make that man pay. Somehow. Some way.

But for now, he needed to focus on Sofia.

"Bastard." He wanted to pound the crap out of the guy. "Who the hell does he think he is?"

"A man who hasn't heard 'no' very often." She walked fast, giving away how angry the incident had made her. "An entitled, self-centered man who has let his reviews go to his head."

"I'm so sorry you had to deal with that. For what it's worth, it sounds like you handled it well."

"That reporter, Delaney, was lurking behind stage and overheard what happened." They crossed Central Park West and headed south to find entry onto a walking path. "At least if Fortier tries to discredit me or lie about what happened, I have a witness."

Hell. That hadn't even occurred to him. Sofia really could take care of herself and he respected the hell out of her for that.

"Would she tell the truth?" Quinn didn't know what to expect of the journalist who had seemed happy to sell anyone out for a story.

"To my surprise, I think she would." Sofia turned into the park ahead of him, still walking fast, as though demons followed close on her heels.

"Sofia." He took her arm gently, needing to get a better handle on what was happening here. "Please slow down. Should we go back there now and confront him? I'd be glad to—"

"No." She shifted her weight from one foot to the other, as if she had too much energy and didn't know where to put it all. "Definitely not. I'll call the ballet mistress tonight and tell her what happened. But I wasn't nervous. I was cool and professional. I danced the best I ever have. So, on some level, it was a good day because I drew on new strengths I didn't know I had." She stood still again, her wide blue eyes landing on his and seeming to really see him for the first time. "I'm only getting nervous again now because...you're here. And you said we needed to talk?"

Right. He'd asked for this audience, not realizing she'd just had one of the hardest days of her life. He tried reaching for her bag again.

"Please. Let me carry this for you."

She bit her full bottom lip for a moment, then passed him the bag. He felt like some medieval knight who'd just gotten his lady's favor tied to his sword.

They kept walking east, roughly following the same path as last time without ever discussing it.

"First, my IT connection put me in touch with the web site that posted—"

"I saw Olena, the matchmaker my father hired. She is just his old friend, by the way, and not a professional. That's probably why my father didn't tell you anything about her when the two of you spoke. I'm sure he didn't want to throw a friend under the bus. But she was the one who gave Cameron my contact details." She waved away the incident like it was no longer a concern. "She didn't understand the kind of site where she posted my photo. She meant well, but she knows I'm taking over my dating life. I will be choosing all future dating prospects."

The words punched a hole through his chest. He felt the sting of cold winter air right in the center of it as they walked down the slope near Tavern on the Green. This time, there was no talk of beauty surrounding them. No mischievous attempts to taste beauty on her tongue.

"About that." He willed all his persuasive powers to the fore. "I didn't sleep last night, thinking about what you said."

"That makes two of us." She wrapped her arms around herself.

He hadn't expected that hint of vulnerability from her after the way she'd ended things the night before.

"Sofia, I didn't mean to mislead you," he said, his boots crunching the frozen patches of snow. He'd dressed casually in boots and jeans today, taking the day off from work to focus on her. He'd take all damn month off if he needed to. "I understand how it might seem that way, but everything between us happened so fast. We went from planning how to stop a media storm to figuring out our dating history, and then getting to know each other for real in those phone calls—which I very much enjoyed—to trying to figure out where the matchmaking leak came from."

"I was focused on recovering from jet lag and impressing a lecherous ass." Her voice wound around him with a comfortable intimacy that he wished could last a lifetime.

She was that damn special to him.

"But we never lacked for conversation, did we?" he prodded, trying to justify his actions. "I didn't mention my grandfather's will at first because I didn't plan on following through. I planned to put his feet to the fire about the thing when he got back from China. Make him see reason. Marriage is too important to use as some bargaining chip in a business transaction."

Sofia glanced at him, giving him an assessing look through her lashes.

"If you really believe that—"

"I swear it. I sat up all night thinking about how I could convince you of it. I woke up my attorney and had her write up contracts to show you where I would renounce all rights to McNeill Resorts so you'd believe me." He opened his coat to show her a sheaf of crumpled papers. "I signed them, then discarded them an hour later, remembering how dismissive you sounded about using contracts in a personal relationship."

She nibbled a snowflake off her bottom lip. "Was I?"

"You suggested we should be able to arrange for dates without the help of a legally binding agreement." He withdrew the crumpled papers and handed them to her. "I'm only showing them to you now to illustrate how hard I tried to figure out how to convince you."

Heading east onto quieter pathways, they passed a horse-drawn carriage full of tourists snapping photos, but other than that there wasn't much traffic here.

"Convince me of what, exactly?" Sofia stopped near a field full of halfhearted snowmen, a few of which wore empty coffee cups for hats.

"I hadn't thought through what it meant to bring up marriage last night since I was wrecked after hearing about Gramps' condition." He reached for her free hand, pulling it from her pocket so he could hold it in both of his. "You haven't known me for long, so you couldn't know how unusual it is for me to talk without having any kind of agenda. But that is what has been so great about you. I got comfortable thinking we could talk about anything. But I had no business putting you in that kind of position."

"So you never meant to propose." She seemed to be tracking the conversation carefully, making him realize she was very much paying attention now.

Because she cared? Because she shared some of his feelings?

Fresh hope filled some of that hole in his chest and he took his time to get the words right for her.

"My brain was telling me to find any way possible to keep a ring on your finger so that that we could keep exploring whatever is happening between us. I sure didn't want to break off our fake engagement right when I realized I'm falling in love with you."

Sofia held a contract in her hand—signed by one of the country's wealthiest men—that stated in no uncertain terms he would relinquish all rights to his grandfather's legacy.

For her, he'd done that incredibly foolish thing.

That had floored her on a day when she thought she couldn't be any more surprised by life.

But then he told her he was falling for her and it was like what her mother had told her about beauty—you didn't see it. You experienced it all around you. She stood inside one of those beautiful moments right now with a man so important to her she could no longer imagine life without him.

"I know it sounds crazy," he started.

She tucked the contract into his pocket and squeezed his hands tightly through her beautiful yellow mittens that made her happy.

The mittens that made her think she had inherited some of her mother's joyous outlook on life.

"It doesn't sound crazy. I was there, remember?" She echoed his words from the night before when she'd told him the sex was so good the first time she'd thought she dreamed it.

"I remember." His voice deepened as he stepped closer.

"I was falling in love, too," she admitted, her voice hoarse in a throat clogged with emotions.

"Was?" He stood toe-to-toe with her now. She had to look up at him.

"Am." She breathed the word between their lips as they stood together in the snowfall. "I am falling in love with you, Quinn. And I do see you for the man you are."

He kissed her, answering all her questions and easing all her doubts. Her heart swelled with new joy that crowded out everything else, making her wonder how she could have ever believed there was any other place for her in the world than at his side.

His arms wrapped around her, sheltering her. She breathed him in, his scent and touch already so familiar to her.

"I don't want to lose you, Sofia," he said between kisses. "Whatever it takes to convince you, to keep you, I will do it." He sealed his mouth to hers and only broke the kiss when an older lady rode past them on a bicycle, ringing her bell at them and giving them a thumbs-up.

Sofia laughed, feeling a ghost of her mother's happy spirit in that sweet, romantic gesture.

"You're not going to lose me." Her whole world felt new and full of possibilities, their lives as mingled as their puffy breaths merging in the cold air.

"Then it's the happiest day of my life so far. How should we celebrate?" he asked, tucking her under his arm to walk past the pond toward East Sixty-First where the Pierre waited.

His home.

"First, we're going to burn that contract." She patted the pocket where she'd shoved the papers. "Because I want you to support your grandfather's business and fulfill his legacy with your brothers."

"That's generous of you, but it sounds too tame for a celebration." Quinn dropped a kiss on top of her hair.

"Then we're going to make love all day," she whispered in his ear as they walked.

"I can't wait for that." The husky note in his voice assured her how much he meant it.

"Then we're going to come up with a plan to help me find a way to have a career after dance that doesn't involve Idris the Idiot."

"I hope it involves me punching him into next year." Quinn's jaw flexed.

"Probably not, but we'll leave it open for negotiation." Sofia let him lead her into the beautiful building where he lived, wondering if she'd ever get used to this kind of opulence.

"Can I make a suggestion?" Quinn asked, hitting the button for his private elevator.

"Of course." She bet he had a hot tub in that extravagant place of his. Her knees, at least, would get used to luxury in a hurry.

"I'd like to replace that monstrosity of a ring from my brother with something that looks more like you." He must have seen the surprise she felt because he rushed to explain. "Not that it's a proposal. We can take all the time you want to date. But as long as the world thinks we're engaged…"

"You weren't kidding about keeping a ring on my finger, were you?" She stepped into the elevator, grateful when the cabin doors shut behind them, sealing them in privacy.

"We don't have to comment on it, or issue any statements, or explain anything to anyone. We can just date and be mysterious about our plans." His blue eyes sparkled with a happiness she hadn't seen in them before. Also, a hint of sensual wickedness that she *had* seen before. And thoroughly enjoyed.

She had the feeling it was the same look in her eyes.

"Right. Because what we do is no one else's business. And we each have a partner we can trust." She felt dizzy from the rush of the elevator up to his floor. The rush of love for a man who knew her better than any other.

A man who had spent all night thinking about how to show her he loved her.

When the elevator door opened and let them out into his apartment, Sofia fell into his arms, dragging him toward the first bed she found.

"I'm going to make you happy, Sofia." He kissed the words into her neck while she walked backward, peeling off her coat.

She smiled against his shoulder as she pushed off his jacket, too.

"You already have."

* * * * *

THE MAGNATE'S
MARRIAGE MERGER

JOANNE ROCK

For Heather Kerzner,
who inspires everyone she knows.
I miss seeing you in person, my friend,
but I smile to think of all the people you meet
who benefit from having you in their lives.
Thank you for being a bright light!

One

"You found her?" Ensconced in his office at the McNeill Resorts headquarters in New York's Financial District, Ian McNeill glanced up from the file folder on his desk at the private investigator standing before him.

Ian had been back stateside for less than twenty-four hours when he'd gotten the message that the PI he'd hired two months ago had news for him. Ian's older brother, Quinn, had asked for his help to locate an anonymous Manhattan matchmaker who'd tried to pair their younger brother, Cameron, with a renowned ballerina. While that sounded harmless enough on the surface, the potential "bride" had had no knowledge she was supposed to meet Cameron, and it had caused a public scandal.

Bad enough in itself.

Except then the next day, the matchmaker responsible had closed up shop. Ian discovered within the week that the woman had been using a fake name and an assistant as a front to do most of her work. But despite a few leads, he hadn't had any luck finding the woman.

Until now.

"That's her." The investigator, Bentley, pointed to the closed file folder on Ian's desk. The guy was a former college roommate and someone he trusted. Bentley's specialty was digital forensics, but he took the occasional job outside the office if the case was interesting enough or, as in Ian's case, if the work was for a friend. With his clean-shaven face, wire-rimmed glasses and a faded pair of camo pants, Bentley looked more like a teenage gamer geek than a successful entrepreneur. "It's no wonder she used an alias for her matchmaking business. She's certainly well-known in Manhattan by her real name."

Ian slid the file closer, tapping a finger on the cover.

"The New York tabloids sold plenty of papers trying to guess her identity last winter after she paired up one of the Brooklyn Nets with that fashion blogger," Bentley explained. The mystery matchmaker had been responsible for a string of high-profile matches between celebrity clients and wealthy movers and shakers, and her success under an assumed name had the New York social scene all trying to guess who she was.

Curious, Ian leaned back in the cherry-red leather executive chair, manila folder in hand. The late-morning sun slanted in through the huge windows with a view of the river. Taking a deep breath, he flipped open the file to the papers inside.

Only to see an eight-by-ten glossy photo of his ex-lover's face on the top page.

Lydia Whitney smiled back at him with that Mona Lisa grin he'd fallen hard for a year ago—before she'd disappeared from his life after a huge argument.

Ian's blood chilled.

He sat up straight and waved the photo at his friend.

"What kind of sick joke is this?" He hadn't told Bentley about his brief affair with Lydia, but the guy specialized in unearthing digital trails. He must have stumbled across some link between them in his investigation.

"What do you mean?" Bentley frowned. Shifting positions, he leaned forward to peer at the folder as if to double-check what Ian was looking at. He shoved the wire-rimmed glasses up into his shaggy dark hair. "That's her. Lydia Whitney. She's the illegitimate daughter of that billionaire art collector and the sexpot nurse he hired before he died. Lydia's mother sued the family for years for part of the inheritance."

Tension kinked Ian's shoulders. A tic started below his right eye.

"I know who she is." *Damn. It.* Just looking at the picture of Lydia—the Cupid's bow mouth, the dimples, the pin-straight dark hair that shone like a silk sheet flowing over one shoulder—brought the past roaring back to life. The best weeks of his entire life had been spent with those jade-green eyes staring back into his. "I'm asking why the hell there's a photo of her here."

"Ian." Bentley straightened. When his glasses shifted

on his head, he raked them off and jammed them in the front pocket of his olive-green work shirt. "You asked me to find the matchmaker who used the name of Mallory West. The woman who hid behind an alias when she worked for Mates, Manhattan's elite dating service. That's her."

The news sank into Ian's brain slowly. Or maybe it was Bentley's expression that made him take a second look at the file in his lap. His former college roommate was a literal guy, and he wasn't prone to pulling pranks. And he appeared serious about this.

Gaze falling back on Lydia's flawless skin, Ian flipped past the photo to see what else the file contained. The first sheet was a timeline of the events of last February when "Mallory West" had paired Cameron McNeill with ballerina Sofia Koslov. There were notes about Mallory's assistant, Kinley, who'd admitted that Mallory was an alias but refused to identify her boss. Then there were pages of notes about Kinley's whereabouts, including photos of Kinley meeting with Lydia at various places on the Upper East Side—where Ian knew Lydia lived.

"Lydia Whitney is the mystery matchmaker?" As he said the words aloud, they made a kind of poetic sense.

Lydia had ended the most passionate affair of his life when she'd discovered Ian's photo and profile were on a dating website while they were seeing each other. He'd understood her anger, but mistakenly assumed she would listen to his very reasonable explanation. He had not posted the profile or created the account. He'd given cursory permission to his grandfather's personal aide to do so after a heated argument with the old man, but had heard no more about it after that day.

Grandpa Malcolm McNeill was so determined his grandsons should marry that he'd since written the condition into his will. None of his grandsons would inherit their one-third share of the global corporation he'd built until they'd been married for at least twelve months. That stipulation had come last winter, prompting Cameron to find a bride with a matchmaker, leading to the fiasco with Sofia Koslov. But the pressure to wed had started long before that. And it had resulted in Ian's offhanded agreement to allow his profile to be listed on a dating website.

But Lydia didn't care about his explanation. She'd been furious and had cut off all contact, accusing him of betrayal. What if she'd gone into the matchmaking business—at the very same agency his grandfather had used—to spite Ian? In the months after that, Ian had indeed received some odd suggestions for dates that he'd ignored. Could Lydia have been behind those, too? Anger rolled hot through his veins. Along with it, another kind of heat flared, as well.

"I was surprised, too," Bentley observed, moving closer to the window overlooking the river and Battery Park. "I thought Mallory West would be someone with more Park Avenue pedigree. An older, well-accepted socialite with more connections among her clientele." The investigator rested a shoulder on the window frame near Ian's bookcase full of travel guides.

It didn't matter that he could get maps of every country on his phone when he traveled for work. Ian liked seeing the big picture of a foldout map, orienting himself on the plane ride to wherever it was he headed to oversee renovations or development work on resorts all over the globe.

"She used to work as an interior designer," Ian observed lightly, tossing aside the file before he gave any more away about the relationship he hadn't shared with anyone. "Do you know if she still does?"

He needed to think through his response to this problem. He had planned to hand over Mallory West's real identity to Vitaly Koslov—the ballerina's father—who had every intention of suing the matchmaker for dragging his daughter through unsavory headlines last winter. But now that Lydia was the mystery matchmaker? Ian needed to investigate this more himself.

"Yes. Throughout the year she worked as a matchmaker, she continued to take jobs decorating. Since she walked away from the dating service, she is back to working more hours at the design business, but she still volunteers a lot of her time with the single mothers' network I mentioned in the notes."

"Single mothers?" Frowning, Ian opened the file again and riffled through it.

"Moms' Connection. She gives a lot of money to the diaper and food banks." Straightening, Bentley backed up a step. "Anyway, mystery solved, and I've got an appointment in midtown I can't miss. Are we good here?"

"Sure. I'll have my assistant send the payment." Setting aside the file, Ian shoved to his feet and extended a hand to his friend. "I appreciate the time you put into this."

Bentley bumped his fist. "Not a problem. I'd forgo the payment if you could get me a meeting with your brother Cameron."

"Cam?" Ian frowned, thinking his friend must have confused his brothers. "Quinn's the hedge fund manager. Were you thinking of doing some investing?"

"No. It's Cameron I'd like to meet with. Word is, he's working on a new video game and I've got some ideas to speed graphics. I'd prefer to work with an independent—"

"Done." Ian wasn't ready to dive into a discussion full of technojargon, but he knew his younger brother would speak Bentley's language. Cameron was the family tech guy since he owned a video game business in addition to his role in McNeill Resorts. "I'll put him in touch with you."

Seeing his friend out the door, Ian returned to the photo of Lydia Whitney he'd left on the window ledge. He felt the kick-to-the-chest sensation all over again. He needed to see her in person to get to the bottom of this. He'd thought they were finished forever when she broke things off last spring. But clearly, there was unfinished business between them.

Pivoting on the heel of one Italian leather loafer, Ian pressed the intercom button on his phone to page his assistant. In seconds, Mrs. Trager appeared in his doorway, tablet in hand.

"Yes, Mr. McNeill?" The older woman was efficient and deferential in a public setting, but she'd been with him long enough that she didn't pull punches when they worked together privately.

"I need to find a consulting gig, and I'm willing to take a pay cut to secure the right one. It doesn't matter where it is in the world, as long as you can get me onto a project where Lydia Whitney is providing the design services."

Despite the highly unusual request, Mrs. Trager didn't even blink as she tapped buttons on the digital tablet. "I just read in an architectural trade that Ms. Whitney recently committed to Singer Associates for a hotel renovation on South Beach."

"Good." He knew Jeremy Singer well. The guy only bought highly specialized properties that he liked to turn into foodie havens. "I'll call Jeremy myself. Once I speak to him, I'll let you know how soon I'll need a flight."

"Very good." His assistant tucked the tablet under one arm. "I forwarded you an article about the property."

"Thank you." Settling back into the chair behind his oversize desk while Mrs. Trager closed the door behind her, Ian had a plan already taking shape.

He had met Lydia on a shared job site a little over a year ago. Working closely together to develop a unique property had meant they spent long hours in each other's company. Once Lydia realized who she'd be working with, she might very well try to detach herself from the Singer project, but she was too much of a professional to simply walk off a job site.

Which gave Ian at least a few days to figure out what in the hell was going on with Lydia Whitney.

She'd taken some anonymous revenge against him,

it seemed, and he had every intention of calling her on it. But first things first, he needed to slip back into her world in a way that wouldn't send her running. Once he had her in his sights, he would figure out how to exact a payback of his own.

He'd never considered himself the kind of man who could blackmail a woman into his bed. But with the surge of anger still fresh in his veins at this betrayal Ian planned to keep all his options open.

Tilting her head back, Lydia Whitney savored the Miami sun. The weather was still beautiful at eight o'clock in the morning before the real heat and humidity set in. Seated at her outdoor table at the News Café on Ocean Drive, she had a breeze off the water and a perfect cup of coffee to start her day before her first meeting for the new interior design job on South Beach.

The swish of the ocean waves rolling onto the shore, along with the rustle of palm fronds, was a persistent white noise. Foot traffic on both sides of Ocean Drive was brisk even though June was a quieter time for the tourist area. The tables near her were both empty, so she felt no need to rush through her coffee or her splurge breakfast of almond brioche French toast. No one was waiting for her table. She could linger over her newspaper, catching up on the Manhattan social scene.

Perhaps, if she was a more dedicated interior designer, she'd be studying the other recent hotel renovations on South Beach so she could ensure she approached her new job with a singular, distinctive style. But she didn't work like that, preferring to let her muse make up her own mind once she saw the plans and the proposed space.

Instead, Lydia read the social pages with the same avid interest that other women devoted to watching the *Real Housewives* series. She soaked in all the names and places, checking to see who was newly single or newly engaged. It was all highly relevant because, in her secret second job, Lydia still did some moonlighting as a matchmaker to Manhattan's most eligible bachelors and bachelorettes. It was a job she couldn't seem to give up, no matter that she'd had to leave the high-end dating service that had allowed her to work under the alias of "Mallory West."

There'd been a bit of a scandal last winter, forcing Lydia to leave town and take a brief hiatus from matchmaking. Her life had been too full of scandals to allow for another, so she'd buried herself in design work for the next few months, ignoring the tabloid speculation about the true identity of Mallory West. But she'd missed the high drama and the lucrative second income of the matchmaking work, especially since she donated 100 percent of those profits to a charity dear to her heart.

"More coffee, miss?" A slim blonde waitress in a black tee and cargo shorts paused by her table, juggling an armful of menus and a coffeepot.

"No, thank you." Lydia switched off the screen on her tablet by habit, accustomed to protecting her privacy at all times. "I'm almost finished anytime you want to bring the check." She should be early for her first meeting, even if she hadn't done a lot of design homework to prep for it.

Singer Associates, the firm that had hired her to overhaul the interior of the landmark Foxfire Hotel, had been good to her over the years. The firm had hired her for the job where she'd met Ian McNeill, she recalled. Perhaps that had been the only time where a Singer Associates job had a snag attached, since her disastrous affair with Ian had broken her heart in more ways than one.

But that certainly hadn't been Jeremy Singer's fault.

Stuffing in one last bite of the almond brioche French toast, Lydia promised herself to arrive earlier for breakfast tomorrow so she could people watch on Ocean Drive. Most of her potential matchmaking clientele fled to the Hamptons or Europe this time of year, not Miami. But there were always interesting international travelers in South Beach, no matter the season. Not to mention the fresh-faced models who were a dime a dozen on this stretch of beach. And wealthy men were always interested in models and actresses. It couldn't hurt to keep her ears and eyes open for prospects as long as she was in town.

Retrieving her leather tote from the chair beside her, Lydia paid her bill and dialed her assistant back in New York as she walked south on Ocean Drive toward the Foxfire Hotel.

Traffic crawled by as tourists snapped photos of the historic art deco buildings in the area. The cotton candy colors of the stucco walls wouldn't work as well anywhere but at the beach. Here, the pinks and yellows blended with the colorful sunrises and sunsets, while the strong, geometric lines balanced the soft colors. The Foxfire Hotel had lost some of its early grandeur in misguided attempts to update the property, with subsequent owners covering up the decorative spandrels and fluting around doors and windows. Her contract with Singer Associates—the new owner—had assured her those details would be recovered and honored wherever possible.

"Good morning, Lydia." Her assistant, Kinley, answered the call with her usual morning enthusiasm. The younger woman was at her desk shortly after dawn, a feat made easier by the fact that she sublet rooms in Lydia's Manhattan apartment for a nominal fee. "Did you need anything for your morning meeting?"

"No. I'm all set, thanks. But it occurred to me that I could collect some contacts while I'm down here for our second business." Pausing outside the Foxfire, she knew Kinley would understand her meaning and her desire to be discreet. "I wondered if you could see who we know is in South Beach this month and maybe wrangle some fun party invites for me?"

"Are we ready to dive back into the dating world?" Kinley asked. In the background, Lydia heard her turn down the brain-tuning music that her assistant used while she was working.

"I think we've lain low for long enough." Lydia had quit working with the bigger dating agency when Kinley had paired a prominent client with a ballerina who was unaware she'd landed on a list of potential brides. The snafu hadn't been Kinley's fault; it was caused by the ballerina's matchmaker, who'd listed her client in the wrong database. The incident had made the New York social pages, implicating "Mallory West" as potentially responsible. Instead of drawing attention to herself and her business, Lydia had simply withdrawn from the matchmaking world, mostly because the prominent client had actually been Ian McNeill's younger brother, Cameron. Lydia hadn't wanted to draw the attention of her former lover just when she'd finally been starting to heal from their breakup.

And from the loss of the pregnancy she'd never told him about. The punch to her gut still happened when she thought about it. But the ache had dulled to a more manageably sized hurt.

"Music to my ears." Kinley's grin was obvious in her tone of voice. "I've been keeping our files up-to-date for just this moment so we'd be ready to go when you gave the okay."

"Excellent. Look for some South Beach parties then." She checked her watch. "I'll touch base with you after the meeting."

"Got it. Good luck." Kinley disconnected the call.

Lydia entered the building, her eyes struggling to adjust to the sudden darkness. The hotel had been closed since the property had changed hands, and was a construction site. Lights were on in the lobby, but some remodeling efforts were already underway with the space torn down to the studs.

"Right this way, ma'am." An older man dressed in crisp blue jeans and wearing a yellow construction hat gestured her toward the back of the lobby where plywood had been laid over the sawdust on the floor. "You must be here for the new owner's meeting." At her nod, he extended a hand. "I'm Rick, the foreman."

She quickened her step, approaching to shake his hand and blinking at the bright white light dangling from an orange electric cord thrown over a nearby exposed rafter.

"Nice to meet you." She'd learned early in her career to make friends with the site supervisor wherever possible since that person usually had a better handle on the job than whatever upper level manager was put on the project.

"We've got you set up at a table in the courtyard." He gestured to two glass doors in the back leading to a broad space of smooth pavers and manicured landscaping open to natural sunlight. "Just through there."

"Great." She straightened the strap on her leather tote and smoothed a hand over her turquoise sheath dress. She wished she'd found a restroom before she left the News Café so she could have touched up her lipstick and checked her hair; she hadn't expected the conditions at the Foxfire to still be so rough. "It's a beautiful day to enjoy the outdoors."

"For another hour, maybe." Rick chuckled to himself. "You New Yorkers all like the heat until you're here for a few days in the summer."

Yes, well. There might be a smidge of truth to that. She'd probably be melting this afternoon. Thanking him, Lydia pushed through the glass door on the right, her eye already picking out a wicker chair off to one side of a large wrought iron table. She was glad to be early so she could pull over the wicker seat and save herself from sitting on wrought iron for however long this meeting lasted.

A small water feature burbled quietly in the open-air courtyard, sending up a soft spray of mist as it tumbled over smooth rocks and landed in a scenic pool surrounded by exotic plantings. Dwarf palms mingled with a few taller species that attracted a pair of squawking green parrots. High up, at the top of the building, a retractable canopy over part of the space dimmed the sun a bit without blocking it completely.

"Lydia." She turned her head sharply to one side to find the source of the familiar baritone.

She hadn't heard that voice in over a year. It couldn't be…

"Ian?" She felt that breathless punch to her gut again, harder than it had been this morning when she'd thought of her lost pregnancy.

Ian McNeill stood in the far corner of the room beside a Mexican-style tea cart laden with silver ice buckets and cold, bottled drinks, his strong arms crossed over his chest. His slightly bronzed skin that hinted at his Brazilian mother's heritage made his blue eyes all the more striking. His dark hair was short at the sides and longer on top, still damp from a morning shower. He was impeccably groomed in his crisp dark suit, gray shirt and blue tie.

Ian McNeill. The lover who'd broken her heart. The man who'd kept his profile on a matchmaker's site while he dated her, prompting her to go into the matchmaking business just so she could try her hand at sending horrible dating prospects his way. She'd outgrown the foolish need for vengeance after she'd lost their baby. So it had been an accident when she'd paired Ian's brother with that famous ballerina.

How much did Ian know about any of that?

"Nice to see you, Lydia," he said smoothly, approaching her with the languid grace of a lifelong athlete. "A real pleasure to be working with you again."

His eyes held hers captive for a long moment while she debated what he meant by "pleasure." The word choice hadn't been an accident. Ian was the most methodical man she'd ever met.

"I didn't know—" She faltered, trying to make sense of how she could have taken a job where Ian McNeill played any role. "That is, Jeremy Singer never told me—"

"He and I agreed to exchange peer review services on a couple of random properties—a recent idea we had to keep our project managers on their toes and revitalize the work environment." Ian brought a bottled water to the table and set it down before tugging over the wicker chair for her. "I was pleased to hear you were in line for this job, especially since you and I work so well together."

He held the chair for her. Waiting.

Her heart thrummed a crazy beat in her chest. She could not take a job where she'd be working under Ian. *Oh, God.*

She couldn't even think about being *under Ian* without heat clawing its way up her face.

And, of course, those blue eyes of his didn't miss

her blush. He seemed to track its progress avidly as the heat flooded up her neck and spilled onto her cheeks, pounding with a heartbeat all its own.

When the barest hint of a smile curved his full, sculpted lips, Lydia knew he wasn't here by accident. It had all been by design. She wasn't sure how she knew. But something in Ian's expression assured her it was true.

She opened her mouth to argue. To tell him they wouldn't be working together under any conditions. But just then the glass doors opened again and the job engineer strode into the room with Rick, the foreman she'd met briefly. Behind them, two other women she didn't know appeared deep in conversation about the history of the Foxfire, comparing notes about the size of the original starburst sign that hung on the front facade.

Lydia's gaze flicked to Ian, but the opportunity to tell him what she thought about his maneuvering was lost. She'd have to get through this meeting and speak to Jeremy Singer herself since she couldn't afford to walk off a job.

But there was no way she could work with the man who'd betrayed her.

Even if he affected her now as much as ever.

TWO

Doing his damnedest not to be distracted by the sight of Lydia's long legs as she sat on the opposite side of the room, Ian paid close attention in the Foxfire meeting, appreciating the favor Jeremy Singer had done by letting Ian step in at the last minute. Having worked with the resort developer on a handful of other projects over the years, Ian understood the man's style and expectations, so he would offer whatever insights he could on the job site. Since launching his own resort development company on a smaller, more exacting scale than his grandfather's global McNeill Resorts Corporation, Ian wasn't normally in the business of overseeing other people's buildings when he was in a position to design his own. Yet he did enjoy having a hand in specialty public spaces like the foodie-centered resort Singer planned for the revamped Foxfire.

One of the drawbacks of running his own business was less day-to-day focus on his clients' concerns, building restrictions and the inevitable permit nightmares. Being on-site now and again gave him renewed awareness of the obstacles in his work. So this brief stint at one of Jeremy Singer's buildings was no hardship.

And the payoff promised to be far greater than the sacrifice of his time.

Ian's gaze slid to Lydia's profile as the meeting broke up. She remained in her seat on the opposite side of the room, speaking to a woman in charge of indoor air quality on the job site. The room was full of people who would only play a limited role in the renovation, but Ian had wanted to attend the meeting and get up to speed as quickly as possible. The enclosed courtyard was crowded, too, ensuring Lydia couldn't walk out the door before he caught up with her.

Her turquoise dress skimmed her slight curves and was accented by a belt with a thin tortoiseshell buckle emphasizing a trim waist. The hem ended just above her knee, showcasing her legs in high-heeled gold sandals. Her straight dark hair slid over one arm as she turned, still in conversation with the other woman, her dimple flashing once as they continued their animated talk. Clearly, the two of them knew each other, but then again, they moved in a small world of elite professionals.

Would Lydia try to leave without speaking to him privately? He didn't think so. She was not a woman to mince words. And while he'd caught her off guard—clearly—by showing up here without her knowledge, she'd had two hours during the meeting to consider her course of action. She would confront him directly.

The idea tantalized far more than it should have. She'd walked away from him. Worse, she'd meddled in his affairs without his knowledge. Even that, he might have forgiven. But how could she extend her vengeance to his family? She'd matched his brother Cameron to an oblivious stranger. The meeting—and Cameron's impulsive proposal in the middle of a private airport—had been caught on film by a dance magazine that was doing a special on the ballerina and would-be bride. The episode put their older brother, Quinn, in the awkward position of trying to smooth things over in the media to placate the woman's furious and embarrassed father.

Lydia had been responsible for all of that, and Ian wasn't about to forget it. Even if things had worked out in the end when Quinn fell hard for the ballerina himself. The two were now engaged. Happy.

Ian exchanged pleasantries with the site manager as the rest of the group filed out through the glass doors and back into the main building, leaving him and Lydia alone in the interior courtyard. A water feature gurgled in the space as yet untouched by the remodel.

The babble of water over a short rock wall softened the impact of the sudden silence. Shoving to his feet, Ian stalked around the wrought iron table to where Lydia sat, gathering her things and tucking a silver pen into the sleeve inside her leather tote bag.

"I need to speak with you privately," she informed him, slinging the tote onto one shoulder as she met his gaze.

He'd forgotten how green her eyes were. He remembered staring into those jade depths while the two of them stood in a languid pool off the Pacific on a beach in Rangiroa, just north of Tahiti. He'd thought then that her eyes matched the color of the water—not really emerald green or aqua that day, but a brilliant green.

He'd thought a whole lot of foolish things then, though. A mistake he would not be repeating.

"I figured you might." He inclined his head. "My car is outside."

For the briefest moment, she nipped her lower lip. *Uncertain? Or unwilling?*

Or tempted? Ah...

"We might as well work while we talk," he explained. He didn't want her to think he planned to cart her off and ravish her at the first opportunity, the way he once would have after a tedious two-hour meeting. "Traffic should be reasonable at this hour. We can drive over to Singer's inspiration hotels and take a look around."

"Of course." She pivoted on her heel and preceded him toward the exit. "Thank you."

His eyes dipped to the gentle sway of her hips in the turquoise silk, the hint of thigh visible in the short slit at the back of her skirt. He didn't recognize the dress, but the thighs were a different story. He and Lydia had been crazy about each other, tearing one another's clothes off at the slightest opportunity. One time, they'd barely made it to an outdoor shower stall on their way up to his villa from the beach.

Now her hair had grown longer, reaching to the middle of her back. Last year, it had been cut in a razor-sharp line across the middle of her shoulder blades. Today, it draped lower, the ends trimmed in a V that seemed to point to the sweet curve of her lovely ass.

He reached around her to open the door for her, leading them into the Miami sun, grown considerably warmer over the last two hours. Once outside, he flicked open the top button on his shirt beneath his tie, knowing full well this noontime excursion wasn't going to be all about work and knowing with even more certainty that his rising temperature had more to do with the woman in step beside him than the sun above him.

"This way." He pointed toward the valet at the next hotel over, grateful the attendant behind the small stand noticed Ian and sent one of the younger workers into the parking garage with a set of keys.

No doubt his rented convertible BMW would be driven out soon enough. He ushered Lydia to one side of the street while they waited, his hand brushing the small of her back just long enough to feel the gentle glide of silk on his fingertips and the warmth of her body underneath.

The South Beach scenery—palm trees, exotic cars, brilliant blue water and beach bodies parading to and from the shore on the other side of the street—was nothing to him. Lydia had his undivided attention.

"You just happened to be in Miami?" She turned on him suddenly, the frustration that had been banked earlier finding fresh heat now that they were alone. "On a job that has nothing to do with McNeill Resorts or your personal development company?"

He caught a hint of her fragrance, something tropical that stood out from the scent of the hibiscus hedge behind her.

"I am here to see you." He saw no need to hide his intentions. "Although even I didn't realize until recently how much unfinished business remained between us."

"So pick up the phone." She bit out the words with careful articulation, though her voice remained quiet. "There was no need to fly fifteen hundred miles to ambush me on my project."

"*Our* project," he reminded her, letting the "ambush" remark slide. "And I saw no sense in calling you when you purposely went into hiding after we left Rangiroa." He'd been furious that she'd blocked him in every way possible, giving him no access to her unless he wanted to be truly obnoxious about seeing her. He refused to be that guy who wouldn't give up on a woman who wanted nothing to do with him.

"You knew how I felt about public scandals." She hugged her arms around herself for a moment, eliciting an unwelcome twinge of empathy from him.

With a very famous father and a mother who was unrepentant about going after his billions, Lydia had received way too much media attention as a child and straight through her teen years. Her parents were the kind of media spectacle that the tabloids cashed in on again and again. In Lydia's eyes, all her mother had done was to destroy Lydia's relationships with her father's family.

"You had no reason to believe I would ever make our affair public." He spotted the silver Z4 rolling out of the parking garage and pointed out the vehicle to her. "You know me better than that."

"I only thought I knew you, Ian."

She didn't need to say any more than that for him to hear the damning accusation behind the words as they headed toward the car.

Tipping the valet service, Ian grudgingly allowed one of the other attendants to close Lydia's door behind her, not surprised the thin veneer of civility between them was already wearing thin. He'd cared deeply about her and he was sure she'd once felt the same about him. The raw hurt of tearing things apart had left them both full of resentments, it seemed.

Indulging those bitter emotions wasn't going to get him what he wanted, however. His objective remained to find out what she was doing messing with his life and his family's welfare through her so-called matchmaking efforts.

"Do you mind having the top down?" he asked. They'd shared a Jeep with no top to roam around the French Polynesian island a year ago, but the stiff-shouldered woman in his passenger seat today bore little resemblance to the laughing, tanned lover of those days.

"It's fine." She reached into the leather tote at her feet and retrieved a dark elastic hair band that she used to twist her hair into a tail and then a loop so the pieces were all tucked away somehow. "Maybe having some fresh air blowing around this conversation will help us keep our tempers."

He pulled out of the hotel parking area and onto Ocean Drive.

"Either that or the Miami heat will only fire things up more." The question was would it result in hot frustration? Or hotter lust?

Seeing her arranging her long, dark hair had already affected him, and he knew his brain had stored away the image to return to later.

In slow motion.

"I prefer to think optimistically." She leaned back in her seat as he slowly drove north through heavy traffic that still didn't come close to the gridlock that plagued this city in the evenings. "So where are we going?" She swiveled in her seat. "There are more of the traditional art deco buildings to the south of us, I think."

"That may be, but I've got a spot in mind that will give us the lay of the land first." He needed to get her alone. Somewhere private where he could focus his full attention on the conversation.

"The lay of the land?" She shielded her eyes and peered ahead of them. "Florida isn't exactly famous for its high ground."

"That's what penthouses are for." He steered into the right lane where the street began to widen even as the traffic didn't seem to lessen.

"A penthouse?" She shifted to face him in her seat, her eyes narrowing. "You can't be serious."

"You'll like this, trust me."

"Not *your* penthouse?" she pressed.

Was that a hint of nervousness in her voice? Either she didn't trust him or she didn't trust herself. He tucked that intriguing thought away.

"I took the penthouse suite at the Setai." He pointed to the luxury hotel looming just ahead of them. "It comes with access to a private rooftop pool. We can speak up there and take in the whole art deco district at the same time."

"You're in the penthouse at the Setai?" She turned her attention to the front of the hotel as he steered the BMW toward the waiting valet. "One of the ten most expensive suites in the known world?"

"Is it?" He didn't usually indulge in that kind of extravagance when he traveled, but then, this wasn't his usual brand of business trip. "Then it's a property that will appeal to the designer in you."

He wondered if she would have agreed if it weren't for the private valet and concierge service already giving them the red carpet treatment as the car pulled up. Lydia's attention was on the attendant who opened her door. Another attendant offered to help with her tote as he discreetly asked what she might require.

That alone made the suite pay for itself, because in the end, Lydia got on the private elevator with Ian and headed to the fortieth floor where they could be alone.

Lydia, you have lost your mind.

She'd been so distracted by the gracious service as she entered the famous hotel that she'd somehow ended up speeding her way toward Ian McNeill's private penthouse suite. She wished it was as simple as the designer in her taking a professional interest in a world-class luxury space, the way Ian had suggested. But she feared that it was more complex than that. Ian had swept her right back into his world today, imposing his will on her work environment, and then staking a claim on her private time, too.

Yes, she'd wanted to speak to him privately. But damn it, that didn't necessitate a trip to a hotel suite with a one-night price tag as high—higher—than what many people paid for an automobile.

"Ian." She took a deep breath before turning to face him.

Just then, the elevator doors swished open, revealing the most gorgeous, Asian-inspired decor imaginable, framed by views of the sparkling sapphire Atlantic out of window after window.

"Wow." Her words dried up.

As a student of architectural design, she did indeed find a lot to savor about the rooms, the layout and the exquisite care taken to render every surface beautiful. She'd read about this suite before in an effort to keep up-to-date on the world's premiere properties, so she'd seen photos of the Steinway in the foyer and—oddly—recalled reading about the absolute black granite in the shower. She guessed the penthouse was close to ten thousand square feet with the double living rooms, a full dining room for ten people and multiple bedrooms. As she walked around the space in admiring silence, her eyes lit on the private terrace overlooking the beach below.

Ian had gotten ahead of her somehow. No doubt she'd been lost in her own thoughts as she'd circled the living areas of the penthouse. But she spotted him in the lounge area of the terrace, speaking to waitstaff who'd set up silver trays in a serving area under a small cabana. White silk had been woven and draped through a pergola, creating a wide swath of shade over the seating.

In all of this exotic, breathtaking space, Ian himself still seemed to be the most appealing focal point. In his crisp blue suit custom-tailored to his athletic frame, he drew the eye like nothing else. His whole family was far too attractive, truth be told. She'd seen photos of his Brazilian mother, who'd left Ian's daredevil father long ago. They'd made a glamorous couple together. Liam McNeill had the dark hair and striking blue eyes of his Scots roots, resulting in three sons who all followed a Gerard Butler mold, although Ian had a darker complexion than the others.

If the gene pool hadn't been kind enough there, Ian was also relentlessly athletic. He'd sailed, surfed and swum regularly while they worked on the hotel property in French Polynesia, and the results of his efforts were obvious even when he was wearing a suit. When he was naked…

Blinking away that thought, she forced her feet forward, refocusing her gaze on the glass half wall surrounding the huge terrace forty stories up. She breathed in the salty scent of the sea that wafted on the breeze while Ian excused the servers.

Soon, she felt his presence beside her more than she heard him. He moved quietly, a man in tune with his surroundings and comfortable enough in his own skin that he never needed to make a noisy entrance. Damn, but she didn't want to remember things that she'd liked about him.

"You were right," she admitted, relaxing slightly as she stared out at the limitless blue of the ocean. "In bringing me here, I mean. It's stunning. Although calling this space a penthouse hardly does justice to how special it is."

"I enjoyed seeing your reaction to it." Out of the corner of her eye, she saw Ian's posture ease. One elbow came up beside hers on the half wall as he joined her at the railing. "Being on the design end of so many projects—and experiencing all the headaches that entails—makes it easy to forget why we enjoy what we do. Then, you see a place like this where they got everything right. It's a reminder that not every project is about a bottom line."

She hesitated. "Yes. Except how many people will ever get to enjoy it?"

"Not enough," he agreed easily. "But if we're inspired, we'll do a better job with properties like Foxfire. And that's an attainable vacation for a lot of people." Turning from the view, he gestured toward the cabana where the food trays waited.

A few minutes later, she had settled herself on a long, U-shaped couch that wrapped around a granite coffee table under the shade of white silk, a plate of fresh fruit and cheese balanced on one knee. Ian poured them each a glass of prosecco even though she'd already helped herself to a bottle of water.

She'd forgotten how extravagantly he lived. While her father had been extremely wealthy, her mother hadn't always been. After suing Lydia's father's estate, she'd eventually taken great joy in overspending once her settlement came through, but by then, Lydia had moved on to her own life. Her father had left her a small amount that she had put toward the purchase of her Manhattan apartment, but his legally recognized children had inherited his true wealth. Besides, Lydia had spent her childhood perpetually worried that her mother would squander their every last cent on frivolous things, so Lydia maintained a practical outlook on finances, careful never to live above her means.

Still, who wouldn't enjoy a day like this?

"You mentioned you wanted to speak to me privately after today's meeting," Ian reminded her as he handed her the sparkling prosecco in a cut crystal glass. A single strawberry rested at the bottom. "Why?"

"Isn't it obvious?" She sipped at the bubbles and set the drink aside. "Ian, I can't work with you on this project."

He'd removed his jacket to expose the gray silk shirt beneath. His muscles stretched the fabric as he moved, reminding her of the honed body beneath.

"You're a professional. I'm a professional. I think we can put aside personal differences for the sake of the project." His expression gave away nothing.

Old hurts threatened to rise to the surface, but she kept a tight rein on those feelings.

"Don't you think you're diminishing what we once meant to each other to call our breakup a 'personal difference'?" Her chest squeezed at all that she'd lost afterward.

One eyebrow lifted as he met her gaze. "No more than you diminished what we meant to one another by playing matchmaker for me afterward, Mallory West."

Three

He knew.

Lydia felt her skin chill despite the bright South Beach sun warming the thin canopy of silk overhead. For a long moment, she only heard the swoosh of waves far below the rooftop terrace, the cry of a few circling gulls and her own pounding heart.

"That's what this is about?" she managed finally, shoving off the deep couch cushions to pace the lounge area near the hot tub. "You found a way to play a role in the same design project as me so you could confront me with this?"

"You don't deny it then?"

"I played a childish game of revenge after we broke up, Ian. You caught me. But it hardly did any damage when you never actually went on a date with any of those women." She'd started her matchmaking career out of spite. She wasn't proud of it, but she had been in a very dark place emotionally.

"No. But I also didn't post my profile on that match-making site, as I tried to tell you from the start. My grandfather's assistant ran the photo and the profile after Grandad twisted my arm about marriage." Ian unfolded himself from his place on the couch to stand, though he did not approach her. "So my grandfather personally reviewed your suggestions that I date…those women." His jaw flexed with annoyance.

She'd sent ridiculous dating suggestions to the man-ager of Ian's profile. She'd been furious to discover he had an active profile on a popular dating website while she'd been falling in love with him. And his refusal to understand why she was upset, his infuriatingly calm insistence that it meant *nothing*, had shredded her.

She'd been tired and overly emotional at the time, but she'd credited it to her broken heart and deep feel-ings for him. Only a week later, she'd discovered she was pregnant.

"I was hurt by your cavalier dismissal of my con-cerns." She moved toward the glass half wall, taking comfort from the sight of the ocean and the relentless roll of incoming waves. "It was petty of me."

"My grandfather was the one who was disappointed." Ian stalked closer, his broad shoulders blocking her view of the water. "But your temporary anger with me doesn't explain why you deceived my younger brother into thinking he was meeting a potential bride, only to have the woman turn out to be completely unaware of his existence." Cool fire flashed in Ian's eyes as he studied her. "It's one thing to lash out at me. But my family?" He shook his head slowly. "No."

"That was an accident." Her temples throbbed with the start of a tension headache as this meeting quickly spiraled out of control. "A genuine accident. Although it didn't help that Cameron signed a waiver saying he didn't care if the matches had been vetted—"

"He clicked a button online to agree to that. Hardly the same as signing something."

"But my assistant explained to him—"

"An assistant who impersonated you, by the way."

Which was something Lydia regretted tremendously. But she'd handed off Cameron McNeill as a client because she hadn't been ready to face Ian's brother with her emotions still raw where Ian was concerned. By the time she'd realized the error in Cameron's match, it was too late to fix it. Jumping in to deal with the aftermath would have meant facing Ian in person—and she hadn't been ready for that at a time when she'd only just started to recover emotionally from the miscarriage.

"I am sorry about that." She pivoted to face him head-on. "I really weighed the options for getting involved after I realized what had happened. But would you really have wanted me to step in when Quinn and Sofia had already announced an engagement? I didn't want to undermine whatever was happening between them by drawing even more attention to the mismatch with Cameron." She'd followed the courtship of Sofia Koslov and Quinn McNeill closely and it had been obvious to her from the photos of them together that they were crazy about each other. "And yes, I was trying to protect my identity. My work had become very important to me by then."

"Very important or very lucrative?"

"Both." She refused to be cowed by him. Straightening to her full height she narrowed her gaze. "I put one hundred percent of the profits after expenses from matchmaking toward a very worthy cause."

"Moms' Connection."

His quick reply unsettled her. How much did he know about her life in the past year? Her shoulders tensed even tighter.

"How did you know that?"

He rested an elbow on the railing, relaxing his posture.

"That's actually one of your less well-guarded secrets. I hired a friend to learn the identity of Mallory West in the hope of sparing Cameron any further embarrassment." Ian shrugged a shoulder. "And to spare Sophia Koslov further embarrassment, since Cameron's potential bride turned out to be the love of Quinn's life."

"I read about that. I'm glad that some good came out of the situation." She hesitated a moment before deciding to press on. "You hired someone to find me?"

What else did he know about the last year of her life? Worry knotted her gut, but she had to hope that the confidentiality of her medical records had withstood his investigation.

"I wasn't expecting to find *you*, Lydia. I hired someone to track Mallory West." His words were clipped. "I can't begin to describe my surprise at discovering you'd had a hand in my affairs ever since you broke things off with me last summer."

"You gave me no choice," she reminded him, remembering the sting of seeing his smiling, handsome face on a friend's page of potential matches on the Mates International dating site. "You not only betrayed me, you did so publicly. If we'd been dating in Manhattan instead of Rangiroa, I can only imagine the fallout." She needed to leave now. To escape whatever dark plans he had in mind by following her to South Beach and insinuating himself back into her life. "But thankfully, that wasn't the case and the rumors of our affair died quickly enough."

Pivoting on her heel, she retrieved her tote bag, prepared to request an Uber.

"I just have one question." Ian followed her across the private terrace, his arms folded over his broad chest as he walked.

"I'm listening." She found her phone and clutched it in one hand.

"Why do all the profits go to a charity benefiting single mothers?"

It was on the tip of her tongue to lie. To tell him that it was a way to help women like her mother, who'd allowed being a single parent to turn her into a bitter person.

But she knew that he wouldn't believe her. He knew her better than that, understood the complex and difficult relationship she had with her mom.

"I met a few women who worked with the group." That was true. Still, her mouth went dry and the heat was beginning to get to her. This whole day was getting to her.

No. Ian McNeill was getting to her.

Those intensely blue eyes seemed to probe all her secrets, seeing right through her.

"How? Where?" he pressed, even as he gestured her toward a seat on the couch again.

He lowered himself to sit beside her as she wondered how much he already knew. She didn't want to equivocate if his personal investigation had already revealed the truth.

"At a support group for single mothers." Her eyes met his. Held. "I attended a few meetings in the weeks after our affair." She had been so touched by those women. So helped by their unwavering support. She took a deep breath. "That was before I lost the pregnancy and... our child."

Ian felt like he'd stepped into the elevator shaft and fallen straight down all forty stories.

"What?" He thought he'd been shocked to discover Lydia was the woman behind Mallory West. Yet the blow he'd felt then was nothing compared to *this*. "You were pregnant when you ended things between us?"

She'd been so fierce and definite. So unwilling to listen to any explanation even though Ian hadn't done a damn thing to post that stupid profile. And all the time she'd been carrying his child? A new anger surged—putting all the other frustrations on the back burner.

How could she hide that from him?

"I didn't realize it at the time. But yes." Lydia unclenched her hand where she'd been holding her cell phone. Setting it carefully aside on the table beside their untouched lunch, she shifted her tote to the outdoor carpet at her feet. She seemed unsure where to look, her eyes darting around the terrace without landing on any one thing. "I realized later that the pregnancy hormones were probably part of the reason why I reacted so strongly to finding your profile online. But it never crossed my mind that I could be pregnant for another week, and then—"

"We were so careful." His mind went back to those long, sultry nights with her. Lydia all wrapped around him in that villa with no walls where they could look straight out into the Pacific Ocean, the sea breezes cooling their damp bodies after their lovemaking. "Every time we were careful."

"There were a couple of nights we went in the water," she reminded him, nibbling on her lower lip. "The hot tub once. And the ocean…remember?"

Her green eyes brought him right back to one of those moments when he'd been looking into them as a rainfall shower sprayed over them in the outdoor Jacuzzi. Her delicate hands had smoothed over his shoulders, nails biting gently into his skin as he moved deeper inside her.

"Yes." His voice was hoarse with how damn well he remembered. "I recall."

She pursed her lips. "Maybe one of those times. I don't know. But I can tell you that I tested positive when it occurred to me I might be pregnant and then—"

"I had a right to know." That part was only just beginning to really take hold in his brain, firing him up even more. "When you first found out, you should have told me."

"Because things had ended so happily between us?" she retorted, her brow furrowed. "Ian, you didn't even deny that you were going to date other people. You said your family wanted you to find a wife."

"That could have been you." He articulated the words clearly, restraining himself when he wanted to roar them for all of South Beach to hear. "And I didn't deny your ludicrous accusation about dating other people because I had no intention of dating anyone but you."

Hell, he'd fallen in love with her. He'd been ready to propose, thought they knew everything about each other there could be to know. And it had insulted him in the very fiber of his being that a woman he cared about so much could think so poorly of him that he would advertise himself for dates with other women. Clearly, they hadn't known each other as well as he thought. He'd been too damn impulsive and mistook intense—very intense—passion for love.

Later, he'd forgotten about his grandfather's plan, pure and simple, because he'd been caught up in his work and in Lydia. Plus, they'd been a million miles from home and the pressure of the McNeill world.

She went so quiet that he wondered what she was thinking. Instead of asking, he helped himself to a swig of the prosecco they'd left out on the table, trying to settle his own thoughts.

"As I said, I was probably operating under the influence of pregnancy hormones. I've spoken to a lot of other mothers since then, and they say it's a powerful chemical change." She surprised him with her practical admission, especially after the matchmaking games she'd played last summer.

Maybe time had softened her initial anger with him. Or showed her that he might not be fully to blame for his grandfather's matchmaking transgression.

"Setting aside the fact that you never informed me about our child—" he took a deep breath as he willed himself to set it aside, too "—can you tell me what happened? Why do the doctors think you miscarried?"

He had a million other questions. How far along had she been? Had she ever considered reaching out to him before she'd lost the baby? What if the pregnancy had gone to full term? Would she have ever contacted him?

That last question, and the possibility that the answer was no, burned right through him.

"The cause was undetermined. My doctor assured me miscarriages happen in ten to twenty-five percent of pregnancies for women in their child-bearing years, so it's not that unusual." She laid a hand across her abdomen as she spoke. An unconscious gesture? "The most common cause is a chromosome abnormality, but there's no reason to believe it would happen to me again."

Hearing the vulnerability in her voice, seeing it for himself in her eyes, made some of the resentment ease away.

"I'm sorry I wasn't there with you." He reached to take her hand resting beside him on the couch.

Her skin felt cool to the touch despite the heat. She

stared down at his fingers clasping hers, but didn't move away from the connection.

"I didn't handle it well." She retrieved her bottle of water and took a long drink. "It might have been hormones, but the sadness was overwhelming. But I spent a lot of time with the mothers' group I told you about. Being with them helped me to heal."

A row of misters clicked on nearby to provide water to the exotic flowers tucked in a planter by the doors to his suite. The cool spray glanced over their skin before the water evaporated in the Miami sun glinting off white stone walls all around the rooftop terrace.

"That's why you support this group now—Moms' Connection." He tried to fit the pieces together in his mind to figure out what she'd been through in the past year.

"Yes. I met some incredibly strong women who inspired me. Seeing their efforts to help other single mothers made me realize how petty it was for me to meddle in the matches that were being sent to you." She hesitated. "I started to put more effort into really matching up people and I discovered I was good at it."

Sliding her hand from his grip, she smoothed it along the hem of her dress, straightening the fabric.

"So you kept at it and used the funds to help the group that helped you." His vision of her shifted slightly, coming into sharper focus. "And what happened with Sofia Koslov and my brother was, as you say, a genuine accident."

"Yes. I shouldn't have taken your brother on as a client, but by that time, Kinley was filling in for me often.

I was away for several weeks last winter doing a job for a singer who moved to Las Vegas for an extended contract and wanted me to design her new home." Lydia picked one red strawberry from a plate on the table. "But the profits from the matchmaking work were doing a lot of good for the mothers' organization by then. I didn't want to let my support of a good cause lapse. I still don't."

She bit into the strawberry, her lips molding to the red fruit in a way that made his mouth go dry.

"You must be aware that Sofia Koslov's father is an extremely wealthy and powerful man. He allowed my family to investigate the matter of Mallory West's identity since she's now engaged to Quinn, but when he finds out who you are, he has every intention of suing." Ian hadn't told a soul about discovering that Lydia was behind the debacle.

He hadn't even told his two brothers, which didn't sit particularly well with him. But he'd been handed an opportunity to bargain with this woman and he wasn't about to lose it.

Initially, he'd entertained fantasies about leveraging his position for revenge. But now he knew that his relationship with Lydia was far more complex than that. There was still an undeniable spark between them—and a connection that went deeper than just the attraction. Otherwise, the news of her losing a pregnancy wouldn't have affected him like a sledgehammer to his chest.

Which meant he was going to be bargaining for something more than sensual revenge.

"I had hoped now that Sofia is marrying your brother

later this month, her father wouldn't want to draw public attention to the matchmaking mishap." The worry in Lydia's eyes was unmistakable as the ocean breeze tousled her dark hair where it rested on her shoulders.

Ian buried any concern he might have had about her feelings. She certainly hadn't taken his into account when she hid the news of his child from him.

"Vitaly Koslov strikes me as a man who does not forget a slight to his family." Ian respected that. He wasn't inclined to let a slight to his go unchecked either. "But I have a suggestion that might help you avoid a civil suit and restore your matchmaking business."

"You do?" The hope that sparked in her gaze ignited a response in him.

This was a good plan. And it was going to solve problems for them both.

"You are aware that, due to familial pressure, I am in the market for a wife?" The terms of his grandfather's will had caused him no end of grief in his relationship with Lydia, after all. "Last summer, my grandfather had already started to apply pressure to wed, but this winter, he created legally binding terms in a rewritten will. In order to retain family control of my grandfather's legacy, my brothers and I each need to marry for at least twelve months."

"But you already have your own successful business—"

"Keeping McNeill Resorts in the family is about legacy, not finances." He wouldn't allow his third of the company to go to strangers. Cameron and Quinn felt the same about the family empire.

"I can help you find someone, if you'd like a private consultation." Her words were stiff and formal.

Did she honestly not guess his intent? Or was she bracing for the inevitable?

"That's kind of you. But I'm perfectly capable of choosing a temporary wife for myself."

"You're taking over that task from your grandfather?" She arched an eyebrow at him, challenging.

With just one fiery look, she reminded him how good it was going to be when he touched her again.

And he would touch her again. Soon.

"Definitely. My search just ended, Lydia." He allowed himself the pleasure of skimming a knuckle down her bare arm. "You will solve both our problems if you agree to be my wife for the next twelve months."

Four

"He proposed to you?" Lydia's assistant, Kinley, squealed in Lydia's ear late that night during a conference call to catch up on business back in New York.

With her feet tucked beneath her on the sofa while she ate her room service salad, Lydia shifted her laptop on the coffee table to reduce the glare from the reading lamp. Kinley's hazel eyes were huge, her face comically close to her webcam as she gestured for Lydia to hurry up with her story.

"Yes." Stabbing a cherry tomato with her fork, Lydia tried to ignore the butterflies in her stomach that the memory invited. Why on earth would she feel flattered to be part of Ian's scheme to use her in order to deceive his grandfather? But the fluttery feeling in her belly had been undeniable—both when Ian suggested marriage, and now as she related the story to Kinley. "He means it strictly as a business arrangement."

Although when he'd asked her, he'd been trailing the back of one knuckle down her cheek, making her think about how good they were together and what the man's touch could do to her. So she hadn't said no as quickly as she would have wished.

"And he would protect you from scandal if it comes to a lawsuit over the match between his brother and Sofia Koslov?"

Lydia watched her assistant on the computer screen. Back in New York, Kinley's pen hovered over a cross-word puzzle in the newspaper, a habit she'd developed once she started skimming the social pages for any interesting leads in the matchmaking world.

"He made it clear he would keep my name out of the headlines and negotiate with Vitaly Koslov if there are legal repercussions." The Ukrainian entrepreneur was the founder of the mega-successful start-up, Safe Sale, and was worth billions. Lydia had read all about him after the bad press she'd received for the misfire with his daughter's matchmaking experience.

And Ian would swoop in and save her. Just like she'd once dreamed a romantic hero would do for the woman he loved, back when she still believed in happily-ever-afters. Foolish, foolish visions for her to indulge when she'd grown up with the most cynical of parents whose relationship was a continual power struggle.

"So what did you say?" Kinley pressed, tapping her pen impatiently against the newspaper.

"I turned him down in no uncertain terms, at which

point he reminded me that if I wanted Mallory's identity kept secret, I should give his offer more careful consideration." Remembering that thinly veiled taunt still made her fume hours afterward. At the time, she'd been too angry to trust herself to speak.

She'd called the elevator and let the Setai's attentive concierge put her in a car the hotel offered her as Ian's guest. No doubt, they would have escorted her all over town if she wished—a reminder of how far apart their lifestyles had always been. For all that her father had been a wealthy man, Lydia worked hard to pay her own bills, refusing to fall into her mother's role of bilking others in order to lead an extravagant lifestyle.

"I'll admit it's not exactly the proposal every girl dreams of." Kinley began tapping the pen against her cheek, her lips pursed thoughtfully. "But still. Ian McNeill?" She whistled softly. "A woman could do worse for herself."

"Marriage isn't a competitive sport." Lydia twirled the hotel bathrobe tie around her finger, agitated at how the day had unfolded—start to finish. "I'm not trying to find the richest or most prestigious partner."

"I was thinking more along the lines of the best looking." Kinley grinned shamelessly. "He's seriously hot." She ran her finger over the screen of her phone before flipping it toward the camera to show Lydia a photo of the man himself. "C'mon, Lydia. You can't deny that he's super yummy."

Those blue eyes were magnetic. No doubt.

But the picture wasn't nearly as appealing as the temptation she'd faced today when he stroked a hand along her cheek or told her he wished he'd been there with her when she lost their baby. Those moments had rattled her resolve far more than the vision of his strong shoulders or disarming smile.

Perhaps the idea of a temporary marriage to Ian wouldn't sting so much if she hadn't once let herself imagine a very real marriage with him. Sure, they'd only dated for six weeks, but it had been an intense affair that dominated both their lives. Things had escalated fast.

"That's hardly a good reason to enter into a complicated relationship." If anything, the sensual pull she felt for him was a strike against the idea. She was so drawn to him that it would be easy to let herself confuse attraction for caring again.

And *that* she could not allow.

"Hmm…twelve months of having the world at your feet and a gorgeous, well-respected billionaire to fend off your enemies and keep you safe?" Kinley shook her head, her expression serious for the first time all evening. "I will go out on a limb and say there's more at work here than you're telling me."

Caught.

Lydia shot her an apologetic smile. "Ancient history better forgotten than relived." She took a deep breath. Lydia had resolved to move on after she shared this crazy turn to her day with Kinley. Now it was time to live up to her promise. "But on to more important things. Did you find some parties I should be attending to meet potential clients or possible matches for our current clients?"

She wanted to spend her time helping the cause dear to her heart by raising money for women who really needed it. That meant no more wallowing in regrets over how things had turned out between her and Ian. She'd find some other way to protect her business, even if he revealed her identity as Mallory West to the powerful Vitaly Koslov.

"I did. I'm emailing you a list as soon as I lock down a few more contacts for you. I want to be sure you don't have any trouble getting into any of the events. There are a few European royals in town this month, so invitations are in high demand." She paused. "Although I'm sure Ian McNeill would get the red carpet treatment at all of these places."

Thinking back to that over-the-top penthouse suite at the Setai, Lydia didn't doubt it. He moved in the circles Lydia's mother had never managed to penetrate. And although there'd been a time when Lydia didn't care about acceptance into that kind of elite, she'd begun to see the benefits if only for the sake of Moms' Connection.

"I'm sure he does. But since he won't be attending any of these functions with me, I will wait for you to work your magic on my behalf. Just do whatever you can with my father's name." She refused to feel guilty about that since her father had been a committed philanthropist. He would have applauded Lydia's efforts, she felt certain.

Not for the first time, she wished she'd had more time with him growing up, but she'd been her mother's bargaining chip from the day of her birth, withheld from her dad whenever her mother was unhappy with him.

Which meant she didn't see him often. And when she did, her mother was close at hand, making sure to take her share of the billionaire's attention.

Finishing up her business with Kinley, Lydia ended the video call and closed her laptop. She was staying at the Calypso Hotel close to the Foxfire, in a small room with an ocean view. The suite needed updating desperately, but as she padded across the black-and-white tile floor to the sliding glass door overlooking the water, she admired the same view that Ian had in his gargantuan spread just twenty blocks away. Her surroundings indoors might pale in comparison, but with the ocean waves lapping the shore below, providing a soothing music despite the stressful day, she too could enjoy the most priceless kind of beauty.

Breathing in the soft, salty air, she tried to let the Atlantic work its magic. But deep down, she knew she hadn't escaped Ian McNeill's marriage offer simply by walking out of his suite. He'd allowed her to leave, no doubt so she could mull over the idea—rage against it—and slowly realize how thoroughly he had her back against the wall.

Revealing her as the woman behind Mallory West threatened to derail all her hard work with Moms' Connection, turning her life back into another scandal-ridden media circus when she'd worked so hard to put the antics of her mother behind her. Furthermore, even if she managed to keep the matchmaking business afloat and somehow turn a profit in spite of all the media attention, she would have Vitaly Koslov to contend with, a powerful business mogul with the power to bankrupt her on every front.

Right now, she could afford to live in Manhattan and run a business she enjoyed. Losing a civil suit to Koslov might ruin her financially for years to come. All she had to do to avoid those consequences was put herself in Ian McNeill's hands for one year. She simply had to wed the man who'd left her heart with the deepest scars.

Just seeing him for one day had threatened to rip those old wounds open again. She couldn't possibly go through with it.

So, turning to enter her hotel room and slip between the sheets for the night, Lydia knew she'd have to refuse him when he asked her again. Because not for a moment did she think he'd dropped the idea of a temporary union between them.

Ian McNeill wasn't a man to take marriage lightly. Even the cold-blooded, contractual kind.

Nodding a greeting to the desk attendant at the Calypso Hotel shortly before dawn, Ian checked his watch as he took up a spot near the main elevators. It was one of South Beach's aging art deco–era properties. Standing on the huge tile inlay featuring a gold starburst design, Ian pulled his phone from his pocket to check his stocks for the day, but in reality all he could think about was Lydia.

It was a risk to surprise her. But when she'd ended their conversation prematurely the day before, she must have known he would find a time to renew their discussion. Sooner rather than later.

She was a woman of habit and that would serve him well now. He hoped. He remembered how much she had enjoyed swimming first thing in the morning when they were working together in the islands of Tahiti. He'd accused her of being a mermaid with her daily need to return to the sea, but even when he'd been bleary-eyed from working late the night before, he never missed a chance to swim with her. For safety purposes, he'd told her, and not just because he enjoyed the occasional chance to slide a hand beneath her bikini top or wind the wet rope of her hair around his hand and angle her sea-salty lips for his kiss.

When the elevator sounded its dull chime, he slowly looked up. The doors opened and Lydia strode into view. His gaze fell on her long, shapely legs, the hem of her black mesh tunic revealing a hint of thigh.

"Ian?" Her voice tugged his attention higher, pulling his focus to her green eyes and creamy skin devoid of makeup.

With her hair scraped back into a ponytail, she looked every inch the part of his earthy, warmhearted lover from last summer. He had to remember that she hadn't been the woman he thought, that he'd been wrong about her, or he might have swept her up into his arms and ridden the elevator back up to her hotel room to remind her how good they were together in at least one respect.

Sex. Raw, sensual, mind-blowing sex.

His pulse ramped up at the steamy memories, so much so that he had to shut down those thoughts and focus on the present or his plan would be doomed before he even started.

"Hope you don't mind if I join you." Ian tucked his phone back into the pocket of the cargo shorts he'd slid on over his swim trunks.

She halted in front of him abruptly. Then, eyes sliding to the desk attendant, she stepped closer. Probably she did it to minimize the chance of being overheard.

Ian liked the opportunity to breathe in the scent of her—the lavender fragrance of the detergent she washed her clothes in and a subtle perfume more complex than that.

"What on earth are you doing here?" She glanced over her shoulder. "You realize most of the consultants working on the Foxfire are staying in this hotel? What will they say if someone sees us together at this hour?"

"They'll think we had a whole lot more fun last night than they did."

Last night, he'd paced the floor of his penthouse suite for far too long, thinking through every aspect of a contract marriage and what details he should include in the paperwork.

In the end, she would sign. But she wasn't going to like him forcing her hand, and that bothered him more than it should have.

"And that doesn't concern you? I happen to enjoy a hard-earned reputation as a professional." Her clipped words and the high color in her cheeks told him he'd gotten under her skin in record time.

"If you don't want anyone to see us together, we might as well hit the beach. Take refuge in the water." His hand itched to touch her. To rest on the small of her back and steer her out the door, across the street and onto the soft sand. But he had to be careful not to push or she could dig her heels in about his suggestion and delay the whole thing.

Now that he'd made up his mind and seen the benefits of a union between the two of them, he couldn't think of one damn reason why he should delay.

After narrowing her green eyes at him for an instant, she pivoted on her wedge sandals and strode toward the exit.

He caught up to her in two long steps, holding the door wide for her before as they headed out onto Ocean Drive, which was strangely quiet in the predawn dark. There were more joggers on the beach than bathers; a few runners kicked up sand as they pounded past them.

"It'll be quieter down here." He pointed out a stretch of the shore where no beach loungers had been set up yet, a spot free from any hotel guests.

In fact, he'd claimed the location for them earlier when he'd ordered a cabana and sunrise breakfast. Lydia apparently didn't notice his preparations, however, instead appearing too absorbed in her frustrated march toward the water, her feet churning through the sand at breakneck pace.

The horizon was starting to smudge from inky black to purple as she reached the shoreline and kicked off her shoes. Then she yanked the black mesh cover-up off and over her head. Mesmerized by her silhouette as his eyes adjusted to the light, Ian watched as she ran into the surf and made a shallow dive under an oncoming wave.

He retrieved her clothes and put them in the cabana where he removed his own shorts and tee, stacking them off to one side out of the way of a server still setting up a tea cart full of trays for their breakfast.

Then Ian sprinted into the ocean after Lydia, seized with memories of other times they'd done this. They'd had plenty of games they played in the water, from him grabbing an ankle and tracing the long line of her leg up to the juncture of her thighs to races of every kind. He didn't think she'd appreciate the former, so he settled for the latter, pacing her as she executed perfect butterfly strokes through the salty water.

With the horizon turning lavender now, he could see her better. Her creamy skin glinted in the soft light each time her arm broke the surface. Only when they were far from the shore did she stop short to tread water.

"You're insane," she accused softly, even though she seemed significantly calmer than when she'd been on her march toward the water. With her dark hair plastered to her head and the long ponytail floating around her shoulders, she looked so beautiful and so damn familiar that it hurt.

"To swim in a dark ocean before the sun rises? Or to brave your wrath and swim beside you when I know you're angry?"

Her huff of frustration rippled the water in front of her. "To propose marriage when we have so much... unhappy history. So much frustration between us. It's crazy and you know it." She swatted aside a drifting clump of seaweed.

"I'm a practical man, Lydia. And by now, I'm sure you've had enough time to realize how practical my suggestion is." He'd wanted her to have cooling off time yesterday, but he guessed she'd been awake as long as he had last night, thinking about the possibilities.

"Practical?" She rose up on her toes to move out of the way of a swell coming toward them. "Ian, we aren't some royal couple needing to secure the family line or keep the castle in the clan. Marriage isn't supposed to be a line item in a business deal."

"And it won't be." He took her hand before the next swell rolled over them. "Come this way so you can touch the bottom."

Even that simple touch—his grip wrapped around her fingers in the cool water—sent a flash of undeniable heat through him. Judging from how fast she pulled back, he would guess she felt it, too.

"I'm fine," she argued despite the goose bumps along her arm.

"You're cold." He pointed to the shore where their server had left a small hurricane lamp burning on the table. "You see the cabana? I ordered some breakfast for us. Let's dry off and talk about this reasonably before the next wave drags you under."

"We're having breakfast there?" She shook her head slowly, but began swimming toward shore. "I have the feeling you could have had the free buffet at the Setai."

He laughed.

"Maybe so. But my hotel lacks your company. A situation I hope to change once you agree to my proposal."

She stopped swimming. But they were so close to the shore now, they were able to stand and walk side by side the rest of the way. She'd stopped arguing, which he took as a positive sign. So he kept his peace for now, shortening his stride to stay beside her as they moved closer and closer to their destination. The all-white tent was closed on three sides but open to the water, the domed roof making it look like something out of *Arabian Nights*.

She nibbled her bottom lip, then released it slowly before shooting a sideways glance his way. "You're really serious about this."

"You doubted it?" He passed her a towel from the stack an attendant left near their clothes.

"Not really." She squeezed the water out of her long ponytail and let it drip onto the sand. "I guess I hoped maybe you were just trying to scare me with the threat of Koslov's lawsuit. Make me regret what I'd done by interfering in your romantic life with the matches I suggested."

She'd sent him suggestions for dates with a reality TV star renowned for her diva-ish behavior and an ex-girlfriend she knew he disliked for using his name to get ahead in her career for long after they'd broken up.

"No." Moving to the sideboard where the food had been set up, he poured them both coffee. "Although I won't deny I let myself imagine all kinds of inventive sensual blackmail once I found out you were the woman behind Mallory West."

She clutched the towel tighter to her lovely body as he set the mugs on the bistro-size table. When she said nothing, he waited another moment to continue, letting his words sink in. He wasn't going to pretend that he wasn't attracted.

Or that he wouldn't act on it.

"But after we had the chance to speak yesterday, I realized you were under an incredible amount of stress at that time, and I regret not being there for you." It made his chest go tight thinking about her alone and losing their child. *Their child.* He had to swallow down the lump in his throat before he could continue. "No matter what else happened between us, you should have known you could contact me."

He hadn't forgiven her for keeping the baby a secret in the first place, but he hated that she'd been through that by herself.

She sank into her chair at the table, stirring sugar into the coffee he'd placed in front of her. She made no protest when he set a plate of food before her, the stoneware loaded down with fruits and cheeses he knew she liked. The scent of eggs and bacon wafted from the warming trays as he prepared a plate for himself and a smaller, second one for her.

"So you didn't suggest marriage as a punishment." She gave him a lopsided smile and slid her arms into the black mesh bathing suit cover-up.

"Far from it." He pulled on his linen button-down shirt and took the seat across from her, letting his knee brush hers under the table and seeing the jolt of awareness in her eyes. "I think a marriage between us could have all kinds of added benefits."

Five

A shock of heat radiated out from that one spot where their legs brushed, seizing Lydia's attention faster than any words. How easy it would be to heed that impulse, to fall under the spell of simmering attraction until she was powerless to resist it. Of course, it didn't help that she remembered so many other times when she'd allowed this very sensation to carry her away, pulling her into his arms to answer the hunger only he could fill.

Urging herself to be stronger than that, she shifted her legs away from him under the table, crossing one knee over the other to put herself farther out of his reach.

"I'm not sure it's fair of you to resort to underhanded tactics to convince me we should try this crazy scheme of yours." Taking a sip of her coffee, she focused on the pink sun rising past the horizon, bathing them both in warm light.

The beach was still quiet at this early hour with a smattering of tourists more focused on the famed night-life than the joys of the early morning. About twenty yards away, a fisherman cast a line and waited to see what was biting, his chair half in the surf. A few inter-ested birds stalked him, sensing the possibility of an easy meal.

"Underhanded?" Ian straightened, as if rearing back from an undeserved slight. But then a smile curved his sculpted lips, sliding right past her boundaries. "Under the table, maybe. But hardly underhanded."

"You know what I mean." She stabbed a half straw-berry with her fork and ignored all the nerve endings urging her to listen to him, to let him woo her back where her body would love to be. "If we can't hash out terms logically, it's not a good idea to start wielding seduction as a weapon."

"Lydia," he began, his tone gently chiding. "Seduc-tion was a very rewarding part of our relationship. I'd never want it to be anything but a pleasure."

He didn't move any closer as he spoke, but somehow the air thickened around them as if he'd grazed against her again. Hearing the word *pleasure* on his lips wasn't good for her defenses.

"Then let's keep it out of the negotiations." She spoke through gritted teeth, she realized, and forced herself to take a breath.

"Of course." He finished his eggs and moved his plate aside, leaning his elbows on the table.

The breeze off the water blew through his dark wavy hair, which was beginning to dry. He was impossibly handsome with his deeply bronzed skin and blue eyes.

"Good." Relaxing a little, she hoped she could still reason with him. "Then we can discuss alternatives to the marriage plan."

"The only alternative is me revealing Mallory West's identity to the world, Vitaly Koslov included." Ian lifted the coffee carafe to pour her more.

Her stomach cramped. He was perfectly serious. Ian might be the peacemaker within the McNeill family, brokering middle ground between his conservative older brother and his playboy, techno-genius younger sibling, but that didn't mean Ian himself ever gave ground. More often than not, the other McNeills let themselves be guided by Ian's position.

"That will ruin any hope of resurrecting my matchmaking career. Aside from the personal loss, I would be saddened by the missed opportunity for the world of good it's doing for so many people," she reminded him, unable to enjoy the fresh fruit on her plate when her nerves were wound tight. She didn't want to lose her ability to give back to Moms' Connection and the women who'd helped her through the darkest time of her life.

He shrugged with a pragmatic air. "Sometimes we make sacrifices for the things that are most important to us."

How could he be so cavalier about love? "And you don't care if I look at marriage to you as sacrificing myself?" Maybe she'd hoped some small part of him still cared about what they had meant to each other once.

"We are both offering something to get what we want." He tapped the table as if jabbing home his point. "I prefer to focus on the positives."

"Like you getting around your grandfather's terms for the will?"

"Precisely." He reached to take her fork from her plate and spear a grape. He then lifted it, offering it to her. "And you avoid a civil suit while growing your business." He paused, fork hovering in midair. "Among other benefits."

That damnable heat returned to her skin. How could she have forgotten how easily he tampered with her ability to think clearly?

"So you mentioned. But I'm not going to suddenly take up where we left off just because we sign on for a year together." She withdrew the fork from his fingers and set it down again, unwilling to play romantic games with him. "Not that I'm seriously considering this idea at all, Ian. If anything, I'm still trying to figure out how to get out of my contract with Singer Associates so I can leave South Beach and the Foxfire project altogether."

"I would never expect you to pick up where we left off a year ago." His gaze was steady and direct. He appeared sincere. "I know the heat is still there, but it would be up to you if we did anything about it—plain and simple."

Her heart beat faster just talking about it. How would she ever find enough strength to resist the man day in and day out for a whole year if she were to actually consider going through with this?

She really didn't want to lose her matchmaking business because the proceeds did so much good for the charity she cared about. Confused and flustered, she stood abruptly.

"I can't do this again." She shook her head, wishing she could shake off the old feelings crowding out reasonable thought. "The first time hurt too much."

Retrieving her towel, she wanted to retreat before she did something foolish. Like throw her arms around his neck and press herself against him, or drag him deeper into the cabana and peel off his clothes.

"Please." Ian stood with her, a hand darting out to capture hers, linking their fingers with an ease from their past relationship. "My grandfather had a heart attack last winter after the debacle of Cameron proposing to Sofia."

Ian's touch curved around her elbow, gentle but firm.

"I'm sorry. I didn't know."

"It happened while he traveled abroad. In China, in fact. That helped us to keep it quiet."

She softened a little, knowing how much Malcolm McNeill meant to all of his grandsons. She recalled how Ian had told her about his fond memories of the older man throughout his childhood.

With the sun just above the horizon now, pink and orange light spilled over them, a spotlight just for them. Ian's fingers caressed the back of her arm lightly and she could feel her resistance ebbing away with the tide.

"Will he be okay?" She read between the lines. If something happened to Malcolm McNeill and Ian had not fulfilled the terms of the trust, the family would lose control of McNeill Resorts.

"We hope so. He had a pacemaker put in and his doctors say he's doing well. But Gramps wouldn't let us take him to see his physician in the States yet until he's certain he can control any rumors spreading about his health."

They stood just inside the cabana's shelter, her bare toes curling in the sand as Ian's fingers stroked lightly over the back of her arm. She wasn't even sure he was aware that he was doing it. His gaze turned sober, his shoulders tense with concern.

"He wants to protect the integrity of the business." She understood the older man's reasons. Even the strongest companies could experience a downturn over rumors about a change in leadership.

"Yes." Ian's touch stilled as he met her gaze. "Even at the expense of his health. But you see why I am all the more concerned about protecting his legacy? Not for me, but for him?"

She understood about wanting approval. She'd craved it her whole life from her father and then, after his death, from her half siblings and the family she'd never gotten to know. But that had eluded her. Ian didn't have those kinds of concern, though. He knew his grandfather loved him.

"If keeping the company in the family was that important to him, don't you think he would alter the terms of the will?" She tipped her face to the sea breeze off the water, feeling off-kilter over having an intimate conversation with Ian at such close range. "Maybe your grandfather is more concerned with your happiness. I can't imagine he'd want you to marry someone just for the sake of keeping the business in the family."

"Malcolm McNeill was raised in a different time. He doesn't see the problem with choosing a bride for practical purposes." Ian released her but didn't move away, which in essence blocked her from leaving the cabana. "So I'm trying to see his reasoning in those terms. You and I make sense together, Lydia. We can help each other."

This would be so much easier if she didn't keep mixing up the past and the present, seeing her former lover in Ian instead of the hard, pragmatic man she knew him to be. Even last year, he'd put his grandfather's wishes before hers, so why should it surprise her that he would marry for the sake of his family? Yet no matter how hard she tried, she saw the man who made love to her in a waterfall at dawn. A man who'd shown her a level of pleasure in bed she'd never imagined possible.

A man who'd held her heart in his strong palm.

"I can't help you." Her words were soft, fragile things, not nearly as fierce as she would have liked.

"What could I do to make you say yes?" He corralled a flyaway strand of hair and smoothed it behind her ear. "Just name it."

He was offering her the chance to keep her matchmaking business and protect her identity from another scandal. He'd keep Vitaly Koslov at bay and give her a kind of respectability she'd never known as the daughter of a notorious tabloid diva. All of which would be very beneficial.

Now, he was even allowing her to dictate her terms.

She couldn't deny she was tempted. Especially now that she knew his motive wasn't payback for the matches she'd sent him last fall. She believed he was truly worried about his grandfather's health and fulfilling one of the old man's wishes.

"Separate rooms." The words came tumbling from her mouth before she'd really thought through all the ways this could go wrong. "Help with my matchmaking business if I need it." She remembered what Kinley had said about the McNeill family's access to A-list events that would be difficult to get into otherwise.

"I don't know a lot about matchmaking," he admitted. "I would have thought you and I were going to be great together."

Her heart squeezed tight, remembering that she'd thought the same thing until she'd discovered he was only using their relationship to fill the time until he found the right woman to marry. Now it seemed Ian didn't mind compromising his standards for a wife when he was in a hurry.

"Not that kind of help. I mean it might aid my work if I could use the McNeill name to meet more potential clients."

"Done." Ian didn't hesitate. "It's a deal then?"

A deal? For real? She must have lost her mind for considering this. But it was only for twelve months, right?

"I would have one other condition." She swallowed hard, needing to be forthright with him if she was going to go through with this.

He stayed silent, which somehow swayed her more than a million words.

She found herself speaking slowly, weighing each

thought, almost like dipping her toe in to test the waters. "I would expect you to honor what you said earlier about not using seduction as a weapon." Her voice did that high, breathy thing again, and she swallowed hard to make it go away. "While I acknowledge there is a pull between us, Ian, I need you to promise me you won't take advantage of that."

"On one condition." His voice lowered. His forehead tipped closer to hers.

Her heart pounded like it wanted to leap free of her chest.

"What?" She should have spelled out that he couldn't even get this close to her.

What had she been thinking?

"I get to kiss you on two occasions."

Kisses. Just kisses. But when had they ever been able to stop at just kisses?

She should protest. End this now. Let Vitaly Koslov sue her into bankruptcy for embarrassing his ballerina daughter by sending her a marriage-minded suitor to propose to her in front of the press.

Instead, Lydia breathed in the feel of having Ian this close to her. So close she caught a hint of his sandalwood aftershave that had occasionally clung to her skin after a night in his bed.

"When would those kisses happen?" Her eyes tracked his. "On what occasions?"

"Once on our wedding day. And once to seal the deal."

"As in…now?" She would not lick her lips even though her mouth went chalk-dry at the thought.

"Right now." His hand found the center of her back, his palm an electric warmth through the mesh fabric of her cover-up. "Do we have a deal, Lydia? One year together and I'll honor all of your terms."

Bad idea, bad idea, her brain chanted, as if to urge the words out of her mouth. But she could not forsake the women—the mothers—who needed her help. And selfishly, she could not put herself through another scandal.

She nodded her assent.

A wicked, masculine smile curved his lips.

"I'm so glad to hear it." His blue eyes glowed with a new heat in that moment of victory right before he lowered his mouth to hers.

If one kiss was all he got until their vows, Ian planned to make it count.

His hands cupped her waist just above the gentle curve of her hips. Her skin was warm through the thin mesh cover-up. She pressed closer, or maybe he did, the space between them shrinking until her breasts teased against his chest, the soft swell of sweet feminine flesh making him ache for a better feel of her.

Hunger for her roared down Ian's spine the moment their lips touched. The electric connection they'd always had sparked to flame, singeing his insides with a need to have her. Here. Now. He could lower the curtains on the cabana for privacy and ease her beautiful body down to the table. With no effort at all he could sweep aside that scrap of fabric that counted as a swimsuit and be deep inside her. He knew her body so well.

Felt the answering heat in the breathless way she kissed him back, her fingernails clutching lightly at his shirt to keep him close.

Even now, she fit her body to his, her hips arching into him. Or maybe her legs felt as weak beneath her as his did and she was simply melting against him.

Yes.

He reached behind her, just above her head, to release the tie holding back one side of the cabana's front curtain. The fabric fell in a rush, cloaking them in shadows. Lydia levered back, blinking up at the change in the light. She focused on the fallen length of white fabric.

"What are you doing?" Her lips trembled. "Why?"

He couldn't take his eyes off her mouth.

"Giving us more privacy." He kissed her again, feeding on the plump softness until her lips parted.

He turned them both, pinning her to him with one hand at the small of her back while he flicked free the other side of the cabana curtain, letting it tumble to the ground and shield them completely from view of anyone else on the beach.

"A kiss." Her words whispered over his mouth in a soft sigh. "We said one kiss."

"We did." He bent to taste the skin just below her ear, feeling her pulse beat fast. "And see how well that turned out for both of us?"

"Ian." She fisted her hands tighter in his shirt for a moment, then edged back from him.

Wide-eyed in the newly dim interior of the closed cabana, she gazed up at him while the white curtains shifted gently in the breeze off the water. He listened to the waves roll in to keep his focus off the way she looked with her cover-up sliding off one shoulder and her lips swollen from his kiss.

He needed to be patient. To not push for more. It would be better when she came to him because she was ready to pick up where they left off. But damn. Keeping his hands off her right now when the air between them pulsed with want and heat proved a staggering test of restraint.

"Yes?" He wanted to trace the fullness of her lower lip. Memorize the feel of her.

"How fast is this going to happen? A marriage, I mean?"

She was talking about marriage? A surge of triumph pumped through him. This deal was all but done.

He held back his victory shout and kept his voice level. "I hope you're asking because you're looking forward to that next kiss as much as I am."

"I'm wondering how to handle us being on the same job in the same city. If we're supposed to look like a couple, and if that's okay while we're working together." She straightened her cover-up and took a step back from him.

He tugged the privacy curtain back into place on one side of the cabana, giving up on the idea of resurrecting their relationship with impromptu sex on the breakfast table.

Patience.

"I'll find a justice of the peace and see how quickly we can put in the paperwork." He would rest easier when he knew he was on track to meet the terms of his grandfather's will. The sooner they got married, the sooner that would happen.

His brother Quinn and his ballerina fiancée were due to wed in two weeks. With any luck, Ian would already be wed to Lydia by then. Not that they needed to announce it until afterward.

"And you think we can stay on this job together as a couple, no emotions, no sex involved?" She seemed worried about that and he wondered why.

He'd never imagined her as overly concerned with finances. She was donating 100 percent of the money she made in her matchmaking business, after all. His friend Bentley's report had confirmed as much.

But then again, if she was so financially stable, he had to wonder about her accommodations at the old, worn-down Calypso Hotel.

"I will honor your wishes every step of the way. But to be certain, I'll speak to Jeremy today. And in the meantime, I have several vacant bedrooms at the suite at the Setai. I'll ask the concierge service to move your things." He sent out two text messages to arrange for her clothes to be delivered to the penthouse.

She'd said separate rooms. But she could hardly quibble when his suite was bigger than most private homes.

"There's one other thing. About the terms I mentioned?" She followed him out of the cabana across the sand, back toward his car. "I'd like to use your name to get into a party later this week. I think I'll get in more easily as your guest."

"I'll put you in touch with my assistant if we need an invitation. I'll go with you and we can debut our romantic relationship publicly." He withdrew his phone and sent a message to Mrs. Trager.

She paused near the Calypso.

"I'm parked this way." He pointed toward his vehicle in a spot up the street.

"But I should at least go shower and change."

"You can do both those things at my suite. For all we know we'll be able to marry by this afternoon." He took her hand and led her forward when she hesitated. "We might as well stick together."

"I can't believe we're really going through with this." She matched her steps to his, heading toward the BMW convertible. "Should we sign an agreement of some sort? I'd feel better if we had things in writing."

"Of course." He would ensure their terms were spelled out clearly. Put her at ease with the plan so she could relax and enjoy the benefits of marriage.

Because the next time they kissed, he planned to take his time reminding her how very rewarding the next twelve months together could be.

Six

Three whirlwind days later, shortly before noon, Lydia stood in front of a Dade County justice of the peace and signed the documents to become Ian's wife.

Privately, they'd already signed the papers spelling out the terms for separation in one year. She'd had a trusted attorney look over it to be sure she understood all aspects of the document and agreed the settlement was fair. Ian had added numerous financial benefits that she'd had stricken from the agreement since she wasn't marrying him for a cash prize, for crying out loud. They'd argued about it more than once, but in the end, he'd capitulated when she'd flat-out refused to sign under those terms.

Now, signing her name beside Ian's in the public register, Lydia clutched her flowers tighter as the simple ceremony got underway. They hadn't even forewarned their families. But though there was no fanfare, she wore an ivory silk cocktail dress that Ian had ordered for the occasion. He'd insisted it was his tailor's idea since her dress matched the accessories on his charcoal silk suit. And she had to admit the lines of the sheath gown with its wide-set straps and square neck were pretty without shouting "bridal" when they'd walked into the courthouse.

So she watched the petals of the peach-colored lilies tremble in her bouquet while the justice of the peace made their temporary marriage official. She'd barely had time to think since agreeing to all this, from moving into the luxury penthouse suite of Ian's hotel to explaining her upcoming nuptials to Kinley and doing her job for the Foxfire after Ian had officially disclosed their relationship to Jeremy Singer. Since that last heated kiss on the beach, Ian hadn't pressed for further physical intimacy, which didn't surprise her since they'd agreed she would set the pace.

And yet, had he thought about those electric moments in the cabana as often as she had? Knowing that another kiss awaited them today—their wedding day—only added to the butterflies in her stomach as the judge made their marriage official. This time, however, things wouldn't spiral out of control the way they had at the beach. For one thing, she was prepared this time.

For another, there were witnesses, for crying out loud. Strangers, perhaps, but legal witnesses nevertheless.

As Lydia peered up into Ian's blue eyes and the rest

of the world seemed to disappear, she acknowledged that he had the power to make her completely forget herself. It was why she'd need to be very careful during the next twelve months or she would lose her heart to him all over again. Because no matter how much her body responded to the chemistry they generated, her head understood that Ian would always put the McNeills—the family and the business bearing their name—before her.

Ian was impeccably dressed in a custom-tailored H. Huntsman two-button gray silk suit, a white shirt with an ivory silk tie and a pocket square that took the outfit to another level of formal. She had to admit his tailor was correct in suggesting the outfits—their wedding photo snapped by the secretary out front was bound to be beautiful. For a wistful moment, Lydia wished she had Kinley with her to share what was normally a momentous occasion in a woman's life. But in the end, she'd thought it was best to simply keep the nuptials quiet until the marriage was a *fait accompli* since Lydia's mother would have been the first to insinuate herself into the media coverage.

"And now for the presentation of the rings," the justice of the peace announced, startling Lydia from her reverie and inducing a moment of panic.

Ian had said he'd take care of that. Had he remembered?

But he was already producing platinum bands. One was plain and masculine with some kind of etching. The other had a square yellow diamond in a cushion-cut setting that made her gasp out loud. The clerk continued, prompting them to repeat after him the standard vows from the simplest ceremony offered. Lydia repeated the words, hoping she wasn't making a colossal mistake, as she slid Ian's ring onto his finger and accepted the gorgeous canary sparkler on her own hand.

"I now declare you man and wife," the justice of the peace intoned, closing the black leather book he read from and shuffling it to one side of the polished oak desk behind him. "You may kiss your bride."

Lydia couldn't have said which idea provided the greater shock to her system. That she was now Ian's wife? Or that his lips were about to covers hers again?

She saw the glow of possessive fire in her groom's eyes—or maybe she just felt the answering fire in her blood. Either way, her heart rate increased to double-time and the silk bodice of her gown seemed to shrink, cutting off her air as she held her breath for a suspended moment.

When Ian dipped closer, however, he merely brushed his lips along her cheek and whispered in her ear.

"I'm banking the real kiss for later," he promised, the deep timbre of his voice smoking over her skin and calling to mind heated scenarios she felt sure no proper bride would be dreaming about at the altar.

Or, in this case, at the courthouse desk.

Off-kilter from that whispered vow and her new marital status, Lydia smiled woodenly for another photo as Ian finished their business and took copies of their paperwork. They didn't speak again until they left the courtroom and their words wouldn't be overheard.

"Congratulations, Mrs. McNeill," Ian told her as he

took her hand and led her from the building out into the heat of a Miami afternoon.

They'd traveled inland and north of the city for the courthouse visit, but Lydia hadn't paid much attention to their surroundings that morning when they'd parked the car. She'd been too nervous. Now she felt even more on edge thinking about Ian's plan to bank that kiss.

She lowered her nose to the bouquet of lilies and roses and inhaled the fresh fragrance to soothe her nerves.

"Congratulations to us both. We've fooled the world into thinking we are in love for the sake of our personal objectives." She hadn't meant to taint the day with the bitterness she felt since it would be easier to simply coast along like none of this was getting to her.

But something about the dress and the beautiful diamond now on her hand—all the trappings of a real wedding—had gotten under her skin.

"We've merely set aside our differences to help one another." He waved over a dark luxury SUV that was not the vehicle they'd arrived in. "Let's celebrate the occasion, shall we?"

Lydia's silk kitten heels skidded on the pavement as she halted. Ian slowed his step to take her elbow. Steady her.

"What do you mean?" She kept her eye on the SUV as it pulled up to the curb beside them, the tinted windows dark enough to prevent her from seeing inside. "I have an online meeting with an overseas supplier this afternoon."

She needed to regain her equilibrium. Work would help with that.

"I remember." Ian gave a nod toward the SUV and at his signal, a liveried driver stepped from the vehicle. "I've got a conference room prepared for you. I was hoping to sit in on some of it since I think this group has some architectural salvage pieces that could be incorporated into the courtyard design."

The driver opened the rear door of the SUV, revealing champagne-colored bucket seats as a blast of air-conditioning cooled Lydia's skin. A passing vehicle honked its horn at them as someone shouted "Congratulations, newlyweds!"

"You see?" Ian's hand slid around her waist to nudge her gently forward. "Everyone else wants us to seize the day. You can work for two hours while we are in the air and by the time you're done we'll be almost ready to land. Tonight, we can toast our marriage while the sun sets over the Pacific."

She didn't budge. The last time she'd been in the Pacific with him, she'd ended up pregnant.

"You know I wouldn't want to go back there—"

"Of course." He shook his head, lowering his voice for her ears only. "I wouldn't take you to Rangiroa. But we can be in Costa Rica in a couple of hours. We could have a decadent dinner overlooking the water, then return in the morning."

Lydia wondered far more about what could happen in the time *between* that decadent dinner and the flight home in the morning. Yet she was relieved to know Ian hadn't tried to resurrect the magic of last spring in the Polynesian islands when she'd fallen head over heels. Too many memories in that part of the world.

"I was not expecting anything like this. I don't have anything packed." She should probably have just said no outright. But the gesture was thoughtful even if it was more over-the-top than something she would have chosen.

"Taken care of. And if we are going to spend a year in close proximity, I think it would benefit us to try and find our footing as friends." He nodded at the driver again, chasing the attendant back to the front of the vehicle without a word.

"Friends." She tested the idea, unable to imagine such a tepid term for the relationship they'd once shared. But since that was in the past, perhaps he had a point. "This seems highly romantic for friendship."

"We just wed, Lydia. The illusion of a quick honeymoon will only cement our story for the rest of the world—our families included."

"So it's also for show." She nodded thoughtfully. She knew Ian would honor their agreement. There would be separate rooms. He would let her make the next move. She trusted in this implicitly because she knew his sense of honor.

It was that damnable kiss that had her rattled.

"And I think you'll enjoy being out of town when the news breaks about our nuptials," he reminded her.

Oddly, that won her over more than anything else he might have said. The thought of being in the papers—for any reason—made her skin crawl after growing up with her attention-seeking mother. As a bonus, she would have every reason in the world to ignore calls from her mom about her marriage for a little while longer.

"Deal." Lydia slid onto her seat inside the SUV and told herself the time together could be put to good use anyhow. She would speak to him about setting boundaries and house rules for living together over the next year once they settled into dinner.

Or, better yet, she would keep that topic for their *after*-dinner conversation. Because as the SUV whisked them away toward the nearest private airport, she knew she needed to figure out a way to fill that mysterious void of time between their meal and the return flight home.

Ian might be entitled to one more kiss, but she planned to make certain it didn't lead to a wedding night.

"I thought you weren't concerned with the terms of Gramps's will." Cameron McNeill scolded during a teleconference Ian was holding on board the chartered Gulfstream currently flying Lydia and him to Costa Rica for the night.

Ian had been sitting in the jet's small conference room with Lydia when his phone went berserk with repeated texts from both his brothers. Excusing himself from the online meeting with the overseas supplier to let Lydia handle it, Ian had taken a seat in the lounge and put his feet up before he dialed Quinn's office in New York, hoping to speak to his older—more cool-headed—sibling first.

But apparently Quinn only found out about the secret wedding because Cameron had barged into his office with an eight-by-ten printer blow-up of the photo taken at the Dade County clerk's office. Who leaked the information was anyone's guess since neither Ian nor Lydia was particularly well-known outside their social and professional circles, but clearly someone had keyed in on the McNeill name and publicized Ian's hasty marriage. The article Cameron had found was on a New York gossip blog, but the story was making the rounds in other places, fueled in part—Ian would guess—by how knockout beautiful Lydia looked in that ivory gown. She had a Mona Lisa smile in the photo, but there was something unmistakably mischievous in her bright green eyes.

No wonder the tabloids couldn't post the story fast enough.

"I didn't marry her just because of the will," Ian argued. "We had a prior relationship. Although I will admit, our grandfather's heart attack gave his terms a new sense of urgency."

Both his brothers were in Quinn's office in the Financial District back in New York. Quinn rested one hip on the window seat with a view of midtown behind him while Cameron paced the large office with the restless energy of a caged animal. Tall and rangy, he almost didn't fit in the frame captured by the webcam as he stalked back and forth in front of the antique bookshelves. Ian adjusted the angle on the fold-down screen above his seat to cut the glare from a nearby window as the plane began its descent.

He'd far rather be staring at his bride right now, but Lydia sat behind a partition in a separate section of the plane intended for teleconferencing on a big screen.

"You both told me Gramps was bluffing," Cameron reminded them. "You said he would back off on this. And now Ian tied the knot in secret and Quinn's getting married in two weeks." Cameron flung himself into the leather chair behind Quinn's oversize desk, wheeling the seat back a few feet. "I'm beginning to think it's you two who are bluffing."

"Our point, Cameron," Quinn interjected, loosening his gray silk tie, "was that you shouldn't marry for Gramps's sake. If you meet the right woman, that's one thing." He turned toward the camera—and Ian. "And I'm assuming this was a serious relationship for Ian to make him think of marrying."

Talking down Cameron's bluster was far easier than working his way around Quinn's canny gaze. The oldest of the three, Quinn had taken on the parenting role early when their mother divorced their father and the three McNeill sons split the year between the two of them. In Rio, with their mother, they were well supervised. The rest of the time, if their thrill-seeking, globe-trotting father, Liam, was in charge, Quinn proved a more reliable guardian for the three of them.

"Of course." Ian's reasons for marrying Lydia were complex enough that he wasn't entirely certain he could pick through them all himself. But he regretted walking out of her life without a fight last spring. He should have stayed. Should have been there for her when she miscarried their child. Now? He might have torched the old feelings for her, but he could damn well build on what they'd had before. He was comfortable with a marriage built on a legal foundation. He understood the terms and knew what was expected—unlike last time when he'd fallen too far too fast.

When both Quinn and Cameron stared at him expectantly, Ian realized he needed to offer up some kind of explanation. Not easy to do when he'd agreed not to reveal the secret of Mallory West.

"Lydia and I met last year when I was supervising the hotel project in Rangiroa." He clicked on his seat belt when he heard the chime overhead from the pilot and saw the sign go on. His gaze went to the conference room door, but it was still closed so Lydia must be buckling in for the descent in there. "We had a strong connection, but we wanted to see if it was because we met in a tropical paradise or if the bond could withstand the real world. Turns out, we're very good for each other."

Quinn frowned. Cameron's eyes widened.

"You dated for a year without telling anyone about her?" Cam asked, spearing his fingers through his dark hair.

"No." Ian should have thought through his response more before having this conversation but he wanted it done, and after the constant texts, he'd realized the McNeills weren't going to let a secret wedding stand without an inquisition. "We had our ups and downs, but we reconnected on the South Beach project and felt drawn to be together. We agreed we didn't want to detract from Quinn and Sofia's wedding so we thought we'd marry quietly. It didn't occur to me that filing for a license would flag any media interest."

"Wrong on that count, dude." Cameron reached for

the eight-by-ten photo of the courthouse wedding and waved it. "This sucker was making the rounds half an hour after you did the deal."

Ian gritted his teeth. "Quinn, please extend my apologies to Sofia if my awkward timing for the marriage upset her. We hoped to wait until after your wedding to announce ours. But if that's all, gentleman, I'm about ten minutes away from touching down in Costa Rica for my honeymoon."

"Sofia doesn't mind sharing the spotlight as a bride, only as a ballerina." The grin on Quinn's face was a new expression that they'd only started to see when the New York City Ballet dancer had entered his life.

Sometimes it still took Ian a second to reconcile that expression with his ever-serious older brother. He envied their complete devotion to one another. A kind of happiness Ian knew he'd never find in his temporary contract marriage.

There would be other rewards, however. For both of them.

Cameron elbowed Quinn. "Tell him why we really called, man."

Instantly on alert, Ian straightened, the fine leather in the chair squeaking as he moved.

"Is it Gramps? Is he okay?" He'd been worried about Malcolm McNeill's transition from Shanghai to New York, a trip that had been delayed twice because of his doctor's concerns and the need to travel with good medical equipment.

"He's fine," Quinn assured him. "But he contacted

us today after your wedding photo circulated online. He wants to meet with all of us."

Ian's gut knotted. Tightened. "Of course. How soon?"

"No immediate rush. He wouldn't want to disrupt the honeymoon." Quinn rose from his spot at the window ledge and flipped a page on the desk calendar. "Three days from now, maybe? I'll be in New York then and so will Cam, right?" He glanced up at their youngest brother.

"Sure thing," Cam answered as the plane broke through the cloud cover and the Costa Rican mountains became visible in a wavy carpet of dark green below.

"I'll be there." Ian's honeymoon would be over by then. "Any idea what he wants?"

"No." Quinn shook his head, brow furrowed. "But I would bring Lydia with you. She's part of the family now."

Ian nodded as he disconnected the call, hating the hollow feeling in his chest. He'd had good reasons for this marriage, but they weren't anything his grandfather was going to understand or approve. Even now, his new wife tended to business just on the other side of that partition. He couldn't hear her conversation, but he knew she would be bargaining for the best price on the decor and artwork she hoped to secure for the Foxfire. But soon, they would be alone and they could figure out what this marriage meant for their future.

His arrangement with Lydia was strictly between the two of them. She understood what was at stake and so did he. No complicated emotions meant they wouldn't crash and burn like they had last year. As for her other terms?

A McNeill knew that everything was open for negotiation. And he still had one kiss to bargain with.

Seven

Mrs. Lydia McNeill.

Seated inside her dressing room at their private villa in Costa Rica late that afternoon, Lydia read the engraved luggage tag on the buttery leather suitcase tucked under a bamboo shelf of the walk-in closet off the bathroom of her suite.

None of this felt real. Not the suite at the Honeymoon House. Not the flight on a Gulfstream jet that she'd boarded with only a few minutes' notice. And certainly not her new name.

Her eyes wandered over the wardrobe selections some unnamed staffer of Ian's had chosen for her. There was a silk tropical print maxi dress with coral-colored hibiscus flowers on a white background. A teal-colored pair of gauzy palazzo pants with a white sequined crepe halter top. A silver evening gown that looked like something a fairy princess would wear with gossamer-thin layers of vaguely iridescent fabric. Designer everything, of course. There were other clothes stacked neatly on the bamboo shelves, as well. Italian-made underthings. A nightgown so soft and sheer it was perfect for a bride with its combination of innocence and sensuality.

Except she wasn't a bride in the real sense. And she would not be putting that gorgeous nightdress on her body tonight.

"Lydia?" Ian called from the other side of the bathroom door. "Can I get you anything?"

Her stomach did a fluttery flip at the sound of his voice so close in this piece of paradise. No doubt he wanted to make sure the clothes fit before the dinner they would share on the open-air patio. He'd seemed pleased to show her their accommodations for the night, stressing the way the separate bedrooms fit her requirements but also gave them a chance to celebrate a new peace between them.

Except she didn't feel one bit peaceful about this marriage. If anything, the tropical retreat on the country's western coast only emphasized all the ways today fell short of what she'd once hoped to share with him. If not for the need to hide the true identity of Mallory West, she never would have said yes to this arrangement. But she needed to protect her matchmaking business and the important income it gave to a cause that meant so much to her, to women who inspired her with their strength and determination to be good mothers no matter what obstacles life handed them. Her mother had afforded parenthood by making herself and her daughter tabloid spectacles. Worse, she'd put her energy into fueling that drama rather than showing up at science fairs or even Lydia's high school graduation, which had unfortunately coincided with a face-lift.

Small wonder Lydia felt called to champion single moms who genuinely adored motherhood.

"No. I'll be out in a moment," she called, forcing herself to her feet. The dressing area was as luxe as some women's living rooms with a comfortable leather chair, plenty of mirrors and soft ambient lighting. But she could hardly afford to languish here, staring at her married name on a luggage tag.

Pulling on the silk maxi dress, Lydia let the fabric fall over the soft, imported lace slip that was too beautiful not to wear. She'd never spend her hard-earned dollars as a decorator on something so extravagant, but a woman would have to be blind not to appreciate the careful stitchwork that went into such a delicate design.

"There's no rush. The sun set won't set for another half hour," he called. After a moment, Lydia could hear the sound of his footsteps as he retreated deeper into the resort villa.

Leaving her to remember how many sunsets they'd watched together last spring when they'd been falling in love.

Twelve.

She'd marked them on a calendar, because that was the kind of silly nonsense young women indulged in when they fell in love. They drew hearts around meaningful days in a date book and scribbled effusive prose punctuated with too many exclamation marks in diaries. Lydia had been guilty on all counts.

Emerging from the dressing area, she stepped into her bedroom where she'd left all the windows open to the fresh air. A white-faced capuchin monkey sat on the low stone wall behind her hammock, munching on a piece of mango. Beyond the terrace, she could see the path down to the ocean, hear the gentle rush of waves to the sand.

Any other time, she would have loved an impromptu trip like this to an exotic destination. Travel was her favorite thing about her job since she couldn't afford it otherwise. But tonight, she was getting ready to face her new husband over the dinner table, and that made her too nervous to fully enjoy the surroundings.

"Wish me luck," she called to the monkey before it hopped off the wall and into the pink glow of the coming sunset.

Then, leaving her bedroom, she climbed the stairs to the third story of their private villa and the open-air deck where a local restaurant had set up the catered meal.

"You look incredible." Ian greeted her near the outdoor stairs, offering his arm to escort her past the lone table in the middle of the wooden deck overlooking the ocean. "I hope you found the clothing options as appealing as I do."

His blue eyes never left hers as he spoke, yet her whole body responded to his words, a tingling sensation skipping along her skin. She couldn't help but notice how handsome he looked in a dark suit with a white linen shirt open at the neck. Formal, but with a touch of the reprobate about him.

And now he was her husband.

"Thank you." Clearing her throat, she thought it better not to linger on how well Ian McNeill wore a suit. "The whole place is beautiful." She gestured to the view overlooking the water, the elegant table for two set with a crisp white cloth and laden with silver dishes, bright tropical flowers in vases and seven wax tapers flickering in a candelabra. "I thought it was nice of your local chef to text us his menu suggestions beforehand."

She'd received a message from the chef on the plane, offering a selection of dishes made from the freshest ingredients his culinary staff obtained that morning.

"Were you brave enough to order the grilled octopus he recommended?" Ian teased, drawing her to the edge of the deck to watch the pink sun slip lower on the horizon. His hand lingered at her waist even after they reached the wooden railing, his fingers separated from her skin by the thinnest silk.

Her heartbeat sped faster and she concentrated on the fragrant angel's trumpet flowers spilling over the railing at their feet, sending their heady perfume into the air to mingle with the salty brine of the ocean. Monkeys and birds called to one another as they hastened to their homes before dark fell. Better to think about monkeys and birds than the way Ian's touch affected her.

"I went with the Thai coconut shrimp and pineapple. The preparation sounded suitably tropical." The breeze blew a strand of hair across her chin.

Before she could fix it, Ian reached to skim it aside and tuck it behind one ear, his touch slow and warm. Deliberate.

Oh. So. Inviting.

"There's fresh mango salsa if you're ready for hors d'oeuvres." His voice rumbled low, vibrating along her sensitive skin. "Are you hungry, Lydia?"

Her gaze flashed up to his. Did he know how hard she struggled with the temptation he presented? Was he teasing her again?

But his blue eyes appeared concerned, not intent on seduction. Perhaps she shouldn't rush to judge him.

"I wouldn't mind a drink while the sun sets." Her mouth was dry and her heart felt more than a little bruised to undergo the trappings of marriage without the feelings that should go along with it. "Maybe we should have our toast now."

"Certainly." He excused himself to pour the champagne from a bucket chilling on a stand near their table. "I hope you don't mind, but we'll be serving ourselves tonight. The honeymoon suite service is…discreet in that way."

"Of course." She tensed, crossing her arms. "That way, if we decide we have to tear each other's clothes off before dessert, we'll have complete privacy to do so."

Ian finished pouring the champagne, but she could see his shoulders stiffen underneath the impeccably tailored suit jacket.

"I guess we would. But since you've been very clear about your expectations in this marriage, I realize that's not going to happen tonight." He stalked toward her, a champagne flute in each hand. "And that's another reason I thought it would be best for the waitstaff not to be around. I want to protect your privacy and respect your wishes about all things."

Somehow that consideration made her heart beat faster still. The sea breeze tickled the silk of her dress against her thighs and toyed with the spaghetti straps on her shoulders, a phantom lover's touch. She needed a dose of reality back in this faux honeymoon.

"You say that." She tugged the flute from his hands with a bit more force than necessary, her emotions getting the better of her as a few bubbles slid over the side of the glass. "And yet you persist in pretending that this is a real marriage with a flight to Costa Rica and a sunset meal in a villa called the Honeymoon House. I can't help but feel the weight of very different expectations."

"Lydia." He set his glass on the railing then guided hers there, too. "We need to present the world with a believable marriage or our agreement isn't worth anything." He folded both of her hands in his, turning her to face him. "I spoke to my brothers on the flight here and they informed me that news of our nuptials has already been leaked. Believe me when I tell you, the world is watching what happens next."

"Leaked?" She tried to imagine how that could happen. "Why? Who would care about our marriage?" Panic tightened in her chest as she thought of all the horrible ways the tabloids could ratchet up interest in a story. She'd been the object of media interest far too often in her life. "What are they saying?"

"Only that we married. Someone in the district court

offices must have leaked the news directly since my brothers had a copy of the wedding photo within thirty minutes of the ceremony."

"If they aren't saying anything ugly yet, they will soon." She needed to sit. Or maybe walk. She didn't know what she needed, but she felt all the makings of a full-blown panic attack coming on. "Excuse me."

Pulling away from his touch, she paced the deck.

"There is nothing ugly to say," Ian assured her, watching her progress but not following her, which she appreciated.

"Then they make something up. That's how the tabloids sell their sordid work." She recalled old headlines from her past—stories about her mother. Stories about her. "Did you know there was a whole year where the media sold papers on the idea that my mother was part of a religious cult that cast a spell on my father?" They'd taken a laughable photo of her mother in a Halloween costume and used it for weeks on end. "Then, there was a whole other year where they used zoom lenses to snap photos of her stomach to analyze it for a baby bump. And one extremely hellish year when *I* was photographed and accused of having a baby bump. At sixteen."

She didn't mention the stories that suggested her mother had pimped her out to rich men for a fat payday. Or the fact that she'd been treated for an eating disorder after being accused of looking pregnant as a vulnerable teenager.

Feeling a wealth of old resentment threaten to wash over her like a rogue wave, Lydia took the wooden stairs leading away from the third-floor deck all the way down to the beach. Vaguely, she heard Ian call out to her, and his footsteps as he followed her. She didn't stop, though. She couldn't get enough air into her lungs no matter how deeply she breathed. Kicking off her jeweled sandals, she let her toes sink into the powdery sand as she hurried down to the water's edge.

By the time Ian reached her side, she had the hem of her long silk maxi dress in one hand, the fabric hiked up to her knees so she could stand in the rolling surf. The warm water soothed her, lapping gently along her calves and beading up on her skin slick with the coconut oil lotion supplied as a resort amenity. Somehow the feel of the water against her skin took her heart rate down a notch, and she tipped her face into the soft sea breeze.

Ian removed his socks and shoes at the water's edge, preparing to join her. She thought about telling him not to bother—that she was okay—but then she wondered why she needed to pretend she was fine when she so often wasn't.

She'd denied herself comfort in life many times out of the need to look like she had her life together and a deep-seated desire to avoid scandal. But no matter what she did, she was a favorite target of the tabloid media. She could live the most pristine, blameless life possible and they'd still find some way to make a tawdry tale out of her.

And right now, as she watched Ian stride toward her with his broad shoulders that looked like they could take on the problems of the world, she had to wonder why she kept denying herself pleasure for the sake of a good reputation she would never achieve.

Ian McNeill was her husband. He was the most generous, amazing lover she'd ever had. And he'd made it very clear that he still wanted her.

As long as she could separate pleasure from a deep emotional commitment, couldn't she at least indulge herself for a little while?

Ian had almost reached Lydia's side when she sent him a look that sizzled over him like a lover's tongue.

The sensation was so tangible he had to halt his forward progress through the shallow surf. No way had he read her expression correctly. He was mixing up his own emotions with hers—seeing what he wanted to see in her bright green eyes. His heart slugged harder in his chest, urging him toward her, while he fought the need with all his might.

She'd just shared some hurtful memories he never knew about, so no way in hell was she thinking what he was thinking.

Get it together.

"Lydia." He forced an even tone into his voice, reminding himself that good men didn't confuse compassion with sex. "I'm so sorry you went through that as a teen."

He reached for her, cupping her cheek in one hand even as he maintained a bit of space between them. Her eyes slid closed at his touch, her cheek tilting into his palm in a way that urged him to give more physical comfort.

Reigniting the war within.

Gritting his teeth against all the ways he wanted to surround her body with his—protect her, pleasure her—Ian shifted closer to slide an arm around her waist. He drew her against him, fitting her to his side, resting his cheek on top of her silky hair. The scent of coconut drifted up from her skin. His mouth watered.

"I promise you," he assured her, stroking along the soft skin of her upper arm while he stared out to sea, "if anyone dares to initiate a story about you that isn't true, I will sue their company into bankruptcy."

"They will say I married you for money." She pulled back to look him in the eye. "The same way my mother pursued my father."

"We both know nothing could be further from the truth." He'd tried to include a financial settlement in their contract, but she'd refused. Had she done so because she anticipated that kind of negative press?

"Your family will have their doubts about my intentions in this marriage. As will all of Manhattan. I received a famously small settlement from my father upon his death." She knotted the silk of her skirt at one knee so she didn't need to hold on to the fabric to keep it out of the water. "There will be questions about my motives for marrying you and the press speculation will only fuel the fire."

He'd seen that trick with a skirt hem in Rangiroa a few times, and he liked this side of her that was a little messier.

"My family has faith in my judgment." He'd already

told them to stand down where she was concerned. "And that means they will trust you."

When she didn't answer right away, he noticed that she was staring out at the horizon where the sun was sliding the rest of the way into the sea. She'd told him once that she liked to make a wish on it before it disappeared.

"I wish *you* could trust me to make you happy for the next twelve months." He got the words out just before the final glowing orange arc vanished.

The sky glowed pink and purple in the aftermath, the ocean reflecting the colors in watery ripples while a heron and a pair of white ibis flew overhead.

"I don't think that's such a good thing to wish for." She turned to face him, her exposed skin reflecting the sunset hues.

"No?"

"No," she told him flatly. "Investing too much in this marriage will only make things all the more complicated when our year together is done." She folded her arms across her chest and stared down into the water where they stood. "We both need to remember this is a business arrangement. Nothing more."

"One thing doesn't have to preclude the other, does it?" He turned his attention to her arm, where the strap of her dress flirted with the edge of her shoulder. "We can be happy and respect the business arrangement, too."

Maybe this time together would help cure him of his preoccupation with her. He'd barely dated since they'd split.

"I've been thinking about that." She glanced down at the water where the gentle swell of the tide lapped at her ankles. She lifted one foot and skimmed it over the surface in a slow arc in front of her. "About the benefits of marriage."

His throat dried up. He stayed very still to keep from touching her the way he wanted to, convincing her with his hands and his mouth how *beneficial* this relationship could be for both of them. He'd promised her she could set the pace with any kind of physical relationship and he wouldn't earn her trust anytime soon if he took that power out of her hands.

But the temptation to draw her into the water—into his arms—was so strong he could barely breathe.

"Like Costa Rican vacations?" He tried for a light tone but failed, his whole body fueled with a biological imperative to take his bride to his bed.

"This is definitely a treat." She quit her game of drawing her toes through the water, turning to face him in air that felt suddenly too still. "But I was thinking more along the lines of how—" she bit her lip for a second before pressing on "—*satisfying* we both found our previous relationship."

Blood pounded through his temples for a split second before surging south.

"Meaning you're reconsidering the idea of separate bedrooms?" He kept his eyes on hers in the growing dimness despite the flickering tiki torches dotting the sand near Honeymoon House. "We need to be very clear about this point, Lydia, since it's your move next."

During the heavy beat of silence that followed, an

owl hooted from a tree nearby. In the distance, Ian spied a party boat on the waves, the music cranked high as the vessel sped through the dark water.

"It occurs to me that no matter how hard I've tried to live beyond reproach, I'm always going to be a target for the tabloids. In their eyes, my mother was a gold digger who duped my father into getting her pregnant. And I'm the bait she used to ensure she got her payoff." Lydia shrugged and the spaghetti strap that had been teetering on the edge of her shoulder gave up the ghost, sliding down her arm. "Why should I create some exaggerated facade of respectability when I'll forever be a tabloid story waiting to happen?"

He dragged his gaze from her bare shoulder and the delicate curve of her neck. "You make it sound like being with me compromises your reputation."

"No. I only mean that I have to stop worrying about what other people think of me and find what happiness I can. Because no matter what I do or how careful I am, I will be a magnet for rumors."

He sifted through her words. Put them in the context of the one question that burned brightest in his brain as the stars began to dot the sky above them.

"You want to find happiness." This seemed highly relevant. "And you agree that there were *satisfying* aspects of our relationship before things fell apart." Heat burned over him despite the fact that he stood ankle-deep in the Pacific. He wanted a taste of her more than he wanted his next breath as the tropical air blanketed his skin with sultry touches.

"Correct." She kept her arms clenched around herself, but there was no mistaking the challenging tilt of her chin. The throaty edge in her voice.

He waded an inch closer. Their bodies weren't touching. But the water swirled between them in circles that seemed to connect them anyway.

"Can I assume that you're open to revisiting those satisfying aspects?" He wouldn't have to use his kiss as a bargaining tool to woo her into his bed tonight.

"I'm starting to think it would be foolish to deny ourselves." Her words were breathless, a barely there sound that caressed his ears.

"I couldn't agree more." He waited for her touch. Watched for it.

Even the cries of birds and monkeys seemed to quiet in the still moment of her decision.

"It's my wedding night," she informed him, her voice picking up strength and volume. "I don't need to sleep alone."

"Not when I want you in my bed for days on end," he assured her, only too happy to describe exactly how thoroughly he would pleasure her if given the opportunity to touch her tonight. "Although I will be very disappointed if we are sleeping."

Despite the growing dark, he could see the convulsive movement of her throat as she swallowed. Licked her lips.

"Ian?"

"Mmm?"

"I think I'd like that kiss now."

Eight

A year ago, they would have fallen on each other with the ravenous hunger of lovers who need to be touching all the time.

Truth be told, she was so ready for his kiss, she felt more than a little ravenous now as they stood in the surf outside Honeymoon House.

But their relationship was much different now. Careful. Tenuous. And—she still couldn't believe it—they were married. Maybe that's why Ian took his time closing the distance between them. Instead of taking her in his arms, he stroked along her bare shoulder where one strap of her gown had fallen away. She hadn't realized how cool her skin was from standing in the water until she felt the warmth of his hand when he made contact. His callus-roughened palms reminded her he wasn't the kind of developer who simply drew plans, although he was talented enough to design his own buildings.

No. She'd seen Ian McNeill clamber up ladders and take a crowbar to stubborn wall supports himself, never afraid of getting his hands dirty on a job site. She liked that his millions hadn't robbed him of the ability to walk among the workmen or appreciate the less glamorous aspects of actual physical construction.

"Are you cold?" he asked, perhaps feeling the difference in their skin temperatures, and yet still he didn't kiss her in spite of her request. He held back, even as the fire in his eyes broadcast how much he wanted her.

"I'm not chilly at all. Thank you, though." She was plenty hot on the inside; in fact, she was anticipating that kiss, aching for him to take her lips. To take her. "I like being outside." She could breathe deeply out here without feeling suffocated by all the expectations weighing her down back home. Without the scandal rocking her world again.

"You're trembling," he observed softly, his other hand coming between them to skim a knuckle along her lower lip, drawing out the moment.

Lydia nipped it to put an end to that line of conversation since she was overwhelmed by her feelings for him. *Sensual feelings*, she told herself. *Nothing deeper.* The trembling didn't have a thing to do with romantic notions about the relationship she was undertaking again.

Finally—*thank goodness*—Ian cupped her face and tipped her chin up, perhaps to see her better in the moonlight. The glow of the tiki torches on the beach and dotting the railing of the deck on the third floor of

Honeymoon House didn't give off enough light to see each other well now that the sun had set.

The look in his eyes sent of a flash fire along her skin. Brooding and intense, he stared at her as if she were a complicated puzzle he'd rather devour than solve. So when his kiss came, she was surprised by its devastating gentleness. His soft, full lips covered hers, coaxing them apart to taste and explore.

Sighing into him, she gave herself up to the wholly masculine feel of his strong arms wrapped around her. The hint of sandalwood on his skin unleashed a torrent of fiery memories. Stripping each other's clothes off in a hotel dining room because they couldn't wait to get to the bedroom. Ian slipping her swimsuit aside to pleasure her behind an island waterfall where no one could see them. Her hoarse shouts of fulfillment when he'd demonstrated a deftness with his tongue that had been her undoing, not just once, but many, many times.

Past and present mingling, Lydia pressed her body to all that hard, masculine heat, wanting to lose herself in him. In pleasure. No holding back. She wanted those memories to be reality now. The good memories. Not the aftermath of lies and deceit.

She worked the buttons of his linen dress shirt, hastily unfastening each one to splay greedy hands over his sculpted chest and abs. The moonlight shone down on his bronzed skin, making her greedy to see more of him. All of him.

"I want to take you inside." He captured her questing fingers, stilling her hungry explorations before he kissed the fingertips, one at a time. "I need to see you."

With a jerky nod, she agreed, even though she could have gladly pulled *An Affair to Remember* moment and wrestled him to the beach to make love in the surf.

Together, they hurried out of the water. He scooped up both pairs of shoes and set them on the first stair leading to the villa. She followed him barefoot up the wooden steps and onto the cool stone patio of the first floor. Here, the light from the small gas torches set at intervals in the stone railing cast plenty of light on them as he led her toward the outdoor shower.

And while she would have also pulled her dress off then and there, Ian turned on the shower spray at foot level just long enough to rinse the beach sand from their toes. She unfastened the knot she'd put in her dress hem to hold it up, letting the silk fall back around her calves while he shut off the nozzle.

She eyed his strong back as he straightened, the ripple of muscles evident through the thin, pale linen of his shirt.

"Damn, Lydia, you're killing me when you look at me like that."

Ian tugged her closer with one hand. Caught openly ogling him, she felt her cheeks heat and was glad for the rosy glow of the torchlight.

"I'm sure I don't know what you mean," she told him archly, turning to head up the stairs since both bedrooms were situated on the second floor.

"What I'd like to know—" he palmed the small of her back, shadowing her movements as his voice overwhelmed her senses "—is what you're thinking about when you look at me that way."

"Probably something really benign," she lied, teasing him only because she knew there would be an end to both their torments soon. "Like what you'll think of the outdoor rugs I chose for the Foxfire courtyard."

She paused in the hallway between the two bedrooms, unsure which way to go. The villa was exposed to the Costa Rican elements on three sides and they'd left all the retractable windows open to savor the mild weather. She could see into his bedroom where a king-size platform bed covered in a black duvet and batik-patterned pillows was illuminated only by the flickering outdoor torches of the master suite's deck.

"Rugs? Not even close," he taunted lightly as he steered her toward his bedroom and the small shelter it offered from the thick, jungle-like branches that brushed against the open half walls. "I'll bet you were thinking about how much you wanted our clothes off."

He turned her to face him and her heart raced a crazy staccato beat as her gaze fell to his bare chest where she'd already undone half the buttons on his shirt.

"If we're being totally honest—" she hooked her finger into the gap of the soft linen and wrangled another button free, her knuckle grazing the warmth of those beautifully chiseled abs "—I was far more fixated on getting your clothes off than my own."

"That can be arranged." He stood in shadow, his back to the glow of torchlight while he shrugged out of the shirt, letting the expensive material float to the floor behind him. "I'll gladly do what it takes to put that gleam in your eyes again."

He tipped her face up and their gazes collided. Her

breathing hitched and her skin tingled everywhere. She was seized with the need to kiss and touch him. To follow all the pent-up emotions their reunion had stirred, leaving her aching for him for days on end.

"There it is." He ran his hands down her shoulders, dragging the only remaining strap of her dress off so the bodice slid loose to sag against her breasts. His eyes remained on hers, however. "There's that look I like. When you watched me walking into the surf tonight, you were staring at me with that expression in your eyes. It was all I could do not to haul you into bed like a caveman."

He turned her inside out with just his words while the heady scent of angel's trumpet and jasmine drifted on the warm breeze.

"I do that to you?" She leaned forward to press a kiss to his chest, savoring the smooth warmth of one pectoral. "I wish I'd known I had that power."

"Lydia." He skimmed a hand down her hair. Stroking. Petting. "You distract me too much already. If I told you everything you do that drives me crazy with wanting you, I'd never get anything done."

Through the veil of her hair, he toyed with the zipper at the back of her dress, flicking at the toggle and tracing the path it would take if he pulled it down. She thought she'd come out of her skin faster than she'd get out of her clothes, the slower pace making her flesh feel too tight and sensitive.

"You say that." She pressed another kiss to his chest, letting her tongue flick along the silken heat of smooth pectoral there. Then, gathering her courage, she arched up on her toes to speak softly in his ear. "But if I was anywhere near as irresistible as you claim, I'd be underneath you already."

With both her hands on his chest now, Lydia could feel the hard shudder go through him. Only then did she understand the restraint he was exercising.

"Is that what you think?" His hands pressed harder against her, molding her to him before he found that zipper again and started to ease it downward. "Because I was doing everything in my power to make tonight different than any time we've been together before. To give us a fresh start."

Her heart turned over in her chest even though she'd told herself a hundred times she wasn't going to let her emotions get all tangled up in this like last time. She couldn't go through that heartbreak again. Right now, she wanted to lose herself in pleasure, not think about a fresh start.

And yet...

How unexpectedly thoughtful of him to want to make tonight a new beginning. To make it different from their past together. She wanted to tell him that was unnecessary, but with the silk dress gliding lower and lower on her body, she found it difficult to argue with him. The sound of the sea rolling in provided a soothing music in harmony with the rustle of palm fronds, drowning out everything else as she shimmied the rest of the way out of her dress. The silk pooled at her feet, leaving her clad in the beautiful imported lace lingerie she thought he'd never see tonight.

"You're my wife now," he reminded her, backing her

toward the bed while his blue eyes moved languidly over her body. They were both more visible now as they neared the bedside sconce. "Not just my lover. We should make tonight the start of something new. Different."

"I like that idea." She was breathless. So turned on she could hardly find enough air to speak. Underneath the coral-colored lace, her breasts tightened to impossibly taut peaks. "A new start, that is."

She remembered—vaguely—that she wanted their relationship to be different than before. So a do-over was a good thing. She could protect her heart from all the ways this marriage could hurt her before they said goodbye. But right now, she mostly wanted Ian McNeill all over her. Inside her.

He lowered her to the bed, her body meeting the soft duvet while Ian loomed over her, shirtless and golden in the torchlight. He unfastened his belt. She held her breath.

"But, Ian?" She chewed her lip as he freed himself from his trousers, her eyes sliding to the gray silk boxers that couldn't conceal how much he wanted her.

"Yes, wife?" He bent over her on the bed, brushing a kiss over one hip, his lips working a decadent magic on her skin.

"We don't need to make *everything* different than it was before." She remembered multiple orgasms—the first of her life. And then there was the tireless lovemaking that woke her in the middle of the night and left her sleeping more deeply—happily—than ever before.

She felt his lips smile against her hip while he kissed

her there, and then licked a path along the hem of her lace underwear.

Her eyes might have crossed before she closed them, giving herself over to him.

"No?" He kissed. Licked. Kissed again.

Behind her eyelids, she was already seeing stars just thinking about what he might do next. Her body tensed with anticipation.

"No. Some things were really quite perfect." She debated shouldering her way out of the strapless lace bra top holding her in, the fabric like a straitjacket when she wanted to feel nothing but Ian's body against hers.

Her breath came in short pants. She licked her lips. Wriggled her hips. Arched her spine to get closer to him because she needed him. Now.

"Perfect." He repeated the word in a whisper over her skin, trailing a kiss into the indent of her waist as he covered her with his body.

Finally. Finally.

A moan of satisfaction hummed through her as the hard length of him pressed at the juncture of her thighs. She dragged him down to kiss her. She nipped his lower lip, unable to stay still beneath him. She couldn't get close enough, her breasts flattening against the hard wall of his chest in a delicious caress that left her wanting more.

The humid air hung heavy on her skin and his too, a salty ocean tang that made the night feel all the more exotic but familiar, as well. Like the past, but different.

When his mouth closed on her breast through the soft lace, she twined her fingers in his hair. Held him close and clung to the sensations he loosed in her with each flick of his tongue. He unfastened the series of hooks at the front until she could sidle free of the confining fabric. She slid one leg around his, wanting him everywhere.

He must have guessed, or else he was as caught up as she was, because he skimmed a touch between her thighs, teasing over the damp lace until she shuddered with the small convulsions that were a precursor to all the pleasure that was to come. She remembered this wildness, the heated, primal joining that had overwhelmed her in the past.

As Ian tugged aside the thin scrap of panties to find her slick core, Lydia forgot everything but the way he made her feel. Mindless. Sensual. Wanted.

With each stroke of his fingers, each press of his palm against her, the tension in her body coiled more tightly. He wound her up, taking her higher. She gripped his shoulders. Breathed his name.

And flew apart in a wave of orgasms that washed over and over her. It was even more amazing than she remembered. A blissful retreat from the world to a place where only pleasure remained. She reeled with the aftershocks for long moments knowing the night was only beginning.

Soon, he would be deep inside her. Joined with her physically to make their marriage legal. Binding.

As he poised above her, his body taut with a hunger he hadn't appeased yet, Lydia had just enough wits about her to wonder how she'd ever survive the onslaught of pleasure while guarding her heart. She

walked an emotional tightrope tonight and—possibly—
for many nights to come.

Heaven help her, she couldn't stop if she tried.

Ian needed her with a fierceness that defied logic.

Beads of sweat popped up along his brow. He ground
his teeth together against the ache of it all. He'd waited
this long to take her. He could wait another minute to
chase the sudden shadows from her gaze.

"Look at me," he commanded, unable to soften the
edge in his voice. Instead, he simply lowered the volume.

His gaze met hers. There were definitely shadows
there. The light was dim, but he knew the nuances of
those green eyes. Time hadn't dimmed his memory of
this woman's moods.

"I want you," she said simply. Urgently.

Was she running from her shadows by losing herself
in this night with him? He was too amped up to figure
out what might have upset her, but he knew she wanted
him, too. She couldn't hide that.

"That's going to happen soon," he promised, already
clutching a condom in one hand. "But I never gave you
the proper kiss to commemorate the day."

Her eyebrows lifted.

"There were kisses," she argued, lifting her neck to
plant another on his cheek, to one side of his mouth. "I
was there for a lot of highly memorable kisses just now."

"Not a 'you may kiss the bride' kind of kiss." He let
go of the foil wrapper, setting it beside the pillow near
her head, where dark hair spilled in every direction.

She was so damn beautiful.

"I'm not sure how that kind is any different." Frowning, she seemed appropriately distracted from whatever had bothered her a moment ago.

And that made holding back worth it, even if he throbbed as though a vise were clamped around him.

"I put it off before because I wanted to get it right." He wanted her to be happy on her wedding day, and he wanted to be the one to banish those shadows in her eyes. Call him old-fashioned, but even if it was a temporary marriage, Lydia was now his wife. She deserved something to mark that occasion—something more than the courthouse visit. "It didn't seem like the kind of kiss to share in front of strangers."

Her eyes locked on his. Curiosity mixed with desire. And he was damn glad he'd taken this moment to remind them both what it meant to be together tonight. Digging under the covers, he found her left hand and held it, running his finger over the platinum band and square-shaped diamond there. He twisted it gently—back and forth a few degrees in either direction before resettling it right where it had been. Resting it there anew.

Then, his gaze lowering to her lips, he kissed her. Savored her. He felt the tension ease out of her as her arms went around him. She returned the kiss with a sweetness that almost made him forget everything else that had passed between them.

And before he let himself think about that, he retrieved the condom and rolled it into place. Never breaking the kiss, he made room for himself between her thighs and pressed deep inside her. Her fingernails scored his chest, scratching lightly as he found a rhythm that pleased them both. Heat flared all over, building gain until it roared up his spine with new urgency. He'd put this off too long. Forced himself to wait and wait. So now when the pressure built, it powered through him with an undeniable force.

He wrapped Lydia in his arms, rolled her on top of him so he could watch her. She bit her lip, her dark hair spilling over her shoulders as she moved in time with him, her narrow hips rocking in time with his.

He remembered so much about her and he used it to his advantage now, recalling exactly where to touch her to send her spiraling into ecstasy. He reached between them, fingering his way to where she was slick with heat. She arched back, still for a moment, before she collapsed over him, her body convulsing all around him. The soft, feminine pulses were his undoing, the feel of her pleasure spiking his own.

Their shouts mingled with the night birds and howler monkeys, a wild coming together that pounded through both of them. When the spasms slowed and stopped, Ian turned her in his arms so they lay side by side, breathing the same humid air of the Costa Rican jungle while the bamboo fan blades turned languidly overhead.

Their marriage was real now. The words they'd spoken in front of the county clerk were only a precursor to this, the ultimate bond that made it legitimate. He had been prepared to wait to consummate the marriage until she was ready, but maybe Lydia had seen that their union could have as many benefits as they allowed themselves.

Tonight might be a shadow of what a real marriage between them could have been like. But he could take a whole lot of pleasure from more nights like this. Whatever had driven her into his arms tonight, Ian wasn't about to argue.

Nine

Seated at the polished stone patio table across from Ian two hours later, Lydia decided she preferred dining while dressed in one of the T-shirts and boxer shorts he'd packed for their trip. Wrapped in a cotton throw blanket that she'd found on the back of the couch, she tucked sock-clad feet beneath her while Ian filled their water glasses from the pewter pitcher, still cold all these hours after they should have eaten.

But the caterers had left several covered trays of food with small candles burning in the stands below them on the buffet, while other dishes had been placed on ice, so everything she'd put on her plate remained delicious. She helped herself to another bite of the baked pineapple that was so good she couldn't wait to recreate it at home. Or maybe everything simply tasted better after multiple orgasms. She didn't think she could shake the pleasurable feeling in her veins if she tried.

Even knowing her marriage was utterly unorthodox and it wouldn't last beyond this time next year, Lydia was determined to savor the joy of the night. There would be worries enough when they returned to the real world.

For now, eating cold lobster at midnight overlooking the Pacific with a fascinating, handsome dinner companion, she couldn't muster the energy to worry just yet. The heady scent of flowers wafted on the sea breeze, and she reveled in how her cooling skin was still warm from a shared shower with Ian.

She flushed just thinking about the things he'd done to her under the shower spray. But better to think about that than the moments when he'd toyed with her wedding ring and kissed her as though she would be his bride forever.

"More wine?" he offered, lifting the decanter of pinot grigio.

With his jaw shadowed by stubble and his dress shirt unbuttoned to his waist, Ian still managed to look completely at home at the formal dining table, his blue eyes hooded from the glow of the candelabra that had remained burning thanks to the glass globes around the tapers.

"No, thank you." She took another drink from her water glass. "Being in Miami and now here, I'm thirstier than usual from the heat."

Or else she was thirstier than usual from the unaccustomed physical activity. Sweet, merciful heaven, but the man could do incredible things to her.

"Do you usually stay in Manhattan over the summer?" he asked as he bit into a slice of fresh mango. It was an innocuous question but one that reminded her of the differences in their worlds.

"Unless a client hires me for a job outside the city, I'm always in Manhattan." She shifted the cotton throw on her shoulders and tucked closer to the table. "I can't afford to get used to the McNeill lifestyle."

All around the deck, tiki torches still burned. The animal life had quieted some so she could hear the roll of waves onto the beach below along with the ever-present swish of palm fronds in the breeze.

Ian frowned. "We have a house in the Hamptons. You could go there on the weekends if you'd like to escape the heat."

"That's just what I mean." She remembered how many times her mother had dragged her to Newport in the summer, couch-surfing with any potential acquaintance while she tried to wrangle an invitation from Lydia's father to stay at the Whitney mansion. "I don't want to get in the habit of living beyond my means."

He wiped his hands on a linen napkin and set it aside, then moved to take the seat next to her at the round table. Just his physical nearness affected her, spiking her heart rate the same way it had every single time he got close to her. It had been this way last year when she'd fallen for him. It had stayed that way even when she'd been angry with him and told him they were finished. Right to the last minute when he'd walked out of her hotel room in Rangiroa, she'd felt the hum of response to his nearness.

"Lydia, we'll be sharing my home in New York. You need to be comfortable there." He took her hand, threading his fingers through hers. "Our marriage needs to be believable."

She stared down at their interlocked hands, wondering what was for show now. His touch? His kiss? She needed to remember that they had a relationship based on mutual needs. Ian's legal need to keep the family business in family hands, and her need to protect the secret of Mallory West so she could continue her more lucrative side business of matchmaking to help struggling mothers. Simple.

And yet it would be so easy to let the chemistry she shared with this man distract her from her goals.

"I don't need to start spending weekends in the Hamptons to have people believe our marriage is real." She plucked a plump berry from a bowl of fresh fruit and took a bite. "Even if we were wildly in love and planning our forever, I wouldn't suddenly quit my job and give up my work with Moms' Connection."

"But you can expand your role there now." He leaned back in his seat, keeping her hand in his and resting their joined palms on his knee while the candelabra candles burned down a little more, dripping wax on the linen tablecloth. "Maybe chair your own fund-raiser for the group when we return to New York."

The possibility shimmered like a beautiful mirage. Help her favorite cause? Aid the women who had given so much to her those weeks when she'd been thinking she would be a single mother to Ian's child? She could do so much good there.

Except that it wouldn't last. Her time as a New York socialite would be short-lived.

"That's what I mean, Ian. In twelve months' time, I won't have the kind of social standing needed to chair Manhattan charity events. If anything, my reputation might very well be in a worse state than ever, and that's saying something considering my past."

"Then take a one-year position on their board. Do what you can to further their goals in that time. All I'm saying is, it would be good to get involved at the level people would expect of my wife." He turned her shoulders toward him so she faced him head-on. "You might as well work with a group you support anyhow."

"Thank you." She couldn't deny the idea intrigued her. "It's generous of you to suggest."

He shrugged like it wasn't a big deal to write a substantial check to a group that struggled for every dime. "You'd be doing the legwork, not me. Besides, I'd like to find ways for you to be happy over the next year." A wicked grin slid over his face. "Outside of bed, I mean. Because that much I believe we have covered."

He drew her forward, his eyes intent on hers before he closed them at the last moment. He nipped her lower lip, and then soothed the spot with his tongue, sending a shiver of pleasure all over her body.

He hadn't been kidding about making her happy in bed. Ian McNeill had that power locked down.

"What about when we go back to the real world?" she asked, her eyes fluttering open. "I'm concerned you may have underestimated the level of interest the press will take in this marriage. Not to mention the interest my mother will have."

"We'll deal with that as it comes," he said firmly. "For now, if you're finished with dinner, I'd like my dessert."

The heated look in his eyes turned her blood molten.

"What about mine?" She pushed the words past lips gone dry.

"You'll get yours, Lydia McNeill," he whispered in her ear before licking along the lobe, his hand already seeking the hem of the T-shirt she wore and tucking underneath it. "That much I promise you."

An hour later—after much taste-testing of the dessert menu and his wife—Ian counted himself a lucky man. The marriage might be fake, but Ian was confident he was having as rewarding a honeymoon as any groom on the planet.

He sure as hell had a hotter wife than anyone else.

He had convinced Lydia to join him in the oversize hot tub off the master suite, another space that was mostly open to the elements. The sinks and bathroom had been situated on an interior wall, but the shower and hot tub could be partially exposed to the villa's private patch of forest on the steep mountainside that led down to the beach. With no other accommodations for miles, the Honeymoon House was the perfect blend of seclusion and luxury, with services available from the local resort.

Ian had shut down all the outdoor torches now that

it was well past midnight. The house was quite dark except for the moonlight spilling across the hot tub's surface and the spa light underwater.

He watched as Lydia stripped off her T-shirt. His T-shirt, actually. He liked seeing her in his clothes. And he really, really liked seeing her out of them. He couldn't take his eyes off her now as she looked back over one shoulder before slipping a thumb into the band of the boxer shorts she'd folded over and tucked to fit her slender frame.

It didn't matter that the shadows were thick around them. He could see the shape of her hips as she wriggled free of the cotton. And, damn, he could see her even better as she faced the tub and hurried—naked—into the bubbling water.

Her high, firm breasts hid just beneath the surface. For a moment he wondered why he'd suggested this since what he really wanted was to bury himself inside her all over again and the hot tub was only going to slow him down. But then, this was her honeymoon, too. And he wanted to make sure he made their time here unforgettable for her.

She was already worried about returning to the real world and facing their families, which reminded him what a good, generous woman she was. He didn't want her to worry about any of that when he could take care of everything. She was his to protect now. He planned to erase all those concerns tonight before they slept.

"It's your turn," she called from the water, her glossy, dark hair spilling around her like a mermaid in the clear bubbles.

"Just admiring the view." He stripped off his shirt that he had hadn't even bothered to button, tossing it onto the wood planks of the deck.

"So am I." She leaned back against one of the neck rests of the molded spa. "Feel free to take your time."

"You saying things like that makes it all the tougher to take my time. I hope you know that." He eased his shorts off, his body ready to go again from just looking at her.

Though her playful words only amped him up more.

"Maybe I like cracking that legendary McNeill control." She watched him as he stepped down into the tub beside her. Her pale skin was a liquid shadow in the water.

"Legendary?" He gathered up the hair floating around her and laid it over her shoulder. "You overestimate me."

"Do I? I've heard you're as coolheaded in the boardroom as you are on the job site—never rattled, utterly restrained, and it's impossible to guess what you're thinking."

Is that how she saw him?

He studied her pretty face washed clean of any makeup, her lips still deeply pink without any added color. Her eyelashes were dark and spiky from the water. And she studied him as thoroughly as he did her. It amazed him they didn't understand each other better.

"I'm actually more of the negotiator of the family. The link between my two brothers, who make a habit of taking the opposite views on just about everything." If he and Lydia were going to spend this year together, it might help if they knew each other better outside the bedroom. "Far from being the guy with legendary control, I'm the one most likely to do the compromising."

She arched her eyebrows and smiled. "Ian McNeill? Compromise? I can think of a whole host of independent contractors working on the luxury hotel in Rangiroa who would have been astounded to hear it. For that matter, most of my colleagues at work on the Foxfire are already nervous about the possibility of budget overruns."

"That's not necessarily a bad thing." He wondered if she was overstating the case. "I respect deadlines and budget constraints. I expect the people who work with me to follow suit."

"And they rush to do just that. All I'm saying is that you're not the easiest of bosses. I can't picture you as the one in your family who compromises."

That bugged him, actually. He forced himself to lean back against the seat though, unwilling to let her see as much.

"My whole life, I've been the one in the middle. In age as well as temperament." He reached for her, lifting her legs and laying them across his lap so she was now sitting sideways in her corner seat. "When Quinn wants a highbrow hotel launch and Cameron thinks we could hit the youth market with a launch during Comic-Con, I'm saddled with finding the halfway point. And that's been true since the time Quinn was old enough to build a soap box derby car and spent all day painting it black with silver stripes, only to wake and find Cameron had used decoupage to paste 'artful nudes' all over the body."

She only half smothered a laugh. "I'd love to hear your compromise on that one."

"Before or after Quinn broke Cam's nose?" That had been the first of some ugly fights. They'd learned to work around each other—and respect their very different approaches—since then. But the learning curve hadn't been pretty. "I tried repainting the car, but since I was only eight at the time and had to paint over decoupage, it lacked the cool refinement of Quinn's version."

Lydia was quiet for a long moment. Feeling that he'd failed to bring the right touch of humor to the story, Ian wished he'd kept it to himself.

"Perhaps not getting your own way in the family dynamic made you all the more disposed to dictating the terms in your life." She tipped her head up to the moonlight for a moment, giving him a tempting view of her long neck and damp shoulders.

But her words had distracted him even more than her body. Did she have a point?

He filed the notion away, unwilling to lose this time with her by getting caught up in their differences.

"What about you?" He turned the tables, only because it was the first conversational tidbit that occurred to him and he didn't want to start analyzing his own situation. "No one defaces your prized possessions when you're an only child."

She tensed, a reaction he felt where he stroked her calves under the water.

"I wasn't, though." She straightened in the tub, but didn't turn away from him or move her feet off his lap. "My mother made sure I was very aware that I had half siblings and that my father treated them very differently from how he behaved with me."

"Damn. I'm sorry, Lydia." He sure as hell hadn't meant to stir up old hurts.

"No." She shook her head and waved a hand as if she could brush aside his concern. "Don't be. I think she hoped throughout my entire childhood that Dad would swoop in and raise me for her, but that never happened. Once she realized that she was going to have to be my mother—well, I was mostly grown by then. But we got along better once I stopped expecting her to be a mom and started enjoying her as a friend."

"Yeah?" He massaged her feet, hoping to ease away the tension that had crept into her body since he started this conversation. He hated to think she'd never been her parents' number one priority. "Maybe I ought to try that approach with Liam. He was the nonparent in my youth. But at least I had my mother and grandfather."

"Although you were the one standing between your siblings when they came to blows." Her green eyes pinned his for a moment before shifting lower. "Maybe that's why you and I ended up getting along so well. For a few incredibly memorable weeks, we put one another first."

Until they didn't.

He wondered if that realization echoed through her with the same dull ache that it did for him. But Lydia was already shifting closer, her naked thighs straddling his on the hot tub seat and making it impossible to think about anything but her. Them.

This moment.

* * *

Lydia needed to lose herself in Ian.

She didn't want to think about how much it had hurt when he put his family before her. When he'd refused to see how painful it might be for her that he'd allowed his grandfather to collect potential bride prospects for Ian when she thought she'd been the most important woman in his life.

All he had to do was deny it. Or explain it. But he'd done neither, drawing a line with her that she had been too hurt and angry to cross.

But even though a year apart had done little to soothe the raw, empty gap he'd left in her life, she was able to breathe all that hurt away enough to kiss his damp shoulder. To plaster her hands to his bare chest and absorb the hard warmth of his strong body. Selfish?

Maybe.

Or maybe there was a tenderness underneath that cold control of his. And maybe she'd kiss her way to it this time.

She could feel the moment when the fire that burned her caught him, too. His body came alive beneath her. His fingers flexed against her lower back, hands palming her spine and drawing her hips closer to his. Her thigh grazed the thick length of his erection, the contact making him groan with a hunger that reverberated through her, too.

"I want you." He said the words even though she understood as much from every single touch on her body.

"Not in here," she cautioned, her too-brief pregnancy coming to mind and causing a fresh pang in her chest.

"Too risky." He spoke into her ear, his hands wrapping around her waist and lifting her higher against him. "I know."

In a flash, he had her on her feet, with him following her. A moment later, he stepped out of the tub and opened the warming drawer full of fresh towels, a billow of dry heat spilling out along with the scent of detergent and lavender. He turned back to her before she'd even stepped all the way out of the spa and extended a towel for her to wrap herself in.

Rather, he wrapped her in the towel and his arms, too. He already had one around his waist and one on the deck where they stood. She couldn't touch him back since her arms were pinned to her sides in the towel, but she arched her neck for his kiss, getting lost in the man and the moment.

Just the way she'd wanted. And better.

"Where should I take you?" He asked the question against her cheek as he trailed kisses there, down her jaw, and onto her neck.

Her whole body came alive for him, like it always had when he touched her. Every single time.

"Anywhere," she murmured, not caring as long as he kept touching her.

When he stopped kissing her, she opened her eyes a moment to see him gather up a stack of more towels before he took her hand and tugged her out on the deck toward a teak porch swing covered in gold-and-turquoise cushions. Gossamer-light mosquito netting was draped over it and there was a table full of hurricane lamps to one side of the swing, which looked like a pasha's bed. Ian paused to light two of the lamps before pulling her into the netting enclosure with him. He tossed the towels into one corner of the bed, a foil packet sliding off to one side.

She smiled at his careful thought to protection, a sweet gesture that made her relax against him as he pulled her underneath him.

"I can't get enough of you." He breathed the words into her skin as he kissed his way down her body, sliding aside the towel and licking over her sensitive breasts.

His thigh pressed between hers, the welcome weight hitting the place where she craved his touch most. Her back bowed off the cushions, hips meeting his despite the lingering barrier of the thick terry cloth at his waist. She tunneled her fingers through his damp hair, holding him to her, feeling the tension build deep inside her.

Still warm from the hot tub, her skin heated to a dull sheen from the humid air. She tugged at the remnants of the towels between them, needing to get rid of all barriers to having him deep inside her.

He touched her before she could finish the job, however, his hand covering her sex and moving in a slow circle that made her head loll back against the cushions while ribbons of pleasure stroked her from the inside. Helpless at that touch, she held herself very still, not wanting to miss the slightest movement of his fingers over the slick warmth.

When he slid a finger inside her, she went mindless, boneless with a melting desire. Delicate convulsions fluttered through her, one after the other, drowning her in sweet fulfillment.

"Please," she urged him. "Please, please. Right now." She patted around the cushions in search of the condom.

Seizing upon it, she clutched it in her fist and passed it to him. But there must have been two, because he already had one in place. She'd been too intent on her own mission to notice his.

He rolled her on top of him and she forgot all about it. He thrust into her and it was all she could do to remain upright. She held very still for a long moment, getting used to the feel of him. Relishing the way they moved together.

A tightly perfect fit.

Ian gripped her hips and held her in place, moving beneath her. She met each thrust, closing her eyes to lose herself completely.

The tension built again, the rapid pace of it catching her off guard. She steadied herself against his shoulders, her hair falling forward to stroke his chest while he moved faster. Harder.

Her release blindsided her before she was ready. Before she knew it would happen. It rolled over her, through her, again and again. She collapsed against him while his climax overtook him. She kissed his shoulder. His face. Whatever she could reach as the pleasure spent itself and their heartbeats quieted.

Slowly.

For long moments she simply listened to Ian's ragged breathing, liking the way the feelings played havoc with him, too. It helped to know she wasn't alone in this. That she affected him as much as he did her.

The force of it, the raw power of the attraction and

the chemistry, was unlike anything she'd ever experienced. Unlike anything she knew could transpire between a man and a woman.

Maybe a small part of her had hoped that this marriage would show her that she'd been wrong about how monumental their relationship had been. If anything, being back together with Ian now only proved that they were more combustible than ever before.

The problem with combustible heat?

It didn't tend to burn itself out quietly.

Ten

By noon the next day, the honeymoon was over.

Ian regretted leaving Costa Rica, but Lydia kept saying she was worried about their families' reactions to the secret marriage. So, wanting to keep her happy, he'd arranged to leave, and now here they were, back on a chartered jet. It touched him that she seemed as concerned about the McNeills as she was about her own mother's response. And, of course, she had a legitimate reason to be concerned about how the tabloid media would choose to spin the story given her unique past. Whatever gossip played out online would be best quieted by a press release of their own.

So shortly after noon, they boarded the same private plane that had delivered them to Central America. The plan had been to return to Miami—and the Foxfire renovation project. But they had the aircraft at their disposal for the day and their bags packed with enough clothes for several days. So Ian needed to speak to her about a change of travel plans that he hadn't wanted to mention previously.

A change of flight plans he'd given to the pilot the night before.

He slid into the soft leather seat beside her, taking her hand before she could boot up her electronics for the trip. He understood she was anxious to check on the media reports about their marriage, but first he needed to clear a side trip with her.

No longer dressed in the honeymoon garments he liked so much—his T-shirts or the silk dress knotted at the knees for wading in the ocean—Lydia was now wearing a peach-colored linen sheath that reached her knees with an ivory jacket buttoned over it. With her dark hair pulled back in a neat ponytail and a heavy gold necklace, she had returned to work mode. His beautiful, endlessly competent wife.

"I've asked the pilot to give us a moment before take-off." *Damn it.* Ian should have brought this up sooner. He'd been too busy enjoying what they'd shared this weekend—the connection and spark he remembered from their early days together. He'd wanted to lose himself in that when he knew damn well they would never return to the time when they offered one another a tenuous trust. Love.

Thinking about the betrayal of that trust—on both sides he could now acknowledge—still burned his gut.

"Why?" Lydia straightened in her seat, immediately alert. "Did you leave something behind?"

"No. Nothing like that." He took both her hands in his, hoping he'd earned back some small amount of her trust during this weekend together. They'd need that to make it through this marriage. "I wanted to speak to you about a possible change in our travel plans today."

She tipped her head to one side, more quizzical than upset.

"You know as well as I do the pilot has to file any alterations to the flight ahead of time—" She cut herself off, understanding lighting her features along with a new coolness. "Of course you know that. You've already changed our plans, haven't you?"

Ian could change the itinerary back again. They'd just need to wait until the plan was approved. He gripped her hands tighter, hoping she'd understand.

"Remember when I told you my brothers contacted me on the flight here yesterday?" At her nod, he continued, "They didn't check in just to let me know the news of our marriage had leaked. Apparently my grandfather has asked to see us—all of his family—as soon as possible. My brother said it wasn't cause to interrupt the honeymoon, but the sooner we could come to New York for a family meeting, the better."

"Is it his health?" The look in her green eyes was compassionate. Concerned.

Something about that quick empathy soothed the raw places inside him.

"I don't know. I would have thought I'd be able to tell by my brothers' faces if they were worried about him. But honestly? I couldn't read them. I don't know if they're putting up a brave front because we just got married." The fear had been in the back of his mind for nearly twenty-four hours and it was a relief to share it.

To feel Lydia squeeze his hands in return.

"Of course. We'll go straight to New York. There's no work in the world that's more important than a loved one's health."

Her reaction humbled him. Even as he gave the nod to the pilot and settled in for takeoff, he recognized that he'd missed out on something special with this caring woman. What might have happened if he'd swallowed his pride last spring and forced her to listen to his explanation about why his profile was circulating on a matchmaker's website even as he dated her? If he'd fought harder for her—hell, fought for her at all—could he have made her see the truth? That he hadn't given a rat's ass about anyone but her?

In all the months since their breakup, he'd been too busy blaming her for believing the worst of him. For not having any faith in him.

But maybe he'd been every bit as guilty as her. More, even.

The realization made him wonder if he could use these next months to turn this marriage into something real. Convince Lydia that they were meant to be together after all.

He was still brooding over the idea when Lydia's soft expletive hit his ears—an unlikely exclamation from the woman who had cultivated a perfect façade to keep scandal-hungry tabloid reporters at bay.

"What's wrong?" He glanced over at her as the plane began to taxi toward the runway to begin the flight.

Lydia squeezed her phone in a white-knuckle grip.

"It's my mother." She shook her head, slowly leaning back in the leather chair with a sigh that blew her dark hair from over one eye. "She's already lining up press interviews for us." Lydia turned an anguished look his way. She caught her lip between her teeth for a long moment, worrying away the slick peach lip gloss. "She wants to meet me at a network television studio in New York tomorrow for a live interview with one of the morning shows." Lydia drew in a long breath. "The host already shared her lead-in to the story." She flipped the phone so he could see a text from her mother in all capital letters.

BILLIONAIRE'S REJECTED LOVE CHILD FINALLY HITS THE JACKPOT AS A MCNEILL BRIDE!

Six hours later, seated beside Ian in a chauffeured limousine transporting them from the private New Jersey airstrip to Malcolm McNeill's residence on Park Avenue in Manhattan, Lydia talked herself through her plan for getting through this day. Ian had taken a business call to handle a few details on the Foxfire Hotel project in South Beach, leaving Lydia alone with her thoughts for their ride through the city.

For which she was grateful.

Trying to steady her trembling hands and jittery nerves, she sipped the bottled water stocked in the limousine's mini bar. The events of the last day and a half had been staggering. Her wedding. Finding out the event had been leaked to the press. The unbelievable honeymoon night in Costa Rica. An unexpected trip to New York because Ian's grandfather wanted to meet with his whole family.

Her mother's sudden interest in her life now that Lydia had tied the knot with one of the wealthiest men in the country.

Lydia's stomach churned as the limo stopped at a red light. Ian had been kind about her mother's meddling notes and eager desire for involvement in her life. He had reassured Lydia that he understood she wasn't responsible for her mother's behavior and promised her that the McNeills would deal with any media stunts her mother pulled.

In the end, Lydia had opted not to contact her mother just yet. For all that Mom knew, Lydia remained on her honeymoon for the next week or more. She had no reason to believe Lydia was back in New York and all too close to the network studio where her mother had committed to an interview.

Lydia thought she was done with this kind of thing— trying to manage her mother's need for the spotlight while staying firmly out of it herself. She hadn't factored in this kind of thing when Ian had offered his proposal for a marriage that would benefit both of them.

Sliding a sidelong glance at him now as the car turned into Central Park and headed east, Lydia braced for the swell of desire that just a simple look inspired. His dark suit was more casual today with his white dress shirt open at the neck. His legs were sprawled, one knee close to hers, his left hand resting on his navy trousers, the platinum wedding band glinting in the sunlight.

She thumbed her own ring as she watched him, her eyes greedily moving over his strong jaw and the dark hair that brushed his collar. Her heart tumbled over itself in an odd rhythm, alerting her to the presence of all the old feelings for him. The ones she wanted so desperately to ignore. The ones that tingled along her senses even now at just sitting near enough to touch him.

When he'd kissed her the night before and told her he wanted them to have a fresh start, she'd felt her defenses tremble. And today, after she'd read the texts from her mother and she'd been hurting and embarrassed on so many levels, Ian had been quick to assure her he could handle any of her mother's media antics, promising to hire a full-time publicist to manage Lydia's image and ensure that the media knew whom to contact for all stories having to do with Lydia McNeill.

It had sounded so smart and reasonable, and it probably was a very real possibility that his solution would work. It helped to have the financial resources, of course. But more than anything, the gesture had spoken of a kindness and consideration for Lydia's feelings that rocked her old perceptions of him.

Had she been too quick to judge him last year? Too insecure in herself to ever believe that Ian might have a reasonable explanation for his presence on a matchmaker's site? Her gaze returned to his platinum wedding band as he finished up his call. He might have pressured her into a marriage that would help him fulfill his grandfather's wishes, but he was helping her at the same time. She couldn't afford the scandal or the financial strain of a legal battle with Vitaly Koslov.

Another kindness Ian had done for her sake.

"I wonder what you're thinking, Mrs. McNeill." His words cut through her daze as the limo emerged on the east side of Central Park.

Startled, she sat bolt upright on her seat, her drink sloshing droplets on her arm. She set the water aside in the cup holder to give herself time to gather her thoughts. When had he finished his phone call? She needed to get her head on straight before they walked into his grandfather's house and faced the full contingent of McNeills. Ian had phoned his brothers from the plane to let them know they were flying to New York earlier than anticipated. Apprehension flitted through her, and Lydia wished she'd taken Ian up on his offer of a light lunch during their flight to New York. Maybe having something in her stomach would have helped ease her nerves.

"Just a few jitters about meeting all the McNeills at one time." She smoothed the hem of the peach-colored dress some anonymous staffer of Ian's had packed for her back in Florida before this trip. She really needed to find out more about him and the people who worked with him, who'd made this trip just a little less stressful by sending some of her own clothes with her. "I know you said that your family trusts your judgment so they will accept your choice of wife, too."

"They will see what I see. A smart, compassionate woman who's battled complicated obstacles to carve out a good career." He took her hand and lifted it to his lips, his blue eyes warm.

Would she ever get used to the way he made her pulse flutter like that?

Then she recalled the whole reason for this trip and cursed herself for becoming sidetracked by her own worries. "But I'm being selfish." She shifted to face him on the bench seat, her knee grazing his. "You have much deeper concerns than that for this visit. More than anything, I hope your grandfather is well."

"Me, too," he said simply, turning to peer out the window as the driver slowed the car. "But we'll know soon enough how he fares because we're here."

Lydia marveled as they came to a stop at the curb outside a six-story limestone building with an Italianate facade and a delicate wrought iron balcony off the second floor. Her designer's eye went to the clay-tiled mansard roof and neo-Renaissance details, but it was difficult to enjoy the beauty of one of New York's turn-of-the-century masterpieces when Ian's family was on the other side of the front door.

No matter what Ian said, she worried what his brothers would think of their unorthodox—and rushed—marriage. But right now, she needed to be there for Ian in case his grandfather's health had taken a turn for the worse.

Resisting the urge to pull a mirror out of her purse and indulge the old insecurity demon her mother had given her, Lydia took a deep breath and stepped out of the vehicle as the chauffeur opened the door. She would remain calm. Composed.

Strong.

Ian had been all of that and more for her in the face of her mother's attempted publicity stunt.

The iron gates of the foyer rolled open before Ian

announced them on the intercom. Clearly, they'd been expected.

"I texted Gramps's housekeeper," Ian explained as they strode into the house without knocking. "She must have been watching for us. She said my brothers are here. Sofia is running late because of a ballet performance earlier in the day, but she's due to arrive shortly."

He closed the door behind them and Lydia did her best not to gawk. She'd read that Malcolm McNeill was an avid art collector, but she hadn't expected to be greeted in the foyer by a Cezanne and a Manet. The pieces were hung to be enjoyed, with the focus on the art. The only piece of furniture was a settee in a shade of cerulean shared by both paintings. Lydia had seen the opposite approach often enough in her time as a designer—boastful collectors who were more interested in having their taste admired and envied.

"Wow." She'd been drawn to the pieces in spite of herself, only realizing after a long moment that Ian was speaking in quiet tones to someone off to one side of the hallway.

Lydia turned to join them, but the older woman in a gray uniform had already hurried away.

"Cindy tells me the family is upstairs," he informed her, pointing the way. "It's two flights to the library, though. Let's take the elevator out of deference to your shoes." He cut a quick sideways glance her way. "Though they make your already-gorgeous long legs look damn amazing."

Before she could think of a response to his outrageous compliment—that yes, she did enjoy—he was already pushing the call button, and the elevator door swished open. She followed him into the cabin. The grand staircase snaked through all six floors with a mammoth skylight at the top, and though beautifully impressive, she didn't relish the idea of testing her heels on the sleek, polished treads. Not that she planned to take them off and walk in to meet Ian's grandfather barefoot.

As the door closed behind them, whisking them upward, her apprehension grew. But Ian stepped nearer, and the warmth of his physical proximity somehow comforted her.

"Thank you for coming with me." He spoke with quiet sincerity. "I'm glad you're here."

The words so perfectly echoed what she'd been feeling at that moment, they slid right past her defenses and burrowed in her heart in a way that made her breath catch.

Before she could think what to say, Ian folded her palm in his and squeezed. "We might as well hold hands." He planted a kiss on her temple. "We're newlyweds, remember?"

The soft warmth of his lips stirred a hungry response in her as she recalled their honeymoon in vivid, passion-saturated detail. But as the full import of his words sank in, she wondered if the display of affection was for his family's sake more than anything.

The elevator cabin halted and the door slid open on a third-floor hallway flooded with light from the skylight over the central staircase. Male voices and laughter sounded from nearby. Ian led her to a partially closed door flanked by carved wood panels that were flawless reproductions in the French eighteenth-century style. Better to focus on the home design than the butterflies in her stomach.

"That's my grandfather's voice," Ian noted, walking faster. "He sounds good."

Lydia squeezed his arm, offering what comfort she could as she followed him into a library where the walls were fitted with historic Chinese lacquer panels between the windows overlooking the street. But not even the superb design details could sway her attention from the impressive men scattered around the room. Even before introductions were made, she knew she was seeing three generations of McNeills. The gray-haired eldest sat in a leather club chair in the corner. Wearing a retro red-and-black smoking jacket belted over his trousers, the patriarch of the family gripped a crystal tumbler half-full of an amber-colored drink, a forgotten copy of the *Wall Street Journal* tucked into the chair at his side. At the window stood an extremely fit man who looked to be in his late fifties. He'd shaved his head completely, and she could see a tattoo on the back of his neck. Was this Liam McNeill? His gray pants and black T-shirt combined to make him look more like hired muscle than Ian's father.

But as the middle-aged man turned toward her, she saw the same ice-blue eyes shared by every man in the room.

Ian introduced her to each member of his family in age order, ending with Quinn and Cameron, who rose from their seats on opposite ends of the room to greet her.

Quinn and Cameron, she thought, looked more alike than Ian, whose bronzed complexion favored their Brazilian mother. But Cameron was very tall, perhaps six foot five. She would have thought him a professional athlete if she'd seen him on the street.

Lydia was saved from making small talk by the arrival of an exquisitely beautiful, petite blonde, hair tightly coiled in a bun at the back of her head.

"I'm so sorry," the woman offered, rushing to Quinn's side. "I thought the train would be faster since traffic was ridiculous after the show, but there were delays." She kissed Quinn. Her eyes darted around the room and, finding Malcolm McNeill, she moved to give the older man a kiss on one cheek that coaxed a smile from him.

"Sofia, my new wife, Lydia." Ian repeated his simple introduction from earlier.

Lydia braced herself for a chilly greeting since she'd unwittingly stolen some of the woman's wedding thunder with their preemptive visit to the justice of the peace, but if Sofia Koslov resented it, she hid it well.

The ballerina winked at Lydia, although she remained at Quinn's side as he guided her to a love seat at the center of the room.

"I've been so eager to meet you." Sofia pulled a silver phone from her small leather hobo purse and waved it. "Let's exchange numbers before you leave."

"I'd like that." Lydia couldn't help smiling, feeling more at ease with another woman in the room full of accomplished, powerful men. She and Ian took a seat on the long couch opposite Quinn and Sofia.

Without preamble, Malcolm McNeill reached for his silver-topped cane and rose to his feet, every bit as tall as Ian, even with his bent knees and back. "Lydia, we're all glad to welcome you into our family." He lifted his glass in a silent toast and took a sip before returning it to the side table. "I hope you will consider a more public celebration this summer so we can show the world how pleased we are to call you a McNeill."

The old man's blue eyes pinned her, inciting gratitude for the warmth of the gesture even as she regretted deceiving him. All of them.

Ian squeezed her hand as if he guessed her thoughts.

"Thank you, sir." She ducked her head, oddly intimidated to be in the hot seat in this room full of strangers who would be her family for such a short time.

Luckily, she didn't need to worry about saying anything else, because Malcolm continued to speak.

"It's Liam who asked me to round up the whole lot of you." Malcolm looked over to his son and gestured to the room. "Go on now. Tell 'em."

"Dad wanted us all here?" Ian rose to offer his grandfather an arm while the older man lowered himself into the large club chair. "Gramps, I thought you called us together to talk about your health. How you're doing since the heart attack and the trip home from Shanghai."

"No, no." Malcolm McNeill waved aside the help and the concern. "I'm healthy as a horse."

Lydia felt the unease all around the room in the shifting of positions. Cameron sat forward in his chair, elbows on his knees.

He then scowled at his father. "Dad, what gives? Ian left his honeymoon for this. Sofia ditched her meet and greet after a ballet performance."

Liam cleared his throat. "It's not easy getting you all together at once." He strode around to the desk, staying on the perimeter of the room, rubbing a hand over his shaved head. "My apologies for the timing, but I've waited long enough to tell you about this."

Quinn spoke up. "That sounds ominous, Dad." The oldest of the McNeill sons turned in his seat to better see his father. Quinn was a hedge fund manager, Lydia knew, and had all the appearances of refinement and wealth. But then, at the end of the day, that's what he sold—access to a world of privilege by gaining the trust of the world's wealthiest investors.

Cameron sighed. "What gives?" the youngest asked again, spreading his hands wide, a note of impatience in his voice.

Ian remained silent at her side.

Then Liam McNeill stopped pacing the perimeter of the room and turned to face the rest of the family. Lydia held her breath.

Liam looked around the room at all of them before speaking. "I have another family I've never told you about. Three more sons, actually." A ghost of a smile flitted across the man's face before vanishing. "Your mother left me because she found out about them, but I could never convince Audrey—my other, er, girlfriend—to move to the States and be a permanent part of my life."

The news landed with all the force of a grenade,

sending shrapnel into the heart of every McNeill. And that was before Cameron McNeill stalked across the room and launched a fist into his father's jaw.

Eleven

Ian hauled a steaming Cameron to one side of the library while Quinn stood in front of their father, blocking further physical confrontation. They might as well be a freaking reality TV show at this rate. *McNeills Gone Mad!*

Ian couldn't believe he'd left his honeymoon and flown to New York for this news, let alone that he'd dragged Lydia into it. Lydia—a woman who had lived her life as carefully as possible to avoid big, messy scandals. He noticed that Sofia had moved to sit beside Lydia on the couch, the two of them silently on the same side without saying a word. What was it about women that they could remain civilized when all hell broke loose around them?

Even Quinn looked the worse for wear after the

dustup, with his shirttails untucked in front and jacket unbuttoned. Ian hadn't fared as well; struggling with six-foot-five inches of pissed-off muscle and impulsiveness had sent him through the wringer. While epithets flew back and forth, it became apparent that Liam had been cheating on Ian's mother for years, fathering sons with a mistress on the West Coast until the woman got fed up with his refusal to divorce his wife and left the United States the year after Cameron was born.

Private investigators had trouble finding her, but then she'd had years of McNeill money stashed to help her make the getaway. Liam had lost touch with her and his sons until a few weeks ago, when one of the old investigators snagged a lead on a McNeill family ring in a pawnshop in the US Virgin Islands. Liam thought it was just a ploy by the PI to resurrect an old job, but he'd contacted Ian's friend Bentley to track it down, and it turned out the ring was real, verified by a family jeweler. Bentley traced it to the servant of a wealthy family—named McNeill—in Martinique.

"They use our name?" Ian barked, feeling more than a little angry with his father himself.

Furious, actually.

"I don't know when the boys started using the name," his father said, hanging his head. "But their mother died long ago and they want nothing to do with us, so you don't have to worry about anyone coming in here and..."

Quinn swore. Cam accused their father of several indecent acts. Ian's eyes went to Lydia, wishing she didn't have to hear all this. She looked calm, however, if a little pale. She held her cell phone in one hand; her other was tucked under her thigh on the couch.

"Quiet down, all of you, and listen here." Gramps stood, using his cane as he moved. "These young men are your half brothers, like it or not. They are your blood. My blood. Every bit as much my grandsons as you are. That doesn't mean, however, that I plan to give them the whole kit and kaboodle of the family portfolio." He straightened as much as his bad back would allow and used the cane to point at Cameron. "I've invited them to New York and we'll take their measure when they arrive."

Ian exchanged glances with Quinn. Family was all well and good. But what did this mean for them? And for McNeill Resorts if their grandfather handed over shares to people who clearly resented them? Ian didn't give a damn about money, but the family business they'd poured their blood, sweat and soul into? That was another matter. Let his father do right by his offspring financially, sure, but protect the business.

"Gramps, that's fine," Ian said reasonably, stepping on Cam's toe to ensure his brother didn't gainsay him. "We understand you want to meet them and provide for them. But what about McNeill Resorts? You've spent our whole lives trying to impart what the company means to you and how you want it developed. You can't honestly mean to start parceling off your business to people who are complete strangers to you?"

Out of the corner of his eye, Ian noticed Lydia straighten in her seat. Belatedly, it occurred to him she might feel differently about this newly unearthed branch of the family. Hell, in her childhood, she'd been the unacknowledged heir, and it had caused pain her whole life.

"I meant it when I said they're as much my grandsons as you are." Gramps leveled a look at each one of the brothers, a stiff set to his jaw, before he put his cane back on the floor and shuffled toward the door. "Now that we have that out of the way, I'm going to change for dinner. You're all invited, but don't stay if you can't act like grown-ups." He paused at the door, almost running into Lydia, who had leaped off the couch to open it for him.

Gramps smiled at her. "You're a pretty thing, aren't you? If it gets too rough in this room, just head down to the dining room and someone will fix you up a cocktail." He patted her arm.

"Yes, sir." She beamed.

Gramps had made one person happy today. As for the rest of the McNeills, Ian couldn't imagine what this meant for the family. He'd just gotten married to secure his portion of his grandfather's company because he had been under the mistaken impression it meant so much to the old man.

Now? The whole damn trust and will were almost assuredly going to be rewritten to incorporate this new branch of the family their father had never bothered to mention.

That bugged Ian on a lot of levels—mostly because he had to contend with the news that his father was a selfish, cheating bastard. Yet what bothered him more than anything was the idea that if the will was altered and it no longer included a stipulation about taking a wife to secure a portion of McNeill Resorts, would Lydia suggest they dissolve their marriage?

You can't honestly mean to start parceling off your business to people who are complete strangers to you?

Ian's words echoed in Lydia's mind long after they left his grandfather's home. They chased around her brain even now, late that night, after they'd arrived at Ian's apartment at the historic Pierre Hotel on Central Park, where both Ian and Quinn owned space. They'd opted to spend another day in New York so that he would have time to meet with his brothers and figure out what their father's news meant for the family.

Lydia hadn't argued, understanding why he would want to talk to his brothers privately. But the events had shaken her. Ian had locked himself in his library to make calls and Lydia found herself walking in aimless circles around the kitchen at midnight.

She and Ian hadn't stayed for dinner with Malcolm after the McNeill family blowup. She understood why a meal together might be uncomfortable with so much unsettled among them, but no wonder she was hungry now. She rifled through the cabinets in the sleek, caterer-friendly kitchen, searching for food.

Lydia had said good-night to Malcolm McNeill in his study while he drank his aperitif before going in to dinner. Liam had left immediately after his father walked out of the library. Quinn and Sofia had made their excuses as well, and Sofia had looked strained, although she'd taken Lydia's number and promised to call her so they could arrange a time to get to know each other.

Cameron alone had remained behind to have dinner with his grandfather. In the car afterward, on the way to Ian's apartment, Ian had sincerely apologized for the family dustup. But Lydia hadn't cared about that half as much as she cared about the fact that Ian didn't believe in welcoming half siblings into the family. He'd called those half brothers "complete strangers," implying they had no right to any McNeill inheritance.

He reacted the same way her half siblings had when they found out about her existence. It didn't matter that they all shared a father. She'd never been good enough in their eyes and it troubled her deeply to think Ian felt that way about people who shared his blood.

Peering into the huge Sub-Zero fridge, she retrieved a bottled water and sat at the breakfast nook overlooking the lights of Central Park. She'd changed into a nightgown and a white spa robe she'd found in the bathroom. Although Ian owned the Pierre apartment, apparently the whole building shared the hotel maid service and— come to think of it—Ian had told her there was twenty-four-hour room service from the kitchens downstairs. She would have phoned for something, but now, as it neared midnight, she tried to talk herself out of it.

Even all these years after that photograph of her in a magazine with a "baby bump" at sixteen, Lydia found herself careful not to overeat. Except, of course, in those weeks where she hugged the news of a real pregnancy close. Then, she'd fed herself like a queen, dreaming of the baby she'd never gotten the chance to meet.

"There you are." Ian's voice from the far side of the kitchen startled her from her thoughts.

He flipped on a pendant lamp over the black granite countertop. The backlight made it so she couldn't see out the window anymore. Instead, her own reflection stared back at her, a pale, negative image in black and white.

"Were you able to resolve anything?" she asked, careful to keep her thoughts to herself about any disappointment with Ian's reaction to his father's news.

It was possible the shock of the moment had colored his response. In time, he might feel differently about welcoming his half brothers into the family.

"Not really." He took a seat in one of the four white armchairs surrounding the polished teak table in the open-plan dining area. He set his phone on the table beside him. His shirtsleeves were rolled to expose strong forearms and he'd removed his jacket and tie. "I spoke at length to Bentley, the same friend who found you when I was looking for Mallory West. My father called him to go to Martinique two days ago and confirm the identity of my half brothers. Bentley said there's no doubt. He has photos of my father with his other family when they were young."

Ian switched the phone on and called up a photo of Liam McNeill standing with one woman and three small boys in front of the Cezanne she recognized from Malcolm McNeill's foyer. The three boys had to be Quinn, Ian and Cameron—all three of them sweet and adorable in jackets and ties, but with mischief in their matching blue eyes.

Below that photo, was another of Liam with an obviously pregnant blonde in a long, white gauzy dress. They stood on a beach at sunset, the sky purple and pink behind them, their arms around two small boys who could have been twins to the three in the photo above. Same blue eyes, same grins. The only difference was that the boys in the beach photo wore white T-shirts and cargo shorts. She wasn't sure why the third half brother wasn't in the photo.

"I can't believe that no one knew about this." Lydia ran a finger over the woman's pregnant belly in the photo. Had she known about Liam's other family when she carried those children? "I think back to all the stories that ran about me as a teen—complete fiction. And yet your father successfully hid a whole double life from the tabloids."

"My mother knew about this." Ian slid the phone from her hands and turned off the screen, setting it facedown on the table. "She just didn't want our lives to turn into a media circus so she kept quiet about it when she left my father."

"Our mothers are cut from very different cloth, aren't they?" Lydia wondered if he had any idea how much she identified with his father's *other* family. "I'm more surprised that his mistress didn't expose the truth."

Ian shook his head. "Maybe she had enough money. Bentley said the house where she raised her sons was paid for in cash."

Lydia drew a deep breath and reminded herself the shock of the news hadn't worn off yet for him. And still, she couldn't keep from pointing out, "It's not always about money. Most women want their children to have a relationship with their father. Don't you wonder why she cut off all contact and her sons never got in touch with the family either?" She turned that over in her mind. "As much as I resented the way my mother tried to get my father's attention by making us a spectacle, I wouldn't have had any relationship with him if she hadn't brought me to his attention."

And in the end, her father had been kind. He'd encouraged her desire to study art and design and introduced her to prominent people in the field in which she now worked. She'd found common ground with him and enjoyed those long, last conversations about beautiful buildings he'd seen all over the world. She treasured those memories.

"If not for that damned ring showing up, we might never have discovered them." Ian stared down at the table and she wondered if he'd heard what she'd said. "And now? Everything my grandfather worked for is going to land in the laps of people who never wanted anything to do with us."

She tried to bite her tongue. And failed.

"They're still your family," she reminded him. "That counts for something."

She wanted—*needed*—him to agree. Even when she had been pregnant with their child—a baby who would not have had the legal protection of marriage—she had thought Ian would embrace his offspring. That he would see beyond those rigid notions of what "family" meant. But if he truly believed that he could only count the legally recognized brothers as worthy of his notice...

Then she didn't know him at all. Then her marriage really was based strictly on a piece of paper and all those tender touches in Costa Rica were just a case of physical attraction.

He turned on her, blue eyes thoughtful. "How can you, of all people, believe that family trumps all? Your half siblings did everything in their power to discredit you and your mother when your mom sued your father's estate. How could you even consider them family when they've gone out of their way to hurt you like that?"

Disappointment prickled all over her, deflating the hope she'd had that Ian was a different kind of man. That they were building a tentative trust again.

"You can't pick family the way you choose your friends. But I still believe those relationships are worth investing in. If I hadn't gotten to know the Whitneys, I would have missed out on knowing my father." She stared down at the yellow diamond on her finger, more confused than ever about what it meant.

About what Ian hoped to gain by playing the part of her husband in a way that had fooled even her.

"Lydia, I'm sorry that this had to come up right now." He took her left hand and kissed the backs of her fingers. "I can see you're upset and I don't blame you. I'm going to order a tray for you from room service and have something brought up."

"There's really no need."

"I insist." The gentle concern in his eyes undid her as he stroked a thumb over the inside of her wrist, still holding her hand. "I haven't forgotten about your mother's attempts to reach you. And with your permission,

I'll invite a publicist over tomorrow and you can plan how you want to manage the news about our marriage and your public image. The woman—Jasmine—is a good friend of Sofia's. Quinn highly recommended her."

"Thank you." Lydia slid her hand away, the diamond weighing heavily on her finger. "I appreciate that. But in all the events of the evening we haven't even spoken about what this news of your father's means for your grandfather's will."

A muscle in Ian's jaw flexed as he leaned back from the breakfast table. "It means nothing."

"Ian, it's not too late to say the wedding photo was—I don't know—a prank?" She held her breath while he looked back at her with stunned eyes. "I'm not trying to add to your problems, but if it simplifies things for you to quietly annul this, we could—"

"No." He bit off the word with a fierceness echoed by the flash of emotion in his eyes. "Absolutely not." He leaned over the table and kissed her—a hard, possessive kiss. "As much as I regret that you had to witness the whole drama with my father, having you with me was the only bright spot in this day."

Her heart contracted, squeezing hopefully around those words. She took a deep breath, no closer to answers than she had been hours ago. Before she could say anything he rose to his feet.

"I'll have the kitchen bring something up and then I've got a few more calls to make." He kissed the top of her head. "If the publicist is here at ten tomorrow morning, is that too early?"

"That's fine. I'll be ready." She knew she needed help

figuring out how to manage her public image. Whether or not she stayed married to Ian for the rest of this year, she'd come to one decision tonight. She'd allowed the fear of a scandal surrounding Mallory West to send her running into his arms for protection from a lawsuit, and that problem wasn't going to go away after twelve months.

Even if Ian ensured Vitaly Koslov never sought legal retribution, there was the fact that Lydia wanted to return to matchmaking. And aside from that one small scandal that she'd never addressed, her alter ego actually had a great, lucrative reputation.

More than ever after tonight, Lydia was convinced she had a mission in life to champion single mothers. Women who were ostracized by family or lovers who refused to recognize their own children.

So, at ten the next morning, she planned to ask Jasmine the publicist how to introduce herself to the world as the mystery matchmaker, Mallory West.

As for Ian? She didn't plan to consult him about that particular decision. She had every reason to believe he wouldn't understand.

Twelve

Two hours later, Ian paced the floor of his study, a restless unease still weighing on his chest even though he was checking things off his mental to-do list with reasonable speed.

He'd exchanged emails with the site manager on the Foxfire project and gotten an update on the South Beach property, a lucky stroke since the guy was as much of a night owl as him. Ian had triple-checked the marriage paperwork to ensure it had all been filed properly, then he faxed his attorney the signed files outlining the provisions Ian was making for Lydia no matter what happened in the next twelve months. She'd made it clear she didn't want any kind of financial settlement in a year's time—an issue he'd revisit—but for now, he made sure she received all the legal and financial protections possible as his spouse.

What she'd said at the kitchen table earlier still needled his brain and he didn't understand why. He had the impression she was unhappy with his response to his father's bombshell about his second family, but he couldn't quite put his finger on what he'd done wrong.

Sure, she'd made the comment that family wasn't all about money. But she'd also seemed upset that he wasn't welcoming the McNeill interlopers into his grandfather's company. And since Ian couldn't untangle what bothered her, he planned to make sure she knew that he didn't equate her position in the family with these pseudo McNeills.

Lydia's case was different. *She* was different.

Special.

Ian made his last call of the night to Quinn, still hoping to dispel some of the tension of the day. He knew none of his brothers would be getting any sleep tonight either.

"I have Jasmine confirmed for tomorrow morning," he informed his older brother, who was probably staring out at this exact same view of Central Park three floors above him right now. "Thank you for the recommendation. She got back to me almost immediately."

"She's a go-getter." Quinn sounded weary on the other end of the call, but no doubt he'd been making calls well into the night too, trying to sort through the news of their half brothers. "Jasmine is very protective of Sofia and her image. They're friends, of course, but I got the impression that she's the kind of person who invests a lot in her clients."

"That's exactly what Lydia needs. Her mother has

tried undermining Lydia's image too many times." It had upset Ian when he made a quick scan of articles about Lydia tonight—so he could give the publicist some background on the situation. "It will help her to have a go-between she trusts to manage the stories that circulate about her."

Lydia had a giving heart and a willingness to help people that was too rare in his world. She should be recognized for her efforts. Or, at the very least, not belittled by sensationalized stories that focused on her personal life.

"You'll be happy with Jasmine." Quinn paused a moment. In the background, Ian could hear the clink of ice cubes in a glass. "And I've been meaning to let you know that Sofia has told me twice to cancel any efforts to find Mallory West."

"Seriously?" Ian stopped his pacing, instantly alert.

"Yes. She mentioned it a couple of weeks ago, saying that we shouldn't hound someone who was responsible for bringing the two of us together." Quinn's tone shifted as he spoke about his fiancée. There was a lightness that had been absent in him until Sofia arrived in his life. "I thought she was just being sentimental, or… I don't know. I didn't think she was serious about it. But last week she raised the issue again, and apparently she's already spoken to her father. So definitely call off any search for the matchmaker."

That was good news for Lydia.

And Ian was happy about it, too. One less thing to worry about that could chip away at Lydia's public image during a time when they were trying to cultivate a new one.

Yet he had to wonder. Would this give Lydia all the incentive she needed to end their marriage early?

"Ian? You there?"

"Yes. Sorry. I'm just surprised. But I'll abandon that project and call in the investigator." No use telling Quinn he'd already found Mallory and that she currently slept in his bed.

"Thanks. And don't be surprised if Sofia knocks on your door tomorrow morning. She has a ballet class to teach at noon, but she mentioned wanting to personally introduce your wife to her friend Jasmine before she heads in to work."

Distracted, Ian agreed to relay the message before disconnecting the call.

His brain was still stuck on the news that the Koslovs no longer cared about finding the matchmaker who'd embarrassed them. Now Sofia had decided it was because of Mallory's matchmaking that she'd met Quinn in the first place.

Ian couldn't keep up. Shutting his phone off for the night, he padded barefoot through the apartment, heading to his bedroom. He craved Lydia's touch. Hell, she was most certainly sleeping already. Even just lying beside her would be enough to chase some of the restlessness away.

But as he stepped into the master suite, he knew right away that she wasn't there. Her suitcase had been moved from his closet where he'd set it himself earlier. His bed was still made.

Maybe she was still in the kitchen? Even as he stalked through the darkened apartment, however, he knew she wouldn't be there. When he passed the closed door to one of the guest suites, he knew she'd found an empty bed to sleep in for the night.

He placed a palm on the door, missing her. He told himself that she was probably just trying to get better sleep. This way, he wouldn't wake her when he went to bed. If that was her reasoning, he could hardly begrudge her the guest room. But the vague unease in his chest all evening took a new form. He'd been worrying about what his father's betrayal meant for the family when he should have been paying attention to Lydia.

He'd let her sleep for now. They would speak in the morning when they were both clearheaded.

Because deep in his gut he knew she hadn't sought that spare room for the sake of a good night's rest. His new wife wasn't happy with him. And more than ever, he feared that she was already dreaming up ways to end this marriage.

As Lydia prepared for her meeting with her new publicist the next morning, she nibbled on the scones that Ian had had delivered to the kitchen, along with a huge platter of other breakfast choices. If this was a real marriage, she would ask him about the possibility of rethinking some of his extravagant expenditures to help others. She could think of five struggling young mothers she helped through Moms' Connection who were probably going without breakfast today so their kids could have something nutritious. It made it hard for Lydia to enjoy the scone when so much food sat there untouched.

She hadn't seen Ian yet this morning. She'd awakened to discover he had a meeting with the McNeill family's private attorney. He had been in the study all morning.

So she prepared for her own meeting with the publicist by herself, asking the morning maid to set out the coffee and pastry treats in the living room to offer her guests. Because apparently Sofia Koslov would be joining them briefly, too, if only to make introductions. She'd texted Lydia this morning to make sure she didn't mind.

Already, Lydia had the impression she would have been truly fortunate to marry into this family for the sake of gaining a sister-in-law like Sofia. Lydia had read a great deal about the principal dancer for the New York City Ballet last winter during the awkward media coverage of Cameron's proposal to her. How would Sofia react one day when she learned that Lydia was actually Mallory West? The possibility of being rejected that way—by someone so warmhearted—stirred a deep regret for how she'd handled the matchmaking mistake.

What struck Lydia now, as she finished her scone and reviewed her notes for her morning meeting, was that Sofia Koslov must share some of Lydia's desire for family. The dancer's mother had died when Sofia was a girl, and she'd never been close to her father, even though the Ukrainian-born billionaire had stepped in to claim control of her life. But as Lydia read about Sofia, she couldn't help but think they might have really enjoyed being sisters.

Too bad Lydia's temporary marriage was proving even more temporary than she'd imagined.

She heard the apartment doorbell chime and checked her watch, guessing that it was Sofia since it wasn't quite 10:00 a.m. and Sofia was scheduled to arrive a little before Jasmine. Letting the maid answer the door, Lydia took another moment to freshen her lipstick and check the fall of her bright green summer dress with big purple flowers embroidered at the hem. She wore a thin yellow sweater around her shoulders to cover up the dress's square halter neck.

When she got to the living room, Sofia darted off the couch. Dressed in slouchy pants and a leotard with a hoodie thrown over it, she could have been a nine-teen-year-old college student with her clean scrubbed face and glowing skin. Her still-damp hair was piled on her head in a bun with a braid wrapped around it. She moved gracefully toward Lydia, meeting her in the center of the room.

"You look so pretty!" Sofia exclaimed, taking in the embroidered hem of Lydia's dress. "You already dress like a publicist's dream. Jasmine is going to love work-ing with you."

They made small talk for a few minutes, compar-ing notes on clothes, but before Lydia could offer her guest a seat, the door to Ian's study opened down the hall. The voices of Ian, Quinn, Cameron and a stranger echoed off the Italian marble floor.

"I forgot Quinn was coming down here for the meet-ing with their attorney." Sofia's smile was infectious, the grin of a woman in love. "He worked so late last night, and then was up at the crack of dawn. Not that I'm supposed to know that since I'm technically living in my own apartment until my wedding." She made a good-natured eye roll. "But how could I leave Quinn alone last night after what they had to deal with yesterday?"

Lydia felt a pang of guilt at Sofia's empathetic words. Should Lydia have kept more of her opinions to herself last night?

Her eyes went straight to Ian as the men walked into the living area, close to the private elevator. Their business conversation must be done, as they joked about their golf handicaps and a charity fund-raiser at a popular course in Long Island the following weekend.

Cameron checked out of the guy talk early, his eyes landing on the plate full of pastries on the coffee table. He made a beeline for it as his brothers said goodbye to the attorney.

Cameron gave Lydia a thumbs-up before speaking around a mouthful of jelly doughnut. "This must be your doing. Ian never has food in this place. Good job."

"I'm glad someone is enjoying it." She smiled in spite of the tension knotting her shoulders at Ian's arrival in the room. Something had shifted between them last night and made her uneasy today. She had slept in another room, but he hadn't spoken to her about it—last night or this morning. Had he thought it peculiar? Or were they back to being strangers with a contractual marriage?

Quinn and Ian joined them in the living area. Sofia and Quinn drew together like magnets, each pulled toward the other irresistibly, splitting the distance between them to meet in the middle. It was beautiful—and painful—to see, making Lydia realize all that she'd sacrificed in tying herself to a man who didn't think in terms of love and family, but business and legal obligations.

Sofia tucked her head to Quinn's chest. "Quinn, did you tell your brothers that we don't want to pursue any investigation into Mallory West?"

Lydia gasped. She covered it with a cough and a murmured, "Excuse me."

She was careful to avoid Ian's gaze, although she felt it on her.

Thankfully, Cameron McNeill spoke over her gaffe. "Are you kidding me? I thought we were going to sue her for all she's worth and donate the money to one of Sofia's favorite charities?" He leaned down to the coffee table to scoop up another pastry and a napkin. "I thought it was a great plan."

Ian was suddenly standing by Lydia's side, his arm sliding beneath her lightweight sweater to palm her back. "Quinn told me you no longer wish to pursue the matchmaker. I've called off the investigator."

When? And had he planned on telling her that the Koslovs no longer cared to sue Lydia's alter ego? She tensed beneath Ian's touch, anger tightening every muscle.

"May I ask why?" Lydia asked, not caring if they all thought her rude to question them about a piece of private family business.

She needed to know. Why had Ian let her think that the lawsuit from Sofia's father was still very much a possibility? Had he been that intent on marrying her to fulfill his grandfather's will? Her chest burned with frustration and her stomach rebelled at the scone she'd eaten earlier.

Sofia smiled warmly. "Of course. I was never upset with Ms. West after I discovered it was my father's matchmaker who truly caused all the trouble with me getting paired with Cameron." She gave a sisterly elbow to Cameron's stomach as he stood beside her. "But I made a point of speaking to my father about it last month and convinced him that there was no need to scare a good matchmaker out of practicing her skills in New York. I mean, thanks to her—and Olga, the matchmaker my dad hired—I found Quinn."

How kind of Ian to let me know.

Lydia felt breathless and immobile, kind of like she'd had the wind knocked out of her. Behind her, she felt Ian's grip tighten on her waist, but she knew that as soon as his family left, she would tell him what she'd known yesterday and hadn't wanted to admit to herself.

She could not possibly stay married to him.

Thirteen

From a leather slipper chair in the corner of the spare bedroom, Ian watched—stunned—as Lydia packed her few things an hour after Jasmine left the apartment following a tense meeting. He'd only stayed for a portion of it, sensing he was the one causing the tension for Lydia. But he'd been able to see for himself that Jasmine had things well in hand for managing Lydia's public presence, making smart suggestions for how to handle Lydia's mother all the while maintaining control of all publicity.

He hoped she was simply preparing for their flight to Miami to return to work on the Foxfire. He feared it was more than that since their plane wasn't scheduled to take off for nine more hours.

Lydia folded a white silk nightgown with unsteady

hands, her focus overly careful. "How long have you known that the Koslovs didn't plan to sue me?"

Her words hung in the air. She smoothed the neatly folded garment on the bed, then tucked it into the small travel bag she'd set on a nearby luggage valet. Her face was still averted. She looked too pretty in her bright dress, and he wished he could twirl her around the room and make her smile the way they had in Costa Rica.

And before that, in Rangiroa.

What was it about their relationship that it only seemed to thrive in vacation mode? He should've never returned to New York with her so soon.

"Quinn told me to call off the investigator last night in a phone call after you'd gone to bed." It was the honest truth.

But it wouldn't be the first time she'd ignored the truth to draw her own conclusions.

She gave a vague nod, hearing his words, but never slowing her pace as she moved to the closet and found the next item of clothing to fold—the sheath dress she'd worn yesterday.

"You didn't have any inkling that your family no longer cared about uncovering Mallory West's identity?" She glanced his way, her green eyes huge and rimmed with red, before she returned to her task. "I asked Jasmine about my double identity in confidence, and she said—if I want her to—she would speak to Sofia about having us reveal the truth together and turn it into a story of happily-ever-afters." Lydia's voice hitched on the phrase and she stopped. She swiped an impatient hand across her cheek as she refolded the dress that wasn't cooperating. "She said it could be the perfect publicity spark to relaunch Mallory's matchmaking career, especially if Sofia were to get behind the Moms' Connection charity."

Ian hated to see Lydia hurt and upset. He wanted to wrap his arms around her and comfort her. Remind her that she knew him better than that.

But she'd never had faith in him, assuming the worst of him when his profile had landed on a matchmaker's site last summer. Assuming the worst of him now, even though he'd told her the truth. That's why he'd kept this marriage agreement *flexible*.

Smart of him, right?

So why did he feel as though her leaving was driving a knife through his chest?

"I had no idea that Sofia had talked her father into giving up the search for Mallory West," he reiterated, hoping if she heard it clearly, a second time, the words might mean more to her. "Lydia, I will tell you honestly that I was confident once I spoke to Vitaly Koslov and told him I knew Mallory's identity and that she meant no harm, he would forget about pursuing legal action."

"Yet you used the threat of a lawsuit to maneuver me into a marriage that would secure your share of McNeill Resorts." She straightened from folding the clothes and faced him. "That in itself seems…disingenuous."

"Perhaps," he conceded. "But don't forget that when I came to Miami to speak to you, I thought you'd been playing revenge games with me by matching me up with inappropriate people through your matchmaking service." He cut her off before she could argue.

"Only you weren't. I jumped to that conclusion about you, not realizing you'd just lost our child and were hurting desperately. And I am sorrier for that than I can ever say."

He rose from the chair, needing to hold her. Hoping she would let him.

"It seems we are both at fault for misjudging each other," she admitted, her voice thin and her expression unhappy. "But I was in the same apartment as you last night when you found out that your family had forgiven me for the matchmaking mistake. You could have told me then, or this morning."

"It would have been easy to do if you'd been in my bed, where I thought you'd be." He wondered why he hadn't knocked on the door to the guest room last night. Asked her what was wrong and shared that good news with her.

Maybe he really hadn't wanted to know that she sided with his new half siblings over him. That once again, he didn't come first with someone he loved—

Loved?

He let the word settle in his head, into his heart. And yes, hell, yes, he realized he loved her.

That's why his chest hurt as though it wanted to bleed out on the floor at her feet. He loved Lydia. And she was already looking for a way out of his life. Again.

"I wasn't half a globe away, Ian. I lay wide-awake in a bed one hundred feet from yours," she reminded him, tears gathering in her green eyes. "I guess I thought after the way our honeymoon went, maybe you wouldn't always have to put the McNeills before me."

He reached out to her, clasping her shoulders in his hands.

"You are a McNeill, damn it." He'd spent half the evening making sure she was legally protected in every way.

But Lydia was already tugging off her wedding ring. She held it out to him, the yellow diamond winking in the afternoon sunlight slanting in through the curtains.

"Not for much longer, Ian." She dropped it into his hand, and it was only then, when he held the cold stone in his palm, that he realized his hands had fallen from her shoulders.

"We still have months together," he informed her, his tone fiercer than he intended.

How could he convince her to make this a real marriage unless she stayed with him?

"It's not too late to admit we made a mistake." She turned her back on him, her green dress swishing as she moved around the room, taunting him somehow. "I thought I could pretend with you for twelve months and somehow survive the emotional fallout, but after how close we got in Costa Rica, I know I can't do that. I can't pretend when it hurts this much."

"And you're not worried about a scandal now, when a divorce after a three-day marriage will put you in the headlines for the rest of the year?" He hated himself for saying it.

Especially right on the heels of realizing he loved this woman. He should let her go with some dignity, damn it. Except he'd tried that once before and it hadn't made him any happier.

"I've realized a scandal is far less painful than a broken heart." She snapped the suitcase closed. "I called for a car, Ian. I'm going to stay at my place and see Kinley before I return to South Beach. I'll send someone up for my bag."

She picked up her purse and walked out of the guest room while Ian scraped his heart off the floor.

Wait a minute.

Why would *her* heart be broken?

He tried to put the pieces together and figure out what she meant. Why she was so upset.

Bloody hell.

Just as the elevator doors shut behind the woman he loved, he realized the truth that should have been obvious ever since they'd peeled each other's clothes off in Costa Rica.

She loved him, too.

By some kind of miracle, Lydia rode the elevator all the way down to the first floor without crying.

She hadn't wanted to walk through the busy lobby past the concierge desk with tears streaming down her face. She'd spent too much of her life trying to avoid making a scene to let herself fall apart publicly.

She hadn't called for a car. That had been total fiction she'd made up for Ian. And she didn't send someone up for her bag the way she'd told Ian she would. The tears behind her eyes were burning, burning, burning, so she blindly hurried out of the Pierre and rushed toward the closest traffic light so she could cross Fifth Avenue and lose herself in Central Park. A sea of tourists crowded the Grand Army Plaza, but she bypassed all of them, feeling the tears already plunking from her eyelashes to her cheeks.

Hugging her purse tighter, she squeezed through a line of city visitors waiting to ride the Big Bus. Couples and families milled around the food vendors, some checking street maps and others negotiating prices with the hansom cab drivers.

Lydia's shoes clicked along the pavement and onto the shady road leading into the park down to the pond. She found an empty bench near Gapstow Bridge, close enough for her to enjoy the view as well as some privacy. Only then did she give in to the crushing feeling in her chest, letting loose a soft wail of sadness that only constricted her lungs more.

Damn him.

She rummaged for tissue in her purse and came up with an antique handkerchief she'd purchased in a vintage shop a year ago. She'd washed it and tucked the linen in her bag, but hadn't found reason to sob her heart out in public until now.

She just couldn't see any reason to remain in a marriage with a man who freely admitted he only wanted to wed her to legally protect his share of a family business. But now, with the news of his half siblings and his grandfather's need to rewrite his legal documents to include the rest of the family, Ian didn't need her to serve that role anymore. Plus, she didn't need Ian's protection from a lawsuit since that wouldn't be happening either.

They'd been hasty. And she'd been too entranced by his kisses to see what a bad idea it was to play house with a man who held your heart in his hands. She'd been foolish.

She'd loved Ian McNeill ever since that first night together in Rangiroa.

"Is this seat taken?" The familiar masculine voice came from over her left shoulder.

She debated her options for running and hiding. She did not want Ian to see her like this. Sniffling loudly behind her handkerchief, she gave an inelegant shrug and tried to collect herself.

"Lydia, I need to talk to you." He lowered himself to the bench beside her.

She felt the warmth of his knee graze hers, but he didn't touch her otherwise. She ducked her head, unwilling to meet his eyes. How on earth had he found her? He must have followed her.

"I feel like you had your say back in the apartment, but I didn't really get to make my case." He draped a hand along the back of the metal bench, but didn't touch her. "I'd like a chance to tell you a few things before you follow through with…whatever you decide to do."

She was going to have their marriage annulled. That was her plan. But she hadn't recovered her voice yet from the crying. And she couldn't deny she was curious.

"I have not been myself for the last twenty hours—ever since I learned about the way my father betrayed my mother. Let me just start by saying that much. I know that I upset you last night, but I was too caught up in the family drama to chase down why, and I regret that. Deeply." He moved closer. "There is no McNeill more important to me than you. Not my brothers. Not my half brothers. And yes—there will be a difference for me until I meet the McNeill doppelgängers in person and decide what I think about them."

She heard a big group of people coming down the path near the bench and wiped her eyes on the handkerchief, not wanting to look like a basket case. But her ears were closely attuned to what Ian was saying. She was surprised he'd come after her at all.

"I swear to you, I didn't know Vitaly Koslov was going to drop the idea of a lawsuit when I proposed to you. I may have hit that angle hard to convince you to marry me, but I genuinely believed he would sue you. Cameron is working closely with Sofia on a new ballet video game, and he's mentioned more than once that bit about suing Mallory West so Sofia could use the proceeds for a charity that helps bring art and dance to underfunded school systems." Ian drew a breath, pausing as the large group of tourists walked past, led by a private tour guide still giving statistics about the Gapstow Bridge's reconstruction.

The pause gave Lydia time to process. Sofia and Cameron were making a video game? Not for the first time, she wished she could have been a part of the family. A real part.

She'd never had that, always on the outside looking in.

"Anyhow, I had every reason to think Sofia's father would make good on that threat until Quinn told me otherwise last night." Beside her, Ian traced a flower on the hem of her dress where the fabric lay between them on the bench. That part of the full skirt didn't touch her body, but still…

The small action felt intimate.

Her heart ached.

"I believe you," she blurted before she'd even planned to speak. "That is, I already regret the way I didn't hear you out about why you were on a matchmaking website last year. I was hasty and misjudged you then, and I'm not making that same mistake again." If only that was the extent of their problems. She shifted beside him, finally daring to turn and face him. "But, Ian, you can't deny that you deliberately put a time limit on our relationship. That you tied up our relationship with a contract because you had no interest in a real marriage."

"A fail-safe," he said simply. "I fell in love in Rangiroa, Lydia. I wanted you to marry me then and bought this ring a whole year ago." He produced the yellow diamond from his pocket. "When you said you never wanted to see me again…it crushed me. But not so much that I pawned the ring."

Her heart tripped over itself, and then lodged somewhere in her throat. She swallowed hard, her smile wobbly with love. And hope.

"You've had the ring—all that time?" It didn't compute. Even when she'd been miscarrying alone? Even when he'd found her in Miami and maneuvered her into a fake marriage?

"Yes, although I have to confess, I couldn't look at it for months." He held it up to the sunlight and the smaller stones ringing the yellow diamond refracted light in a dazzling pattern. "But when I went to South Beach—a job I took specifically because I knew you were working there—I brought the ring with me and thought I'd see what happened."

"But you wanted a contract. You said it was only temporary." She thought back to that day on the rooftop of the Setai when it felt as if she had no options but to say yes to him.

"How many times could I risk breaking my heart on one woman? Or at least, that was the logic I used then." He took her left hand in his and stroked over the finger where the ring once rested. "But after what we shared in Costa Rica, after having you fall asleep in my arms again, I knew that my heart is yours to break, Lydia. However many times it takes."

Emotions swelled and burst inside her. She had to clutch a hand to her chest to keep them all in. But she couldn't hold back a shocked gasp as he handed her the ring again.

And then he got down on one knee in front of the bench in Central Park for all the tourists to see.

"Will you marry me, Lydia? For real, and forever? I love you, and if you think you can love me, too, we can say our vows again in front of our family. All of them." His lips curved in a smile more compelling than that gorgeous, one-of-a-kind diamond. "Even the Caribbean McNeills, if you want."

She could sense people nearby stopping and staring. It was the first time in her life she didn't mind being a spectacle.

"Yes." A half cry, half laugh hiccuped out of her throat. She nodded fast. "Yes, Ian. I will marry you again and again. I'm far too in love with you to do anything else."

All around them, people clapped. Whistled. Cheered. The whole tour that had passed them before had stopped to watch the Central Park proposal.

Lydia let Ian slide the ring onto her finger, and then hauled him up onto the bench to kiss him, not caring who saw.

When he stopped, he whispered in her ear, "You think your publicist will mind we didn't clear this with her? I'm pretty sure there were some cameras around."

"I'm returning to matchmaking," she whispered back, her heart swelling with happiness. "I need to show I can at least get it right for myself."

Ian leaned away to look in her eyes and cupped her cheek in his hand. "You just made your first customer the luckiest man on earth. If you want, I can give you a testimonial."

She couldn't withhold a grin. She traced a finger over his mouth and watched heat flare in his blue eyes. "I'd rather have an encore."

To his credit, he didn't hesitate.

* * * * *

HIS
ACCIDENTAL HEIR

JOANNE ROCK

For Barbara Jean Thomas, an early mentor
and role model of hard work. Thank you, Barbara, for
teaching me the value of keeping my chin up and
having faith in myself. During my teens, you were so
much more than a boss… You were a friend, a
cheerleader and a sometimes mom on those weekend
trips with the crew. I'll never forget my visit to
New York to see Oprah, courtesy of you!
Much love to you, always.

One

"Rafe, I need you in the Antilles Suite today." Maresa Delphine handed her younger brother a gallon jug of bubble bath. "I have a guest checking in who needs a hot bath on arrival, but he isn't sure what time he'll get here."

Her twenty-one-year-old sibling—who'd recently suffered a traumatic brain injury in a car accident—didn't reach to take the jug. Instead, his hazel eyes tracked the movements of a friendly barmaid currently serving a guest a Blackbeard's Revenge specialty drink on the patio just outside the lobby. The Carib Grand Hotel's floor-to-ceiling windows allowed for views of the tiki bar on Barefoot Beach and the glittering Caribbean Sea beyond. Inside the hotel, the afternoon activity had picked up since Maresa's mad dash to the island's sundries shop for the bath products. All of her runners had been busy fulfilling other duties for guests, so she'd made the trip herself. She had no idea what her newest runner—her recovering brother who still needed to work in a monitored environment—had been doing at that hour. He hadn't answered his radio and he needed to get with the program if he wanted to remain employed. Not to mention, Maria might be blamed for his slipups. She was supporting her family, and couldn't afford to lose her job as concierge for this exclusive hotel on a private island off Saint Thomas.

And she really, really needed him to remain employed where she could watch over him. Where he was eligible for better insurance benefits that could give him the long-term follow-up care he would need for years. She knew she held Rafe to a higher standard so that no one on staff could view his employment as a conflict of interest. Sure, the hotel director had approved his application, but she had promised to carefully supervise her brother during his three-month trial period.

"Rafe." She gently nudged her sibling with the heavy container of rose-scented bubbles, remembering his counselor's advice about helping him stay on task when he got distracted. "I have some croissants from the bakery to share with you on your next break. But for now, I really need help. Can you please take this to the Antilles Suite? I'd like you to turn on the hot water and add this for a bubble bath as soon as I text you."

Their demanding guest could stride through the lobby doors any moment. Mr. Holmes had phoned this morning, unsure of his arrival time, but insistent on having a hot bath waiting for him. That was just the first item on a long list of requests.

She checked her slim watch, a gift from her last employer, the Parisian hotel where she'd had the job of her dreams. As much as Maresa loved her former position, she couldn't keep it after her mother's car accident that had caused Rafe's head injury almost a year ago. Going forward, her place was here in Charlotte Amalie to help with her brother.

She refused to let him fail at the Carib Grand Hotel. Her mother's poor health meant she couldn't supervise him at home, for one thing. So having him work close to Maresa all day was ideal.

"I'll go to the Antilles Suite." Rafe tucked the bubble bath under one arm and continued to study the barmaid, a sweet girl named Nancy who'd been really kind to him when Maresa introduced them. "You will call me on the phone when I need to turn on the water."

Maresa touched Rafe's cheek to capture his full attention, her fingers grazing the jagged scar that wrapped beneath his left ear. Her mother had suffered an MS flare-up behind the wheel one night last year, sending her car into a telephone pole during a moment of temporary paralysis. Rafe had gone through the windshield since his seatbelt was unbuckled; he'd been trying to retrieve his phone that had slid into the backseat. Afterward, Maresa had been deeply involved in his recovery and care since their mother had been battling her own health issues. Their father had always been useless, a deadbeat American businessman who worked in the cruise industry and used to visit often, wooing Maresa's mother with promises about coming to live with him in Wisconsin when he saved up enough money to bring them. That had never happened, and he'd checked out on them by the time Maresa was ten, moving to Europe for his job. Yet then, as now, Maresa didn't mind adapting her life to help Rafe. Her brother's injuries could have been fatal that day. Instead, he was a happy part of her world. Yes, he would forever cope with bouts of confusion, memory loss and irritability along with the learning disabilities the accident had brought with it. Throughout it all, though, Rafe was always… Rafe. The brother she adored. He'd been her biggest supporter after her former fiancé broke things off with her a week before their wedding two years ago, encouraging her to go to Paris and "be my superstar."

He was there for her then, after that humiliating experience. She would be there for him now.

"Rafe? Go to the Antilles Suite and I'll text you when it's time to turn on the hot water." She repeated the instructions for him now, knowing it would be kinder to transfer him to the maintenance team or landscaping staff where he could do the same kinds of things every day. But who would watch out for him there? "Be sure to add the bubbles. Okay?"

Drawing in a breath, she took comfort from the soothing scent of white tuberoses and orchids in the arrangement on her granite podium.

"A bubble bath." Rafe grinned, his eyes clearing. "Can do." He ambled off toward the elevator, whistling.

Her relief lasted only a moment because just then a limousine pulled up in front of the hotel. She had a clear view out the windows overlooking the horseshoe driveway flanked by fountains and thick banks of birds-of-paradise. The doormen moved as a coordinated team toward the vehicle, prepared to open doors and handle baggage.

She straightened the orchid pinned on her pale blue linen jacket. If this was Mr. Holmes, she needed to stall him to give Rafe time to run that bath. The guest had been curt to the point of rudeness on the phone, requiring a suite with real grass—and it had to be ryegrass only— for his Maltese to relieve himself. The guest had also ordered a dog walker with three years' worth of references and a groomer on-site, fresh lilacs in the room daily and specialty pies flown in from a shop in rural upstate New York for his bedtime snack each evening.

And that was just for starters. She couldn't wait to see what he needed once he settled in for his two-week stay. These were the kinds of guests that could make or break a career. The vocal kind with many precise needs. All of which she would fulfill. It was the job she'd chosen because she took pride in her organizational skills, continually reordering her world throughout a chaotic childhood with an absentee father and a chronically ill mother. She took comfort in structuring what she could. And since there were only so many jobs on the island that could afford to pay her the kind of money she needed to support both her mother and her brother, Maresa had to succeed at the Carib Grand.

She calmed herself by squaring the single sheet of paper on her podium, lining up her pen beside it. She tapped open her list of restaurant phone numbers on her call screen so she could dial reservations at a moment's notice. The small, routine movements helped her to feel in control, reminding her she could do this job well. When she looked up again—

Wow.

The sight of the tall, chiseled male unfolding himself from the limousine was enough to take her breath away. His strong, striking features practically called for a feminine hand to caress them. Fraternizing with guests was, of course, strictly against the rules and Maresa had never been tempted. But if ever she had an inkling to stray from that philosophy, the powerful shoulders encased in expensive designer silk were exactly the sort of attribute that would intrigue her. The man towered over everyone in the courtyard entrance, including Big Bill, the head doorman. Dressed in a charcoal suit tailored to his long, athletic frame, the dark-haired guest buttoned his jacket, hiding too much of the hard, muscled chest that she'd glimpsed as he'd stepped out of the vehicle. Straightening his tie, he peered through the window, his ice-blue gaze somehow landing on her.

Direct hit.

She felt the jolt of awareness right through the glass. This supremely masculine specimen couldn't possibly be Mr. Holmes. Her brain didn't reconcile the image of a man with that square jaw and sharp blade of a nose ordering lilacs for himself. Daily.

Relaxing a fraction, Maresa blew out a breath as the newcomer turned back toward the vehicle. Until a silky white Maltese dog stepped regally from the limousine into the man's waiting arms.

In theory, Cameron McNeill liked dogs.

Big, slobbery working canines that thrived outdoors and could keep up with him on a distance run. The long-haired Maltese in his arms, on the other hand, was a prize-winning show animal with too many travel accessories to count. The retired purebred was on loan to Cam for his undercover assessment of a recently acquired McNeill Resorts property, however, and he needed Poppy's cooperation for his stint as a demanding hotel guest. If he walked into the financially floundering Carib Grand Hotel as himself—an owner and vice president of McNeill Resorts—he would receive the most attentive service imaginable and learn absolutely nothing about the establishment's underlying problems. But as Mr. Holmes, first-class pain in the ass, Cam would put the staff on their toes and see how they reacted.

After reviewing the Carib Grand's performance reports for the past two months, Cameron knew something was off in the day-to-day operations. And since he'd personally recommended that the company buy the property in the first place, he wasn't willing to wait for an overpriced operations review by an outside agency. Not that McNeill Resorts couldn't afford it. It simply chafed his pride that he'd missed something in his initial research. Besides, his family had just learned of a long-hidden branch of relations living on a nearby island—his father's sons by a secret mistress. Cam would use his time here to check out the other McNeills personally.

But for now? Business first.

"Welcome to the Carib Grand," an aging doorman greeted him with a deferential nod and a friendly smile.

Cam forced a frown onto his face to keep from smiling back. That wasn't as hard as he thought given the way Poppy's foolishly long fur was plastering itself to his jacket when he walked too fast, her topknot and tail bobbing with his stride and tickling his chin. It wouldn't come naturally to Cam to be the hard-to-please guest this week. He was a people-person to begin with, and appreciated those who worked for McNeill Resorts especially. But this was the fastest way he knew to find out what was going on at the hotel firsthand. He'd be damned if anyone on the board questioned his business acumen during a time when his aging grandfather was testing all his heirs for their commitment to his legacy.

The Carib Grand lobby was welcoming, as he recalled from his tour six months ago when the property had been briefly shut down. The two wings of the hotel flanked the reception area to either side with restaurants stacked overhead. But the lobby itself drew visitors in with floor-to-ceiling windows so the sparkling Caribbean beckoned at all times. Huge hanging baskets of exotic flowers framed the view without impeding it.

The scent of bougainvillea drifted in through the door

behind him. Poppy tilted her nose in the air and took a seat on his forearm, a queen on her throne.

The front desk attendant—only one—was busy with another guest. Cameron's bellhop, a young guy with a long ponytail of dreadlocks, must have noticed the front desk was busy at the same time as him, because he gestured to the concierge's tall granite counter where a stunning brunette smiled.

"Ms. Delphine can help you check in, sir," the bellhop informed him while whisking his luggage onto a waiting cart. "Would you like me to walk the dog while you get settled?"

Nothing would please him more than to off-load Poppy and the miles of snow-white pet hair threading around his suit buttons. Cameron was pretty sure there was a cloud of fur floating just beneath his nose.

"Her name is Poppy," Cameron snapped at the helpful soul, unable to take his eyes off the very appealing concierge, who'd snagged his attention through the window the second he'd stepped out of the limo. "And I've requested a dog walker with references."

The bellhop gave a nod and backed away, no doubt glad to leave a surly guest in the hands of the bronze-skinned beauty sidling out from her counter to welcome Cameron. She seemed to have that mix of ethnicities common in the Caribbean. The burnished tint of her skin set off wide, tawny gold eyes. A natural curl and kink in her dusky brown hair ended in sun-blond tips. Perfect posture and a well-fitted linen suit made her look every inch a professional, yet her long legs drew his eye even though her skirt hit just above her knees. Even if he'd been visiting the property as her boss, he wouldn't have acted on the flash of attraction, of course. But it was a damn shame that he'd be at odds with this enticing female for the next two weeks. The concierge position was the linchpin in the hotel staff, though, and his mission to rattle cages began with her.

"Welcome, Mr. Holmes." He was impressed that she'd greeted him by name. "I'm Maresa. We're so glad to see you and Poppy, too."

He'd spoken to a Maresa Delphine on the phone earlier, purposely issuing a string of demands on short notice to see how she'd fare. She didn't look nervous. Yet. He'd need to challenge her, to prod at all facets of the management and staff to pinpoint the weak links. The hotel wasn't necessarily losing money, but it was only a matter of time before earnings followed the decline in performance reviews.

"Poppy will be glad to meet her walker." He came straight to the point, ignoring the eager bob of the dog's head as Maresa offered admiring words to the pooch. Cameron could imagine what the wag of the tail was doing to the back of his jacket. "Do you have the references ready?"

"Of course." Maresa straightened with a sunny smile. She had a hint of an accent he couldn't place. "They're right here at my desk."

Cameron's gaze dipped to her slim hips as she turned. He'd taken a hiatus from dating for fun over the last few months, thinking he ought to find himself a wife to fulfill his grandfather's dictate that McNeill Resorts would only go to the grandsons who were stable and wed. But he'd botched that, too, impulsively issuing a marriage proposal to the first woman his matchmaker suggested in order to have the business settled.

Now? Apparently the months without sex were conspiring against him. He ground his teeth against a surge of ill-timed desire.

"Here you go." The concierge turned with a sheet of paper in hand and passed it to him, her honey-colored gaze as potent as any caress. "I took the liberty of checking all the references myself, but I've included the numbers in case you'd like to talk to any of them directly."

"That's why I asked," he replied tightly, tugging the paper harder than necessary.

He could have sworn Poppy slanted him a dirty look over one fluffy white shoulder. Her nails definitely flexed into his forearm right through the sleeve of his suit before she fixed her coal-black eyes on Maresa Delphine.

Not that he blamed Poppy. He'd rather be staring at Maresa than scowling over dog walker references. Being the boss wasn't always a rocking-good time. Yet he'd rather ruffle feathers today and fix the core problems than have the staff jump though the hoops of an extended performance review.

Cameron slid the paper into his jacket pocket. "I'll check these after I have the chance to clean up. If you can have someone show us to our room."

He hurried her on purpose, curious if the room extras were ready to go. The bath wasn't a tough request, but the flowers had most likely needed to be flown in. If he hadn't been specifically looking for it, he might have missed the smallest hesitation on her part.

"Certainly." She lifted a tablet from the granite countertop where she worked. "If you can just sign here to approve the information you provided over the phone, I'll escort you myself."

That wasn't protocol. Did Ms. Delphine expect additional tips this way? Cam remembered reading that the concierge had been with the company since the reopening under McNeill ownership two months ago.

Signing his fake name on the electronic screen, he fished for information. "Are you understaffed?"

She ran a pair of keycards through the machine and slid them into a small welcome folder.

"Definitely not. We'll have Rudolfo bring your bags. I just want to personally ensure the suite is to your liking." She handed him the packet with the keys while giving a nod to the bell captain. "Can I make a dinner reservation for you this evening, Mr. Holmes?"

Cameron juggled the restless dog, who was no doubt more travel-weary than him. They'd taken a private jet, but even with the shorter air time, there'd been limo rides to and from airports, plus a boat crossing from Charlotte Amalie to the Carib Grand since the hotel occupied a small, private island just outside the harbor area in Saint Thomas. He'd walked the dog when they hit the ground at the airfield, but Poppy's owner had cautioned him to give the animal a certain amount of rest and play each day. So far on Cam's watch, Poppy had clocked zero time spent on both counts. For a pampered show dog, she was proving a trouper.

As soon as he banished the hotel staff including Maresa Delphine, he'd find a quiet spot on the beach where he and his borrowed pet could recharge.

"I've heard a retired chef from Paris opened a new restaurant in Martinique." He would be spending some time on that island where his half brothers were living. "I'd like a standing reservation for the rest of the week." He had no idea if he'd be able to get over there, but it was the kind of thing a good concierge could accommodate.

"I've heard La Belle Palm is fantastic." Maresa punched a button on the guest elevator while Rudolfo disappeared down another hall with the luggage. "I haven't visited yet, but I enjoyed Chef Pierre's La Luce on the Left Bank."

Her words brought to mind her résumé that he'd reviewed briefly before making the trip. She'd worked at a Paris hotel prior to accepting her current position.

"You've spent time in Paris, Ms. Delphine?" He set Poppy on the floor, unfurling the pink jeweled leash that had matched the carrying case Mrs. Trager had given him. He'd kept all the accessories except for that one—the huge pink pet carrier made Cam look like he was travelling with Barbie's Dreamhouse under his arm.

"She's so cute." Maresa kept her eyes on the dog and not on him. "And yes, I lived in Paris for a year before returning to Saint Thomas."

"You're from the area originally?" He almost regretted setting the dog down since it removed a barrier between them. Something about Maresa Delphine drew him in.

His gaze settled on the bare arch of her neck just above her jacket collar. Her thick brown hair had been clipped at the nape, ending in a silky tail that curled along one shoulder. A single pearl drop earring rolled along the tender expanse of skin, a pale contrast to her rich brown complexion.

"I grew up in Charlotte Amalie and worked in a local hotel until a foreign exchange program run by the corporate owner afforded me the chance to work overseas." She glanced up at him. Caught him staring.

The jolt of awareness flared, hot and unmistakable. He could tell she felt it, too. Her pupils dilated a fraction, dark pools with golden rims. His heartbeat slugged heavier. Harder.

He forced his gaze away as the elevator chimed to announce their arrival on his floor. "After you."

He held the door as she stepped out into the short hall.

They passed a uniformed attendant with a gallon-sized jug stuffed under his arm, a pair of earbuds half-in and half-out of his ears. After a quick glance at Maresa, the young man pulled the buds off and jammed them in his pocket, then shoved open a door to the stairwell.

"Here we are." Maresa stepped aside so Cam stood directly in front of the entrance to the Antilles Suite.

Poppy took a seat and stared at the door expectantly.

Cameron used the keycard to unlock the suite, not sure what to expect. Was Maresa Delphine worthy of what the company compensated her? Or had she returned to her hometown in order to bilk guests out of extra tips and take advantage of her employer? But she didn't appear to be looking for a bonus gratuity as her gaze darted around the suite interior and then landed on him.

Poppy spotted the patch of natural grass just outside the bathroom door. The sod rested inside a pallet on carpeted wheels, the cart painted in blues and tans to match the room's decorating scheme. The dog made a break for it and Cam let her go, the leash dangling behind her.

Lilacs flanked the crystal decanters on the minibar. Through the open door to the bathroom, Cameron could see the bubbles nearing the edge of the tub, the hot water still running as steam wafted upward.

So far, Maresa had proven a worthy concierge. That was good for the hotel, but less favorable for him, perhaps, since her high standards surely precluded acting on a fleeting elevator attraction.

"If everything is to your satisfaction, Mr. Holmes, I'll leave you undisturbed while I go make your dinner reservations for the week." She hadn't even allowed the door to close behind them, a wise practice, of course, for a female hotel employee.

Rudolfo was already in the hall with the luggage cart.

Cameron could hear Maresa giving the bellhop instructions for his bags. And Poppy's.

"Thank you." Cameron turned his back on her to stare out at the view of the hotel's private beach and the brilliant turquoise Caribbean Sea. "For now, I'm satisfied."

The room, of course, was fine. Ms. Delphine had passed his first test. But was he satisfied? No. He wouldn't rest until he knew why the guest reviews of the Carib Grand were lower than anticipated. And satisfaction was the last thing he was feeling when the most enticing woman he'd met in a long time was off-limits.

That attraction would be difficult to ignore when it was imperative he uncover all her secrets.

Two

As much as Maresa cursed her alarm clock chirping at her before dawn, she never regretted waking up early once she was on the Carib Grand's private beach before sunrise. Her mother's house was perched on a street high above Saint Thomas Harbor, which meant Maresa took a bike to the ferry each morning to get to the hotel property early for these two precious hours of alone time before work. Her brother was comfortable walking down to the dock later for his shift, a task that was overseen by a neighbor and fellow employee who also took the ferry over each day.

Now, rolling out her yoga mat on the damp sand, she made herself comfortable in child's pose, letting the magic of the sea and the surf do their work on her muscles tight with stress.

One. Two. Three. Breathe.

Smoothing her hands over the soft cotton of her bright

pink crop top, she felt her diaphragm lift and expand. She rarely saw anyone else on the beach at this hour, and the few runners or walkers who passed by were too busy soaking up the same quiet moments as she to pay her any mind.

Maresa counted through the inhales and exhales, trying her damnedest to let go of her worries. Too bad Cameron Holmes's ice-blue eyes and sculpted features kept appearing in her mind, distracting her with memories of that electric current she'd experienced just looking at him.

It made no sense, she lectured herself as she swapped positions for her sun salutations. The guest was demanding and borderline rude—something that shouldn't attract her in the slightest. She hated to think his raw masculinity was sliding under her radar despite what her brain knew about him.

At least she'd made it through the first day of his stay without incident. But while that was something to celebrate, she didn't want her brother crossing paths with the surly guest again. She'd held her breath yesterday when the two passed one another in the corridor outside the Antilles Suite, knowing how much Rafe loved dogs. Thankfully, her brother had been engrossed in his music and hadn't noticed the Maltese.

She'd keep Rafe safely away from Mr. Holmes for the next two weeks. Tilting her face to the soft glow of first light, she arched her back in the upward salute before sweeping down into a forward bend. Breathing out the challenges—living in tight quarters with her family, battling local agencies to get her brother into support programs he needed for his recovery, avoiding her former fiancé who'd texted her twice in the last twenty-four hours asking to see her— Maresa took comfort in this moment every day.

Shifting into her lunge as the sun peeked above the horizon, Maresa heard a dog bark before a small white ball of fluff careened past her toward the water. Startled by the sudden brush of fur against her arm, she had to reposition her hands to maintain her balance.

"Poppy." A man's voice sounded from somewhere in the woods behind the beach.

Cameron Holmes.

Maresa recognized the deep baritone, not by sound so much as by the effect it had on her. A slow, warm wave through the pit of her belly. What was the matter with her? She scrambled to her feet, realizing the pampered pet of her most difficult guest was charging into the Caribbean, happily chasing a tern.

"Poppy!" she called after the dog just as Cameron Holmes stepped onto the beach.

Shirtless.

She had to swallow hard before she lifted her fingers to her lips and whistled. The little Maltese stopped in the surf, peering back in search of the noise while the tern flew away up the shore. The ends of Poppy's glossy coat floated on the surface of the incoming tide.

The man charged toward his pet, his bare feet leaving wet footprints in the sand. Maresa was grateful for the moment to indulge her curiosity about him without his seeing her. A pair of bright board shorts rode low on his hips. The fiery glow of sunrise burnished his skin to a deeper tan, his square shoulders rolling with an easy grace as he scooped the animal out of the water and into his arms. He spoke softly to her even as the strands of long, wet fur clung to his side. Whatever he said earned him a heartfelt lick on the cheek from the pooch, its white tail wagging slowly.

Maresa's heart melted a little. Especially when she

caught a glimpse of Cameron Holmes's smile as he turned back toward her. For a moment, he looked like another man entirely.

Then, catching sight of her standing beside her yoga mat, his expression grew shuttered.

"Sorry to interrupt your morning." He gave a brief nod. Curt. Dismissive. "I thought the beach would be empty at this hour or I wouldn't have let her off the leash." He clipped a length of pink leather to the collar around Poppy's neck.

"Most days, I'm the only one down here at this time." She forced a politeness she didn't feel, especially when she wasn't on duty yet. "Would you like a towel for her?"

The animal wasn't shivering, but Maresa couldn't imagine it would be easy to groom the dog if she walked home with wet fur dragging on the ground.

"I didn't think to bring one with me." He frowned, glancing around the deserted beach as if one might appear. "I assumed towels would be provided."

She tried not to grind her teeth at the air of entitlement. It became far easier to ignore the appeal of his shirtless chest once he started speaking in that superior air.

"Towels are available when the beach cabana opens at eight." Bending to retrieve the duffel on the corner of her mat, she tugged out hers and handed it to him. "Poppy can have mine."

He hesitated.

She fought the urge to cram the terry cloth back in her bag and stomp off. But, of course, she couldn't do that. She reached toward the pup's neck and scratched her there instead. Poppy's heart-shaped collar jangled softly against Maresa's hand. She noticed the "If Found" name on the back.

Olivia Trager?

Maybe the animal belonged to a girlfriend.

"Thank you." He took the hand towel and tucked it around the dog. Poppy stared out of her wrap as if used to being swaddled. "I really didn't mean to interrupt you."

He sounded more sincere this time. Maresa glanced up at him, only to realize how close they were standing. His gaze roamed over her as if he had been taking advantage of an unseen moment, the same way she had ogled him earlier. Becoming aware of her skimpy yoga crop top and the heat of awareness warming her skin, she stepped back awkwardly.

"Ms. Trager must really trust you with her dog." She hadn't meant to say it aloud. Then again, maybe hearing about his girlfriend would stop these wayward thoughts about him. "That is, no wonder you want to take such good care of her."

Awkward much? Maresa cursed herself for sticking her nose in his personal business.

His expression remained inscrutable for a moment. He studied her as if weighing how much to share. "My mother wouldn't trust anyone but me with her dog," he said finally.

She considered his words, still half wishing the mystery Ms. Trager was a girlfriend on her way to the resort today. Then Maresa would have to take a giant mental step backward from the confusing hotel guest. As it stood, she had no one to save her from the attraction but herself. With that in mind, she raked up her yoga mat and started rolling it.

"Well, I hope the dog walker and groomer meet your criteria." She stuffed the mat in her duffel, wondering why he hadn't let the walker take the animal out in the first place. "I'm happy to find someone else if—"

"The walker is fine. You're doing an excellent job, Maresa."

The unexpected praise caught her off guard. She nearly dropped her bag, mostly because he fixed her with his clear blue gaze. Heat rushed through her again, and it didn't have anything to do with the sun bathing them in the morning light now that it was fully risen.

"Thank you." Her throat went dry. She backed up a step. Retreating. "I'm going to let you enjoy the beach."

Maresa turned toward the path through the thick undergrowth that led back to the hotel and nearly ran right into Jaden Torries, her ex-fiancé.

"Whoa!" Jaden's one hand reached to steady her, his other curved protectively around a pink bundle he carried. Tall and rangy, her artist ex-boyfriend was thin where Cameron was well-muscled. The round glasses Jaden wore for affectation and not because he needed them were jammed into the thick curls that reached his shoulders. "Maresa. I've been trying to contact you."

He released her, juggling his hold on the small pink parcel he carried. A parcel that wriggled?

"I've been busy." She wanted to pivot away from the man who'd told the whole island he was dumping her before informing her of the fact. But that shifting pink blanket captured her full attention.

A tiny wrinkled hand reached up from the lightweight cotton, the movement followed by the softest sigh imaginable.

Her ex-fiancé was carrying a baby.

"But this is important, Maresa. It's about Isla." He lowered his arm cradling the infant so Maresa could see her better.

Indigo eyes blinked up at her. Short dark hair complimented the baby's medium skin tone. A white cotton headband decorated with rosettes rested above barely there eyebrows. Perfectly formed tiny features were molded into a silent yawn, the tiny hands reaching heavenward as the baby shifted against Jaden.

Something shifted inside Maresa at the same time. A maternal urge she hadn't known she possessed seized her insides and squeezed tight. Once upon a time she had dreamed about having this man's babies. She'd imagined what they would look like. Now, he had sought her out to...taunt her with the life she'd missed out on?

The maternal urge hardened into resentment, but she'd be damned if she'd let him see it.

"Congratulations. Your daughter is lovely, Jaden." She straightened as the large shadow of Cameron Holmes covered them both.

"Is there a problem, Ms. Delphine?" His tone was cool and impersonal, yet in that awkward moment he felt like an ally.

She appreciated his strong presence beside her when she felt that old surge of betrayal. She let Jaden answer since she didn't feel any need to defend the ex who'd called off their wedding via a text message.

"There's no problem. I'm an old friend of Maresa's. Jaden Torries." He extended his free hand to introduce himself.

Mr. Holmes ignored it. Poppy barked at Jaden.

"Then I'm sure you'll respect Maresa's wish to be on her way." Her unlikely rescuer tucked his hand under one arm as easily as he'd plucked his pet from the water earlier.

The warmth of his skin made her want to curl into him just like Poppy had, too.

"Right." Jaden dropped his hand. "Except Rafe's old girlfriend, Trina, left town last night, Maresa. And since

Trina's my cousin, she stuck me with the job of delivering Rafe's daughter into your care."

Maresa's feet froze to the spot. She had a vague sense of Cameron leaning closer to her, his hand suddenly at her back. Which was helpful, because she thought for a minute there was a very real chance she was going to faint. Her knees wobbled beneath her.

"Sorry to spring it on you like this," Jaden continued. "I tried telling Trina she owed it to your family to tell you in person, and I thought I had her talked into it, but—"

"Rafe?" Maresa turned around slowly, needing to see with her own eyes if there was any chance Jaden was telling the truth. "Trina broke up with him almost a year ago. Right after the accident."

Jaden stepped closer. "Right. And Trina didn't even find out she was pregnant until a couple of weeks afterward, while Rafe was still in critical condition. Trina decided to go through with the pregnancy on her own. Isla was born the end of January."

Maresa was too shaken to even do the math, but she did know that Trina and Rafe had been hot and heavy for the last month or two they were together. They'd been a constant fixture on Maresa's social media feed for those weeks. Which had made it all the more upsetting when Trina bailed on him right after the accident, bursting into tears every time she got close to his bedside before giving up altogether. Had she been even more emotional because she'd been in the early stages of pregnancy?

"Why wouldn't she have called me or my mother?" Her knees wobbled again as her gaze fell on the tiny infant. Isla? She had Rafe's hairline—the curve of dark hair encroaching on the temples. But plenty of babies had that, didn't they? "I would have helped her. I could have been there when the baby was born."

"Who is Rafe?" Cameron asked.

She'd forgotten all about him.

Maresa gulped a breath. "My brother." The very real possibility that Jaden was telling the truth threatened to level her. Rafe was in no position to be a father with the assorted symptoms he still battled. And financially? She was barely getting by supporting her family and paying some of Rafe's staggering medical bills since he hadn't been fully insured at the time.

"Look." Jaden set a bright pink diaper bag down on the beach. Cartoon cats cartwheeled across the front. "My apartment is no place for a baby. You know that, right? I just took her because Trina showed up last night, begging me for help. I told her no, but told her she could spend the night. She took off while I was sleeping. But she left a note for you." He looked as though he wanted to sort through the diaper bag to find it, but before he leaned down he held the baby out to Maresa. "Here. Take her."

Maresa wasn't even sure she'd made up her mind to do so when Jaden thrust the warm, precious weight into her arms. He was still talking about Trina seeming "unstable" ever since giving birth, but Maresa couldn't follow his words with an infant in her arms. She felt stiff and awkward, but she was careful to support the squirming bundle, cradling the baby against her chest while Isla gurgled and kicked.

Maresa's heart turned over. Melted.

Here, the junglelike landscaping blocked out the sun where the tree branches arced over the dirt path. The scent of green and growing things mingled with the sea breeze and a hint of baby shampoo.

"She's a beauty," Cameron observed over her shoulder. He had set Poppy on the ground so he could get closer to Isla and Maresa. "Are you okay holding her?"

"Fine," she said automatically, not wanting to give her up. "Just…um…overwhelmed."

Glancing up at him, she caught her breath at the expression on his face as he looked down at the child in her arms. She had thought he seemed different—kinder—toward Poppy. But that unguarded smile she'd seen for the Maltese was nothing compared to the warmth in his expression as he peered down at the baby.

If she didn't know better—if she hadn't seen him be rude and abrupt with perfectly nice hotel staffers—she would have guessed she caught him making silly faces at Isla. The little girl appeared thoroughly captivated.

"Here it is." Jaden straightened, a piece of paper in his hand. "She left this for you along with some notes about the kid's schedule." He passed the papers to Cameron. "I've got to get going if I'm going to catch that ferry, Maresa. I only came out here because Trina gave me no choice, but I've got to get to work—"

"Seriously?" She had to work, too. But even as she was about to say as much, another voice in her head piped up. If Isla was really Rafe's child, would she honestly want Jaden Torries in charge of the baby for another minute? The answer was a crystal clear *absolutely not*.

"Drop her off at social services if you don't believe me." Jaden shrugged. "I've got a rich old lady client paying a whole hell of a lot for me to paint her portrait at eight." He checked his watch. "I'm outta here."

And with that, her ex-fiancé walked away, his sandy-gold curls bouncing. Poppy barked again, clearly unimpressed.

Social services? Really?

"If only I had Poppy around three years ago when I got engaged to him," she muttered darkly, hugging the baby tighter.

Cameron's hand briefly found the small of her back as he watched the other man leave. He clutched the letter from Rafe's former girlfriend—Isla's mother.

"And yet you didn't go through with the wedding. So you did just fine on your own." Cameron glanced down at her, his hand lingering on her back for one heart-stopping moment before it drifted away again. "Want me to read the letter? Or would you like me to take Isla so you can do the honors?"

He held the paper out for her to decide.

She liked him better here—outside the hotel. He was less intimidating, for one thing.

For another? He was appealing to her in all the ways a man could. A dangerous feeling for her when she needed to be on her guard around him. He was a guest, for crying out loud. But she was out of her depth with this precious little girl in her arms and she didn't know what she'd do if Cameron Holmes walked away from her right now. Having him there made her feel—if only for a moment—that she wasn't totally alone.

"Actually, I'd be really grateful if you would read it." She shook her head, tightening her hold on Isla. "I'm too nervous."

Katrina—Trina—Blanchett had been Rafe's girlfriend for about six months before the car accident. Maresa had never seen them together except for photos on social media of the two of them out playing on the beach or at the clubs. They'd seemed happy enough, but Rafe had told her on the phone it wasn't serious. The night of the accident, in fact, the couple had gotten into an argument at a bar and Trina had stranded him there. Rafe had called their mother for a ride, something she'd been only too happy to provide even though it was late. She'd never had an MS attack while driving before.

Less than ten days after seeing Rafe in the hospital, Trina had told Maresa through tears that she couldn't stand seeing him that way and it would be better for her to leave. At the time, Maresa had been too focused on Rafe's prognosis to worry about his flighty girlfriend. If she'd taken time to talk to the girl, might she have confided the pregnancy news that followed the breakup?

"Would you like to have a seat?" Cameron pointed toward a bench near the outdoor faucet where guests could rinse off their feet. "You look too pale."

She nodded, certain she was pale. What was her mother going to say when she found out Rafe had a daughter? If he had a daughter. And Rafe? She couldn't imagine how frustrated he would feel to have been left out of the whole experience. Then again, how frustrated would he feel knowing that he couldn't care for his daughter the way he could have at one time?

Struggling to get her spinning thoughts under control, she allowed Cameron to guide her to the bench. Carefully, she lowered herself to sit with Isla, the baby blanket covering her lap since the kicking little girl had mostly freed herself of the swaddling. While she settled the baby, she noticed Cameron lift Poppy and towel her off a bit more before setting her down again. He double-checked the leash clip on her collar then took the seat beside Maresa.

"I'm ready," she announced, needing to hear whatever Isla's mother had to say.

Cameron unfolded the paper and read aloud. "'Isla is Rafe's daughter. I wasn't with anyone else while we were together. I was afraid to tell him about her after the doctor said he'd be…'" Cameron hesitated for only a moment "'…brain damaged. I know Rafe can't take care of her, but his mother will love her, right? I can't do this. I'm going to see my dad in Florida for a few weeks, but I'll sign papers to give you custody. I'm sorry."

Maresa listened to the silence following the words, her brain uncomprehending. How could the woman just take off and leave her baby—Rafe's baby—with Jaden Torries while she traveled to Florida? Who did that? Trina wasn't a kid—she was twenty-one when she'd dated Rafe. But she'd never had much family support, according to Rafe. Her mother was an alcoholic and her father had raised her, but he'd never paid her much attention.

A fierce surge of protectiveness swelled inside of Maresa. It was so strong she didn't know where to put it all. But she knew for damn sure that she would protect little Isla—her niece—far better than the child's mother had. And she would call a lawyer and find out how to file for full custody.

"You could order DNA testing," Cameron observed, his impressive abs rippling as he leaned forward on the bench. "If you are concerned she's not a biological relative."

Maresa closed her eyes for a moment to banish all thoughts of male abs, no matter how much she welcomed the distraction from the monumental life shift taking place for her this morning.

"I'll ask an attorney about it when I call to find out how I can secure legal custody." She wrapped Isla's foot back in a corner of the blanket. "For right now, I need to find suitable care for Isla before my shift at the Carib begins for the day." Throat burning, Maresa realized she was near tears just thinking about the unfairness of it all. Not to *her*, of course, because she would make it work no matter what life threw at her.

But how unfair to *Rafe*, who wouldn't be able to parent his child without massive amounts of help. Perhaps he wouldn't be interested in parenting at all. Would he be angry? Would Trina's surprise be the kind of thing that unsettled his confused mind and set back his recovery?

She would call his counselor before saying anything to him. That call would be right after she spoke to a lawyer. She wasn't even ready to tell her mother yet. Analise Delphine's health was fragile and stress could aggravate it. Maresa wanted to be sure she was calm before she spoke to her mother. They'd all been in the dark for months about Trina's pregnancy. A few more hours wouldn't matter one way or another.

"I noticed on the dog walker's résumé that she has experience working in a day care." Cameron folded the paper from Trina and inserted it into an exterior pocket of the diaper bag. "And as it happens, I already walked the dog. Would you like me to text her and ask her to meet you somewhere in the hotel to give you a hand?"

Maresa couldn't imagine what that would cost. But what were her options since she didn't want to upset her mother? She didn't have time to return home and give the baby to her mother even if she was sure her mother could handle the shocking news.

"That would be a great help, thank you. The caregiver can meet me in the women's locker room by the pool in twenty minutes." Shooting to her feet, Maresa realized she'd imposed on Cameron Holmes's kindness for far too long. "And with that, I'll let you and Poppy get back to your morning walk."

"I'll go with you. I can carry the baby gear." He reached for the pink diaper bag, but she beat him to it.

"I'm fine. I insist." She pasted on her best concierge smile and tried not to think about how comforting it had felt to have him by her side this morning. Now more than ever, she needed job security, which meant she couldn't let an important guest think she made a habit of bringing her personal life to work. "Enjoy your day, Mr. Holmes."

Enjoying his day proved impossible with visions of Maresa Delphine's pale face circling around Cameron's head the rest of the morning. He worked at his laptop on the private terrace off his room, distracted as hell thinking about the beautiful, efficient concierge caught off guard by a surprise that would have damn near leveled anyone else.

She'd inherited her brother's baby. A brother who, from the sounds of it, was not in any condition to care for his child himself.

Sunlight glinted off the sea and the sounds from the beach floated up to his balcony. The noises had grown throughout the morning from a few circling gulls to the handful of vacationing families that now populated the beach. The scent of coconut sunscreen and dense floral vegetation swirled on the breeze. But the temptation of a tropical paradise didn't distract Cam from his work nearly as much as memories of his morning with Maresa.

Shocking encounter with the baby aside, he would still have been distracted just remembering her limber arched back, her beautiful curves outlined by the light of the rising sun when he'd first broken through the dense undergrowth to find her on the private beach. Her skimpy workout gear had skimmed her hips and breasts, still tantalizing the hell out of him when he was supposed to be researching the operations hierarchy of the Carib Grand on his laptop.

But then, all that misplaced attraction got funneled into protectiveness when he'd met her sketchy former fiancé. He'd met the type before—charming enough, but completely self-serving. The guy couldn't have come up with a kinder way to inform her of her niece's existence?

On the plus side, Cameron had located some search results about her brother. Rafe Delphine had worked at the hotel for one month in a hire that some might view as unethical given his relationship to Maresa. But his application—though light on work history—had been approved by the hotel director on-site, so the young man must be fit for the job despite his injury in a car wreck the year before. That, too, had been an easy internet search, with local news articles reporting the crash and a couple of updates on Rafe's condition afterward. The trauma the guy had suffered must have been harrowing for his whole family. Clearly the girlfriend had found it too much to handle.

Now, as a runner for the concierge, Rafe would be directly under Maresa's supervision. That concerned Cameron since Maresa would have every reason in the world to keep him employed. As much as Cam empathized with her situation—all the more now that she'd discovered her brother had an heir—he couldn't afford to ignore good business practices. He'd have to speak to the hotel director about the situation and see if they should make a change.

The ex-fiancé was next on his list of searches. Not that he wanted to pry into Maresa's private life. Cameron was more interested in seeing how the guy connected to the Carib Grand that he'd come all the way to the hotel's private island to pass over the baby. That seemed like an unnecessary trip unless he was staying here or worked here. Why not just give the baby to Maresa at her home in Charlotte Amalie? Why come to her place of work when it was so far out of the way?

Cam had skimmed halfway through the short search results on Jaden Torries's portraits of people and pets before his phone buzzed with an incoming call. Poppy, snoozing in the shade of the chair under his propped feet, didn't even stir at the sound. The dog was definitely making up for lost rest from the day before.

Glimpsing his oldest brother's private number, Cam hit the button to connect the call. "Talk to me."

"Hello to you, too." Quinn's voice came through along with the sounds of Manhattan in the background—horns honking, brakes squealing, a shrill whistle and a few shouts above the hum of humanity indicating he must be on the street. "I wanted to give you a heads-up I just bought a sea plane."

"Nice, bro, But there's no way you'll get clearance to land in the Hudson with that thing." Cameron scrolled to a gallery of Torries's work and was decidedly unimpressed.

Not that he was an expert. But as a supporter of the arts in Manhattan for all his adult life, he felt reasonably sure Maresa's ex was a poser. Then again, maybe he just didn't like a guy who'd once commanded the concierge's attention.

"The aircraft isn't for me," Quinn informed him. "It's for you. I figured it would be easier than a chopper to get from one island to another while you're investigating the Carib Grand and checking out the relatives."

Cam shoved aside his laptop and straightened. "Seriously? You bought a seaplane for my two-week stay?"

As a McNeill, he'd grown up with wealth, yes. He'd even expanded his holdings with the success of the gaming development company he'd started in college. But damn. He limited himself to spending within reason.

"The Carib Grand is the start of our Caribbean expansion, and if it goes well, we'll be spending a lot of time and effort developing the McNeill brand in the islands and South America. We have a plane available in the Mediterranean. Why not keep something accessible on this side of the Atlantic?"

"Right." Cam's jaw flexed at the thought of how much was riding on smoothing things out at the Carib Grand. A poor bottom line wasn't going to help the expansion program. "Good thinking."

"Besides, I have the feeling we'll be seeing our half brothers in Martinique a whole lot more now that Gramps is determined to bring them into the fold." Quinn sounded as grim about that prospect as Cameron felt. "So the plane might be useful for all of us as we try to…contain the situation."

Quinn wanted to keep their half siblings out of Manhattan and out of the family business as much as Cameron did. They'd worked too hard to hand over their company to people who'd never lifted a finger to grow McNeill Resorts.

"Ah." Cam stood to stretch his legs, surprised to realize it was almost noon according to the slim dive watch he'd worn for his morning laps. "But since I'm on the front line meeting them, I'm going to leave it up to you or Ian to be the diplomatic peacemakers."

Quinn only half smothered a laugh. "No one expected you of all people to be the diplomat. Dad's still recovering from the punch you gave him last week when he dropped the I-have-another-family bombshell on us."

Definitely not one of his finer moments. "It seemed like he could have broached the topic with some more tact."

"No kidding. I kept waiting for Sofia to break the engagement after the latest family soap opera." The background noise on Quinn's call faded. "Look, Cam, I just arrived at Lincoln Center to take her out to lunch. I'll text you the contact details for a local pilot."

Cam grinned at the thought of his stodgy older brother

so head over heels for his ballerina fiancée. The same ballerina fiancée Cam had impulsively proposed to last winter when a matchmaker set them up. But even if Cam and Sofia hadn't worked out, the meeting had been a stroke of luck for Quinn, who'd promptly stepped in to woo the dancer.

"Thanks. And give our girl a kiss from me, okay?" It was too fun to resist needling Quinn. Especially since Cameron was two thousand miles away from a retaliatory beat-down.

A string of curses peppered his ear before Quinn growled, "It's not too late to take the plane back."

"Sorry." Cameron wasn't sorry. He was genuinely happy for his brother. "I'll let you know if the faux McNeills are every bit as awful as we imagine."

Disconnecting the call, Cameron texted a message to the dog groomer to give Poppy some primp time. He'd use that window of freedom to follow up on a few leads around the Carib Grand. He wanted to find out what the hotel director thought about Rafe Delphine, for one thing. The director was the only person on-site who knew Cameron's true identity and mission at the hotel. Aldo Ricci had been successful at McNeill properties in the Mediterranean and Malcolm McNeill had personally appointed the guy to make the expansion program a success.

With the McNeill patriarch's health so uncertain, Cameron wanted to respect his grandfather's choices. All the more so since he still hadn't married the way his granddad wanted.

Cameron would start by speaking to his grandfather's personally chosen manager. Cam had a lot of questions about the day-to-day operations and a few key personnel. Most especially the hotel's new concierge, who kept too many secrets behind her beautiful and efficient facade.

Three

Seated in the hotel director's office shortly after noon, Cameron listened to Aldo Ricci discuss his plans for making the Carib Grand more profitable over the next two quarters. Unlike Cameron, the celebrated hotel director with a crammed résumé of successes did not seem concerned about the dip in the Carib Grand's performance.

"All perfectly normal," the impeccably dressed director insisted, prowling around his lavish office on the ground floor of the property. A collector of investment-grade wines, Aldo incorporated a few rare vintages into his office decor. A Bordeaux from Moulin de La Lagune rested casually on a shelf beside some antique corkscrews and a framed invitation from a private tasting at Château Grand Corbin. "We are only beginning to notice the minute fluctuations now that our capacity for data is greater than ever. But those irregularities will not even be noticeable by the time we hit our performance and profit goals for the end of the year."

The heavyset man tugged on his perfectly straight suit cuffs. The fanciness of the dark silk jacket he wore reminded Cameron how many times the guy had taken a property out of the red and into the ranks of the most prestigious places in the world. To have enticed him to McNeill Resorts had been a coup, according to Cameron's grandfather.

"Nevertheless, I'd like to know more about Maresa Delphine." Cameron didn't reveal his reasons. He could see her now through the blinds in the director's office. She strode along the pool patio outside, hurrying past the patrons in her creamy linen blazer with an orchid at the lapel. Her sun-splashed brown hair gleamed in the bright light, but something about her posture conveyed her tension. Worry.

Was she thinking about Isla?

He made a mental note to check on the sitter and be sure she was doing a good job with the baby. Little Isla had tugged at his heartstrings this morning with her tiny, restless hands and her expressive face. That feeling—the warmth for the baby—shocked him. Not that he was an ogre or anything, but he'd decided long ago not to have kids of his own.

He was too much like his father—impulsive, fun-loving, easily distracted—to be a parent. After all, Liam McNeill had turfed out responsibility for his sons at the first possible opportunity, letting the boys' grandfather raise them the moment Liam's Brazilian wife got tired of his globe-trotting, daredevil antics. Cameron had always known his father had shirked the biggest responsibility of his life and that, coupled with his own tendency to follow his own drummer, had been enough to convince Cam that kids weren't for him. And that had been before discovering his dad had fathered a whole other set of kids with someone else.

Before an accident that had compromised Cameron's ability to have a family anyhow.

"Maresa Delphine is a wonderful asset to the hotel," the director assured him, coming around to the front of his desk to sit beside Cameron in the leather club chairs facing the windows. "If you seek answers about the hotel workings, I urge you to reveal your identity to her. I know you want to remain incognito, but I assure you, Ms. Delphine is as discreet and professional as they come."

"Yet you've only known her for…what? Two months?"

"Far longer than that. She worked at another property in Saint Thomas where I supervised her three years ago. I personally recommended her to a five-star property in Paris because I was impressed with her work and she was eager to…escape her hometown for a while. I had no reservations about helping her win the spot. She makes her service her top priority." The director crossed one leg over the other and pointed to a crystal decanter on the low game table between them. "Are you sure I can't offer you anything to drink?"

"No. Thank you." He wanted a clear head for deciding his next move with Maresa. Revealing himself to her was tempting considering the attraction simmering just beneath the surface. But he couldn't forget about the gut instinct that told him she was hiding something. "What can you tell me about her brother?"

"Rafe is a fine young man. I would have gladly hired him even without Maresa's assurances she would watch over him."

"Why would she need to?" He was genuinely curious

about the extent of Rafe's condition. Not only because she seemed protective of him, but also because Maresa hadn't argued Trina's depiction of her brother as "brain damaged."

"Rafe has a traumatic brain injury. He's the reason Maresa gave up the job in Paris. She rushed home to take care of her family. The young man is much better now. Although he can become agitated or confused easily, he has good character, and we haven't put him in a position where he will have much contact with guests." Aldo smiled as he smoothed his tie. "Maresa feels a strong sense of responsibility for him. But I've seen no reason to regret hiring her sibling. She knows, however, that Rafe's employment is on a trial basis."

Aldo Ricci seemed like the kind of man to trust his gut, which might be fine for someone who'd been in the business for as long as he had, but Cameron still wondered if he was overlooking things.

Maybe he should confide in Maresa if only to discover her take on the staff at the Carib Grand. Specifically, he wondered, what was her impression of Aldo Ricci? Cameron found himself wanting to know a lot more about the operations of the hotel.

"Perhaps I will speak to Ms. Delphine." Cameron wanted to find her now, in fact. His need to see her has been growing ever since she'd walked away from him early that morning. "I'd like some concrete answers about those performance reviews, even if they do seem like minute fluctuations."

He rose from his seat, liking the new plan more than he should. *Damn it.* Spending more time with Maresa didn't mean anything was going to happen between them. As her boss, of course, he had a responsibility to ensure it didn't.

And, without question, she had a great deal on her

mind today of all days. But maybe that was all the more reason to give her a break from the concierge stand. Perhaps she'd welcome a few hours away from the demands of the guests.

"Certainly." The hotel director followed him to the door. "There's no one more well-versed in the hotel except for me." His grin revealed a mouth full of shiny white veneers. "Stick close to her."

Cameron planned to do just that.

"Have you seen Rafe?" Maresa asked Nancy, the waitress who worked in the lobby bar shortly after noon. "I wanted to eat lunch with him."

Standing beside Nancy, a tall blonde goddess of a woman who probably made more in tips each week than Maresa made in a month, she peered out over the smattering of guests enjoying cocktails and the view. Her brother was nowhere in sight.

She had checked on Isla a few moments ago, assuring herself the baby was fine. She'd shared Trina's notes about the baby's schedule with the caregiver, discovering Isla's birth certificate with the father's name left blank and a birth date of ten weeks prior. And after placing a call to Trina's mother, Maresa had obtained contact information for the girl's father in Florida, who'd been able to give her a number for Trina herself. The girl had tearfully confirmed everything she said in her note—promising to give custody of the child to Rafe's family since she wasn't ready to be a mother and she didn't trust her own mother to be a good guardian.

The young woman had been so distraught, Maresa had felt sorry for her. All the more so because Trina had tried to handle motherhood alone when she'd been so conflicted about having a baby in the first place.

Now, Maresa wanted to see Rafe for herself to make sure he was okay. What if Jaden had mentioned Isla to him? Or even just mentioned Trina leaving town? Rafe hadn't asked about his girlfriend since regaining consciousness. She suspected Rafe would have been walking onto the ferry that morning the same time as Jaden was walking off.

Earlier that day, she'd left him a to-do list when she'd had an appointment to keep with the on-site restaurant's chef. She'd given Rafe only two chores, and they were both jobs he'd done before so she didn't think he'd have any trouble. He had to pick up some supplies at the gift shop and deliver flowers to one of the guests' rooms.

"I saw him about an hour ago." Nancy rang out a customer's check. "He brought me this." She pointed to the tiny purple wildflowers stuffed behind the engraved silver pin with her name on it. "He really is the sweetest."

"Thank you for being so kind to him." Maresa had witnessed enough people be impatient and rude to him that he'd become her barometer for her measure of a person. People who were nice to Rafe earned her respect.

"Kind to *him*?" Nancy tossed her head back and laughed, her long ponytail swishing. "That boy should earn half my tips since it's Rafe who makes me smile when I feel like strangling some of my more demanding customers—like that Mr. Holmes." She straightened the purple blooms with one hand and shoved the cash drawer closed with her hip. "These flowers from your brother are the nicest flowers any man has ever given me."

Reassured for the moment, Maresa felt her heart squeeze at the words. Her brother had the capacity for great love despite the frustrations of his injury. Maybe he'd come to accept his daughter as part of his life down the road.

Until then, she needed to keep them both safely employed and earning benefits to take care of their family.

"It makes me happy to hear you say that." Maresa turned on her heel, leaving Nancy to her job. "If you see him, will you let him know I'm having lunch down by the croquet field?"

"Sure thing." Nancy lifted a tray full of drinks to take to another table. "Sometimes he hangs out in the break room if the Yankees are on the radio, you know. You might check if they play today."

"Okay. Thanks." She knew her brother liked listening to games on the radio. Being able to listen on his earbuds was always soothing for him.

Maresa hitched her knapsack with the insulated cooler onto her shoulder to carry out to the croquet area. The field didn't officially open again until late afternoon when it cooled down, so no one minded if employees sat under the palm trees there for lunch. There were a handful of places like that on the private island—spots where guests didn't venture that workers could enjoy. She needed a few minutes to collect herself. Come up with a plan for what she was going to do with a ten-week-old infant after work. And what she would tell Rafe about the baby since his counselor hadn't yet returned her phone call.

Her phone vibrated just then as her sandals slapped along the smooth stone path dotted with exotic plantings on both sides. Her mother's number filled the screen.

"Mom?" she answered quietly while passing behind the huge pool and cabanas that surrounded it. The area was busy with couples enjoying outdoor meals or having cocktails at the swim-up bar and families playing in the nearby surf. Seeing a mother share a bite of fresh pineapple with her little girl made Maresa's breath catch.

She'd once dreamed of being a mother to Jaden's children until he betrayed her.

Now, she might be a single mother to her brother's baby if Trina truly relinquished custody.

She scuttled deeper into the shade of some palms for her phone conversation, knowing she couldn't blurt out Isla's existence to her mom on the phone even though, in the days before her mother's health had taken a downhill spiral, she might have been tempted to do just that.

"No need to worry." Her mother's breathing sounded labored. From stress? Or exertion? She tired so easily over the past few months. "I just wanted to let you know your brother came home."

Maresa's steps faltered. Stopped.

"Rafe is there? With you?" Panic tightened her shoulders and clenched her gut. She peered around the path to the croquet field, half hoping her brother would come strolling toward her anyhow, juggling some pilfered deck cushions for her to sit on for an impromptu picnic the way he did sometimes.

"He showed up about ten minutes ago. I would have called sooner, but he was upset and I had to calm him down. I guess the florist gave him a pager—"

"Oh no." Already, Maresa could guess what had happened. "Those are really loud." The devices vibrated and blinked, setting off obnoxious alarms that would startle anyone, let alone someone with nervous tendencies. The floral delivery must not have been prepared when Rafe arrived to pick it up, so they gave him the pager to let him know when it was ready.

"He got scared and dropped it, but I'm not sure where—" Her mother stopped speaking, and in the background, Maresa heard Rafe shouting "I don't know, I don't know, I don't know" in a frightened chorus.

Her gut knotted. How could she bring a ten-week-old into their home tonight, knowing how loud noises upset her brother?

"Tell him everything's fine. I'll find the pager." Turning on her heel, she headed back toward the hotel. She thought the device turned itself off after a few minutes anyhow, but just in case it was still beeping, she'd rather find it before anyone else on staff. "I can probably retrace his steps since I sent him on those errands. I'll deliver the flowers myself."

"Honey, you're taking on too much having him there with you. You don't want to risk your job."

And the alternative? They didn't have one. Especially now with little Isla's care to consider.

"My job will be fine," she reassured her mother as she tugged open a door marked Employees Only that led to the staff room and corporate offices. She needed to sign Rafe out for the day before she did anything else.

Blinking against the loss of sunlight, Maresa felt the blast of air conditioning hit her skin, which had gone clammy with nervous sweat. She picked at the neckline of her thin silk camisole beneath her linen jacket.

"Ms. Delphine?" a familiar masculine voice called to her from the other end of the corridor.

Even before she turned, she knew who she would see. The tingling that tripped over her skin was an unsettling mix of anticipation and dread.

"Mom, I'll call you back." Disconnecting quickly, she dropped the phone in her purse and turned to see Cameron Holmes striding out of the hotel director's office, her boss at his side.

"Mr. Holmes." She forced a smile for both men, wondering why life was conspiring so hard against her today. What on earth would a guest be doing in the hotel director's office if not to complain? Unless maybe he had something extremely valuable he wanted to place in the hotel safe personally.

Highly unorthodox, but that's the only other reason she could think of to explain his presence here.

"Maresa." Her hotel director nodded briefly at her before shaking hands with Cameron Holmes. "And sir, I appreciate you coming to me directly. I certainly understand the need for discretion."

Aldo Ricci turned and re-entered his office, leaving Maresa with a racing heart in the presence of Cameron Holmes, who looked far more intimidating in a custom navy silk suit and a linen shirt open at the throat than he had in his board shorts this morning.

The level of appeal, however, seemed equal on both counts. She couldn't forget his unexpected kindness on the beach no matter how demanding he'd been as a hotel guest.

"Just the woman I was hoping to see." His even white teeth made a quick appearance in what passed for a smile. "Would you join me for a moment in the conference room?"

No.

Her brain filled in the answer even as her feet wisely followed where he led. She didn't want to be alone with him anywhere. Not when she entertained completely inappropriate thoughts about him. She couldn't let her attraction to a guest show.

Furthermore? She needed to sign her brother out of work, locate the pager he'd lost and deliver those flowers before the florist got annoyed and reported Rafe for not doing his job. Now was not the time for fantasizing about a wealthy guest who could afford to shape the world to his liking, even if he had the body of a professional surfer underneath that expensive suit.

As she crossed the threshold into the Carib Grand's private conference room full of tall leather chairs around an antique table, Maresa realized she couldn't do this. Not now.

"Actually, Mr. Holmes," she said, spinning around to face him and misjudging how close he followed behind her.

Suddenly, she stood nose-to-nose with him, her thigh grazing his, her breast brushing his strong arm. She stepped back fast, heat flooding her cheeks. The contact was so brief, she could almost tell herself it hadn't happened, except that her body hummed with awareness where they'd touched.

And then, there was the fact that he gripped her elbow when she wobbled.

"Sorry," she blurted, tugging away from him completely as the door to the conference room closed automatically behind them.

Sealing them in privacy.

Sunlight spilled in behind her, the Caribbean sun the only illumination in the room that hadn't been in use yet today. The quiet was deep here, the carpet muffling his step as he shifted closer.

"Are you all right?" His forehead creased with concern. "Are you comfortable with the caregiver for Isla?"

She glanced up at him, surprised at the thoughtful question. He really had been supportive this morning, giving her courage during an impossible situation. Right now, however, it was difficult to focus on his kind side when the man was simply far too handsome. She wished fervently he had that adorable little dog with him so she could pet Poppy instead of thinking about how hot Mr. Holmes could be when he wasn't scowling.

"I'm fine. I have everything under control." *Um, if*

only. Clearly, she needed to date more often so she didn't turn into a babbling idiot around handsome men during work hours. "It's just that you caught me on my lunch hour, so I'm not technically working."

"Unfortunately, Maresa, I am." He folded his arms across his chest before he paced halfway across the room.

Confused, she watched him. He was not an easy man to look away from.

"I don't understand." She wondered how it happened that being around him made her feel like there wasn't enough air in the room. Like she couldn't possibly catch her breath.

"I'm doing some work for the hotel," he explained, pacing back toward her. "Secretly."

Confusion filled her as she tried to sort through his words that didn't make a bit of sense.

"So you're not actually on vacation at all? What kind of work?" She could think better now that he was on the opposite side of the room. "Is that why you were in the hotel director's office?"

"Yes. My real name is Cameron McNeill and I'm investigating why guest satisfaction has been declining over the last two months." He kept coming toward her, his blue eyes zeroing in on her. "And now I'm beginning to think you're the only person who can help me figure out why."

Cameron could feel her nervousness as clearly as if it was his own.

She stood, alert and ready to flee, her tawny eyes wide. She bit her full lower lip.

"McNeill? As in McNeill Resorts?" She blinked slowly.

"The same."

"Why do you think I can help you?" She smoothed the

cuff of her ivory-colored linen jacket and then swiped elegant fingers along her forehead as if perspiring in spite of the fact she looked cool. So incredibly smooth and cool.

He hated doing this to her today of all days. The woman had just found out her brother had a child who would—he suspected—become her financial and familial dependent. What he'd gathered about Rafe Delphine's health suggested the man wouldn't be in any position to care for a newborn, and Aldo Ricci had made it clear Maresa put her family before herself.

"Preliminary data indicates the Carib is floundering in performance reviews and customer satisfaction." That was true enough. "You have a unique perspective on the hotel and everyone who works here. I'd like to know your views on why that might be?"

"And my boss told you I would talk to you about those issues?" Her gaze flitted to the door behind him and then back to him as if she would rather be anywhere else than right here.

Truth be told, he was a little uncomfortable being alone with her under these circumstances himself. She was far too tempting to question in the privacy of an empty conference room when the attraction was like a live wire sending sparks in all directions.

How could he ignore that?

"Your hotel director assured me you would be discreet."

She'd garnered the respect of her peers. The praise of superiors. All of which only made Cameron more curious about her. He stopped in front of her. At a respectable distance. He held her gaze, not allowing his eyes to wander.

"Of course, Mr. McNeill." She fidgeted with a bracelet—a shiny silver star charm—partially hidden by the sleeve of her jacket. "But what exactly did he hope I could share with you?"

"Call me Cam. And I hope you will share any insights about the staff and even some of the guests." He knew the data could be skewed by one or two unhappy visitors, particularly if they were vocal about their displeasure with the hotel.

"A difficult line to walk considering how much a concierge needs to keep her guests happy. It doesn't serve me—or McNeill Resorts—to betray confidences of valued clients."

Cameron couldn't help the voice in his head that piped up just then, wanting to know what she might have done to keep *him* happy as her guest.

Focus, damn it.

"And yet, you'll want to please the management as well," he reminded her. "Correct?"

"Of course." She nodded, letting go of the silver star so the bracelet slipped lower on her wrist.

"So how about if I buy you lunch and we'll begin our work together? I'll speak to Mr. Ricci about giving you the afternoon off." He needed to take her somewhere else. A place where the temptation to touch her wouldn't get the better of him. "We can bring Isla."

Nothing stifled attraction like an infant, right?

"Thank you, Mr. Mc—er, Cam." Maresa's face lit up with a glow that damn near took his breath away; her relief and eagerness to be reunited with the little girl were all too obvious. "That would be really wonderful."

Her pleasure affected him far more than it should, making him wonder how he could make that smile return to her face again and again. Had he really thought a baby would dull his desire for Maresa?

Not a chance.

Four

"You rented a villa here," Maresa observed as she held the ends of her hair in one hand to keep it from flying away in the open-top Jeep Cameron McNeill used for tooling around the private island. "In addition to the hotel suite."

The Jeep bounced down a long road through the lush foliage to a remote part of the island. In theory, she knew about the private villas that the Carib Grand oversaw on the extensive property, but the guests who took those units had their own staff so she didn't see them often and she'd never toured them. She turned in her seat to peer back at Isla, in the car seat she'd procured from the hotel. The baby faced backward with a sunshade tilted over the seat, but Maresa could see the little girl was still snoozing contentedly.

The caregiver had fed and changed her, and before Maresa could compensate her, Cameron had taken care of the bill, insisting that he make the day as easy as possible for Maresa to make up for the inconvenience of working with him. Spending the day in a private villa with yet another caregiver—this one a licensed nurse from the hospital in Saint Thomas who would meet them there—was hardly an inconvenience. Truth be told, she was grateful to escape the hotel for the day after the stress of discovering Isla and finding out that Rafe had left work without authorization. Luckily, she'd signed him out due to illness and found the pager he dropped on her way to pick up Isla from the caregiver. Maresa had assigned the flower delivery to another runner before leaving.

Now, all she had to do was get through an afternoon with her billionaire boss who'd only been impersonating a pain-in-the-butt client. But what if Cameron McNeill turned out to be even more problematic than his predecessor, Mr. Holmes?

"The villas are managed by a slightly different branch of the company," Cameron informed her, using a remote to open a heavy wrought-iron gate that straddled the road ahead. "My privacy is protected here. I'll return to the hotel suite later tonight to continue my investigation work under Mr. Holmes's name. Unless, of course, you and I can figure out the reason behind the declining reviews before then."

The ocean breeze whipped another strand of Maresa's hair free from where she'd been holding it, the wavy lock tickling against her cheek and teasing along her lips. What was it about Cameron's physical presence that made her so very aware of her own? She'd never felt so on edge around Jaden even when they'd been wildly in love. Cameron's nearness made her feel…anxious. Expectant.

"From my vantage point, everything has been running smoothly at the Carib." Maresa didn't need a poor performance review. What if Cameron McNeill thought that the real reason for the declining ratings was her? A concierge could make or break a customer's experience of any hotel. Maybe this meeting with the boss wasn't to interview her so much as to interrogate her.

But damn it, she knew her performance had been exemplary.

"We'll figure it out, one way or another," Cameron assured her as the Jeep climbed a small hill and broke through a cluster of trees.

The most breathtaking view imaginable spread out before her. She gasped aloud.

"Oh wow." She shook her head at the sparkling expanse of water lapping against White Shoulders Beach below them. On the left, the villa sat at the cliff's edge, positioned so that the windows, balconies and infinity pool all faced the stunning view. "I grew up here, and still—you never grow immune to this."

"I can see why." He pulled the Jeep into a sheltered parking bay beside a simple silver Ford sedan. "It looks like the sitter has already arrived. We can get Isla settled inside with some air conditioning and then get to work."

Unfastening her gaze from the view of Saint John's in the distance, and a smattering of little islands closer by, Maresa turned to take in the villa. The Aerie was billed as the premiere private residence on the island; she thought she recalled the literature saying it was almost twenty thousand square feet. It was a palatial home decorated in the Mediterranean style. The white-sashed stucco and deep bronze roof tiles were an understated color combination, especially when accented with weathered gray doors. The landscaping dominated the home from the outside, but there were balconies everywhere to take advantage of the views.

Sliding out of the Jeep, she smoothed a hand over her windblown hair to try to prepare herself for what was no doubt the most important business meeting of her life. She couldn't allow her guard to slip, not even when Cameron McNeill spared a kind smile for Baby Isla as he carefully unbuckled her from the car seat straps.

"Need any help?" she asked, stepping closer to the Jeep again.

"I've got it." He frowned slightly, reaching beneath the baby to palm her head in his big hand. He supported her back with his forearm, cradling her carefully until he had her tucked against his chest. "There." He grinned over at Maresa. "Just like carrying a football. You take the fall yourself before you fumble."

"Ideally, there's no falling involved for anyone." She knew he was teasing, but she wondered if she should have offered to carry Isla just the same.

She couldn't deny she was a bit overwhelmed, though. She didn't know much about babies, and now she would be lobbying for primary custody of Rafe's little girl, even if Trina changed her mind. Maresa knew Rafe would have wanted to exercise his parental rights, and she would do that in his place. Still, it was almost too much to get her brain around in just a few hours, and she had no one she could share the news with outside of Rafe's counselor. Oddly, having Cameron McNeill beside her today had anchored her when she felt most unsteady, even as she knew she had to keep her guard up around him.

Half an hour later, Maresa finally managed to walk out of the makeshift nursery—a huge suite of rooms adapted for the purpose with the portable crib the hospital nurse had brought with her. The woman had packed a bag full of other baby supplies for Maresa including formula, diapers, fresh clothes and linens, a gift funded by Cameron McNeill, she'd discovered. And while Maresa understood that the man could easily afford such generosity, she couldn't afford to accept any more after this day.

Today, she told herself, was an adjustment period. Tomorrow, she would have a plan.

Clutching the baby monitor the caregiver had provided, Maresa followed the scent of grilled meat toward the patio beside the pool. A woman in a white tuxedo shirt and crisp black pants bustled through the kitchen, her blond ponytail bobbing with her step. She nodded toward the French doors leading outside.

"Mr. McNeill said to tell you he has drinks ready right out here, unless you'd like to swim first, in which case there are suits in the bathhouse." She pointed to the left where a small cabana sat beside a gazebo.

"Thank you." Maresa's gaze flicked over the food the woman was assembling on the kitchen island—tiny appetizers with flaked fish balanced on thin slices of mango and endive, bright red crabmeat prepped for what looked like a shellfish soup and chopped vegetables for a conch salad. "It all looks delicious."

Her stomach growled with a reminder of how long it had been since her usual lunch hour had come and gone. Now, stepping outside onto the covered deck, Maresa spotted Cameron seated at a table beneath the gazebo, a bottled water in hand as he stared down at his laptop screen. Tropical foliage in colorful clay pots dotted the deck. The weathered teak furniture topped by thick cream-colored cushions was understated enough to let the view shine more than the decor. The call of birds and the distant roll of waves on the beach provided the kind

of soundtrack other people piped in using a digital play-
list in order to relax.

Seeing her, Cameron stood. The practice wasn't un-
common in formal business meetings, and happened
more often when she'd worked in Europe. But the gesture here, in this private place, felt more intimate since
it was for her alone.

Or maybe she was simply too preoccupied with her
boss.

"Did you find everything you needed?" he asked, tugging off the aviators he'd been wearing to set them on
the graying teak table.

It was cool in the shade of the pergola threaded with
bright pink bougainvillea, yet just being close to him
made her skin warm. Her gaze climbed his tall height,
stalling on his well-muscled shoulders before reaching
his face. She took in the sculpted jaw and ice-blue eyes
before shifting her focus to his lips. She hadn't kissed a
man since her broken engagement.

A fact she hadn't thought about even once until right
this moment.

"I'm fine," she blurted awkwardly, remembering she
was there to work and not to catalog the finer masculine
traits of the man whose family owned the company she
worked for. "Ready to work."

Beneath the table, a dog yapped happily.

Maresa glanced down to see Poppy standing on a
bright magenta dog bed. Beside the bed, a desk fan os-
cillated back and forth, blowing through the dog's long
white fur at regular intervals.

"Hello, Poppy." She leaned down to greet the fluffy
pooch. "That's quite a setup you have there." She let the
dog sniff her hand for a moment before she scratched
behind the ears, not sure if Poppy would remember her.

"I had the dog walker pick up a few things to be sure she was comfortable. Plus, with a baby in the house, I thought she might be…you know. Jealous."

She looked up in time to see him shrug as if it was the most natural thought in the world to consider if his dog would be envious of an infant guest.

"That's adorable." She knew then that the Cameron Holmes character she'd met the day before had been all for show. Cameron McNeill was another man entirely. Although his jaw tightened at the "adorable" remark. She hurried to explain. "I mean, the dog bed and all of Poppy's matching accessories. Your mom found a lot of great things to coordinate the wardrobe."

Maresa rose to her feet, knowing she couldn't use the pup as a barrier all day.

"Actually, I borrowed Poppy from my brother's administrative assistant." He gestured to the seat beside him and turned the laptop to give her a better view. "I figured a fussy white show dog was a good way to test the patience and demeanor of the hotel staff. But I'll admit, she isn't nearly as uptight as I imagined." He patted the animal's head; the Maltese was rubbing affectionately against his ankles while he talked about her. "She's pretty great."

Coming around to his side of the table, Maresa took the seat he indicated. Right beside him. He'd changed into more casual clothes since she'd last seen him, his white cotton T-shirt only slightly dressed up by a pair of khakis and dark loafers. He wore some kind of brightly colored socks—aqua and purple—at odds with the rest of his outfit.

"The Carib is pet friendly, but I understand why you thought there might be pushback on demands like natural grass for the room." She glanced down at the laptop to see he'd left open a series of graphs with performance rankings for the Carib.

The downturn in the past two months was small, but noticeable.

"Ryegrass only," he reminded her. "I don't enjoy being tough on the staff, but I figured that playing undercover boss for a week or two would still be quicker and less painful for them than if I hire an independent agency to do a thorough review of operations."

"Of course." She gestured to the laptop controls. "May I look through this?"

At his nod, Maresa clicked on links and scrolled through the files related to the hotel's performance. Clearly, Cameron had been doing his homework, making margin notes throughout the document about the operations. Her name made frequent appearances, including a reference to an incident of misplaced money by a guest the week before.

"I remember this." Maresa's finger paused on the comment from a post-visit electronic survey issued to the guest. "An older couple reported that their travelers' checks had gone missing during a trip to the beach." She glanced up to see Cameron bent over the screen to read the notes, his face unexpectedly close to hers.

"The guy left the money in his jacket on the beach. It was gone when he returned." Cameron nodded, his jaw tense. "Definitely a vacation-ruiner."

She bristled. "But not the staff's fault. Our beach employees are tasked with making sure there are pool chairs and towels. We serve drinks and even bring food down to the cabanas. But we can't police everyone's possessions."

"On a private island where everyone should either be a guest or a staff member?" he asked with a hint of censure in his voice.

"That amounts to quite a few people," she pointed out, without hesitation. "And don't forget, many of our guests feel comfortable indulging in extra cocktails while vacationing."

"A few drinks won't make you think you had a thousand dollars in your pocket when you only had ten."

"Maybe not." She thrummed her fingernails on the teak table, remembering some of the antics she'd seen on the beach. Even before her work at the Carib, she'd seen plenty of visitors to Saint Thomas behave like springbreakers simply because they were far from home. Her father included. "However, a few drinks could make you think you put your money in your jacket when you actually had it in the pocket of the shorts you wore into the water, where you lost it while you tried to impress your trophy wife by doing backflips off a Jet Ski."

"And is that what happened in this case?" He glanced over at her, the woodsy scent of his aftershave teasing her senses.

"No." She shook her head, regretting the candid speech as much as the memory of her father's easy transition of affection from Maresa's mother to a wealthy female colleague. Today had rattled her. Her mind kept drifting back to Isla and what she would do tonight to keep her comfortable. "I'm sure it wasn't. I only meant to point out that the staff can't guard against some of the questionable decisions that guests make while vacationing."

Cam regarded her curiously. "I don't suppose your ex-fiancé has a trophy wife?"

"Jaden is still happily single from what I hear." She couldn't afford to share any more personal confidences with this man—her boss—who already knew far too much about her. To redirect their conversation, she tapped a few keys on his laptop. "These other incidents that guests wrote about on their comment forms—slow bar service, a disappointing gallery tour off-site—I assume you've looked into them?"

Both were news to her.

"The bar service, yes. The gallery tour, no. I don't suppose you know which tour they're referencing?"

"No one has asked me to arrange anything like this." She might not remember every hotel recommendation, but she certainly recalled specialty requests. "I can speak to some of the other staff members. Some guests like to ask the doormen or the waiters for their input on local sites."

"Good." He cleared a space in front of them on the table as a server came onto the patio with covered trays. "That's one of the drawbacks of maintaining a presence as a demanding guest—I can't very well quiz the staff for answers about things that happened last month."

Maresa watched as the server quickly set the table, filled their water glasses and left two platters behind along with a wine bottle in a clay pot to maintain the wine's temperature. The final thing the woman did was set out a fresh bowl of water for Poppy before she left them to their late lunch.

"I'm happy to help," Maresa told him honestly, relieved to know that the downturn in performance at the Carib was nothing tied to her work. Or her brother's. Their jobs were more important than ever with a baby to support.

"For that matter, I can't reveal the positive feedback we've received about the staff members either." Cameron lifted the wine bottle from the cooling container and inspected the label before pouring a pale white wine into her glass. "But I can tell you that Rafe received some glowing praise from a guest who referenced him by name."

"Really?" Pleased, Maresa helped herself to some of

the appetizers she'd seen inside, arranging a few extra pieces of mango beside the conch salad. "Did the guest say what he did?"

Cameron loaded his plate with ahi tuna and warm plantain chips with some kind of spicy-looking dipping sauce.

"Something about providing a 'happy escort' to the beach one day and lifting the guest's spirits by pointing out some native birds."

Rafe? Escorting a guest somewhere?

Maresa realized she'd been quiet a beat too long.

"Rafe loves birds," she replied truthfully, hating that she needed to mask her true thoughts with Cameron after he'd trusted her to give him honest feedback on the staff. "He does know a lot about the local plants and animals, too," she rushed to add. "That's one area of knowledge that his accident left untouched."

"Does it surprise you that he was escorting a guest to the beach?" Cameron studied her over his glass as he tasted the wine.

His blue eyes missed nothing.

Clearly, he would know Rafe's job description—something he'd have easy access to in his research of the performance reviews. There was no sense trying to deny it. Still, she hated feeling that she needed to defend her brother for doing a good job.

"A little," she admitted, her shoulders tense. Wary.

Before she could explain, however, a wail came through the baby monitor.

Cam hung back, unsure how to help while Maresa and the nurse caregiver discussed the baby's fretful state. Maresa held the baby close, shifting positions against her shoulder as the baby arched and squirmed.

Over half an hour after the infant's initial outburst, the

little girl still hadn't settled down. Her face was mottled and red, her hands flexing and straining, as if she fought unseen ghosts. Cam hated hearing the cries, but didn't have a clue what to offer. The woman he'd hired for the day was a nurse, after all. She would know if there was anything they needed to worry about, wouldn't she?

Still. He didn't blame Maresa for questioning her. Cameron had done some internet searches himself, one of the few things he knew to contribute.

A moment later, Maresa stepped out of the nursery and shut the door behind her, leaving Isla with Wendy. The cries continued. Poppy paced nervously outside the door.

"I should leave." Worry etched her features. She scraped back her sun-lightened curls behind one ear. "You've been so kind to help me manage my first day of caring for an infant, finding Wendy and the baby supplies, but I really can't impose any longer—"

"You are not anywhere close to an imposition." He didn't want her to leave. "I'm trying to help with Isla because I want to."

Maresa's hands fisted at her side, her whole body rigid. "She's my responsibility."

Her stubborn refusal reminded him of his oldest brother. Quinn never wanted anyone to help him either—a trait Cam respected, even when Quinn became too damn overbearing.

"You've know about her for less than twenty-four hours. Most families get nine months to prepare." He settled a hand on Maresa's shoulder, wanting to ease some of the weight she insisted on putting there.

"That doesn't make her any less my obligation." She folded her arms across her chest in a gesture that hovered between a defensive posture and an effort to hold herself together.

Another shriek from the nursery sent an answering spike of tension through Maresa; he could feel it under his fingertips. He'd have to be some kind of cretin not to respond to that. Still, he dropped his hand before he did something foolish like thread his fingers through her brown hair and soothe away the tension in her neck. Her back.

"Maybe not, but it gives you a damn good reason to accept some help until you get the legalities sorted out and come up with a game plan going forward." He extended his arms to gesture to the villa he'd taken for two weeks. "This place is going to be empty all evening once I head back to the hotel to put the Carib staffers through their paces. Stay put with Isla and the nurse. Have something to eat. Follow up with your lawyer. Poppy and I can sleep at the hotel tonight."

She shook her head. "I can't possibly accept such an offer. Even if you didn't own the company I work for, I couldn't allow you to do that."

"Ethics shouldn't rule out human kindness." Cameron wasn't going to rescind the offer because of some vague notion about what was right or proper. She needed help, damn it.

He drew her into a study down the hallway where indoor palm trees grew in a sunny corner under a series of skylights. Poppy trailed behind them, her collar jingling. Even here, the view of the water and the beach below was breathtaking. It made him want to cliff dive or wind surf. Or kiteboard.

He ground his teeth together on the last one. He hadn't been kiteboarding since the accident that ensured he'd never have children of his own. As if the universe had conspired to make sure he didn't repeat his father's mistakes.

"Is that what this is?" She stared up at him with questioning eyes. Worried. "Kindness? Because to be quite honest, this day has felt like a bit more than that, starting down at the beach this morning."

Starting yesterday for him, actually.

So he couldn't pretend not to know what she meant.

"There may be an underlying dynamic at work, yes. But that doesn't mean I can't offer to do something kind for you on an impossibly hard day." He had that ability, damn it. He wasn't totally self-absorbed. "And it's not just for you. It's for your brother, who might need more time to deal with this. And for Isla, who is clearly unhappy. Why not make their day easier, too?"

Maresa was quiet a long moment.

"What underlying dynamic?" she asked finally.

"It's not obvious?" He turned on his heel, needing a minute to weigh how much he wanted to spell things out. Go on the record. But he did, damn it. He liked this woman. He liked her fearless strength for her family, taking on their problems with more fierceness than she exercised for herself. Who took care of her? "I'm attracted to you."

He wasn't sure what kind of reaction he expected. But if he had to guess, he wouldn't have anticipated an argument.

"No." Her expression didn't change, the unflappable concierge facade in full play. "That's not possible."

There was a flash of fire in her tawny eyes, though. He'd bank on that.

"For all of my shortcomings, I'm pretty damn sure I know what attraction feels like."

"I didn't mean that. It's just—" She closed her eyes for a moment, as if she needed that time in the dark to collect her thoughts. When she opened them again, she took a deep breath. "I don't think I have the mental and emotional wherewithal to figure out what that means right now and what the appropriate response should be." She tipped two fingers to the bridge of her nose and pressed. "I can't afford to make a decision I'll regret. This job is…everything to me. And now I need it more than ever if I'm going to take proper care of Isla and my brother."

"I understand." Now that he'd admitted the attraction, he realized how strong it was, and that rattled him more than a little. He was here for business, not pleasure. "And I'm not acting on those feelings because I don't want to add to the list of things you need to worry about."

"Okay." She eyed him warily. "Thank you."

"So here's what I propose. I'm going to need your help on this project. It's important to me." He couldn't afford trouble at the Carib with so much riding on the Caribbean expansion program. The McNeills had their hands full with their grandfather's failing health and three more heirs on the horizon to vie for the family legacy. "Take a couple of days off from the hotel. Stay here with Isla and get acquainted with her while you prepare your family and plan your next steps. I'll stay at the hotel with Poppy."

"Cam—"

"No arguments." He really needed to leave her be so she could settle in and connect with the baby. He understood the crying and the newness of the situation would upset anyone, especially a woman accustomed to running things smoothly. "You can review those files I showed you earlier in more detail. I'd like your assessment of a variety of hotel personnel."

Finally, she nodded. It felt like a major victory. And no matter what he'd said about ignoring the attraction, he couldn't help but imagine what it would be like to have her agree to other things he wanted from her. Having dinner with him, for instance. Letting him taste her full lips. Feeling her soft curves beneath his palms.

"Isla and I can't thank you enough." She backed away from him and reached for the door. "I should really go check on her."

"Don't wear yourself out," he warned. "Share the duties with the nurse."

"I will." She smiled, her hand pausing on the door-knob, some of the tension sliding off her shoulders.

"And that Jeep we used to get here actually goes with the property. I'll leave the keys on the kitchen counter and have a plate sent up from the kitchen for you." He wasn't going out of his way, he told himself. It was easy enough to do that for her.

Or was he deluding himself? He wanted Maresa—pure and simple. But he knew it was more than that. Something about her drew him. Made him want to help her. He could do this much, at least, with a clear conscience. It benefitted McNeill Resorts to have her review those reports. He was simply giving her the time and space to do the job.

"But how will you get back to the hotel?"

"Poppy is ready for a walk." He could use a long trek to cool off. Remind himself why he had no business acting on what he was feeling for Maresa. "We'll take the scenic route along the beach." He held up his phone. "I'll leave my number with the keys downstairs. Call if you need anything."

"Okay." She nodded, then tipped her head to one side, her whole body going still. "Oh wow. Do you hear that?"

"What?" He listened.

"She stopped crying." Maresa looked relieved. Happy. So it was a total surprise that she burst into tears.

Five

If Maresa hadn't needed her job so badly, she would have seriously considered resigning.

Never in her life had she done anything so embarrassing as losing control in front of an employer. But the day had been too much, from start to finish. After the intense stress of listening to Isla cry for forty minutes, she'd been so relieved to hear silence reign in the nursery. The sudden shift of strong emotions had tipped something inside her.

Now, much to her extreme mortification, Cameron McNeill's arms were around her as he drew her onto a cushioned gray settee close to the door. Even more embarrassing? How much she wanted to sink into those arms and wail her heart out on his strong chest. She cried harder.

"It's okay," he assured her, his voice beside her ear and his woodsy aftershave stirring a hunger for closeness she could not afford.

"No, it's really not." She shook her head against his shoulder, telling herself to get it together.

"As your boss, I order you to stop arguing with me."

She couldn't stop a watery laugh. "I don't know what's the matter with me."

"Anyone would be overwhelmed right now." His arms tightened, drawing her closer in a way that was undeniably more comfortable. "Don't fight so damn hard. Let it out."

And for a moment, she did just that. She didn't let herself think about how deeply she'd screwed up by sobbing in his arms. She just let the emotions run through her, the whole great big unwieldy mess that her life had become. She hadn't cried like this when the doctor told her Rafe might not live. Day after day, she'd sat in that hospital and willed him to hang on and fight. Then, by the time he finally opened his eyes again, she couldn't afford to break down. She needed to be strong for him. To show him that she was fighting, too.

She'd helped him relearn to walk. Had that really been just six months ago? He'd come so far, so fast. But she knew there were limits to what he could do.

Limits to how much he could do because she willed it. She knew, in her heart, he would not be able to handle a crying baby even if she could make him understand that Isla was his. It wouldn't be right to thrust this baby into his life right now. Or fair.

She didn't need the counselor to tell her that, even though the woman had finally returned her call and left a message to come by the office in the morning. Maresa knew that the woman was trying to find a way to tell her the hard truth—this baby could upset him so much he could have a setback.

And she cried for that. For him. Because there had

been a time in Rafe's life when the birth of his daughter would have been a cause for celebration. It broke her heart that his life had to be so different now.

With one last shuddering sigh, she felt the storm inside her pass. As it eased away, leaving her drained but more at peace, Maresa became aware of the man holding her. Aware of the hard plane of his chest where her forehead rested. Of the warm skin beneath the soft cotton T-shirt that she'd soaked with her tears. Amidst all the other embarrassments of the day she was at least grateful that her mascara had been waterproof. It would have been one indignity too many to leave her makeup on his clothes.

His arm was around her shoulders, his hand on her upper arm where he rubbed gentle circles that had soothed her a moment before. Now? That touch teased a growing awareness that spread over her skin to make her senses sing. With more than a little regret, she levered herself up, straightening.

"Cameron." Her voice raspy from the crying, his name sounded far too intimate when she said it that way.

Then again, maybe it seemed more intimate since she was suddenly nose-to-nose with him, his arm still holding her close. She forgot to think. Forgot to breathe. She was pretty sure her heart paused, too, as she stared up at him.

A sexy, incredibly appealing man.

Without her permission, her fingers moved to his face. She traced the line of his lightly shadowed jaw, surprised at the rough bristle against her fingertips. His blue eyes hypnotized her. There was simply no other explanation for what was happening to her right now. Her brain told her to extricate herself. Walk away.

Her hands had other ideas. She twined them around his neck, her heart full of a tenderness she shouldn't feel. But he'd been so good to her. So thoughtful. And she wanted to kiss him more than she wanted anything.

"Maresa." Her name on his lips was a warning. A chance to change her mind.

She understood that she was pushing a boundary. Recognized that he'd just drawn a line in the sand.

"I didn't mind giving up my dream job in Paris to care for Rafe and help my mother recover," she confided, giving him absolutely no context for her comment and hoping he understood what she was saying. "And I will gladly give eighteen years to raise my niece as my own daughter." She'd known it without question the moment Jaden handed her Isla. "But I'm not sure I can sacrifice the chance to have this kiss."

She'd crossed the boundary. Straight into "certifiable" territory. She must have cried out all her good sense.

His blue eyes simmered with more heat than a Saint Thomas summer. He cupped her chin, cradling her face like she was something precious.

"If I thought you wouldn't regret it tomorrow, I'd give you all the kisses you could handle." The stroke of his thumb along her cheek didn't begin to soothe the rejection.

Her eyes burned again, reminding her just how jumbled her emotions were right now. Knowing he had a point did nothing to salvage her pride.

"You told me you were attracted to me." She unwound her hands from his neck.

"Too much," he admitted. "That's why I'm trying to be smart about this. I'm willing to wait to be with you until a time when you won't have any regrets about it."

"You say that like it's a foregone conclusion." She straightened, her cheeks heating.

"Or maybe it's using the power of positive thinking." His lips kicked up in a half smile, but she needed air. Space.

"You should go." She wanted time to clear her head.

Tipping her head toward him, he kissed her forehead with a gentle tenderness that made her ache for all she couldn't have.

"I'll see you in the morning," he told her, shoving to his feet.

"I thought I was taking time off?" She tucked her disheveled hair behind one ear, eager to call her mother and figure out what to do about Isla.

"From the hotel. Not from me." He shoved his hands in his pockets, and something about the gesture made her think he'd done it to keep from touching her.

She knew because she felt the same need to touch him.

"When will I see you?"

"Text me when you and Isla are ready in the morning and I'll come get you. I'm traveling to Martinique tomorrow and I'd like you with me."

She arched an eyebrow. "You need a tour guide with an infant in tow?"

"We could talk through some of the data in those reports a bit more. You could help give me a bigger picture of what's going on here." He opened the door into the quiet hallway of the expansive vacation villa. "Besides, I want to be close by if you decide you want to share kisses you won't regret down the road."

He strode away, whistling softly for Poppy as he headed toward the main staircase. He left Maresa alone in the extravagant house with a baby, a nurse and all kinds of confused feelings for him. One thing was certain, though.

A man like Cameron McNeill might tempt her sorely. But he was a fantasy. A temporary escape from the reality of a life full of obligations she would never walk away from. So until her heart understood how thoroughly off-limits he was, Maresa needed to put all thoughts of kisses out of her head.

An hour later, Maresa had her mother in the Jeep with her as she pulled up to the gated vacation villa. She'd calmly explained the Isla situation on a phone call on the way over to her house, arranging for their retired neighbor to visit with Rafe for a couple of hours while Maresa brought her mom to meet her grandchild.

After hearing back from Rafe's counselor that a mention of his daughter could trigger too much frustration and a possible memory block, Maresa had simply told her brother she wanted to bring their mother to meet a girlfriend's new baby.

She'd kept the story simple and straightforward, and Rafe didn't mind the visit time with Mr. Leopold, who was happy to play one of Rafe's video games with him and keep an eye on him. The paperwork requesting temporary legal custody of the baby would be filed in the morning by her attorney, so she'd taken care of that, too.

Now, driving through the gates, Maresa enjoyed her mother's startled gasp at the breathtaking view of the Caribbean.

"I had the same reaction earlier," she admitted, halting the Jeep in the space beside the nurse's sedan. "But this isn't half as beautiful as Isla."

"I cannot wait to meet her." Analise Delphine opened the car door slowly, the neuropathy in her hands one of many nerve conditions caused by her MS. "But I'm still so angry at Trina for not telling us sooner. Can you imagine what happiness it would have given us in those dark hours with your brother if we had only known about his daughter?"

Maresa hurried around the car to help her mother out since it did no good to tell her to wait. Analise had struggled more with her disease ever since the car crash that injured Rafe. Maresa worried about her since her mother seemed to blame herself—and her MS—for the injury to her beloved son, and some days it appeared as if she wanted to suffer because of her guilt. For months, Maresa had encouraged her mother to get into some more family counseling, but Analise would only go to sessions that were free through a local clinic, not wanting to "be a burden."

Maresa had tread lightly around the topic until now, but if they were going to be responsible for this baby, she needed her mother to be strong emotionally even if her physical health was declining.

"Trina is young," Maresa reminded her as she helped her up the white stone walkway to the main entrance of the villa. "She must have been scared and confused between finding out she was pregnant and then learning Rafe wasn't going to make a full recovery."

Analise breathed heavily as she leaned on Maresa's arm. Analise had always been the most beautiful girl on the block, according to their neighbor Mr. Leopold. She'd worked as a dancer in clubs and in street performances for tourists, earning a good living for years before the MS hit her hard. Her limber dancer's body had thickened with her inability to move freely, but her careful makeup and her eye for clothing meant she always looked stage-ready.

"She is old enough to make better choices." Her mother stopped abruptly, squinting into the sunlight as she peered up at the vacation home. "Speaking of which, Maresa, I hope you are making wise choices by staying here. You said your boss is allowing you to do this?"

"Yes, Mom." She tugged gently at her mother's arm, drawing her up the wide stone steps. "He was there when Jaden handed me Isla, so he knew I had a lot to contend with today."

She wasn't sure about the rest of his motives. She was still separating Cameron McNeill from surly Mr. Holmes, trying to understand him. He'd walked out on her today when she would have gladly lost herself in the attraction. Some of her wounded pride had been comforted by his assurance that he wanted her.

So where did that leave them for tomorrow when he expected her to accompany him to a neighboring island?

"Most men don't share their expensive villas without expectations, Maresa. Be smarter than that," her mother chastised her while Maresa unlocked the front door with the key Cameron had left behind. "You need to come home."

Before she could argue, Wendy appeared in the foyer, a pink bundle in her arms. Her mother oohed and aahed, mesmerized by her new grandchild as she happily cataloged all the sleeping baby's features. Maresa paid scant attention, however, as Analise declared the hairline was Rafe's and the mouth inherited was from Analise herself.

Maresa still smarted from her mother's insistence that she wasn't "being smart" to stay in the villa with Isla tonight. Perhaps it stung all the more because that had been Maresa's first instinct, as well. But damn it, Cameron had a point about the practicality of it. The Carib did indeed comp rooms to special guests who provided services. Why couldn't she enjoy the privilege while she helped Cameron McNeill investigate the operations of his luxury hotel?

Putting aside her frustration, she tried to enjoy her mother's pleasure in the baby even as Maresa worried about the future. It was easy for her mom to tell her that she should simply bring Isla home, but it would be Maresa who had to make arrangements for caregiving and Maresa who would wake up every few hours to look after the child. All of their lives were going to change dramatically under the roof of her mother's tiny house.

Maybe she needed to look for a larger home for all of them. She'd thought she couldn't afford it before, but now she wondered how she could afford *not* to buy something bigger. She would speak to her mother about it, but first, it occurred to her she could speak to Cameron. He was a businessman. His brother—she'd once read online—was a hedge fund manager. Surely a McNeill could give sound financial advice.

Besides, talking about the Caribbean housing market would be a welcome distraction in case the conversation ever turned personal tomorrow. If ever she was tempted to kiss him again, she'd just think about interest rates. That ought to cool her jets in a hurry.

"Look, Maresa!" Her mother turned the baby on her lap to show her Isla's face as they sat on the loveseat of a sprawling white family room decorated with dark leather furnishings and heavy Mexican wood. The little girl's eyes were open now, blinking owlishly. "She has your father's eyes! We need to call him and tell him. He won't believe it."

"Mom. No." She reached for the baby while Analise dug in her boho bag sewn out of brightly colored fabric scraps and pulled out a cell phone. "Dad never likes hearing from us."

She'd been devastated by her father's furious reaction to her phone call the night of Rafe's accident.

I've moved on, Maresa. Help your mother get that through her head.

"Nonsense." Analise grinned as she pressed the screen. "He'll want to hear this. Isla is his first grandchild, too, you know."

In Maresa's arms, the infant kicked and squirmed, her back arching as if she were preparing for a big cry. Maresa resisted the urge to call to Wendy, needing the experience of soothing the little girl. So she patted her back and spoke comforting words, shooting to her feet to walk around the room while her mother left a message on her father's voice mail. No surprise he hadn't picked up the call.

"I bet he'll book a flight down here as soon as he can," Analise assured her. "I should be getting home so I can make the house ready for company. And a baby, too!"

She levered slowly out of her chair to her feet, her new energy and excitement making her wince less even though the hurt had to be just the same as it was an hour ago.

"I don't think Dad will come down here," Maresa warned her quietly, not wanting her mom's hopes raised to impossible levels.

Jack Janson hadn't returned once since moving overseas. He hadn't even visited Maresa in Paris; she'd briefly hoped that since he lived in the UK, he might make the effort to see her. But no.

"Could you let me be excited about just this one thing? We have enough to worry us, Maresa. Let's look for things to be hopeful about." She put her hand on Maresa's shoulders, a touch that didn't comfort her in the least.

If anything, Maresa remembered why she needed to be all the more careful with Cameron McNeill. Like her father, he was only here on business. Like her father, he might think it was fun to indulge himself with a local woman while he was far from his home and his real life.

But once he left Saint Thomas and solved the problems at the Carib Grand, Maresa knew all too well that he wasn't ever coming back.

Cameron had new respect for the running abilities of Maltese show dogs.

He sprinted through the undergrowth on the beach the next morning, about an hour after sunrise, trying to keep up with the little pooch.

"Poppy!" he called to her, cursing himself for giving her a moment off the leash. He'd scoped the beach and knew they were alone on the Carib Grand's private stretch of shore, so he'd figured it was okay.

He could keep up with the little dog on her short legs after all. But Poppy was small and shifty, darting and zigzagging through the brush where Cam couldn't fit. The groomer was going to think he'd gotten the pup's fur tangled on purpose, but damn it, he was just trying to let her have some fun. She seemed so happy chasing those terns.

If only it was as easy to tell what would make Maresa Delphine happy. He'd spent most of the day with her and still wasn't sure how to make her smile again. The concierge had the weight of the world on her straight shoulders.

Catching sight of muddy white fur, Cameron swooped low to scoop up the dog in midstride.

"Gotcha." He held on to the wriggling, overexcited bundle of wet canine while she tried her best to lick his face.

He'd have to shower again before his day in Martinique with Maresa since he was now covered with beach sand and dog fur, but it was tough to stay perturbed with the overjoyed animal. Chiding her gently while he attached the leash, Cam turned to go back up the path to the hotel.

Only to spot Rafe Delphine walking toward the beach beside a well-dressed, much older woman.

Surprised that Rafe had come in to work with Maresa taking the day off, Cameron watched the pair from a hidden vantage point in the bushes.

"Do you know this painter I'm meeting, young man?" the woman asked, her accent sounding Nordic, maybe. Or Finnish.

The woman was probably in her late sixties or early seventies. She had a sleek blond bob and expensive-looking bag. Even the beach sandals she wore had the emblem of an exclusive designer Cam recognized because a long-ago girlfriend had dragged him to a private runway show.

"Jaden paints." Rafe nodded his acknowledgement of the question but his eye was on the ground where a bird flapped its damp wings. "Look. A tern."

Poppy wriggled excitedly. The movement attracted the older woman's attention, giving up Cam's hiding place She smiled at him.

"What a precious little princess!" she exclaimed, eyes on Poppy. "She looks like she's been having fun today."

Rafe's tawny eyes—so like his sister's—turned his way. He gave Cam a nod of recognition, or maybe it was just politeness. Effectively called out of his spot in the woods, Cameron stepped into the sunlight and let the woman meet Poppy, who was—as always—appropriately gracious for the attention.

After a brief exchange with the dog, Cameron continued toward the hotel. He'd known that Jaden Torries was probably trolling for work at the Carib, so it shouldn't be a huge surprise that one of the hotel guests was meeting him at the beach. But why was Rafe bringing her to meet him?

Given how much Maresa disliked her ex-fiancé, it seemed unlikely she would be the one facilitating Jaden doing any kind of work with hotel patrons. Especially since she wasn't even working today. Then again, what if she had found a way to make a little extra income by helping Jaden find patrons? Would she set aside her distaste for him if it made things easier for her?

Deep in thought, Cam arrived at the pool deck. He didn't want to think his attraction to Maresa would influence his handling of the situation, but his first instinct was to speak to her directly. He would ask her about it when he picked her up at the villa, he decided.

Except then he spotted her circulating among the guests by the pool. She'd been here all along?

Suspicion mounted. Grinding his teeth, he charged toward her, more than ready for some answers.

Six

Morning sun beating down on her head, Maresa noticed Cameron McNeill heading her way and she braced herself for the resurrection of Mr. Holmes. She knew he needed to be undercover to learn more about the hotel operations, but did he have to be quite so convincing in his "difficult guest" role? The hard set of his jaw and brooding glare were seriously intimidating even knowing how kind he could be.

She straightened from a conversation with one of her seasonal guests from Quebec who rented a suite for half the year. Pasting on a professionally polite smile to greet Cameron, she told herself she should be grateful to see this side of him so she wouldn't be tempted to throw herself at him again.

Even if his bare chest and low-slung board shorts drew every female eye.

"Good morning, Mr. Holmes." She reached to smooth

her jacket sleeves, only to remember she'd worn a sundress today for the trip into Martinique. *Oh, my.* Her skin had goose bumps of awareness just from standing this close to him.

"May I speak to you privately?" He handed off Poppy to the dog groomer who scurried over from where he'd been waiting by the tiki bar.

Cameron certainly couldn't have any complaints about the service he was receiving, could he? People seemed to hurry to offer him assistance.

"Of course." She excused herself from the other guests, following him toward the door marked Employees Only.

He didn't slow his step until they were in the same conference room where they'd spoken yesterday. The cool blast of air almost matched the ice chips in his blue eyes. He shoved the door shut behind them before he turned to face her.

"I thought you were taking the day off from the hotel." His jaw flexed and he crossed his arms over his bare chest, the board shorts riding low on his hips.

She tried not to stare, distracting herself by focusing on the hint of confrontation in his tone.

"I am." She gestured to her informal clothing. "I only stopped by this morning to see my brother and make sure he felt comfortable about his workday."

"And is he comfortable escorting guests to the beach?" Cameron's arctic glare might have made another woman shiver. Maresa straightened her spine.

"I never give him jobs like that. Why do you ask?" Defensiveness for her brother roared through her.

"Because I just saw him walking one of our overseas guests to the shore to meet Jaden Torries."

Surprised, she quickly guessed he must be mistaken.

He had to be. Still a hint of tension tickled her gut. "Rafe doesn't even arrive until the next ferry." She checked her watch just to be sure the day hadn't slipped away from her. "He should be walking in the employee locker rooms any minute to punch his time card."

"He's already here." Cameron pulled out one of the high-backed leather chairs for her, all sorts of muscles flexing as he moved, distracting her when she needed to be focused. "I saw him myself at the beach with one of the hotel guests just a few minutes ago."

"I don't understand." Ignoring the seat, she paced away from all that tempting male muscle to peer out the windows overlooking the croquet lawn near the pool, hoping to get a view of the path to the beach. How could she relax, wondering if her brother might be doing jobs around the Carib without her knowing? She was supposed to watch over him during his first few months of employment. She'd promised the hotel director as much. "I got here early so I wouldn't miss him when he came to work. I want everything to go smoothly for him if I'm not here to supervise him myself."

Cameron joined her at the window, his body warm beside hers as he peered out onto the mostly empty side lawns. A butterfly garden near the window attracted a handful of brightly colored insects. His shoulder brushed hers, setting off butterflies inside, too. She hated feeling this way—torn between the physical attraction and the mental frustration.

"Did you know Jaden was soliciting business from hotel guests?" Cameron's question was quiet. Dispassionate.

And it offended her mightily. How dare he question her integrity? Her work record was impeccable and he should know as much if he was even halfway doing *his* job.

Anger burned through her as she whirled to face him, her skirt brushing his leg he stood so close to her. She took a step back.

"Absolutely not. Until yesterday, I hadn't seen Jaden since I left for Paris two years ago." She frowned, not understanding why Cameron would think she'd do such a thing. "And while I don't wish him ill, my relationship with him is absolutely over. I certainly don't have any desire to risk my job to help a man I dislike profit off our guests."

"I see." Cameron nodded slowly, as if weighing whether or not to believe her.

Worry balled in her stomach and she reined in her anger. She couldn't afford to be offended. She needed him to believe her.

"Why would you think I'd do such a thing?" She didn't want to be here. She wanted to find her brother and ask him what was going on.

Did Rafe even understand what he was doing by helping Jaden meet potential clients for his artwork? Was Jaden asking him for that kind of help?

"That type of business is probably lucrative for him—"

Understanding dawned. Indignation flared, hot and fast. "And you thought I would be a part of some sordid scheme with my ex-fiancé for the sake of extra cash? Even twisting my brother's arm into setting up meetings when I do everything in my power to protect him?"

If it had been anyone else, she would have stormed out of the meeting room. But she needed this job too much and, at the end of the day, Cameron McNeill was still an owner of the Carib.

He held all the cards.

"I don't know what to think. That's why I wanted to speak to you privately." He picked up a gray T-shirt from the back of a chair in the conference room and pulled it over his head.

She watched in spite of herself, realizing he must have been doing work in the conference room earlier that morning since a laptop and phone sat on the table.

"I won't have any answers until I speak to my brother." She was worried about him. For him. For the baby. Oh God, when had life gotten so complicated?

What had her brother gotten into?

"You realize this isn't the first time he's done it." Cameron's voice softened as he headed toward her again. "That customer review that I shared with you yesterday was from someone who said he provided a 'happy escort' to the beach." Cameron's blue eyes probed hers, searching for answers she didn't have.

As much as she longed to share her fears with him, she couldn't do that. Not when he was in charge of her fate at the hotel, and Rafe's, too.

"I remember." She itched to leave, needing to see Rafe for herself. "And now that you've put that comment in context, I'm happy to speak to my brother and clear this up."

She turned toward the door, desperate to put the complicated knot of feelings her boss inspired behind her.

"Wait." Cameron reached for her hand and held it, his touch warm and firm. "I realize you want to protect him, Maresa, but we need to find out what's going on."

"And we will," she insisted, wishing he didn't make her heart beat faster. "Just as soon as I speak to him."

Cameron studied her for a long moment with searching eyes, then quietly asked, "What if he doesn't have a clear answer?"

Some of the urgency eased from her. She couldn't deny that was a possibility.

"I can only do my best to figure out what's going on." She couldn't imagine who else would be giving him extra chores to do around the hotel. Rafe had never particularly liked Jaden. Then again, her brother was a different man since the accident.

"I know that. And what if we learn more by observing him for a few days? Maybe it would be better to simply keep a closer eye on him now that we know he's carrying out duties for the hotel—or someone else—that you haven't authorized." His tone wasn't accusing. "Maybe you shouldn't upset him unnecessarily."

She wanted to tell him she already spent hours supervising her brother. More than others on her staff. But she bit her lip, refusing to reveal a piece of information that could get Rafe terminated from his position.

"I don't want him getting hurt," she argued, worried about letting her brother's behavior continue unchecked. "And I don't know who he's speaking to that would advise him to take risks like this with his job."

The day had started out so promising, with Isla sleeping for five hours straight and waking up with a drooly baby smile, only to take this radical nosedive. Anxiety spiked. Rafe was going to lose this job, damn it. She would never be able to afford a caregiver for Isla and a companion to supervise Rafe, too. Especially not once they lost Rafe's income. Heaven only knew how much he would recover from the brain injury. What kind of future he would have? How much he could provide for himself, much less a child? All the fears of the unknown jumped up inside her.

Cameron hissed a low, frustrated breath between his teeth. "What if we compromise? You confront him now, but if you don't get a direct answer or if you sense there's more to his answer than what he shares, you back off.

Then, we can keep a closer eye on him for the next week and see who is setting up these meetings."

She didn't like the idea of waiting. She knew there was a good chance Rafe wouldn't give her a direct answer. But what choice did she really have? She wouldn't be able to push him anyhow, since his health and potential recovery were more important than getting answers to any mystery going on at the Carib.

"Fine." She turned to the door, eager to see her brother, but she paused when Cameron followed her. "I'd prefer to speak to him alone."

He followed her so closely that she needed to tilt her head to peer up at him.

"Of course." He stood near enough that she could see the shades of blue in his eyes, as varied as the Caribbean. "I'm going to change for our trip. I'll have a car meet you out front in fifteen minutes."

She wondered if it was wise to risk being seen leaving the hotel with surly Mr. Holmes. But then, that wasn't her problem so much as his. She had enough to worry about waiting for the DNA tests to come back so she could finally tell Rafe about Isla. Her lawyer and his psychologist had advised her and her mother to wait until then.

Hurrying away from all that distracting masculine appeal, Maresa rushed into the employee lounge to look for her brother. She'd already called in a favor from Big Bill, the head doorman, to help keep an eye on Rafe for the next few days. Bill was a friend of her mother's from their old neighborhood and he'd been kind enough to agree, but Maresa knew the man could only do so much.

Inside the lounge, the scent of morning coffee mingled with someone's too-strong perfume. A few people from the maintenance staff gossiped around the kitchen table where a box of pastries sat open. Moving past the kitchen,

Maresa peered into the locker area between the men's and women's private lounges. Rafe sat in the middle row of lockers, carefully braiding the stems of yellow buttercups into a chain. Flowers spilled over the polished bench as he straddled it, his focus completely absorbed in the task.

Any frustration she felt with him melted away. How could Cameron think for a moment that her brother would knowingly do anything unethical at work? It was only because Cameron didn't know Rafe. If he did, he'd never think something like that for a moment.

"Hey, Rafe." She took a seat on the bench nearby, wishing with all her heart he could be in a work program designed for people with his kinds of abilities. He had so much to offer with his love of nature and talent with green and growing things. Even now, his affinity for plants was evident, the same as before the accident when he'd had his own landscaping business. "What are you making?"

He glanced up at her, his eyes so like the ones she saw in the mirror every day.

"Maresa." He smiled briefly before returning his attention to the flowers. "I'm making you a bracelet."

"Me?" She had worried he was heaping more gifts on Nancy. And while she liked the server, she didn't want Rafe to have any kind of romantic hopes about the woman. Hearing the flowers were for her was a relief.

"I felt bad I left work." He lifted the flower chain and laid it on her wrist, his shirt cuffs brushing her skin as he carefully knotted the stems together. "I'm sorry."

Her heart knotted up like the flowers.

"Thank you. I love it." She kissed him on the cheek, smiling at the way his simple offering looked beside the silver star bracelet he'd given her two years ago before she left for Paris.

He was as thoughtful as ever, and his way of showing it hadn't changed all that much.

"Rafe?" She drew a deep breath, hating to ruin a happy moment with questions about Jaden. But this was important. The sooner she helped Cameron McNeill figure out what was going on at the Carib Grand, the sooner their jobs would be secure and they could focus on a new life with Isla—if Isla was in fact his child. And even though their lives would be less complicated without the child, Maresa couldn't deny that the thought of Isla leaving made her stomach clench. "Why did you go to the beach this morning?"

She kept the question simple. Direct.

"Mr. Ricci asked." Rafe rose to his feet, dusting flower petals off his faded olive cargoes. "Time to go to work. Mom said I don't work with you today."

She blinked at the fast change of topic. "Mr. Ricci asked you to bring a guest to the beach?"

"It's eight thirty." Rafe pointed to his watch. "Mom said I don't work with you today."

Damn it. Damn it. She didn't want to throw his whole workday off for the sake of a conversation that might lead nowhere. Maybe Cameron was right and they were better off keeping an eye on the situation.

"Right. I have to work off-site today. You'll be helping Glenna at the concierge stand, but Big Bill is on duty today. If you need help with anything, ask Bill, okay?"

"Ask Big Bill." Rafe gave her a thumbs-up before he stalked out of the locker room and into the hotel to start work.

Watching him leave, Maresa's fingers went to the bracelet he'd made her. He was thoughtful and kind. Surely he would have so much to give Isla. She needed to speak to his counselor in more detail so they could brainstorm ideas for the right way to introduce them. It seemed wrong to deprive the little girl of a father when her mother had already given up on her.

For now, however, she needed to tell Cameron that Rafe was escorting guests to the beach because the hotel director told him to. Would Cameron believe her? Or would he demand to speak to her brother himself?

Cameron's seductive promise floated back to her. *If I thought you wouldn't regret it tomorrow, I'd give you all the kisses you could handle.* She'd replayed those words again and again since he'd said them.

She walked a tightrope with her compelling boss—needing him to allow Rafe to stay in his job, but needing her own secured even more. Which meant she had to help him in his investigation.

Most of all, to keep those objectives perfectly clear, she had to ignore her growing attraction to him. His kindness with Isla might have slid past her defenses, but in order to protect the baby's future, Maresa would have to set aside her desire to find out what "all the kisses she could handle" would feel like.

The flight to Martinique was fast and efficient. They took off from the private dock near the Carib Grand's beach and touched down in the Atlantic near Le Francois on the east coast of Martinique. The pilot landed the new seaplane smoothly, barely jostling Baby Isla's carrier where she sat beside Maresa in the seats facing Cameron.

Cameron tried to focus on the baby to keep his mind off the exotically gorgeous woman across from him. The task had been damn near impossible for the hour of flight time between islands. Maresa's bright sundress was so different from the linen suits he'd seen her in for work. He liked the full skirt and vibrant poppy print, and he admired that she wore the simple floral bracelet around one wrist. With her hair loose and sun-tipped around her face, she looked impossibly beautiful. Her movements with Isla were easier today and her fascination with the little girl was obvious every time she glanced Isla's way.

Before she unbuckled the baby's carrier, she pressed a kiss to the infant's smooth forehead. A new pink dress with a yellow bunny on the front had been a gift from Maresa's mother, apparently. They'd spoken about that much on that flight. Maresa had given him an update on the custody paperwork with the lawyer, the paternity test she'd ordered using Rafe's hair and a cheek swab of Isla's, and she'd told him about her mother's reaction to her granddaughter. They'd only discussed Rafe briefly, agreeing not to confront him any further about bringing guests to meet Jaden Torries. They would watch Rafe more carefully when they returned to Saint Thomas. Until then, Bill the doorman knew to keep a close eye on him.

Cameron hadn't pushed her to discuss her theory about what might be going on, knowing that she was already worried about her brother's activities at the hotel. But at some point today, they would have to discuss where to go next with Rafe, and Jaden, too. For now, Cameron simply wanted to put her at ease for a few hours while he gathered some information about this secret branch of his family. The Martinique McNeills had a home in Le Francois, an isolated compound that was the equivalent of Grandfather Malcolm's home in Manhattan—a centrally located hub with each of the brothers' names on the deed. The family had other property holdings, but their mother had lived here before her death and the next generation all spent time there.

Cameron had done his homework and was ready to

check out this group today. Later, after Maresa had time to relax and catch her breath from the events of the last few days, he would talk to her about a plan for the future. For her and for Isla, too. The little girl in the pink dress tugged at his heart.

"So you have family here?" Maresa passed the baby carrier to him while the pilot opened the plane door.

Fresh air blew in, toying lightly with Maresa's hair.

"In theory. Yes." He wasn't happy about the existence of the other McNeills. "That is—they don't know we're related yet. My father kept his other sons and mistress a secret. When his lover tired of being hidden, she sold the house he'd bought her and left without a forwarding address. He didn't fight her legally because of the scandal that would create." As he said it aloud, however, he realized that didn't sound like his father. "Actually, he was probably just too disinterested to try and find them. He never paid us much attention either."

Liam McNeill had been a sorry excuse for a father. Cameron refused to follow in those footsteps.

Cam lifted the baby carrier above the seats, following Maresa to the exit. They'd parked at a private dock for the Cap Est Lagoon, a resort hotel in Le Francois close to the McNeill estate.

"But at least he's still a part of your life, isn't he?" Maresa held her full skirt with one hand as she descended the steps of the plane. A gusty breeze wreaked havoc with the hem.

The view of her legs was a welcome distraction during a conversation about his dad.

"He is part of the business, so I see him at company meetings. But it's not like he shows up for holidays to hang out. He's never been that kind of father." Even Cameron's grandfather hadn't quite known what to do to create a sense of family. Sure, he'd taken in Quinn, Ian and Cameron often enough as teens. But they were more apt to travel with him on business, learning the ropes from the head of the company, than have fun.

Luckily, Cam had had his brothers.

And, later, his own reckless sense of fun.

Maresa held her hair with one hand as they walked down the dock together, the baby between them in her seat. Behind them, the hotel staff unloaded their bags from the seaplane. Not that they'd travelled with much, but Cam had taken a suite here so Maresa would have a place to retreat with Isla. The Cap Est spread out on the shore ahead of them, the red-roofed buildings ringing the turquoise lagoon. Birds called and circled overhead. A few white sailing boats dotted the blue water.

"A disinterested father is a unique kind of hurt," Maresa observed empathetically—so much so it gave him pause for a moment. But then he was distracted by a hint of her perfume on the breeze as she followed him to the villa where their suite awaited. A greeter from the hotel had texted him instructions on the location so they could proceed directly there. "Do you think your half brothers will be glad to see him again? Has it been a long time that they've been apart?"

"Fifteen years. The youngest hasn't seen his father— my father—since the kid was ten." Cameron hadn't thought about that much. He'd been worried about what the other McNeills might ask from them in terms of the family resort business. But there was a chance they'd be too bitter to claim anything.

Or so bitter that they'd want revenge.

Cameron wouldn't let them hurt his grandfather. Or the legacy his granddad had worked his whole life to build.

"Wow, fifteen? That's not much older than I was the last time I saw my dad." Maresa's words caught him by surprise as they reached the villa where a greeter admitted them.

Cameron didn't ask her about it until the hotel representative had shown them around the two-floor suite with a private deck overlooking the lagoon. When the woman left and Maresa was lifting Isla from the carrier, however, Cameron raised the question.

"Where's your father now?" He watched her coo and comfort the baby, rubbing the little girl's back through her pink dress, the bowlegs bare above tiny white ankle socks.

The vacation villa was smaller than the one near the Carib Grand, but more luxuriously appointed, with floor-to-ceiling windows draped in white silk that fluttered in the constant breeze off the water. Exotic Turkish rugs in bright colors covered alternating sections of dark bamboo floors. Paintings of the market at Marigot and historic houses in Fort-de-France, the capital of Martinique, hung around the living area, providing all the color of an otherwise quietly decorated room. Deep couches with white cushions and teak legs and arms were positioned for the best views of the water. There was even a nursery with a crib brought in especially for their visit.

"He lives outside London with his new wife. I spoke to him briefly after Rafe's accident, but his only response was a plea that I tell my mother he's *moved on* and not to bother him again." She stressed the words in a way that suggested she would never forget the tone of voice in which they'd been spoken. Shaking her head, she walked Isla over to the window and stared out at the shimmering blue expanse. "I won't be contacting him anymore."

Cameron sifted through a half dozen responses before he came up with one that didn't involve curses.

"I don't blame you. The man can't be bothered to come to his critically injured son's bedside? He doesn't deserve his kids." Cameron knew without a doubt that he'd suck as a father, but even he would never turn his back like that on a kid.

Maresa's burden in caring for her whole family became clearer, however. Her mother wasn't working because of her battle with MS, her father was out of the picture and her brother needed careful supervision. Maresa was supporting a lot of people on her salary.

And now, an infant, too. That was one helluva load for a person to carry on her own. Admiration for her grew. She wasn't like his dad, who disengaged from responsibilities and the people counting on him.

"What will you do if your half brothers don't want to see your father?" she asked him now, drifting closer to him as she rubbed her cheek against the top of Isla's downy head.

Cameron was seized with the need to wrap his arms around both of them, a protective urge so strong he had to fight to keep his hands off Maresa. He jammed his fists in the pocket of his khakis to stop himself. Still, he walked closer, wanting to breathe in her scent. To feel the way her nearness heated over his skin like a touch.

"I'll convince them that my grandfather is worth ten of my father and make sure they understand the importance of meeting him." He lowered his voice while he stood so close to her, unable to move away.

Fascinated, he watched the effect he had on her. The goose bumps down her arm. The fast thrum of a tiny vein at the base of her neck. A quick dart of her tongue over her lips that all but did him in.

He wanted this woman. So much that telling himself to stay away wasn't going to help. So much that the baby in her arms wasn't going to distract him, let alone dissuade him.

"I should change," Maresa said suddenly, clutching Isla tighter. "Into something for the trip to your brothers' house. That is, if you want me to accompany you there? I'm not sure what you want my role to be here."

His gaze roamed over her, even knowing it was damned unprofessional. But they'd passed that point in this relationship the day before when Maresa had wrapped her arms around him. He'd used up all his restraint then. Time for some plain talk.

"Your role? First, tell me honestly what you think would happen between us this week if I wasn't your boss." He couldn't help the hoarse hunger in his voice, and knew that she heard it. He studied her while she struggled to answer, envious of the way Isla's tiny body curved around the soft swell of Maresa's breast.

"What good does it do to wonder what if?" Frustration vibrated through her, her body tensing. "The facts can't be changed. I'd never quit this job. It's more important to me than ever."

Right. He knew that. She'd made that more than clear. So why couldn't he seem to stay away? Stifling a curse at himself, he stepped back. Swallowed.

"I need to visit my brothers' place. You can relax here with Isla and review the files I started to show you yesterday. Make whatever notes you can to help me weed through what's important." He had to get some fresh air in his lungs if he was going to keep his distance from Maresa until the time was right.

"Okay. Thank you." She nodded, relief and regret both etched in her features.

"When I get back, I'll have dinner ordered in. We can eat on the upstairs deck before we fly back tonight, unless of course, you decide you'd like to stay another day."

Her eyes widened, a flush of heat stealing along the skin bared by the open V of her sundress. He couldn't look away.

"I'm sure that won't be necessary." She clung to her professional reserve.

"Nevertheless, I'll keep the option open." He reached for her, stroking the barest of touches along her arm. "Just in case."

Seven

Just in case.

Hours later, Cameron's parting words still circled around in Maresa's brain. She'd been ridiculously productive in spite of the seductive thoughts chasing through her mind, throwing herself into her work with determined intensity. Still, Cameron's suggestion of spending the night together built a fever in her blood, giving her a frenetic energy to make extensive notes on his files, research leads on Carib Grand personnel, and review her and Rafe's performance in depth. She hadn't found any answers about Rafe's additional activities, but at least she'd done the job Cameron asked of her to the best of her ability.

Now, walking away from the white-spindled crib where she'd just laid Isla for a nap with a nursery monitor by the bedside, Maresa was drawn across the hallway into the master bedroom while she waited for Cameron to return.

What would happen between us if I wasn't your boss?

Why had he asked that? Hadn't she already made it painfully clear when she'd confided how much she wanted a kiss in those heated moments in his arms yesterday? She'd relived that exchange a million times already and it had happened just twenty-four hours ago.

Now, lowering herself to a white chaise longue near open French doors, Maresa settled the nursery monitor on the hardwood floor at her feet. She would hear Isla if the baby needed anything. For just a few moments at least, she would enjoy overlooking the terrace and the turquoise lagoon below while she waited for Cameron to return. She would inhale the flower-scented sea air of her home, savor the caress of that same breeze along her skin. When was the last time she'd sat quietly and simply enjoyed this kind of beauty, let herself just soak in sensations? Sure, the beach around the Cap Est hotel in Martinique was more upscale than the Caribbean she'd grown up with—public beaches where you brought your own towels from home. But the islands were gorgeous everywhere. No one told the beach morning glory where to grow. It didn't discriminate against the public beaches any more than the yellow wedelia flowers or the bright poinciana trees.

It felt as if she hadn't taken a deep breath all year, not since she'd returned from Paris. There'd been days on the Left Bank when she'd sat at Café de Flore and simply enjoyed the scenery, indulged in people-watching, but since coming home to Charlotte Amalie? Not so much. And now? She had an infant to care for.

If Trina didn't want her baby back—and given the way she'd abandoned Isla, Maresa vowed to block any effort to regain custody—Maresa would have eighteen years of hard work ahead. Her time to stare out to sea and enjoy a few quiet moments would be greatly limited. Given the responsibilities of her brother, mother and now the baby, she couldn't envision many—if any—men who would want to take on all of that to be with her. This window of time with Cameron McNeill might be the last opportunity she had to savor times like this.

To experience romantic pleasure.

Closing her eyes against the thought, she rested her head on the arm of the chaise, unwilling to let her mind wander down that sensual road. She was just tired, that was all.

She'd nap while Isla napped and when she woke up she'd feel like herself again—ready to be strong in the face of all that McNeill magnetism…

"Maresa?"

She awoke to the sound of her name, a whisper of sound against her ear.

Cameron's voice, so close, made her shiver in the most pleasant way, even as her skin warmed all over. The late afternoon sun slanted through the French doors, burnishing her skin to golden bronze—or so it felt. She refused to open her eyes and end the languid sensation in her limbs. The scent of the sea and Cam's woodsy aftershave was a heady combination, a sexy aphrodisiac that had her tilting her head to one side, exposing her neck in silent invitation.

"Mmm?" She arched her back, wanting to be closer to him, needing to feel his lips against her ear once more.

It'd been so long since she'd known a man's touch. And Cameron McNeill was no ordinary man. She bet he kissed like nobody's business.

"Are you hungry?" he asked, the low timbre of his voice turning an everyday question into a sexual innuendo.

Or was it just her imagination?

"Starving," she admitted, reaching up to touch him. To feel the heat and hard muscle of his chest.

She hooked her fingers along the placket of his button-down, next to the top button, which was already undone. She felt his low hiss of response, his heart pumping faster against the back of her knuckles where she touched him. He lowered his body closer, hovering a hair's breadth away.

Breathing him in, she felt the kick of awareness in every nerve ending, her whole body straining toward his.

"Are you sure?" His husky rasp made her skin flame since he still hadn't touched her.

Her throat was dry and she had to swallow to answer. "So sure. So damn certain—"

His lips captured hers, silencing the rest of her words. His chest grazed her breasts, his body covering hers and setting it aflame. Still she craved more. She'd only known him for days but it felt as though she'd been waiting years for him to touch her. His leg slid between hers, his thigh flexing against where she needed him most. A ragged moan slid free...

"Maresa?" He chanted her name in her ear once more, and she thought she couldn't bear it if she didn't start pulling his clothes off.

And her clothes off. She needed to touch more of him.

"Please," she murmured softly, her eyes still closed. She gripped his heavy shoulders. "Please."

"Maresa?" he said again, more uncertainly this time. "Wake up."

Confused, her brain refused to acknowledge that command. She wanted him naked. She did not want to wake up.

Then again…wasn't she awake?

Her eyes wrenched open.

"Cameron?" His name was on her lips as she slid to a sitting position.

Knocking heads with the man she'd been dreaming about.

"Ow." Blinking into the dim light in the room now that the sun had set, Maresa came fully—painfully—awake, her body still on fire from her dream.

"Sorry to startle you." Cameron reached for her, cradling the spot where his forehead had connected with her temple. "Are you okay?"

No. She wasn't okay. She wanted things to go back to where they'd been in her dream. Simple. Sensual.

"Fine." Her breathing was fast. Shallow. Her heartbeat seemed to thunder louder than the waves on the shore. "Is there a storm out there?" she asked, realizing the wind had picked up since she'd fallen asleep. "Is Isla okay?"

The white silk curtains blew into the room. The end of one teased along her bare foot where she'd slid off her shoes. She spotted the nursery monitor on the floor. Silent. Reassuring.

"I just checked on her. She's fine. But there's some heavy weather on the way. The pilot warned me we might want to consider leaving now or—ideally—extending our stay. This system came out of nowhere."

She appreciated the cooler breeze on her overheated skin, and the light mist of rain blowing in with it. Only now did she realize the strap of her sundress had fallen off one shoulder, the bodice slipping precariously down on one side. Before she could reach for it, however, Cameron slid a finger under the errant strap and lifted it into place.

Her skin hummed with pleasure where he touched her.

"Sorry." He slid his hand away fast. "The bare shoulder was…" He shook his head. "I get distracted around you, Maresa. More than I should when I know you want to keep things professional."

The room was mostly dark, except for a glow from the last light of day combined with a golden halo around a wall sconce near the bathroom. He must have turned that on when he'd entered the master suite and found her sleeping.

Dreaming.

"What about you?" Her voice carried the sultriness of sleep. Or maybe it was the sound of desire from her sexy imaginings. Even now, she could swear she remembered the feel of his strong thigh between hers, his chest pressed to aching breasts. "I can't be the only one who wants to keep some professional objectivity."

She slid her feet to the floor, needing to restore some equilibrium with him. Some distance. They sat on opposite sides of the chaise longue, the gathering storm stirring electricity in the air.

"Honestly?" A flash of lightning illuminated his face in full color for a moment before returning them to black-and-white. "I would rather abdicate my role as boss where you're concerned, Maresa. Let my brother Quinn make any decisions that involve you or Rafe. My professional judgment is already seriously compromised."

She breathed in the salty, charged air. Her hair blew silky caresses along her cheek. The gathering damp sat on her skin and she knew he must feel it, too. She was seized with the urge to lean across the chaise and lick him to find out for sure. If she could choose her spot, she'd pick the place just below his steely jaw.

"I don't understand." She shook her head, not following what he was saying. She was still half in dreamland, her whole body conspiring against logic and reason. Rebelling against all her workplace ethics. "We haven't done anything wrong."

Much. They'd talked about a kiss. But there hadn't been one.

His eyes swept her body with unmistakable want.

"Not yet. But I think you know how much I want to." He didn't touch her. He didn't need to.

Her skin was on fire just thinking about it.

"What would your brother think of me if he knew we…" Images of her body twined together with this incredibly sexy man threatened to steal the last of her defenses. "How could he be impartial?"

Another flash of lightning revealed Cam in all his masculine deliciousness. His shirt was open at the collar, just the way it had been in her dream. Except now, his shirt was damp with raindrops, making the pale cotton cling like a second skin.

Cameron watched her steadily, his intense gaze as stirring as any caress. "You know the way you have faith in your brother's good heart and good intentions? No matter what?"

She nodded. "Without question."

"That's how I feel about Quinn's ability to be fair. He can tick me off sometimes, but he is the most level-headed, just person I know."

She weighed what he was saying. Thought about what it meant. "And you're suggesting that if we acted on this attraction…you'd step out of the picture. Your brother becomes my boss, not you."

"Exactly." Cameron's assurance came along with a roll of ominous thunder that rumbled right through the villa.

Right through her feet where they touched the floor.

Maresa felt as if she were standing at the edge of a giant cliff, deciding whether or not to jump. Making that leap would be terrifying. But turning away from the tantalizing possibilities—the lure of the moment—was no longer an option. Even before she'd fallen asleep, she'd known that her window for selfish pleasures was closing fast if Isla proved to be Rafe's daughter and Maresa's responsibility.

How could she deny herself this night?

"Yes." She hurled herself into the unknown and hoped for the best. "I know that you're leaving soon, and I'm okay with that. But for tonight, if we could be just a man and a woman…" The simple words sent a shiver of longing through her.

Even in the dim light, she could see his blue eyes flare hotter, like the gas fireplace in the Antilles Suite when you turned up the thermostat.

"You have no idea how much I was hoping you'd say that." His words took on a ragged edge as his hands slid around her waist. He drew her closer.

Crushed her lips to his.

On contact, fireworks started behind her eyelids and Maresa gave herself up to the spark.

Cameron was caught between the need to savor this moment and the hunger to have the woman he craved like no other. He'd never felt a sexual need like this one. Not as a teenager losing it for the first time. Not during any of the relationships he'd thought were remotely meaningful in his past.

Maresa Delphine stirred some primal hunger different than anything he'd ever experienced. And she'd said *yes*.

The chains were off. His arms banded around her,

pressing all of those delectable curves against him. He ran his palms up her sides, from the soft swell of her hips to the indent of her waist. Up her ribs to the firm mounds of beautiful breasts. Her sundress had tortured him all damn day and he was too glad to tug down the wide straps, exposing her bare shoulders and fragrant skin.

Any hesitation about moving too fast vanished when she lunged in to lick a path along his jaw, pressing herself into him. A low growl rumbled in his chest and he hoped she mistook it for the thunder outside instead of his raw, animal need.

"Please," she murmured against his heated flesh, just below one ear. "Please."

The words were a repeat of the sensual longing he'd heard in her voice when he had first walked into the room earlier. He'd hoped like hell she'd been dreaming about him.

"Anything," he promised her, levering back to look into her tawny eyes. "Name it."

Her lips were swollen from his kiss; she ran her tongue along the top one. He felt a phantom echo of that caress in his throbbing erection that damn near made him light-headed.

"I want your clothes off." She held up her hands to show him. "But I think I'm shaking too badly to manage it."

He cradled her palms in his and kissed them before rising to stand.

"Don't be nervous." He raked his shirt over his head; it was faster than undoing the rest of the buttons.

"It's not that. It's just been such a long time for me." She stood as well, following him deeper into the room. Closer to the bed. "Everything is so hypersensitive. I feel so uncoordinated."

The French doors were still open, but no one would be able to look in unless they were on a boat far out in the water. And then, it would be too dark in the room for anyone out there to see inside. He liked the feel of the damp air and the cool breeze blowing harder.

"Then I'd better unfasten your dress for you." He couldn't wait to have her naked. "Turn around."

She did as he asked, her bare feet shifting silently on the Turkish rug. Cameron found the tab and lowered it slowly, parting the fabric to reveal more and more skin. The bodice dipped forward, falling to her hips so that only a skimpy black lace bra covered the top half of her.

He released the zipper long enough to grab two fist-fuls of the skirt and draw her backward toward him. Her head tipped back against his shoulder, a beautiful offering of her neck. Her body. Her trust. He wanted to lay her down on the bed right now and lose himself inside her, but she deserved better than that. All the more so since it had been a long time for her.

"Can I ask you a question?" He nipped her ear and kissed his way down her neck to the crook of her shoulder. There, he lingered. Tasting. Licking.

"Anything. As long as you keep taking off some clothes." She arched backward, her rump teasing the hard length of him until he had to grind his teeth to keep from tossing her skirt up and peeling away her panties.

A groan of need rumbled in his chest as the rain picked up intensity outside. He cupped her breasts in both hands, savoring the soft weight while he skimmed aside the lace bra for a better feel.

"What were you dreaming when I first walked in here?" He rolled a taut nipple between his thumb and forefinger, dying to taste her. "The soft sighs you were making were sexy as hell."

Her pupils widened with a sensual hint of her answer before she spoke.

"I was dreaming about this." She spun in his arms, pressed her bare breasts to his chest. Her hips to his. "Exactly this. And how much I wanted to be with you."

Her hands went to work on his belt buckle, her trembling fingers teasing him all the more for their slow, inefficient work. He tipped her head up to kiss her, learning her taste and her needs, finding out what she liked best. He nipped and teased. Licked and sucked. She paid him in kind by stripping off his pants and doing a hip shimmy against his raging erection. Heat blasted through him like a furnace turned all the way up.

Single-minded with new focus, he laid her on the bed and left her there while he sorted through his luggage. He needed a condom. Now.

Right. Freaking. Now.

He ripped open the snap on his leather shaving kit and found what he was looking for. When he turned back to the bed, Maresa was wriggling out of her dress, leaving on nothing but a pair of panties he guessed were black lace. It was tough to tell color in the dim light from the wall sconce near the bathroom. The lightning flashes had slowed as the rain intensified. He stepped out of his boxers and returned to the bed.

And covered her with his body.

Her arms went around him, her lips greeting him with hungry abandon, as though he'd been gone for two days instead of a few seconds. His brain buzzed with the need to have her. Still, he laid the condom to one side of her on the bed, needing to satisfy her first. And thoroughly.

She cupped his jaw, trailing kisses along his cheek. When he reached between them to slip his hand beneath the hem of her panties, her head fell back to the bed, turning to one side. She gave herself over to him and that jacked him up even more. She was impossibly hot. Ready. So ready for him. He'd barely started to tease and tempt her when she convulsed with her release.

The soft whimpers she made were so damn satisfying. He wanted to give that release to her again and again. But she wasn't going to sit still for him any longer. Her long leg wrapped around his, aligning their bodies for what they both craved.

He tried to draw out the pleasure by turning his attention to her breasts, feasting on them all over again. But she felt around the bed for the condom and tore it open with her teeth, gently working it over him until he had to shoo her hand away and take over the task. He was hanging by a thread already, damn it.

She chanted sweet words in his ear, encouraging him to come inside her. To give her everything she wanted. He had no chance of resisting her. He thrust inside her with one stroke, holding himself there for a long moment to steel himself for this new level of pleasure. She wrapped her legs around him and he was lost. His eyes crossed. He probably forgot his own name.

It was just Maresa now. He basked in the feel of her body around his. The scent of her citrusy hair and skin. The damp press of her lips to his chest as she moved her hips, meeting his thrusts with her own.

The rain outside pelted harder, faster, cooling his skin when it caught on the wind blowing into the room. He didn't care. It didn't come close to dousing the fire inside him. Maresa raked her nails up his back, a sweet pain he welcomed to balance the pleasure overwhelming him and...

He lost it. His release pounded through him fast and

hot, paralyzing him for a few seconds. Through it all, Maresa clung to him. Kissed him.

When the inner storm passed, he sagged into her and then down on the bed beside her, listening to the other storm. The one picking up force outside. He lay beside her in the aftermath as their breathing slowed. Their heartbeats steadied.

He should feel some kind of guilt, maybe, for bringing her here. For not being able to leave her alone and give her that professional distance she'd wanted. But he couldn't find it in himself to regret a moment of what had just happened. It felt fated. Inevitable.

And if that sounded like him making excuses, so be it.

"Should I shut those?" he asked, kissing her damp forehead and stroking her soft cheek. "The doors, I mean?"

"Probably. But I'm not sure I can let you move yet." A wicked smile kicked up the corner of her lips.

"What if I promise to come back?" He wanted her again. Already.

That seemed physically impossible. And yet…damn.

"In that case, you can go. I'll check on Isla." She untwined her legs from his and eased toward the edge of the bed.

He wanted to ask her if they were okay. If she was upset about what had happened, or if she regretted it.

Then again, did he really want to know if she was already thinking about ways to back off? Now more than ever, he wanted to help her figure out a plan for her future and for Isla's, too. He could help with that. A pragmatic plan to solve both their problems had been growing in his head all day, but now wasn't the time to talk to her about it.

The morning—and the second-guessing that would come with it—was going to happen soon enough. He didn't have any intention of ruining a moment of this night by thinking about what would happen when the sun came up.

Eight

A loud crack of thunder woke Maresa later that night.

Knifing upright in bed, she saw that the French doors in the master bedroom had been closed. Rain pelted the glass outside while streaks of lightning illuminated the empty spot in the king-size bed beside her. Reaching a hand to touch the indent on the other pillow, she felt the warmth of Cameron McNeill's body. The subtle scent of him lingered on her skin, her body aching pleasantly from sex on the chaise longue before a private catered dinner they'd eaten in bed instead of on the patio. Then, there'd been the heated lovemaking in the shower afterward.

And again in the bed before falling asleep in a tangle just a few hours ago. It was after midnight, she remembered. Close to morning.

Isla.

Her gaze darted to the nursery monitor that she'd placed on the nightstand, but it was missing. Cameron must have it, she thought, and be with the baby. But it bothered her that the little girl hadn't been the first thought in her head when she'd opened her eyes.

Dragging Cam's discarded T-shirt from the side of the bed, she pulled it over her head. The hem fell almost to her knees. She hurried out of the master bedroom across the hall to the second room where the hotel staff had brought in a portable crib. There, in a window seat looking out on the storm, lounged Cameron McNeill, cradling tiny Isla against his bare chest.

The little girl's arms reached up toward his face, her uncoordinated fingers flexing and stretching while her eyes tracked him. He spoke to her softly, his lips moving. No. He was singing, actually.

"Rain, rain, go away," he crooned in a melodic tenor that would curl a woman's toes. "Little Isla wants to play—" He stopped midsong when he spotted Maresa by the door. "Hey there. We tried not to wake you."

Her emotions puddled into a giant, liquid mass of feelings too messy to identify. She knew that her heart was at risk because she'd just given this man her body. Of course, that was part of it. But the incredible night aside, she still would have felt her knees go weak to see this impossibly big, strong man cradling a baby girl in his arms so tenderly.

Not just any baby girl, either. This was Rafe's beautiful daughter, given into Maresa's care. Her heart turned over to hear Cameron singing to her.

"It was the storm that woke me, not you." She dragged in a deep breath, trying to steady herself before venturing closer.

He propped one foot on the window seat bench, his knee bent. The other leg sprawled on the floor while his back rested against the casement.

"I gave her a bottle and burped her. I think I did that part all right." He held up the little girl wrapped in a light cotton blanket so Maresa could see. "Not sure how I did on my swaddle job, though."

Maresa smiled, stepping even nearer to take Isla from him. Her hands brushed his chest and sensual memories swamped her. She'd kissed her way up and down those pecs a few hours ago. She shivered at the memory.

"Isla looks completely content." She admired the job he'd done with the blanket. "Although I'm not sure she'll ever break free of the swaddling." She loosened the wrap just a little.

"I wrapped her like a baby burrito." He rose to his feet, scooping up an empty bottle and setting it on the wet bar. "You may be surprised to know I worked in the back of a taco truck one summer as a teen."

"I would be very surprised." She paced around the room with the baby in her arms, taking comfort from the warm weight. Earlier, Maresa had put Isla to bed in a blue-and-white-striped sleeper. Now, she wore a yellow onesie with cartoon dragons, so Cameron must have changed her. "Did your grandfather make you all take normal jobs to build character?"

"No." Cameron shook his head, his dark hair sticking up on one side, possibly from where she'd dragged her fingers through it earlier. He tugged a blanket off the untouched double bed and pulled it over to the window seat. "Come sit until she falls asleep."

She followed him over to the wide bench seat with thick gray cushions and bright throw pillows. The sides were lined with dark wooden shelves containing a few artfully arranged shells and stacks of books. She sat with her back to one of the shelves so she could look out at the storm. Cameron sat across from her, their knees touching. He pulled the blanket over both of their laps.

"You were drawn to the taco truck for the love of fine cuisine?" she pressed, curious to know more about him. She rocked Isla gently, leaning down to brush a kiss across the top of her downy forehead.

"Best tacos in Venice Beach that summer, I'll have you know." He bent forward to tug Maresa's feet into his lap. He massaged the balls of her feet with his big hands. "I was out there to surf the southern California coast that year and ended up sticking around Venice for a few months. I learned everything I know about rolling burritos from Senor Diaz, the dude who owned the truck."

"A skill that's serving you well as a stand-in caregiver," she teased, allowing herself to enjoy this blessedly uncomplicated banter for now. "You'll have to show me your swaddling technique."

"Will do."

"How did your visit to the McNeill family home go?" she asked, regretting that she hadn't done so earlier. "I was so distracted when you got back." She got tingly just thinking about all the ways he'd distracted her over the past few hours.

"You won't hear any complaints from me about how we spent our time." He slowed his stroking, making each swipe of his hands deliberate. Delectable. "And I didn't really visit anyone today. I just wanted to see the place with my own eyes before we contact my half brothers."

"But you will contact them?" She couldn't help but identify with the "other" McNeills. Her mother had been the forgotten mistress of a wealthy American businessman. She knew how it felt to be overlooked.

"My grandfather is insistent we bring them into the fold. I just want to be sure we can trust them."

She nodded, soothed by the pleasure of the impromptu foot massage. "You're proceeding carefully," she observed. "That's probably wise. I want to do the same with Isla—really think about a good plan for raising her." She wanted to ask him what he thought about buying a house, but she didn't want to detract from their personal conversation with business. "I have a lot to learn about caring for a baby."

"Are you sure you want to go for full custody?" His hands stilled on her ankles, his expression thoughtful while lightning flashed in bright bolts over the lagoon. "There's no grandparent on the mother's side that might fight for Isla?"

"I spoke to both of them briefly while I was trying to track down Trina. Trina's mother is an alcoholic who never acknowledged she has a problem, so she's not an option. And the father told me it was all he could do to raise Trina. He's not ready for a newborn." Maresa hadn't even asked him about Isla, so the man must have known that Trina was looking for a way out of being a parent.

"Rafe doesn't know yet?" he said, with a hint of surprise, and perhaps even censure in his voice. He resumed work on her feet, stroking his long fingers up her ankles and the backs of her calves.

"His counselor said we can tell him once paternity is proven, which should be next week. She said she'd help me break the news, and I think I'll take her up on that offer. I know I was floored when I heard about the baby, so I can't imagine how he might feel." She peered down at Isla, watching the baby's eyelids grow heavy. "I'm not sure that Rafe will participate much in Isla's care, but I'll have my mother's help, for as long as she stays healthy."

"You've got a lot on your plate, Maresa," he observed quietly.

"I'm lucky I still have a brother." She remembered how close they'd been to losing him those first few days. "The doctors performed a miracle saving his life, but it took Rafe a lot of hard work to relearn how to walk. To communicate as well as he does. So whatever obstacles I have to face now, it's nothing compared to what Rafe has already overcome."

She brushed another kiss along Isla's forehead, grateful for the unexpected gift of this baby even if her arrival complicated things.

"Does your mother's house have enough room for all of you?" Cameron pressed. "Have you thought about who will care for Isla during the day while you and Rafe are working? If your mother is having more MS attacks—"

"I'll figure out something." She had to. Fast.

"If it comes to a custody hearing, you might need to show the judge that you can provide for the baby with adequate space and come up with a plan for caregiving."

Maresa swallowed past the sudden lump of fear in her throat. She hadn't thought that far ahead. She'd been granted the temporary custody order easily enough, but she hadn't asked her attorney about the next steps.

A bright flash of lightning cracked through the dark horizon, the thunder sounding almost at the same time.

She slid her feet out of Cameron's lap and stood, pacing over to the crib to draw aside the mosquito netting so she could lay Isla in it.

"I'll have to figure something out," she murmured to herself as much as him. "I can't imagine that a judge would take Isla away when Trina herself wants us to raise her."

"Trina could change her mind," he pointed out. His level voice and pragmatic concern reminded her that his business perspective was never far from the surface. "Or one of her parents could decide to sue for custody."

An idea that rattled Maresa.

She whirled on him, her bare feet sticking on the hardwood.

"Are you trying to frighten me?" Because it was working. She'd had Isla in her care for a little less than forty-eight hours and already she couldn't imagine how devastated she would be to lose her. It was unthinkable.

"No, the last thing I want to do is upset you." He stood from the window seat, the blanket sliding off him. "I'm trying to help you prepare because I can see how much she means to you. How much your whole family means to you."

"They're everything," she told him simply, stepping out of the baby's room with the nursery monitor in hand. When her father left Charlotte Amalie, she had been devastated. But her mother and her brother were always there for her, cheering her on when she yearned to travel, helping her to leave Saint Thomas and take the job in Paris when Jaden dumped her. "I won't let them down."

"And I know you'd fight for them to the end, Maresa, but you might need help this time." Cameron closed the door of the second bedroom partway before following Maresa downstairs into the all-white kitchen.

She was wide-awake now, tense and hungry. She'd been more focused on Cameron than eating during dinner, and she was feeling the toll of an exhausting few days. Arriving in the eat-in kitchen with a fridge full of leftovers from the catered meal that they'd only half eaten, she slid a platter of fruits and cheeses from the middle shelf, then grabbed the bottle of sparkling water.

"What kind of help?" she asked, pouring the water into two glasses he produced from a high cabinet lit from within so that the glow came through the frosted-glass front.

Cameron peeled the plastic covering off the fruit and put the platter down in the breakfast nook.

"I have a proposition I'd like to explain." He found white ceramic plates in another cabinet and held out one of the barstools for her to take a seat. "A way we might be able to help one another."

She tucked her knees under the big T-shirt of his that she'd borrowed.

"I'm doing everything I can to help you figure out why the Carib's performance reviews are declining." She couldn't imagine what other kind of help he would need.

"I realize that." He dropped into the seat beside her and filled his plate with slices of pineapple and mango. He added a few shrimp from another tray. "But I've got a much bigger idea in mind."

She tore a heel of crusty bread from the baguette they hadn't even touched earlier. "I'm listening."

"A few months ago, I proposed to a woman I'd never met."

"Seriously?" She put down the bread, shocked. "Why would anyone do that?"

"It was impulsive of me, I'll admit. I was irritated with my grandfather because he rewrote his will with a dictate that his heirs could only inherit after they'd been married for twelve months."

"Why?" Maresa couldn't imagine why anyone would attach those kinds of terms to a will. Especially a rich corporate magnate like Malcolm McNeill. She knew a bit about him from reading the bio on the McNeill Resorts website.

"We're still scratching our heads about it, believe me. I was mad because he'd told me he'd change the terms over his dead body—which is upsetting to hear from an eighty-year-old man—and then he cackled about it like it was a great joke and I was too much of a kid to understand." Cameron polished off the shrimp and reached for the baguette. "So I worked with a matchmaker and picked a woman off a website—a woman who I thought was a foreigner looking for a green-card marriage. Sounded perfect."

"Um. Only if you're insane." Maresa had a hard time reconciling the man she knew with the story he was sharing. Although, when she thought about it, maybe he had shown her his impulsive side with the way he'd taken on her problems like they were his own—giving her the villa while he stayed in the hotel, paying for the caregiver for Isla while Maresa worked. "That's not the way most people would react to the news that they need a bride."

"Right. My brothers said the same thing." Cameron poured them both more water and flicked on an overhead light now that the storm seemed to be settling down a little. "And anyway, I backed out of the marriage proposal when I realized the woman wasn't looking to get married anyhow. My mistake had unexpected benefits, though, since—surprise—my oldest brother is getting married to the woman I proposed to."

Maresa's fork slid from her grip to jangle on the granite countertop. "You're kidding me. Does he even *want* to marry her, or is this just more McNeill maneuvering for the sake of the will?"

"This is the real deal. Quinn is big-time in love." Cameron grinned and she could see that he was happy for his brother. "And Ian is, too, oddly. It's like my grandfather waved the marriage wand and the two of them fell into line."

As conflicted as Cameron's relationships might be

with his father and grandfather, it was obvious he held his siblings in high regard.

"Which leaves you the odd man out with no bride."

"Right." He shoved aside his plate and swiveled his stool in her direction. "My grandfather had a heart attack last month and we're worried about his health. From a financial standpoint, I don't need any of the McNeill inheritance, but keeping the company in the family means everything to Gramps."

She wondered why he thought so if the older man hadn't made his will more straightforward, but she didn't want to ask. Tension crept through her shoulders.

"So you still hope to honor the terms of the will." Even as she thought it, she ground her teeth together. "You know, I'm surprised you didn't mention you had plans to marry when you wooed me into bed with you. That's not the kind of thing I take lightly."

"Neither do I." He covered her hand with his. "I am not going to march blindly into a marriage with someone I don't know. That was a bad idea." He stroked his thumb over the back of her knuckles. "But I know you."

Her mouth went dry. A buzzing started in her ears.

Surely she wasn't understanding him. But she was too dumbfounded to speak, let alone ask him for clarification.

"Maresa, you need help with Isla and your family. Rafe needs the best neurological care possible, something he could get in New York where they have world-class medical facilities. Likewise, for your mother—she needs good doctors to keep her healthy."

"I don't understand." She shook her head to clear it since she couldn't even begin to frame her thoughts. "What are you saying?"

"I'm saying a legal union between the two of us would be a huge benefit on both sides." He reached below her to turn her seat so that she faced him head-on. His blue eyes locked on hers with utter seriousness. "Marry me, Maresa."

Cameron knew his brothers would accuse him of being impulsive all over again. But this situation had nothing in common with the last time he'd proposed to a woman.

He knew Maresa and genuinely wanted to help her. Hell, he couldn't imagine how she could begin to care for a baby with everything she was already juggling. He could make her life so much easier.

She stared at him now as if he'd gone off the deep end. Her jaw unhinged for a moment. Then, she snapped it shut again.

"Maybe we've both been working too hard," she said smoothly, trotting out her competent, can-do concierge voice. "I think once we've gotten some rest you'll see that a legal bond between us would complicate things immeasurably."

Despite the cool-as-you-please smile she sent his way, her hand trembled as she retrieved her knife and cut a tiny slice of manchego from a brick of cheese. With her sun-tipped hair brushing her cheek as she moved and her feminine curves giving delectable shape to his old T-shirt, Maresa looked like a fantasy brought to life. Her lips were still swollen from his kisses, her gorgeous legs partially tucked beneath her where she sat. Yet seeing her hold Isla and tuck the tiny girl into bed had been…

Touching. He couldn't think of any other way to describe what he'd felt, and it confused the hell out of him since he'd never wanted kids. But Maresa and Isla brought a surprise protectiveness out of him, a kind of caring he wasn't sure he'd possessed. And while he wasn't going to turn into a family man anytime soon, he could certainly imagine himself playing a role to help with Isla for the next year. That was worth something to Maresa, wasn't it? Besides, seeing Maresa's tender side assured him that she wasn't going to marry him just for the sake of a big payout. She had character.

"I appreciate you trying to give me a way out." He smoothed a strand of hair back where it skimmed along her jaw. "But I'm thinking clearly, and I believe this is a good solution to serious problems we're both facing."

"Marriage isn't about solving problems, Cam." She set down the cheese without taking a single bite. "Far from it. Marriage *causes* problems. You saw it in your own family, right?"

She was probably referring to his parents' divorce and how tough that had been for him and his brothers, but he pushed ahead with his own perspective.

"But we're approaching this from a more objective standpoint." It made sense. "You and I like each other, obviously. And we both want to keep our families safe. Why not marry for a year to secure my grandfather's legacy and make sure your brother, mother and niece have the best health benefits money can buy? The best doctors and care? A home with enough room where you're not worried about Rafe being upset by the normal sounds of life with an infant?"

"In New York?" She spread her arms wide, as if that alone proved he was crazy. "My work is here. Rafe's job is here. How could we move to New York for the health care? And even if we wanted to, how would we get back here—and find work again—twelve months from now?"

"By focusing on the wheres and hows, I take it you're at least considering it?" He would have a lot of preparations to make, but he could pull it off—he could relocate all of them to Manhattan next week. He just needed to finish up his investigation into the Carib Grand and then he could return to New York.

With the terms of his grandfather's will fulfilled. It would be a worry off his mind and it would be his pleasure to help her family. It would be even more of a pleasure to have her in his bed every night.

The more he thought about it, the more right it seemed.

"Not even close." She slid off the barstool to stand. "By focusing on the wheres and hows, I'm trying to show you how unrealistic this plan is. I'm more grateful to you than I can say for trying to help me, but I will figure out a way to support my family without imposing on the McNeills for a year."

"What about your brother?" Cam shoved aside his plate. "In New York, Rafe could work in a program where he'd be well supervised by professionals who would respect his personal triggers and know how to challenge him just enough to move his recovery forward."

She folded her arms across her breasts, looking vulnerable in the too-big shirt. "You've been doing your research."

"I read up on his injury to be sure you had him doing work he could handle." Cam wouldn't apologize for looking into Rafe's situation. "You know that's why I came to the Carib in the first place—to make sure everyone was doing their job."

"It hardly seems fair to use my brother's condition to convince me."

"Isn't it less fair to deny him a good program because you wouldn't consider a perfectly legitimate offer? I'm no Jaden Torries. I'm not going to back out on you, Maresa." And she would be safe from the worry of having children with him since he would never have any of his own. That would be a good thing in a temporary marriage, right?

"We'll sign a contract that stipulates what will happen after the twelve months are up—"

"I don't want a contract," she snapped, raising her voice as she cut him off. "I've already got a failed engagement in my past. Do you think I want a failed marriage, too?" Her eyes shone too bright and he realized there were unshed tears there.

She didn't want to hear all the reasons why they would work well together on a temporary basis.

He'd hurt her.

By the time he'd figured that out, however, he was standing in the kitchen by himself. The thunder had stopped, but it seemed the storm in the villa wasn't over.

Nine

Two days later, Maresa sat behind the concierge's desk typing an itinerary for the personal assistant of an aging rock-and-roll star staying at the Carib. The guitar legend was taking his entourage on a vacation to detox after his recent stay in rehab. Maresa's job had been to keep the group occupied and away from drugs and alcohol for two weeks. With her help, they'd be too busy zip-lining, kayaking and Jet Skiing to think about anything else.

The project had been a good diversion for her since she'd returned from her trip to Martinique with Cameron. She still couldn't believe he'd proposed to her for the sake of a mutually beneficial one-year arrangement and not out of any romantic declaration of interest. Great sex aside, a proposal of a marriage of convenience really left her gut in knots.

Leaning back in her desk chair, she blinked into the afternoon sun slanting through the lobby windows and hit the send button on the digital file. She wished she could have stretched out the project a bit longer to help her from thinking about Cam. He'd been kind to her since she'd turned down his proposal, promising her that the marriage offer would remain open until he returned to New York. She shouldn't be surprised that his engagement idea had an expiration date since he wasn't doing it because he'd fallen head over heels for her. It was just business to him. Whereas for her? She had no experience conducting affairs for the sake of expedience. It sounded tawdry and wrong.

Shoving to her feet, she tried not to think about how helpful the arrangement would be for her family. For her, even. He'd dangled incredible enticement in front of her nose by promising the best health care for her brother. Her mom, too. Maresa felt like an ogre for not accepting for those reasons alone. But what was the price to her heart over the long haul? Her self-respect? Maybe it would be different if they hadn't gotten involved romantically. If they'd remained just friends. But he'd waited to spring the idea on her until after she'd kissed him. Peeled off all her clothes with him and made incredible love.

Of course her heart was involved now. How could she risk it again after the way Jaden had shredded her? Things were too murky with Cameron. There were no boundaries with him now that they'd slept together. She could too easily envision herself falling for him and then she would be devastated a year from now when he bought her a first-class ticket back to Saint Thomas. She sagged back in the office chair, the computer screen blurring because of the tears she just barely held back.

Foot traffic in the lobby was picking up as it neared five o'clock. Guests were returning from day trips. New visitors were checking in. A crowd was gathering for happy hour at the bar before the dinner rush. Maresa smiled and nodded, asking a few guests about their day as they passed her. When her phone rang, she saw Cameron's number and her stomach filled with unwanted butterflies. Needing privacy, she stepped behind the concierge stand to take the call. Her heart ached just seeing his number, wishing her brief time with him hadn't imploded so damn fast.

"Hello?" She smoothed a hand over her hair and then caught herself in the middle of the gesture.

"Rafe is on the move with a guest," Cameron spoke quietly. "Meet me on the patio and we'll follow him."

Fear for her brother stabbed through her. What was going on with him? Would this be the end of his job? She might not want to be involved with Cameron personally, but she needed him to support her professionally. She hoped it wouldn't come down to calling in the oldest McNeill brother, Quinn, to decide Rafe's fate, but they'd agreed that Cameron couldn't supervise her after what had happened between them.

"On my way." Her feet were already moving before she disconnected the call. She hurried through the tiki bar where a steel drum band played reggae music for the happy hour crowd. Dodging the waitstaff carrying oversize drinks, Maresa also avoided running into a few soaked kids spilling out onto the pool deck with inflatable rings and toys.

Another time, she would gently intervene to remind the parents they needed to be in the kids' pool. But she wouldn't let Cameron confront Rafe alone. She needed to be there with him.

And then, there he was.

The head of McNeill Resorts waited on the path to the beach for her, his board shorts paired with a T-shirt this time, which was a small favor considering how much the sight of his bare chest could make her forget all her best resolve. He really was spectacularly appealing.

"Where's Rafe?" she asked, gaze skipping past him to the empty path ahead.

"They just turned the corner. Rafe and a young mother who checked in two days ago with her husband for a long weekend."

Maresa wondered how he'd found that out so quickly. She fell into step beside him. "How did you know Rafe was with a guest? I sent him on an errand to the gift shop about twenty minutes ago."

"I hired a PI to keep tabs on things here for a few days."

Her heeled sandal caught on a tree root in the sand. "You're having someone spy on Rafe?"

"I can't assign the task to anyone in the hotel, especially if Aldo Ricci really has anything to do with assigning Rafe the extra duties." Cameron's hand snaked out to hold her back, his attention focused on the beach ahead. "Look."

Maresa peered after her brother and the petite brunette. Her short ponytail swung behind her as she walked. Rafe didn't bring her to the regular beach, but waved her through a clearing to the east. Maresa wanted to charge over there and split them up. Ask Rafe who told him to bring the woman to a deserted beach.

"What's the plan?" she asked, fidgeting with an oversize flower hanging from a tropical bush.

"We see who he's meeting and confront him when he turns back."

"We'll make too much noise tramping through there." She pointed to the overgrown foliage. "I can't believe that

woman is following a total stranger into the unknown."
Why didn't vacationers have more sense?

"He's a hotel employee at one of the most exclusive resorts in the world," Cameron reminded her, his jaw tensing as he drew her into the dense growth. "She paid a lot of money to feel safe here."

Right. Which meant Rafe was so fired. Panic weighted down her chest. Today, every penny of Rafe's check would go to extra care for Isla—an in-home sitter to help Maresa's mom with the baby. What would they do when they lost that money?

She would have to marry Cameron.

The truth stared her in the face as surely as Rafe waved at Jaden Torries on the beach right now. Her ex-fiancé stood by the water's edge with his easel already set up—a half-baked artist trolling for clients at the Carib and using Rafe to deliver them off-site so he could paint them. Rafe was risking his job for…what? He never made any money from this scheme.

"I'm going to strangle Jaden," she announced, fury making her ready to launch through the bushes to read him the riot act.

"No." Cameron's arm slid around her waist, holding her back. He pressed her tightly to him so he could speak softly in her ear. "Say nothing. Follow me and we'll ask Rafe about it when we're farther away so Jaden can't hear."

She wanted to argue. But Cameron must have guessed as much because he covered her lips with one finger.

"Shh." The sound was far more erotic than it should have been since she was angry.

Her body reacted to his nearness without her permission, a fever crawling over her skin until she wanted to turn in his arms and fall on him. Right here.

Thankfully, he let her go and tugged her back to the hotel's main beach where they could wait for Rafe.

"Someone is using him," she informed Cameron while they waited. "He didn't orchestrate this himself, and he doesn't receive any money. I would know if someone was paying him."

"That woman he just took down to the beach is partners with the investigator I hired," Cameron surprised her by saying. "We'll find out what's going on. But for now, ask him who sent him and see what he says. Do you want me to stay with you or do you want to speak to him alone?"

"Um." She bit her lip, her anger draining away. He was helping Rafe. And her. The PI was a good idea and could prove her brother's innocence. "It might be better if I speak to him privately. And thank you."

Cameron's blue eyes held her gaze. His hand skimmed along her arm, setting off a fresh heat inside her. "We'd make a great team if you'd give us a chance."

Would they? Could she trust him to look out for her and her family if she gave in and helped him to secure his family legacy? Sure, Cameron could help her family in ways she couldn't. He already had. But what would it be like to share a home with him for a year while they fulfilled the terms of the marriage he needed? Still, while she worried about all the ways a legal union would be risky for her, she hadn't really stopped to consider that he was already holding up his end of the promised bargain—helping all the Delphines—while she'd given him nothing in return.

Maybe she already owed him her help for all that he'd done for her. Even if the fallout twelve months from now was going to hurt far more than Jaden's betrayal.

"You're right." She squeezed Cameron's hand briefly,

then let go as she saw her brother step onto the beach. "If you're still serious about that one-year deal, I'll take it."

"Maresa?" Rafe stopped when he spotted her standing underneath a date palm tree.

She was nervous about confronting him, wishing she could talk to him about everything at once. His secret meeting on the beach. His daughter. His future.

But she worried about how he would handle the news of Isla and she wanted his counselor there. The paternity results were in, and the woman had agreed to meet them at the Delphine residence after work today, so at least Maresa would be able to share that with him soon. For now, she just needed to ask who sent him here. Keep it simple. Nonthreatening.

He got confused and agitated so easily. Which was understandable, considering the long-and short-term memory loss that plagued him. She'd be agitated too if she couldn't remember what she was doing.

"Hi, Rafe." Forcing herself to smile, she hurried over to him. Slipped an arm through his. "Gorgeous day, isn't it?"

"Nancy says, 'another day in paradise.' Every day she says that." Rafe grinned at her.

His work uniform—mostly khaki, but the short sleeves of his staff shirt were white—was loose on him, making her worry that Rafe had lost weight without her noticing. She needed to care for him more and worry about his job less. Maybe, assuming Rafe agreed, a move to New York could be a real gift for their family right now. She needed to focus on how much Cameron was trying to help her brother, mother and niece, instead of thinking about how this growing attachment to him was only going to hurt in the end.

Cameron McNeill was a warmhearted, generous man, and he'd been that way before she agreed to help him, so it wasn't as though he was self-serving. She admired the careful way he'd gone about investigating the happenings at the Carib. It showed a decency and respect for his employees that she'd bet most billionaire corporate giants wouldn't feel.

"We're lucky like that." Maresa tipped her head to his shoulder for a moment as they walked together, wanting to feel that connection to him. "What brought you down to the beach?"

Overhead, a heron flew low, casting a shadow across her brother's face before landing nearby.

"A guest wanted her picture painted. Mr. Ricci said so."

Again with the hotel director?

Maresa found that hard to believe. The man had been extremely successful in the industry for years. Why would he undermine his position by promoting solicitation on the Carib's grounds? Why would he allow his guests to think they were receiving some kind of luxury experience through a session with Jaden, whose talents were…negligible.

"Rafe." She paused her step, tugging gently on his arm to stop him, too. She needed to make sure, absolutely sure, he understood what she was asking. "Did Mr. Ricci himself tell you to escort that woman here, or did someone else tell you that Mr. Ricci said so?"

She'd tried to keep the question simple, but as soon as she asked it, she could see the furrow between Rafe's brows. The confusion in his eyes, which were so like Isla's. Ahead on the path, she could hear the music from the tiki bar band, the sound carrying on the breeze as the sun dipped lower in the sky.

"Mr. Ricci said it." A storm brewed in Rafe's blue gaze, turning the shade from sapphire to cold slate. "Why don't you believe me?"

"I do believe you, Rafe."

He shook off her hand where she touched him.

"You don't believe me." He raised his voice. He walked faster up the path, away from her. "Every day you ask me the same things. Two times. Everything. Everyday."

He muttered a litany of disjointed words as he stomped through the brush. She closed her eyes and followed him without speaking, not wanting to upset him more. Maybe she should have asked Cameron to stay with her for this.

She craved Cameron's warm touch. His opinion and outside perspective. He'd become important to her so quickly. Was she crazy to let him draw her even more deeply into his world? All the way to New York?

But as she followed Rafe up the path toward the Carib, watching the way his shoulders tensed with agitation, she knew that his job wouldn't have lasted much longer here anyway. She'd wanted this to be the answer for him— for them—until they caught up on the medical bills and she could get him in a different kind of program to support TBI sufferers. Now, she knew she'd been deceiving herself that she could make it work. In truth, she'd been unfair to her brother, setting him up to fail.

No matter how much she loved Rafe, she needed to face the fact that he would never be the brother she once knew. For his own good, she needed to start protecting him and his daughter, too. Tonight, she'd give her notice to the hotel director.

For her family's sake, she would become Mrs. Cameron McNeill. She just hoped in twelve months' time, she'd be able to resurrect Maresa Delphine from the wreckage.

* * *

Back in the Antilles Suite rented out to his alter-ego, Mr. Holmes, Cameron reread Maresa's text.

Rafe said Mr. Ricci sent him on the errand. Became agitated when I asked a second time but stuck to the same facts.

Turning off the screen on his phone, Cam stroked Poppy's head. The Maltese rested on the desk where he worked. She liked being by his laptop screen when they were indoors, maybe because he tended to pet her more often. He was going to hate returning her to Mrs. Trager when they went back to New York and his stint as an undercover boss was over.

His stint as a temporary groom was up next. He'd been surprised but very, very pleased that Maresa had said yes to his proposal. He needed to make it more official, of course. And more romantic, too, now that he thought about it. Hell, a few months ago, he'd proposed to a woman he'd never met before with flowers and a ring. Maresa, on the other hand, had gotten neither and he intended to change that immediately.

He needed to romance her, not burden her with every nitnoid detail that was going into the marriage contract. She hadn't been interested in thinking about the business details, so he would put them in writing only. It didn't matter that she didn't know about his inability to father children. She was focused on her own family. Her own child. And for his part, Cameron would make sure she didn't regret their arrangement for a moment by making it clear she had twelve incredible months ahead.

He dialed his brother Quinn to give him an update on

the situation at the Carib, wanting to lay some ground-work for his hasty nuptials.

"Cam?" His brother answered the phone with a wary voice. "Before you ask, the answer is no. You don't get to fly the seaplane yourself."

Quinn was messing with him, of course. A brotherly jab about his piloting skills—which were actually ex-cellent. But the fact that they were the first words out of his brother's mouth made Cam wonder about the way the rest of the world perceived him. Reckless. Impulsive.

And his quickie engagement wouldn't do anything to change that.

"I'm totally qualified, and you know it," he returned, straightening Poppy's topknot that she'd scratched side-wise. He'd gotten his sport pilot certification years ago and he kept it updated.

"Technically, yes," Quinn groused, the sound of clas-sical music playing in the background. "But I know the first thing you'll do is test the aerial maneuvering or see how she handles in a barrel roll, so the controls are off-limits."

Funny, that had never occurred to him. But a few years ago, it might have. Yeah. It would have. He'd totaled Ian's titanium racing bike his first time on, seeing how fast it would go. He'd felt bad about that. Ian replaced it, but Cameron knew the original had been custom-built by a friend.

He hated being like his father.

"If I stay out of the cockpit, will you do me a favor?" He thought about bringing Maresa to New York and in-troducing her to his family. Would she look at him the same way when she discovered that he was considered the family screwup, or would she take the first flight back to Saint Thomas?

"Possibly." Quinn lowered his voice as the classical music stopped in the background. "Sofia's just finishing up a rehearsal, though. Want me to call you back?"

"No." The less time Quinn had to protest the move, the better. "I'm bringing my new fiancée home as soon as possible," he announced, knowing he had a long night ahead to make all the necessary arrangements.

"Not again." His brother's quick assumption that Cameron was making another mistake grated on Cam's last nerve.

Straightening, he moved away from the desk to stare out the window at the Caribbean Sea below.

"This time it's for real." He trusted Maresa to follow through with the marriage for the agreed-upon time. "Maresa deserves a warm welcome from the whole family and I want your word that she'll receive it."

"Cam, you've been in Saint Thomas for just a few days—"

"Your word," Cam insisted. "And I'll need Ian's co-operation, too."

For a moment, all he heard was Vivaldi's "Spring" starting up in the background of the call. Then, finally, Quinn huffed out a breath.

"Fine. But the plane better damn well be in one piece."

Cameron relaxed his shoulders, realizing now how tense he'd been waiting for an answer. "Done. See you soon, Brother, and I'll give you a full report on the Martinique McNeills plus an update on the Carib."

Disconnecting the call, Cameron went through a mental list of all he needed to do in order to leave for a few days. He had to have the PI take a close look at Aldo Ricci, no matter how stellar the guy's reputation was in the industry. Cameron needed to make arrangements for a ring, flowers and a wedding. He had to find a nanny, narrow down some options for good programs for Rafe and research the best neurosurgeon to have a consultation with Analise Delphine. He could farm out some of those tasks to his staff in New York. But before anything else, he needed to phone his lawyer to draw up the contracts that would protect his interests and Maresa's, too. He felt a sense of accomplishment that he'd be able to help someone he'd come to care about. This was surprisingly easy for him. As long as they both went into this marriage with realistic expectations, it could all work.

Only when that was done would he allow himself to return to Maresa's place and remind her why marrying him was going to be the best decision of her life. He might have his impulsive and reckless side, but he could damn well take good care of her every need for the upcoming year.

With great pleasure for them both.

Ten

I need to see you tonight.

Standing in her mother's living room, Maresa read the text from Cameron, resisting the urge to hug the phone to her chest like an adolescent.

She stared out the front window onto the street, reminding herself he wanted a business arrangement, not a romantic entanglement. If she was going to commit herself to a marriage in name only, she needed to stop spending so much time thinking about him. How kind he'd been to her. How good he could make her feel. How sweet he was with Isla.

Because Cameron McNeill didn't spend his free hours dreaming about her in those romantic ways. He was too busy investigating business practices at the Carib Grand and fulfilling the legal terms of his grandfather's will. Those things were important to him. Not Maresa.

The scent of her mother's cooking lingered in the air—plantains and jerk chicken that she'd shared with Mr. Leopold earlier. Her mom had warmed up a plate for Rafe when they returned from work, but Maresa's stomach was in too many knots to eat. Huffing out a sigh of frustration, Maresa typed out a text in response to Cameron.

The counselor just arrived. Any time after nine is fine.

She shut off her phone as soon as the message went through to stop herself from looking for a reply. If she wasn't careful, she'd be sending heart emojis and making an idiot of herself with him the way she had with Jaden. At least with this marriage, she knew the groom would really go through with it since he wanted to secure his millions. Billions? She had no clue. She only knew that the McNeills lived on a whole other level from the Delphines.

Here, they were a family of four crowded into her mother's two-bedroom apartment. For now, Isla's portable crib was in Analise's bedroom so they could shut the door if she started to cry. They'd told Rafe the little girl was a friend's daughter and that Maresa was babysitting for the night, but he'd barely paid any attention since he was still upset with his sister.

"Mom?" Maresa called as she opened the door for their guest—Tracy Seders, the counselor who would help them tell Rafe about his daughter. "She's here."

Analise Delphine shuffled out of the kitchen, dropping an old-fashioned apron behind a chair on her way out. The house was neat and clean, but their style of housekeeping meant you needed to be careful when opening closets or junk drawers. The mess lurked dangerously below the surface. How would they merge their lifestyle with Cameron's for the next year? Maresa would speak to him in earnest tonight, to make sure he knew what he was getting into by taking on a whole, chaotic family and not just one woman.

"Thank you for coming." Maresa ushered Tracy Seders inside, showing her to a seat in the living area where Maresa had slept since returning from Paris. She'd tucked away the blanket and pillow for the visit.

The three women spent a few minutes talking while Rafe finished his dinner and Isla bounced in a baby seat on the floor, her blue eyes wide and alert. She wore a pastel yellow sleeper with an elephant stitched on the front, one of a half dozen outfits that had arrived from the hotel gift shop that morning, according to Analise. The card read, "Congratulations from McNeill Resorts."

More thoughtfulness from Cameron that made it difficult to be objective about their arrangement.

Now, the counselor turned to Analise. "As I told Maresa on the phone, there's a good chance Rafe doesn't remember his relationship with Trina. He's never once mentioned her to me in our sessions." She smoothed a hand through her windblown auburn hair. The woman favored neat shirtdresses and ponytails most days, and made Maresa think of a kindergarten teacher. Today, the reason for the ponytail was more apparent: her red curls were rioting. "If that's the case, we'll have a difficult time explaining about Isla."

Analise nodded as she frowned, her eyes turned to where Rafe sat alone at the kitchen table, listening to a Yankees game on an old radio and adjusting the antennae.

Maresa repositioned the crochet throw pillow behind her back, fidgeting in her nervousness. "But we don't need to press, right? We can always just end the discussion and reinforce the relationship down the road when he's less resistant."

"Exactly." Tracy Seders tucked her phone in her purse and sat forward on the love seat. "Rafe, would you like to join us for a minute?" she called.

Maresa's stomach knotted tighter. She hadn't told her mother about Cam's proposal yet, but she'd mentioned it to the counselor on the phone in the hopes the woman would help her feel out Rafe about a move to New York. She feared it was too much at once, but the counselor hadn't seemed concerned, calling it a potential diversion from the baby news if Rafe didn't react well to that.

Now her brother ambled toward them. He'd changed out of his work clothes. In his red gym shorts and gray T-shirt, he looked much the same as he had as a teen, only now there were scattered scars in his hair from the surgery that had saved his life. More than the scars though, it was the slow, deliberate movements that gave away his injury. He used to dart and hurry everywhere, a whirling force of nature.

"Ms. Seders. You don't belong here." He grinned as he said it and the counselor didn't take offense.

"You aren't used to me in your living room, are you, Rafe?" She laughed and patted the seat beside her. "I heard your family has exciting news for you."

"What?" He lowered himself beside her, watching her intently.

Maresa held her breath, willing the woman to take the reins. She didn't know how to begin. Especially after she'd hurt his feelings earlier.

"They heard from your old girlfriend, Rafe. Trina?" She waited for any show of recognition.

There was none.

The counselor plowed ahead. "Trina had a baby this

spring, Rafe. Your baby." The woman nodded toward Maresa, gesturing for her to show him Isla.

She bent to lift the little girl from the carrier.

"No." Rafe said, shaking his head. "No. No girlfriend. No baby."

He got to his feet and would have walked away if Tracy hadn't taken his hand.

"Rafe, your sister will watch over Isla for you. But the baby is your daughter. One day, when you feel better—"

"No baby." Rafe looked at Maresa. Was it her imagination, or did his eyes narrow a bit? Was he still angry with her? "No."

He stalked out of the room this time and Analise made a strangled cry. Of disappointment? Maresa couldn't be sure. She'd been so focused on Rafe and trying to read his reaction she hadn't paid attention to her mother. Gently, Maresa returned Isla to the baby carrier, buckling her in to keep her safe.

"Rafe?" the counselor called after him. "I have a friend in New York City I would like you to meet. Another counselor. She lives near where the Yankees play."

Maresa's mother drew a breath as if to interrupt, but Maresa put her hand on her mom's arm to stop her. Analise's eyes went wide while Rafe spun around, his eyes bright.

"The Yankees?" He stepped toward them again, irresistibly drawn. "I could go to New York?" He looked at Maresa, and she realized how much she'd become a parent figure to him in the last months.

"Maresa." Her mother's voice was stern, although she kept her words low enough that Rafe wouldn't hear. "You know that's not possible."

Maresa squeezed her mom's hand, while she kept her

eyes on Rafe. "We could all go if you don't mind seeing a new doctor."

Rafe raised his arm above his head and it took Maresa a moment to realize he was pumping his fist.

"Yankees." He smiled crookedly. "Yankees! Yes."

The counselor shared a smile with Maresa while Rafe went to turn up the radio louder, a happy expression lingering on his face as he sank into a chair at the table.

"Maresa?" Analise asked. "What on earth?"

They both rose to their feet to walk the counselor to the door, and Maresa gave her mother an arm to lean on. Thanking the woman for her help that had gone above and beyond her job description, Maresa waved to her while she walked to her car. Only then did she face her mother, careful to keep Analise balanced on her unsteady feet.

"I'm getting married, Mom." The announcement lacked the squealing joy she'd had when she told her mother about Jaden's proposal. But at least now, with a contract sure to come that would document what she was agreeing to, Maresa knew the marriage would happen as surely as she knew the divorce would, too. "He cares, Mom, and wants to help with Rafe however he can."

Analise bit her lip. "Maresa. Baby." She shook her head. "After everything I went through with your daddy? You ought to know men don't mean half of what they say."

Maresa couldn't have said what surprised her more—that her mother recognized her father had played her false, or that Analise sounded protective on Maresa's behalf.

"I know, Mom." Maresa watched as the counselor sped away from the curb. "But this is different, trust me. I don't have any illusions that he loves me."

"No love?" Her mother grabbed her hand and squeezed—probably as hard as her limited mobility allowed. "There is no other reason to marry, Maresa Delphine, and you know it."

Right. And fairy tales came true.

But Maresa wasn't going to argue that with her mother right now. Instead, she hugged her gently.

"It's going to be okay. And this is going to be good for Rafe. I want us all to move to New York where he can get into a supervised care program that will really help him." She remained on the front step, breathing in the hot air as the moon came out over the Caribbean. Palm trees rustled in the breeze.

"Honey, once you get your heart broke, you can't just unbreak it." Her mother's simple wisdom was a good reminder for her.

She would be like Cameron and look at this objectively. They could be a good team. And just maybe, she could keep her heart intact. But in order to do that, she really shouldn't be sleeping with her charismatic future husband. It was while she was in his arms, kissing him passionately and sharing her body with him, that her emotions got all tangled up.

"I understand," she promised, just as Isla let out a small cry. Her mother insisted on being the one to check on the baby. Before Maresa could follow, a pair of headlights streaked across her as a vehicle turned up her street.

A warm tingle of anticipation tripped over her skin, telling her who it was. What kind of magic let her know when Cameron McNeill was nearby? It was uncanny.

Yet sure enough, on the road below, a dark Jeep slid into the spot that Rafe's counselor had vacated just a short time ago.

Maresa's fiancé had arrived.

* * *

Half an hour later, Cameron had Maresa in the passenger seat of the Jeep. They'd left Isla at her mother's house since the women agreed the baby was out for the night after a final feeding. Or at least until the 3:00 a.m. bottle feeding, which had been her pattern the last few nights.

He'd kept silent in front of Maresa's mom about the fact that he'd been the one to provide that bottle to the baby two nights before. Analise Delphine had been cordial but not warm, unmoved by the bouquets of tropical wildflowers he'd brought for each of them. No doubt Maresa's mother was concerned about the quick engagement, the same way Quinn had been concerned. Both women were worried about Rafe's reaction to his daughter, which had been adamant denial that she belonged to him. Just hearing as much made Cameron's heart ache for the little girl. He knew Maresa would be a good mother figure to her. But how hard must it be for a girl to grow up without a father? Or worse, a father who was a presence but didn't care to acknowledge her?

Of course, one day, she would know that Rafe suffered an injury that changed his personality. But still…he hated that for Isla, who deserved to grow up with every advantage. With a lot of love. Cameron didn't know why he felt so strongly about that. About her. Was it because of the baby's connection to Maresa? Or did he simply have a soft spot for kids that he'd never known about? He'd never questioned his comfort with giving up fatherhood before, but he wondered if he'd always feel as adamant about that.

Now, the breeze whipped through the Jeep since he'd taken the top down. With the speed limit thirty-five everywhere, they were safe enough. Poppy was buckled into her pet carrier in the backseat, her nose pressed to the grates for a better view.

Maresa had shown him how to leave the city and climb the winding road at the center of the island to get to Crown Mountain where he'd rented a place for the night. He hadn't mentioned the destination because they weren't staying there for long, but he didn't want to give her a ring on the doorstep of her mother's home. They might be marrying for mutual benefit, but that didn't mean the union had to be devoid of romance.

She'd had a rough year with her brother's injury and now the surprise baby. And he could tell she'd had a rough evening, the stress of the day apparent in her quietness. The tension in her movements. He wanted to do something nice for her. The first of many things.

"You're very mysterious tonight," she observed as she pointed to another turn he needed to take.

"I don't mean to be." He ignored her directions now that they were close to the cottage he'd rented. He recalled how to get there from here. "But I do have a surprise for you."

She twisted in her seat, her hair whipping across her cheek as she looked backward. "It will be a surprise if we don't get lost since you didn't follow my directions."

"I've got my bearings now." He used the high beams to search for a road marker the owner of the secluded property had mentioned. "There it is." He spotted a bent and rusted road work sign that looked like it had been there for a decade.

Behind the sign lurked a driveway and he turned the Jeep onto the narrow road.

"I'm sure this is private property," Maresa ducked when he slowed for a low tree limb.

"It is." He could see the house now in the distance high up the mountainside. "And I have a key."

"Of course you do." She slouched back in her seat. "I'm sleeping on a couch while you have a seemingly infinite number of places to lay your head at night."

"It helps to own a resort empire." He wouldn't apologize for his family's hard work. "And soon you'll be a part of it. We've got properties all over the globe."

"Including a mountain cottage in Saint Thomas?" She folded her arms, edgy and tense.

"No. I rented this one." He turned a corner and spotted the tropical hideaway that promised amazing views from the terraces. "Come on. I'm anxious to show you your surprise."

"There's more?" She unbuckled her seatbelt as he parked the Jeep in the lighted driveway surrounded by dense landscaping.

Night birds called out a welcome, the scent of fragrant jasmine in the air. The white, Key West-style home was perched on stilts, the dense forest growing up underneath it, although he spotted some kayaks and bikes stored down there. The main floor was lit up from within. Visible through the floor-to-ceiling window, the simple white furnishings and paint contrasted with dark wood floors and ceiling fans.

"Yes and I'm hoping you're more impressed with the next one than you are with the cottage." He stepped down from the Jeep and went around to free Poppy, attaching her leash so she didn't run off after a bird.

"I'm impressed," Maresa acknowledged, briefly brushing against him as she hopped out, unknowingly tantalizing the hell out of him. "I'm just frazzled after the way I upset Rafe down by the beach tonight and then again when we tried to tell him about Isla." She blinked up at Cameron in the moonlight, her shoulders partly bared by the simple navy blue sundress she wore. "It hurts to be the one causing him so much distress after all the months I've tried to take care of him and help his recovery."

The pain in her words was so tangible it all but reached out to sucker punch him. He wanted to kiss her. To offer her the comfort of his arms and his touch, but he didn't want to take anything for granted when the parameters of their relationship had shifted. He settled for brushing a hair from her forehead while Poppy circled their legs.

"They say we often lash out at the people we feel most comfortable with. The people who make us feel safe." His hand found the middle of her back and he palmed it, rubbing gently for a moment. Then he ushered her ahead on the path to the house where he punched in the code he'd been given for the alarm system.

A few minutes later, they'd found enough lights to illuminate the way to the back terrace, which was the main feature he'd brought her here for.

Poppy claimed a chair at the back of the patio and Cam added an extension to the leash to give her lots of freedom to explore. She looked as though she was done for the night, however, settling into the lounger with a soft dog sigh.

"Oh, wow. It's so beautiful here." Maresa paused at the low stone wall that separated them from the brush and trees of the mountainside.

Peering down Crown Mountain, they could see into the harbor and the islands beyond. With a cruise ship docked in the harbor and a hundred other smaller boats in the water nearby, the area looked like a pirate's jewel box, lit up with bright colors.

"Would you like to swim?" He pointed to the pool that overlooked the view, the water lit up to show the natural stone surround and a waterfall feature.

"No, thank you." She wrapped her arms around herself. "It's a beautiful night. I'm happy to just sit and enjoy this." Her tawny eyes flipped up to his. "But I'm curious why you texted me. You said you needed to see me tonight?"

It occurred to him now that part of the reason she'd been tense and edgy on the ride was because she'd been nervous. Or at least, that's how he read her body language now. Wary. Worried.

He wanted to banish every worry from her pretty eyes. And he wanted it with a fierceness that caught him off guard.

"Only because I wanted to make sure we were on the same page about this marriage." He dragged two chairs to the edge of the stone wall so they could put their feet up and look out over the view. "That you felt comfortable about it. That if you had any worries or concerns, I could address them."

Also, he just plain wanted to see her again. Spend time with her when they weren't working. When the whole of the Carib Grand hotel wasn't looking over their shoulders. He didn't want her to feel like he was rushing her into something she wasn't ready for.

"I'm not worried for my sake." She tipped her chin at him as she took her seat and he did the same. "But I'd be lying if I said I wasn't worried about my family. My brother seems excited to go to New York, but my mother thinks it's crazy, of course." She wrapped her arms around herself. "And Isla... I worry that a year is a long time for a baby. How can she help but get attached to you in that time?"

It was a question that had never crossed his mind. But even as he wanted to deny that such a thing would happen, how could he guarantee it? The truth was, he was already growing attached to the little girl and he'd known her less than a week.

"She'll have a nanny," he offered, not sure how else to address the concern. "I've already asked my staff to arrange for candidates for you to interview when we get to New York. And whoever you choose will have the option of returning to Saint Thomas with you if you want to return next year."

"Where else would I go?" She frowned.

"Maybe you'll decide to stay in New York." He couldn't imagine why she'd want to leave. "I've already found a program for Rafe that he's going to love. There's a group of gardeners who work in Central Park under excellent supervision—"

"Don't." She cut him off, shaking her head. Her eyes were over-bright. "We'll never be able to afford to stay there after the year is up and—"

"Maresa." Hadn't he made this clear? The guilt that he might have contributed to her stress by not explaining himself stung. Yes, he'd kept quiet about his inability to father children since they were entering a marriage of convenience, and it wouldn't be a factor anyway. But there were plenty of other things—positive, happy things—he could have shared with her to reassure her about this union. "I'll provide for you afterward. And your whole family. I'm having my attorney work on a fair settlement for you to review, but I assure you that you'll be able to stay in New York if you choose." Maybe the time had come to make things more concrete. He dug in his pocket and found the ring box.

A jingle sounded behind them as Poppy leaped down

from her perch and dragged her leash over to see what was happening. She sat at his feet, expectant. The animal was too smart.

"That's kind of you," Maresa said carefully, not seeing the ring box while she looked down at the harbor. The hem of her navy blue sundress blew loosely around her long legs where she had them propped. "But when you say the marriage will be real, how exactly do you mean that?"

He cracked open the black velvet and leaned closer to show her what was inside.

"I mean this kind of real." He pulled out the two carat pear-shaped diamond surrounded by a halo of smaller diamonds in a platinum band. It was striking without being overdone, just like Maresa. "Will you marry me, Maresa Delphine?"

He heard her breath catch and hoped she liked the surprise, but her eyes remained troubled as she took in the ring.

"I don't understand." Sliding her feet to the stone terrace, she stood. She paced away from him, her blue dress swirling around her calves. "Is it a business arrangement? Or are we playing house and pretending to care about one another as part of some deal?" She spun to face him, her hands fisting on her hips. "Because I don't think I can do both."

Carefully, he tucked the ring back in its box and set it on the seat before he followed her.

"I'm not sure we'll be *playing* at anything," he replied, weighing his words. "My house is real enough. And I care about you or I wouldn't have asked you to do this with me in the first place."

He studied her, looking for a hint of the woman who'd come apart in his arms not once, but three times on that night they'd spent together in Martinique. He'd felt their connection then. She had, too. He'd bet his fortune on it.

"You might think you care about me, but I'm not the efficient and organized concierge that you met when you were pretending to be Mr. Holmes." She folded her arms over her chest. "Maybe I was pretending then, too. I fake that I'm super capable all day to make up for the fact that I keep failing my family every time I turn around. The real me is much messier, Cameron. Much less predictable."

He weighed her rapid-fire words. *O-kay.* She was worried about this. Far more than she'd let on initially. But he was glad to know it now. That's why they were here. To talk about whatever concerned her. To make a plan for tomorrow.

For their future.

"The real you is fascinating as hell." Maybe it was his own impulsive streak responding, but a little straight talk never scared him off. "No need to hide her from me." He reached to touch her, his hands cupping her shoulders, thumbs settling on the delicate collarbone just beneath the straps of her dress.

"Then answer one thing for me, because I can't go into this arrangement without knowing."

"Anything."

"Why me?"

Eleven

It was all too much.

The moonlight ride to this beautiful spot. A fairytale proposal from a man who promised to take care of her struggling family. A man who wasn't scared off by the fact that she'd just inherited a baby.

With her mother's warning still ringing in her ears—that there was no other reason to marry if not for love—Maresa needed some perspective on what was happening between them before she signed a marriage certificate to be Cameron's wife.

"Are you asking me what I find appealing about you?" He lifted a dark eyebrow at her, his gaze simmering as it roamed over her. "I must not have done my job the other night in Martinique."

"Not that." She understood the chemistry. It was hot enough to make her forget all her worries. Hot enough to make her lose herself. "I mean, with all the women in the world who would give their right arm to marry a McNeill, why would you ever choose a bride with a new baby, an ailing mother and a brother who will need supervision for the rest of his adult life? Why go for the woman with the most baggage imaginable?"

As she said the words aloud, they only reinforced how ludicrous the notion seemed. Women like her didn't get the fairytale ending. Women like Maresa just put their heads down and worked harder.

He never stopped touching her, even at her most agitated, his fingers smoothing over her shoulders, brushing aside her hair, rubbing taut muscles she didn't know were so tense. "Let's pretend for a moment that Rafe had never been injured and he was just a regular, twenty-two-year-old brother. How disappointed would you be in him if he chose who to date—who to care about—based on a woman's family life? Based on, as you call it, who had the least baggage?"

Was it Cam's soothing hands that eased some of her tension? Or were his words making a lot of sense? Listening to him made her feel that she'd denigrated her own worth—and damn it, she knew better than that.

"All I'm saying is that you could have made your life a lot simpler by dating someone else." She edged closer to him, drawn by the skillful work of his fingers. He smelled good. And she'd missed him these last two days. "Is that what we're doing, by the way? Dating?"

She wished she didn't need so much assurance. But she'd been jilted before. And she would be making a big leap to follow him to New York, leaving her job behind.

"Married people can date," he assured her, his voice whispering over her ear in a way that made her shiver. "And much more. The two aren't mutually exclusive."

Closing her eyes, she leaned into him, soaking up his

hard male strength. She inhaled the woodsy pine scent of his aftershave, not fighting the chemistry that happened every time he came near her. He tilted her face up to his and she closed her eyes. Waiting.

Wanting.

His thumb traced the outline of her jaw. Brushed her cheek. Trailed delicious shivers in its wake.

When his lips covered hers she almost felt faint. Her knees were liquid and her legs were shaky. She wound her arms around his neck, savoring the brush of five o'clock shadow against her cheek when he kissed her. The gentle abrasion tantalized her, reminding her of the places on her body where she'd found tiny patches of whisker burn after the night they'd spent together.

"You rented this house for the night," she reminded him, her thoughts already retreating to the bedroom indoors.

"I did." He plucked her off her feet, lifting her higher against him so their bodies realigned in new and delicious ways.

"And you haven't even asked me inside." She arched her neck for him to kiss her there, inhaling sharply as he ran his tongue behind her ear.

"I didn't want to be presumptuous." His fingers found the zipper in the back of her dress and tugged the tab down, loosening the soft cotton.

"Gallant." She kissed his jaw. "Chivalrous, even." She kissed his cheek. "But right now, you should start presuming."

He chuckled quietly as he lowered Maresa to her feet again and whistled for Poppy, unhooking the pup's leash where he'd fastened it earlier.

"Let me just grab the chairs." He opened the door for

Maresa and then jogged back to return the furniture to where they'd found it.

Cam was back at her side in no time, hauling her toward the bedroom that he must have scoped out earlier. As if walking on a cloud of hope, she followed him into the large, darkened room where pale blue moonlight streamed through open blinds overlooking the ocean, spotlighting the white duvet of a king-size bed.

It smelled like cypress wood and lemon polish and possibility. Then Cameron's arms were around her again. He slid his hands into her dress, watching with hungry eyes as the fabric slid to the floor and all the possibilities became reality. She hadn't worn much underneath and he made quick work of it now, peeling down the red satin bra and bikini panties that had been her one splurge purchase in Paris. She'd liked the feel of that decadent lace against her skin, but Cameron's hands felt better. Much, much better.

He cupped between her thighs and stroked her with long fingers until she was mindless with want. Need. She felt a deep ache for them to connect in any way possible to help alleviate the nerves in her belly. To ease her reservations about marriage that she desperately didn't want to think about.

Especially not now.

She tugged at his shirt, wanting it gone. But the longer he touched her, the less her limbs cooperated. She couldn't think. She could only feel. Or there was something inherently perfect about only feeling, about abandoning concerns and taking this moment for the two of them, only them, the rest of the world be damned for now.

When the first shudders began, he covered her mouth with a kiss, catching her cries of release. He was so generous. So good to her. He held her while she recovered from the last aftershock. She wanted to return all that generosity with her hands and lips, but he was already lifting her, depositing her where he wanted her on the bed while he stripped off his clothes.

Another time, she would ask him to strip slower so she could savor the ways his muscles worked together on his sculpted body. But right now, she craved the feel of him inside her. Deeply. Sooner rather than later. She waited until he'd found a condom, then sat up on the bed, pulling him down to her.

With unsteady hands, she stroked him, exploring the length and texture of him, wanting to provide the same pleasure he'd given her. He cupped her breasts, molding them in his hands. Teasing the sensitive tips with his tongue. Sensation washed through, threatening to draw her under again. He reached for the condom and passed it to her, letting her roll it into place.

He spanned her thighs with his palms, making room for himself before he thrust into her deeply, fully. She stared up at him and found his gaze on her. He lined up their hands and fit his fingers between each of hers before drawing her arms over her head, holding them there as she took in the moment of them, connected, as one, and a shimmer rippled along her skin.

With the moonlight spilling over their joined bodies, she had to catch her breath against a wave of emotion. Hunger. Want. Tenderness. A whole host of feelings surged and she had to close her eyes against the power of the moment.

He started a rhythm that took her higher. Higher. She lifted her hips, meeting his thrusts, relishing the feel of him as the tension grew taut. Hot.

He still held her hands, her body stretched beneath

his, writhing. He didn't touch her anywhere else. He only leaned close to speak into her ear.

"All mine." The words were a rasp. A breath.

And her total undoing.

Her back arched, every nerve ending tightening for a moment before release came in one wrenching wave after another. She squeezed his hands tight and she felt the answering shock in his body as he went utterly still. His shout mingled with her soft cries while the sensations wrapped around them both.

Replete, Maresa splayed beneath him, waiting to catch her breath. Eventually he rolled to her side but he kissed her shoulder as he went. He brushed her damp hair from her face, smoothing it, pulled the white duvet over her cooling skin and fluffed her pillow. Her body was utterly content. Sated. Pleasurable endorphins frolicked merrily in her blood.

But her heart was already heading back toward wariness. The sex had been powerful. Far more than just chemistry. And she wasn't ready to think about that right now. Not by a long shot.

Yet how long could she delay? Not more than a moment apparently. She didn't have a choice when all too soon she felt Cameron lean over the bed and dig in the pile of clothes. When he came back, he slid something cold along her hand and then onto her left ring finger.

"You should wear this." He left the diamond there and tugged her hand from the covers so they could see the brilliant glint of the stones in the moonlight.

The engagement ring.

She swallowed hard, trying not to think about what it would have been like to have him slide it into place for real, kissing her fingers to seal the moment.

Maresa turned to look at his handsome profile in the

dark, his face so close to hers. He must have felt her stare because he turned toward her, too.

"It's beautiful," she told him honestly, feeling that he deserved some acknowledgement of all his hard work to make this night special for her, even if this marriage might very well break her heart in a million pieces. "Of course I love it. Who wouldn't?"

The words were out of her mouth before she could rethink them. Cameron smiled and kissed her, pleased with her assessment.

But Maresa feared she wasn't just talking about the ring. She was talking about the night and what they'd just shared. Her emotions were too raw and this was all happening way too fast. But somehow, in spite of her better judgment and the mistakes of her past, she was developing deep feelings for him. Very real feelings.

How on earth was she going to hide it from him for the next twelve months? He'd brought her here tonight to discuss their plans for a future. A move to New York. A union that would benefit both of them on paper.

If she had any hope of holding up her end of the agreement to walk away in twelve months, she needed to do a better job of shoring up her defenses.

Starting right now.

Twelve

Two weeks after he first placed a rock on Maresa's finger, Cameron prepared to introduce her to his family. Seated in the third-floor library of his grandfather's house on Manhattan's Upper East Side, Cam sipped the Chivas his brother Ian had just handed him. The three brothers had gathered in the late afternoon to discuss the other McNeill situation before a dinner with their wives, their father and grandfather. He hadn't wanted Maresa to arrive at the house unescorted this evening but she'd been excited to visit Rafe on-site at his new work program during his first full day. It was the first sign of genuine happiness Cameron had seen from her since they'd signed the marriage certificate.

He was trying to give her time to get acclimated to New York before meeting the McNeills, not wanting to make her transition more stressful with the added pressure of a family meeting. He'd even kept the courthouse marriage a secret for the first week—a ceremony conducted by a justice of the peace in Saint Thomas to help keep the McNeill name out of the New York papers. But he could keep things quiet for only so long. Quinn had known a marriage was in the works and finally harassed the truth out of him—that Cam had relocated all the Delphines, including baby Isla, to his place in Brooklyn. Rafe was so excited to see his favorite baseball team play that Cameron had finagled a friend's corporate box for the season, an extravagance Maresa had chided him about, but not for too long after seeing how happy it made Rafe. She didn't know it yet, but Cameron was flying in Bruce Leopold, the Delphines' neighbor in Charlotte Amalie, to attend the team's next home series with Rafe.

Cameron ran a finger over one of the historic Chinese lacquer panels between the windows overlooking the street while he waited for his brothers to finish up a conversation about a hotel Ian had been working on. Cameron felt good about where things stood with all of Maresa's family now. Analise had warmed to him considerably after seeing the in-law suite, thanking him personally for the modifications he'd made so she could get around more easily. It hadn't taken a construction crew long to add handrails to the tub and a teak bench to the shower stall, along with new easier-to-turn doorknobs in all the rooms and an intercom system in case she needed anything.

Isla was sleeping longer stretches at night and Maresa had personally hired a live-in nanny and a weekend caregiver who were settling in well. She seemed pleased with them, and her legal suit for permanent custody of the baby should be settled within the week now that Cameron had gotten his legal team involved to expedite things. Trina wasn't interested in visitation, which made

Maresa sad, but Cameron told her she might change her mind one day. For his part, he enjoyed spending time with a twelve-week-old far more than he ever would have imagined. He liked waving off the nanny at 5:00 a.m. and walking around his house with the baby, showing her the view from the nursery window and discussing his plans for the day. Sometimes, when she stared up at him with her big blue eyes, Cameron would swear she was really listening.

If only his new wife seemed as content. She'd been pulling away from him ever since the night he'd slid the ring onto her finger and he wanted to know why.

"Earth to Cam?" Ian waved his own glass of dark amber Scotch in front of Cameron's nose. "You ready to join us or are you too busy dreaming of the new bride?"

Cam shook his head. "I'm waiting for you to quit talking business so we can figure out our next move with Dad's secret sons."

He wasn't going to talk about Maresa when she wasn't around. He would introduce his brothers to her soon enough and they would be impressed. Hell, they'd be downright envious of him if they hadn't recently scooped up impressive women themselves.

Lowering himself into a leather club chair near one of the built-in bookshelves full of turn-of-the-century encyclopedias that had amused him as a kid, Cameron waited for his brothers to grill him on his fact-finding mission to Martinique.

Quinn took the couch across from Cam and Ian paced. One of them must have hit the button on the entertainment system because an Italian aria played in the background. Quinn must be refining his musical tastes now that he was marrying a ballerina.

"You didn't give us much to go on," Ian noted, pausing

by an antique globe. "You said all three of them—Damon, Gabe and Jager—keep a presence in Martinique?"

Cameron remembered that day of sleuthing well. The only thing that had kept him from feeling resentful as hell about seeing the McNeill doppelgängers had been knowing that Maresa was waiting for him back at the Cap Est Lagoon villa. They'd shared an incredible night together.

"Correct. Jager runs the software empire." They'd all read the report from the PI who'd found the brothers in the first place. "Damon actually founded the company, but he's been noticeably absent over the last six months since his wife disappeared shortly after their wedding." From all accounts, the guy was shredded about the loss, even though he hadn't made the disappearance public. Talking to a few people close to the family about it had made Cameron all the more determined to figure things out with Maresa. "And Gabe, the youngest, runs a small resort property. Ironic coincidence or a deliberate choice to mirror the McNeill business, I can't say."

Frowning, Quinn set down his glass on a heavy stone coaster with a map of Brazil—a gift from their mother. "I thought they were all involved in software? Didn't the PI's report say as much?"

"They are. But they each have outside specialties and interests," Cameron clarified.

Ian took a seat on the arm of the couch at the opposite end from Quinn. He picked up a backgammon piece from a set that remained perpetually out and flipped it in his hand. "Just like us."

Quinn leaned forward. "One obvious way to bring them into the fold is to see if the one who has a resort— Gabe?" He looked to Cam for confirmation before continuing. "We ask him if he's interested in stepping into Aldo Ricci's spot at the Carib now that Cam ousted him.

With good reason, I might add." He lifted his Scotch in a toast.

Ian did the same. "Here, here. Good job figuring that one out, Cam."

Enjoying a rare moment of praise from his brothers, Cam lifted the glass in acknowledgement and took a sip along with them. With the help of another investigator, Cameron had confirmed that Aldo Ricci had been taking kickbacks from low-end artists passing their work off as far more valuable than it was to the guests. With Ricci's worldly demeanor and contacts around the globe, he was someone that guests trusted when he assured them a sitting with a famous artist was difficult to procure.

But for a fee, he could arrange it.

Ricci hadn't just done so with Jaden Torries, but a whole host of artists at the Carib Grand and at properties he worked for before coming to McNeill Resorts. Cameron had released him from his contract and the company lawyers would decide if it was worth a lawsuit. Certainly, there would be public relations damage control. But at least the Carib was free of a man who gladly preyed on employees like Rafe to facilitate meetings—employees who were working on a trial basis and could be terminated easily. Cameron was certain the performance reviews would improve with the manipulative director out of the picture.

Good riddance to Aldo Ricci. The arrogant ass.

"You want to ask Gabe McNeill to take Aldo Ricci's job?" Cameron went on to explain that the youngest McNeill's resort was on a much smaller scale.

"All the more reason to get him accustomed to the way we do business," Quinn insisted. "You know Gramps insists we bring them in—"

A scuffle at the library door alerted them to a newcomer's arrival. Malcolm McNeill pushed his way through the door with his polished mahogany walking stick before Ian could reach him to help.

"I heard my name," the gray-haired, thinning patriarch called without as much bluster as he would have even a few months ago. "Don't think you can conduct family business without me."

Cameron worried to see the toll his grandfather's heart attack had taken on him in the past months. Malcolm had booked a trip to China after initially changing his will, saying he didn't want to discuss the new terms. But having his heart attack while abroad had meant the family couldn't see him for weeks afterward, and they hadn't been able to find out much about treatments or the extent of damage until he was well enough to travel home. It had really scared them.

More than ever, Cam was grateful to Maresa for agreeing to this marriage. Crappy relationship with his father notwithstanding, Cam's family meant everything to him. And even though he'd resented having his grandfather dictate his personal life, it seemed like a small thing compared to the possibility of losing him. For most of Cameron's life, he wouldn't have been able to imagine a world without Malcolm McNeill in it. Now, he sure didn't want to, but he could envision it all too well when he saw how unsteady Gramps was on his feet as Quinn helped him into a favorite recliner.

"We need the women, I think, to really make this a party," Gramps observed once he caught his breath. He peered around the room, piercing blue eyes assessing each the brothers. "Family business needs a woman's touch."

Ian lifted his phone before speaking. "Lydia just texted

me. She and Maresa are waiting for Sofia downstairs before they join us."

Cameron resisted the urge to bolt to his feet, strongly suspecting Maresa would rather meet the other women on her own terms. She was great with people, after all. It was part of what made her so good at her job. Still, it bothered him that he wasn't with her to make the introductions himself.

"Good." Gramps underscored the sentiment by pounding his walking stick on the floor. "In the meantime, Cameron, you can give me the update you already shared with these two." He nodded to Quinn and Ian. "When are the rest of my grandsons coming to New York to meet me?"

Cameron was secretly relieved when Ian stepped in to field the question for him. Maybe, as a recently married man himself, Ian knew that Cam was nervous about tonight. Finishing off the Scotch more quickly than he'd intended, he got to his feet and prowled around the room, looking at antique book spines on the walls without really seeing them.

He was uneasy for a lot of reasons tonight. One reason was that discussion of the other McNeills stirred old anger about his father's faithlessness to the woman he'd married. Cam resented that his father's selfish actions resulted in three other sons and a whole life they'd known nothing about. But, as he now watched his grandfather listen to Ian with obvious interest, Cam had to respect the old man for refusing to limit his idea of family. Gabe, Damon and Jager were all as important to Gramps as Ian, Quinn and Cameron.

It didn't matter that he'd never met them.

For the first time, it occurred to Cam that he had more in common with his grandfather than he'd realized. All his life, Cam had been compared to his reckless, impulsive father. But Cameron would never be the kind of man who cheated on his wife. More importantly, he was the kind of man who could—like his grandfather Malcolm—embrace a wider definition of family.

Because Rafe was Cam's brother now. And Analise's health and safety were as important to him as his own mother's.

As for Isla?

Could he adore that little girl more if he'd fathered her himself? Like Malcolm McNeill, Cameron would never let go of the Delphines. He would use all his resources to protect them. Most of all, he would love them.

The insight hit him with resounding force, as sudden and jarring as the impact of that old kiteboarding crash that had stolen his ability to father children of his own. He didn't need to avoid having a real family for fear of repeating his father's mistakes. He already had a real family and he needed to start treating all of them—especially Maresa—like more than contractual obligations.

Because twelve months weren't ever going to be enough time to spend with her. Twelve years weren't going to cover it, in fact. He needed to make this marriage last and now that he knew as much, he didn't want to wait another second to let her know. Because, yes, he'd always have some of that impulsiveness in his character. Only now he knew he'd never let it hurt the woman—the family—he loved.

"Will you excuse me?" he said suddenly, stalking toward the library door. "I need to see my wife."

"We've been dying to meet you," Sofia Koslov told Maresa in the foyer of the impressive six-story Italianate mansion that Malcolm McNeill called home.

Maresa tried not to be intimidated by the tremendous wealth of her surroundings and the elegance of the beautiful women who had greeted her so warmly. Dark-haired Lydia McNeill, a pale-skinned, delicate nymph of a woman who worked in interior design, was married to Cam's brother Ian. The blonde ballerina Sofia was engaged to Quinn and due to marry within the month.

Both of them appeared completely at home on the French baroque reproduction benches situated underneath paintings Maresa was pretty sure she'd seen in art history books. Cushions of bright blue picked up the color scheme shared by the two huge art pieces. Dark wooden banisters curled around the dual stone staircases leading up to the second floor. A maid had told her the men were on the third floor and they were welcome to take the elevator.

Un-freaking-believable. Maresa had been overwhelmed by Cameron's generosity ever since arriving in New York, but seeing the roots of his family wealth, she began to understand how easy it was for him to re-order the world to his liking. He might have grown his own fortune with his online gaming company, but he'd been raised in a world of privilege unlike anything she'd ever known.

"Thank you." Maresa hoped she was smiling with the same kind of genuine warmth that her sister-in-law and soon-to-be sister-in-law demonstrated. But it was difficult to be so out of her element. Knowing she was going to be a part of this family for only eleven and a half more months hurt, too. "I will confess I've been nervous to meet Cameron's family."

Lydia nodded in obvious empathy. She wore a smartly cut sheath dress in a pink mod floral. "Who wouldn't be nervous? They are the *McNeills*—practically a New York institution." She gestured vaguely to the painting above her head. "This is a Cézanne, for crying out loud. I was a wreck my first time here."

Sofia slanted a glance at Lydia. "With good reason, since we witnessed our first McNeill brawl." She shook her head and tugged an elastic band from her long blond hair, releasing the pretty waves from the ballerina bun. She wore dark leggings with a gray lace top, but her style was definitely understated. No makeup in sight and still incredibly lovely. Sofia turned to Maresa and winked. "Your husband is a man of intense passion, we discovered."

"Cam?" Maresa asked, since she couldn't imagine him getting into a physical fight with anyone, least of all his family. He'd been incredibly good to hers, after all.

Lydia opened her purse and found a roll of breath mints, offering them each one before explaining, "It wasn't really a brawl. But Quinn, Ian and Cameron were devastated to learn that their father had a whole other family he'd kept secret for twenty-plus years. Cam landed a fist on his dad's jaw before they all settled down."

Maresa found it impossible to reconcile her knowledge of Cameron with the image they painted. But then again, he had proposed to Sofia mere months ago in a moment of impulsiveness. Maresa knew he'd gone on to extend the offer of marriage to Maresa because he thought he knew her much better. Because they had a connection. But was she really just another impulsive choice on his part?

Her stomach sank at the thought. No matter how hard she struggled to keep her feelings a secret from him these past two weeks, she feared they'd only gotten deeper. Seeing him walk around Isla's nursery with the little girl in his arms at the crack of dawn the past few mornings chinked away at the defenses she needed around him. How effective were those defenses when just the idea that he'd chosen her in a moment of rashness was enough to rattle her?

Drawing a fortifying breath, she sat up straighter on the bench seat. "He's been incredibly good to me and to my family," she said simply.

From somewhere down the hall she thought she heard the swish of an elevator door opening. Maybe the maid was returning to call them in for dinner?

Sofia flexed her feet and pointed her toes, stretching her legs while she sat. "That doesn't surprise me. We were all glad to hear that he's so taken with your little girl."

Lydia leaned forward to lower her voice. "And for a man who swore he'd never have kids, that's incredible." She reached to squeeze Maresa's hand. "His brothers are relieved you've changed his mind."

Footsteps sounded nearby. But Maresa was too distracted by the revelation to pay much attention. Her world had just shifted. Cameron had never said anything about his stance on children.

"Cam doesn't want kids?" She thought about him singing to Isla in the temporary nursery he'd outfitted for her personally while his construction crew worked to remodel an upstairs suite for her that would be ready the following week.

Had his show of caring been as fake as their marriage?

A male shadow fell over her right as her eyes began to burn. "Maresa."

Cameron stood in the foyer at the foot of the stairs, his face somber. Lydia and Sofia greeted him briefly but he didn't so much as flick a gaze their way before the other women excused themselves.

Maresa stood too quickly, feeling suddenly light-headed at the news that she was being carefully deceived. He'd never wanted children. Did that mean he'd also never wanted a wife? That their marriage was even more of a pure necessity than she'd realized? She felt duped. Betrayed.

And just how many other secrets was her husband keeping from her in order to secure the McNeill legacy?

She cleared her throat. "I don't feel well. If you can make my excuses to your family, I need to be leaving." Picking up her purse, she took a half step toward the massive entryway.

Cameron sidestepped, blocking her path. "We need to talk."

Even at a soft level, their voices echoed off all the marble in the foyer.

"What is there to talk about? Your wish not to have children? Too late. I already heard about it." Hurt tore through her to think she was letting Isla grow attached to him.

"I should have told you sooner—" he began, but she couldn't listen. Couldn't hear him explain how or why he'd decided he didn't enjoy kids.

"Please." She brushed past him. "I spent so many hours interviewing potential nannies and caregivers. I should have devoted more time to interviewing my husband." She couldn't help but remember all the ways he'd stepped into a fatherly role.

All those little betrayals she hadn't seen coming.

"It's not that I don't like children, Maresa." He cupped her shoulders with gentle hands. "I had an accident as a stupid twenty-year-old kid. And as a result—medically speaking—I can't father children."

Thirteen

Cameron was losing her.

He could tell by the way Maresa's face paled at the news. He should have told her about this sooner. He'd disclosed his net worth and offered her a prenup with generous financial terms and special provisions for her family.

Yet it had never crossed his mind to share this part of his past. A part that would have had huge implications for a couple planning a genuine future together. A real marriage. He'd been so focused on making a sound plan for the short-term, he hadn't thought about how much he might crave something more.

Something deeper.

"Please." He shifted his grip on her shoulders when she seemed to waver on her feet. "There's a private sitting room over here. Just have a seat for a minute, and let me get you a glass of water."

She looked at him with such naked hurt in her tawny eyes that it felt like a blow to him, too.

"Isla has to be my highest priority. Now and always." Her words were firm. Stern. But, thankfully, her feet followed him as he led her to the east parlor where they could close a door and speak privately.

"I understand that." He drew her into the deep green room with a marble fireplace and windows looking out onto Seventy-Sixth Street. The blinds were tilted to let in sunlight but blocked any real view. Cameron flicked on the sconces surrounding the fireplace while he guided her to a chair near the fireplace. "I admire that more than I can say."

He wanted to tell her about the realization he'd had upstairs with his grandfather. That he was more like Malcolm McNeill than he'd realized. But that would have to wait and he'd be damn lucky if she even stayed and listened to him for that long. He had the feeling the only reason she'd followed him in here was because she was too shell-shocked to decide what to do next.

He needed to talk fast before that wore off. He made quick work of pouring the contents of a chilled water bottle from a hidden minifridge into a cut-crystal glass he pulled off the tea cart.

"It's not fair to Isla to let her grow attached to you." Maresa closed her eyes as he brought over the cold drink, opening them only when he sat down in the chair next to her. "Even if what you say is true—that you like kids—I should have been thinking about it more before I agreed to this marriage." She accepted the drink and took a sip. "Not that I'm backing out since we signed a binding agreement, but maybe we need to reconsider how much time you spend with her, given that you won't be a part of her life twelve months from now."

The hits just kept coming. And feeling the full brunt of that one made him realize how damned unacceptable he found this temporary arrangement. He needed to help her see that they could have a real chance at something more.

"I hope you will change your mind about that, Maresa, but I understand if you can't." He wanted to touch her. To put his hands on her in any way possible while he made his case to her, but she sat with such brittle posture in the upholstered eighteenth-century chair that he kept his hands to himself. "I never knew how much I would enjoy a baby until I met you and Isla. I never had any experience with kids and told myself it was just as well because my father sucked at fatherhood and everyone has always compared me to him."

She looked down at the glass she balanced on one knee but made no comment. Was she waiting? Listening?

Hell, he sure hoped so.

He plowed ahead. "Liam McNeill is reckless and impulsive, and even my brothers said I was just like him. I've always had a lot of restless energy and I channeled it into the same kind of stuff he did—skydiving and hang gliding. Whitewater rafting and surfing big waves. It was a rush and I loved it. But when a kiteboarding accident nearly killed me I had to rethink what I was doing."

Her gaze flew up to meet his. She had been listening. "How did it happen?"

"Too much arrogance. Not enough sense I wanted to catch big air. I jumped too high and got caught in a crosswind that slammed me into some trees." He'd been lucky he remained conscious afterward or he might have died hanging there. "The harness I was wearing got wrapped around my groin." He pantomimed the constriction. "The pain was excruciating, but I needed to cut myself down to alleviate the pressure threatening to cut off all circulation to my leg."

"Wasn't anyone else there to help?" Her eyes were wide. She set her glass aside, turning toward him as she listened.

"Not even close. That crosswind blew me a good half mile out of the water. My friends had to boat to shore and then drive and search for me. They called 911 and the paramedics found me first." He felt the warmth of her leg close to his. He wanted to touch her but he held back because he had to get this right.

"Thank God. You could have lost a limb." She frowned, shaking her head slowly, empathy in her eyes.

For the moment, anyway, it seemed as though she was too caught up in the tale to think about how much distance she wanted to put between the two of them. Between him and Isla. His chest ached with the need to fix this, because losing his new family was going to hurt worse than if he'd lost that leg. If she chose to stay with him, she needed to make that decision for the right reasons. Because he'd told her everything.

"Right. And that's how I always looked at it." He took a deep breath. "A lifetime of compromised sperm count seemed like I got off easy—at the time. I lost my option of being a father since my own father sucked at it and I was already too much like him. Right down to the daredevil stupidity."

She eased her hand from under his, twisting her fingers together as if restraining herself from touching him again. "Do you do things like that anymore?"

"Hell no." He realized he still clutched the water bottle in his hand. He took a sip from it now, needing to clear his thoughts as much as his mind. "I channeled all that restless energy into building the gaming company.

I designed virtual experiences that were almost as cool as the real thing. But safer. I know life is too precious to waste."

"Then you're not all that much like your father, after all," she surprised him by saying. She set down the cut-crystal glass and stood, walking across the library to the fireplace where she studied a photo on the mantle.

It was an image from one of the summers in Brazil with his brothers and their mother. They all looked tan and happy. He'd had plenty of happy times as a kid and he wanted to make those kinds of memories with Maresa and Isla. Maybe he'd convinced himself he didn't care about having a family because he'd never met Maresa. He'd been holding on to his heart, waiting for the right person.

"That's what I came down from the library to tell you tonight." He crossed to stand beside her, reaching to lay his hand over hers. "It's taken me a lifetime to realize it, but I've got plenty of my grandfather's influence at work in me, too."

"How so?" She turned to face him. Listening. Dialed in.

She was so damned beautiful to him, her warmth and caring apparent in everything she did. In every expression she wore. He wanted to be able to see her face every day, forever. To see how she changed as they grew older. Together.

Cameron prayed he got the words right that would make her understand. He couldn't lose this woman who'd become so important to him in a short span of time. Couldn't afford to lose the little girl that he wanted to raise with as much love as he'd give his own child. In fact, he wanted Isla to be his child.

"Because Gramps would never turn his back on family." He gathered up her hands and held them. "He insists we bring my half brothers to New York and cut them in on the McNeill inheritance, even though he's never met any of them. I was upset about that at first, mostly because I'm still mad at my father for keeping such a hurtful secret from Mom."

"I don't like hurtful secrets." Maresa's eyes still held traces of that pain he'd put there and he needed to fix that.

"I didn't withhold that information about my accident on purpose," he told her honestly. "I didn't give it any thought. And that's still my fault for being too concerned about the physical whys and wherefores of making the move to New York work instead of thinking about the intangibles of sharing...our hearts."

"Our what?" She blinked at him as though she'd misunderstood. Or hadn't heard properly.

"I got too caught up in making this a business arrangement without thinking about how much I would come to care about you and your whole family, Maresa." He tugged her closer, trapped her hands between his and his chest so that her palm rested on his heart. "I'm in love with you. And I don't care about the business arrangement anymore. I want you in my life for good. Forever."

For a long moment, Maresa couldn't hear anything outside of her heart pounding a thunderous answer to Cameron's words. But she wasn't sure she could trust her feelings. She didn't plan to let her guard down long enough for him to shatter her far worse than Jaden could have ever dreamed of doing.

Except, when her heart quieted a tiny bit and she began to hear the traffic sounds out on Seventy-Sixth Street—the shrill whistle of someone hailing a cab and the muted laughter of a crowd passing the windows—Maresa realized that Cameron was still here. Still clutching her hands tight in his. And the last words he'd said to her had been that he wanted her to be a part of his life forever.

That hadn't changed.

And since he'd done everything else imaginable to make her happy these last two weeks, she wondered if maybe she ought to let down her guard long enough to at least check and see if he could be serious about a future together.

Her mind reeled as her heart started that pounding thing all over again.

"Cameron, as tempting as it might be to just believe that—"

"You think I would deceive you about being in love?" He sounded offended. He angled back to get a clear view of her eyes.

"No." She didn't mean to upset him when he'd just said the most beautiful things to her. "But I wonder if you're interpreting the emotions correctly. Maybe you simply enjoy the warmth of a family around you and it doesn't have much to do with me."

"It has everything to do with you." He released her hands to wrap one arm around her waist. He slid the other around her shoulders. "I want every night to be like that last night we spent in Saint Thomas when we made love in the villa at Crown Mountain. Do you remember?"

She remembered all right. That was the night she'd understood she was falling for him and decided she needed to be more careful with her heart. As much as she'd treasured their nights together since then, she'd been holding back a part of herself ever since. Her heart. "I do."

"Even if it was just us, I would want you in my life

forever. But it's a bonus that I get your mom and your
brother and your niece." His touch warmed her while his
words wound around her heart and squeezed. "Getting
to be a part of Isla's life would be an incredible gift for
me since I can't have children of my own. But I understand that could be enough reason alone for you to want
to walk away. I don't want to deny you the chance to be
a biological mother."

She could see the pain in his eyes at the thought. And
the love there, too. He wasn't pushing her away, but he
loved her enough that he would be willing to give her
up so she could have that chance. That level of love—
for her—stunned her. And she knew, without question,
she didn't need a child of her own to find fulfillment
as a mother. She was lucky to have a baby who already
shared her family's DNA, something she was reminded
of every time she peered down into Isla's sweet face.
If they wanted more children, she felt sure they could
open their hearts to more through adoption. If Cameron
could already love Isla so completely, Maresa knew he
could expand his sense of family to other children who
needed them.

"I have a lifetime of mothering ahead of me no matter
what since Isla isn't going anywhere." She would make
sure Rafe's daughter grew up loved and happy, even if
Rafe never fully understood his connection to her. He
smiled now when he saw Isla, and that counted as beautiful progress. "Isla is going to fill my life and bring me
a lot of joy so I'm not thinking about other children down
the road. If I was, however, I agree with your grandfather
that we can stretch the definition of what makes a family. We could reach out to a child who needs a home."

"We?" His eyes were the darkest shade of blue as

they tracked hers. "Are you considering it then? A real marriage?"

The hope in his voice could never be faked. Any worries she'd had about him deceiving her in order to secure his family legacy melted away. He might act on instinct, but he did so with honest intentions. With integrity. She'd seen the love in his gaze when he'd held Isla. She should have trusted it. He was so different from Jaden, and she'd already let her past rob her of enough happiness. Time to take a chance on this incredible man.

Even when he'd been masquerading as Mr. Holmes, she'd seen the real man beneath the facade. She'd known there was someone worthy and good, someone noble and kind inside.

"Cameron." She pulled in a deep breath to steady herself. "I've been holding back from loving you because I've been terrified of how much it would hurt to let you go a year from now."

He tipped his head back and seemed to see her with new eyes. "That's why you've pulled away. Ever since—"

"That night on Crown Mountain." She nodded, knowing that he'd seen the difference in her since then. The way she'd been holding herself tightly so she didn't fall the rest of the way in love.

She was failing miserably. Magnificently.

"I'm so sorry if I hurt you that night," he began, stroking her face, threading his fingers into her hair tenderly.

"You did nothing wrong." She cupped his beard-stubbled cheeks in both hands. "I just couldn't afford to love a man who didn't love me back. Not again. I went halfway around the world to get over the hurt and humiliation of Jaden, so I couldn't begin to imagine how much a truly incredible guy like you could hurt me."

For her honesty, she was rewarded with a hug that

left her breathless. Cameron's arms wrapped around her tight. Squeezed. He lifted her against him, burying his face in her hair.

"I love you, Maresa Delphine. So damn much the thought of losing you was killing me inside." His heart-felt confession mirrored her own emotions so perfectly she felt her every last defense fall away.

She closed her eyes, swallowed around the lump in her throat. And hugged him back, so tightly, her body tingling with happiness.

"I love you, Cam. And I'm not going anywhere in twelve months." She arched back to see his face, loving the happiness she saw in his eyes. "I'm going to stay right here with you and be as much a part of your family as you already are of mine."

He grinned, setting her on her feet again and sweeping her hair back from her face. "You have to meet them first."

She laughed, her heart bubbling with joy instead of nerves. With this man at her side, the future stretched out beautifully before her. It wouldn't necessarily be perfect or have no bumps along the way, but it was a real-life fairy tale because they would take on life together. "I do."

"And that's not happening today." He kissed her cheek and temple and her closed eyes.

"It isn't?" She wondered how she got so lucky to find a man who loved her the way Cameron did. A man who would do anything to protect his family.

A man who extended that protectiveness to her and everyone important to her.

"No." He cupped her face in his hand and brushed a kiss over her lips, sending a shiver of want through her. "Or at least, it's not happening until the dessert course."

"We can't leave them all waiting and wondering what's happened."

"They'll get hungry. They'll eat." He nipped her bottom lip, driving her a little crazy with the possessive sweep of his tongue over hers. "I have a whole private suite on the fifth floor, you know."

"Of course you do." She wound her arms around him as heat simmered all through her. "Maybe it would be a good time to celebrate this marriage for real."

"The lifetime one," he reminded her, drawing her out of the parlor and toward the elevator. "Not the twelve-month one."

"Or we could wait until we got home tonight," she reminded him. "And we could celebrate it after we tuck Isla in after her last feeding, when we are at home."

"Our home," he reminded her as he stepped inside the elevator cabin. "So you really want to go meet the McNeills?"

"Every last one of them." She didn't feel nervous at all now. She felt like she belonged.

Cameron had given her that, and it was one of many things she would treasure about him.

About their marriage.

"As my wife wishes." He stabbed at the button for the third floor. "But don't be surprised when I announce a public wedding ceremony to the table."

She glanced up at him in surprise. "Even though we're already married?"

"A courthouse wedding isn't nearly enough of a party to kick off the best marriage ever." He lifted their clasped hands and kissed her ring finger right over the diamond set. "We're going to make a great team, Maresa."

He'd told her that once before and she hadn't believed him nearly enough. With his impulsive side tempered by his loving nature, he was going to make this marriage fun every day.

"I know we will." Squeezing his hand, she felt like a newlywed for the first time and knew in her heart that feeling would last a lifetime. "We already are."

* * * * *

COMING SOON!

We really hope you enjoyed reading this book. If you're looking for more romance, be sure to head to the shops when new books are available on

Thursday 24th January

To see which titles are coming soon, please visit

millsandboon.co.uk/nextmonth